KING'S X

Stephen T. Harper

A NOVEL ENDEAVOR BOOK

For Christie

All that you are, all that you have ever been,
the King's X will reveal...

A lifetime is an arc of lightning. Potent. Unique. Impermanent. What happens when we die? Is it nothing? Is it something?

So much is hidden. So much forgotten. What knowledge remains falls to us in ancient stories of a time lost in shadow. Stories of jealous gods and tormented thieves. Prometheus and the stolen secret of fire. Eve, the Tree of Knowledge, and the taste of forbidden fruit. The clever Raven, who tricked the Sky to steal a piece of the Sun.

Long ago the King's X was stolen from its makers. The Thief is hunted to this day. There can be no rest, not even in death. Because to carry the King's X is to know a truth long hidden, forever outlawed, and all but forgotten.

No one dies.

What follows is a story of secrets, forbidden knowledge, and stolen fire. This is a story of the King's X. One of many.

"I will tell you an old-world story, which I heard from an aged man."

--Plato

Prologue

Avignon, 1307

A prisoner and her jailor moved single file within underground corridors of grim stone and weak torchlight. Far from where her life began in the bright heat of Palestine, Khali neared the moment when it would end, a woman alone in a place where only the worst qualities of men exist. There was no justice here, only rules jealously defended through unspeakable horrors as only the most righteous minds could devise. Cold. Dark. Inquisitor's chamber. Executioner's hall.

A man who spent his days in tunnels without sunlight, his body made of thick, moist flesh which gave him the appearance of a great hulking worm, pulled her deeper into the darkness on a short leash attached to her bound hands by a cord of mildewed leather. To distract from the sound of his open-mouthed, liquid wheeze, she focused on the mingled echoes of their footfalls in the shallow black puddles. To control the fear of what lay ahead, she looked back along the winding and bloody trail of time that had led to this moment. But memory is an uncertain path to the past. She could discern no great wisdom in the tale of her life, only a sense of mystery upon mystery, and a dim awareness of depth upon depth.

The final turn opened into a chamber, large enough that the pulsing firelight could just hint at four walls and several faintly illuminated figures watching from shadow. The air was stale and thick with the atmosphere of death. This was a place where shameful acts could be performed in peace, hidden.

At the deepest level of the catacombs, concealed from all but the weakest light, she came once more and at last to Broussard. His battered and faltering body lay stretched and helpless, lashed to the obscene machine of the Inquisitor. She did not cry out at the sight. She could offer him little aid, but what she could give, as always before, she would.

Masked to declare his work impersonal and blameless, the Inquisitor snarled a pale hand within her beloved's hair and lifted his head to look upon her. She caught her breath quickly as his eyes opened. She steeled herself for his sake, offering all that she had left, the only thing they could not take. She held out to him the last of her strength through the warmth of her eyes.

From beneath his mask, the Inquisitor made his demand again to the fading man in his grasp, "Speak your secret."

She had wondered what she could possibly know that these men would bring her here, to threaten her with these horrors, or to hope that she might break at the sight of her ruined husband. But when the calloused hand of her guide yanked her hair from behind, his rattling breath moved close to her ear, and his cold blade pressed against the soft flesh of her exposed throat, she understood how foolish she had been. They did not believe she knew anything at all. She was not here to watch her husband die. After all, it was *his* secret they craved.

The Inquisitor kept Broussard's eyes fixed upon her, the bargain clear. If he failed to comply he would witness the result. "Speak your secret."

Above his head, coarse, biting rope bound his hands at the wrists to the machine. Broussard pondered the glaze of scar tissue where his finger, lost these many years, once had been. He thought to speak of it, to tantalize and torture his own tormentors with a taste of it in words. *King's X.* But through his ebbing strength he could only offer in weak defiance, "Lost."

This secret they demanded, he could not give. They wanted to know *where.* Of course, through careful planning and desperate deeds, that was the one thing he had made certain he did *not* know. It moved on the trade winds of unknown seas, in the hands of one without destination, elusive as a corsair. He had seen to it that no depth of atrocity they might reach in this pit could possibly cause him to reveal anything of real value. Thus, he had seen to it that there could be no escape. None for him. And now, as he saw the true depth of his failure, none for her.

The Inquisitor signaled the man behind her, and even as she felt the slow sting of the edge, her beloved reached to embrace her once more with his failing gaze. Through battered lips and bruised flesh, his face contorted into what she understood to be a smile, he breathed her name and spoke only for her, "Do not be afraid."

Unable to turn from her eyes while there was still life in them, he held her quiet and still as he offered his last words. Strange, gentle, a tender command or a reassuring plea, Khali felt within them the unfathomable possibility of a story much larger than this moment could reveal. "Wait for me."

"…and so you have to begin all over again like children, and know nothing of what happened in ancient times…"

--Plato

Chapter One

There was no special alignment of the stars at the time of her birth. The event was not preceded by any particular omens. In the spring of 1952, Molly Reed arrived in Alexandria, Virginia.

An awakening is a step from one world into another. Whether the coming day brings good fortune or bad, there can be no preparation for it. The eyes open, the world is new, and the sleeper is suddenly there, right in the middle of it, breathing it in. Molly's eyes first opened to bright lights and the gentle features of her mother's face as she breathed in the cool, antiseptic air of a hospital room.

Molly grew up with her older brother, Brian, in the sheltered environment of the suburbs, in a home provided by adoring and devoted parents. She was a pretty girl who quickly learned the power her beauty gave her over others. She had noticed how it could cause men to soften, and other girls to bristle. She was also a very smart girl who understood that there was an edge in beauty and practical uses for tears. For most of her life she wasn't shy about using either of them to her advantage.

When they failed to stop her parents from divorcing, she learned that the power of tears had strict limits. Soon after her father moved out of the house, Brian died in a far off place called Viet Nam, and Molly began to see the world as much larger than it had always seemed, filled with far greater tragedies than her own. She cried less often and more deeply when she did.

She wept alongside her mother with passions she could not quite understand when President Kennedy was murdered in Dallas. Five years later, she wept with just as little understanding when Martin Luther King Jr. was murdered in Memphis. She knew little of those men, only that they were great enough that people listened to what they said. She felt very far away from these events that happened in other cities and deep into the world of adults, but she still felt the pain of loss. It seemed that when great men were taken away, they were taken from everyone.

She saw pictures of the assassins on television along with everyone else in the country. Maybe her questions were too childish for good answers. *Why would anyone do such a thing?* It always seemed that no one really knew for certain, or if they did, they wouldn't say, like it was some kind of secret.

Molly's tears over such things came less powerfully with the simple passage of time, as if she had been numbed by successive shocks. She wondered if being older and wiser might just mean that old wounds had turned to unfeeling scar tissue.

In the summer of 1968, somewhere in the middle of her sixteenth year, Molly began to receive answers about many secret things. It was the summer of her awakening, when everything changed. It began, as all awakenings must, in her sleep. It began with shadows, whispers, and fear. It began hot like stale breath, cold like stone walls in the dark, and with pain like a thousand pin-pricks to soft skin. Molly's awakening began with very bad dreams.

Chapter Two

Los Angeles, June 1968

James Ford did not remember too much about how he had come to be here. He knew that he was supposed to kill a man. He had purchased a . 22 caliber Smith & Wesson handgun, along with a small box of bullets from a La Brea Avenue pawnshop just for that purpose. But where the facts were fragmented in his mind, like a man straining to pick up the thread of a disturbing dream, he remained dimly aware that he had never fired a gun in his life, much less ever killed anyone. Elsewhere on that poorly illuminated level of thought, close enough to the surface for him to sense, but still too obscured to grasp, it seemed that if he were really going to kill someone, he ought to at least know who he was killing and why that person might deserve to die.

He tried to think about these things, but no answers came to him. He knew only that his chance would come soon, in downtown Los Angeles. A man would be moving within a crowd, and he would shoot that man dead with as many shots as it might take to be sure. James had brought everything he would need with him from home. The driving glasses that helped him see clearly from a distance waited with his new gun, tucked within his powder blue windbreaker. All that remained was the wait. For some reason, one that also escaped him, he chose to wait here in the Hollywood Rose Motel.

Danger gathers slowly around men who are not what they seem, and

Sara's senses were bristling at it now. He had seemed before to be just a frustrated husband looking for an escape, but finding a gun on him changed everything. As the other girls soothed him and slowly stroked his bared flesh, Sara moved his jacket, and the heavy black weapon within it, further out of reach to the chair by the nightstand.

She reminded herself of the things Donnie always said, the things that would make the game foolproof. If she and the other girls pick the right kind of mark, a man with a family and a reputation to protect, nothing will even be reported. No one ever gets hurt. Donnie was very clever. So far, his plan had worked every time. They had played this game half-a-dozen times and never even fired a shot. Still, this man hadn't seemed the type to carry a gun.

James knew in the inner recesses of his mind that he was not a killer. He knew, or at least thought he knew, that he was a manager of New Accounts at a Wells Fargo bank in Cheyenne, Wyoming. He knew that he lived with a quiet and steady woman named Laurie, that she was his wife, that she had given him two children, and that he loved her at least most of the time. He knew that he kept to ten cigarettes a day and drank one martini most evenings, and two at the end of the week. Yet he found himself struggling even to wonder how he had come to be in this room.

There were three young women with him. Attracted by the roll of cash he had withdrawn from his market rate savings account before leaving Cheyenne two days earlier, they had secured for him two cubes of black, sticky sweet hashish from the streets of Hollywood. He had smoked the strangely familiar substance with them from a pipe as if he had done it a thousand times in the past. Still, he knew he had never done any such thing before this day. He tried to remember the names of his children. There were two.

When she heard the muffled scratch of the key against the lock, Sara watched as if a premonition was unfolding before her. James Ford's clouded eyes snapped into focus. His body, once softened and relaxed by the soft red tracks gently scratched into his skin by her companions, tensed like a primed coil.

The door burst open. The men rushed in. Donnie and his two partners waved their guns and shouted in the fearsome choreography she had seen many times before. That was supposed to be it. The girls had done their part and their mark was naked and helpless on the bed. All that was left was for him to cry out, maybe burst into tears at the shame of it, beg for his life, and hand over everything he had with a promise of more.

As the girls pulled away, James Ford grabbed Sara by the hair and yanked her across the bed, opening a clear path to his weapon. Sara fell hard into the corner. She did not look up again until the shooting started. The first thing she saw was fire spitting from Donnie's gun and the look of shock on his face as three holes seemed to explode outward from his denim jacket, ejecting pieces of fabric, bone, and blood directly from above his heart. She sank, hunkered and small, into the corner as the grim spectacle played out in front of her.

With unwavering precision and determination, under a storm of fire from the three panic-stricken intruders, James Ford killed them all. It had only taken an instant, but when the deafening volleys finally stopped, they were all dead. All but one.

Sara crawled from behind the bed, spurred by terror and her own rushing pulse, and climbed quaking to her feet. She reached for Tammy, almost touching her before she saw the blood pooling on the carpet beneath her head. Sara recoiled at the sight of her once pretty face after a bullet from James Ford's gun had passed through it from behind. Horror gave way to panic. She was alone. For the last four months, Donnie and his friends had been her life, her livelihood and her family. Recalling out of instinct what it is like to exist on the streets of Los Angeles without money, she managed to cross the room to where James Ford's devastated body lay crumpled against the wall, to the chair that held his clothes. His chest still rose and fell with a wet sucking sound as he watched her move past his feet.

She reached into his coat and he stirred. Sara froze within his long stare. He seemed to be looking right through her. He raised his weapon. Despite his fading strength, despite his glazing vision, he held the gun steady. His aim was still perfect. Less than three feet away, she could smell the smoke drifting in acrid tendrils from the hot barrel. Even as she imagined the bullet passing through her own head, she could not force herself to move. A strong part of her even wanted it to happen, an ending to fear. She remained transfixed.

He spoke with the conviction of a man who knew he was speaking for the last time. From a deeper sadness he offered the words, to her, to himself, or to someone hidden in the dark well of his thoughts. Sara did not understand them, but even as the blood from his punctured lungs choked the words in his throat, she heard them clearly enough.

"Nothing is true. All is permitted."

He pulled the trigger. The hammer clicked harmlessly over the empty chamber. As his lung collapsed a little more upon itself, it pushed the blood in his throat out through his nostrils and past his lips. Still, he watched her. The last part of his body to hold its strength, his gun hand, began to tremble. He pulled the trigger again. Another hollow click. With his life rapidly leaving him, James Ford wondered again what he was doing in this place. Like a man trying to find his way back into his own waking mind after a bad dream, he struggled to recall someone who had been important. A woman. Laurie.

Sara tore herself away from the sight of life leaving James Ford's body and hurriedly dug through his powder blue windbreaker.

Chapter Three

The oddest thing about Wendell Book might have been that he had never set foot outside the city limits of Los Angeles in his entire life. Not even once.

In a very real sense, through orphanages and foster homes, he had been raised by Los Angeles. He had once dreamed of travel and had prepared for a career that would have shown him the world, or at least the rest of the country. But things changed.

He could once run a distance of forty yards a full two tenths of one second faster than any above-average man his size and lift more than twice his weight in iron. When he was 18, Book received a scholarship to play linebacker for the University of California at Los Angeles. That was as close as he ever came to any kind of glory. Before even stepping on the field in uniform, an unlucky instant on the practice field resulted in two mangled tendons in his right knee, and a permanent limp which rendered him, at best, significantly slower than the average man his size.

Book was left with a natural warrior's body that had never seen a fight. He had volunteered for the Marine Corps, but the injury that had kept him off the playing field also kept him safe from the jungles of Viet Nam. And so he stayed. He stayed in school for four years and in Los Angeles, it seemed, forever. He now worked for the city as a policeman, a detective in the Hollywood Vice Division. At only 27, Book knew he was getting old too fast, but somehow, almost against his will, he was still in the same place, waiting.

A knock at the door is a rare thing in Hollywood apartment buildings. His neighbors generally kept to themselves anyway, but Book's odd working hours often made it seem like he had the entire building to himself.

It was six o'clock in the evening. Book was just getting dressed for his shift. Still in his underwear, wearing one sock and holding the other in his hand, Book opened his door. A fragile old man in a finely tailored new suit that seemed to defy his sagging skin and forward curving spine, craned his neck upward in slow surprise at the much taller young man. "Wendell Book?"

"Yeah," Book answered, instinctively cautious. His bills and taxes were paid as far as he could remember, but no other reason jumped to mind for this man to knock on his door. "Who are you?"

"My name is Grissom." Mr. Grissom reached into his coat, digging within the breast pocket as he spoke. "I am your father's attorney."

"My father?" Book's caution began to blend with deeper suspicion at the sudden invoking of an unpleasant memory. "Carl Book?"

"That's correct." Grissom continued to dig in his coat.

Book listened to the sound of bending and crumpling paper as the old man struggled to free an oversized article from the undersized pocket he had stuffed it into. "I don't remember my father ever having a lawyer."

"Yes, well," Grissom dispassionately countered. "I only met the man once." At last he freed a thick envelope from his coat and offered it to Book. "Sixteen years ago, he retained my services. He wanted me to deliver this letter to his son. In person and in private."

Book stared at the envelope without taking it. It was heavily taped, yellowed with age, and it bulged at the middle. "Aren't you a little late?"

"Not at all. I am precisely on time. My instructions were specific.

This letter was to be delivered today. I hope you haven't been waiting for it for too long."

Wendell Book was ten years old when he first realized that his father was a lunatic. In the last days of his life, the old man had blossomed into the kind of lunatic easily picked out from any crowd as crazy. His expression was both wild and hollow at once, standing in stark contrast to the sane. Carl Book saw many things that simply weren't there, and toward the end, he had taken to talking to his son about them quite a bit.

Book's earliest memories as a son were of taking pride in his father's work at the munitions plant where he turned scrap metal donated by patriotic Californians into artillery shells bound for the fight against the Nazis, a fight the old man had always seemed to take personally. Shortly after that, everything changed, and the boy's pride turned to something else entirely.

It had been sixteen years since his father had last spoken to him - sixteen years since the old man walked out to the garage to end his tormented life by putting a bullet through his own head. Some memories leave impressions, some memories leave scars. If a father is a window to what a child might become, then no child could forget witnessing his father's disintegration into madness. And no boy could truly forgive him for the ultimate act of cowardice without the risk of becoming a coward himself. Wendell Book had memories of his father that cut to the bone. In the years since he last saw the old man, he had grown into a strong, decent man with one great vice, a single self-indulgence. Book hated his father. He worked hard to leave the past unexamined, resting in peace, far from the surface of his thoughts. What Mr. Grissom brought to him now was an unwelcome invasion of his most secret and shameful thoughts.

Book looked from the letter to the old man, whose hand was beginning to shake from the effort to hold it between them. "You're saying that in 1952, my father gave you a letter to be delivered to me on June 4th, 1968?"

"That's correct."

The information coming from Mr. Grissom was simple enough, but Book still felt like he was trying to solve a complex mathematical equation in his head. "How did you know where to find me?"

Grissom raised his shaggy eyebrows before offering the obvious. "Phone book."

"Oh." Book stared for a moment longer, but no further explanation seemed forthcoming from Mr. Grissom. Finally, he took the envelope. "Thanks."

Grissom nodded politely before heading on delicate legs toward the stairs. "Good evening."

Book closed the door again, alone now in his home with his father's apparent last words in his hand. He stared at the hasty scrawl of a single word address, *Wendell*. Whatever was inside must have come very shortly before the end.

In his other hand Book still held his sock. Leaning past his bad knee to dress his right foot was generally the hardest thing he had to do before heading to work. It only took a moment for Book to decide what to do next. He dropped the old yellow envelope into the wastepaper basket by his desk with a heavy, satisfying thud and returned to getting dressed. He would not be late for work.

Chapter Four

Book stepped into the killing room at the Hollywood Rose Motel at a slow, deliberate pace designed to ease the permanent sting of his knee and hide its weakness.

He had seen dead people before, but he was a vice detective, only a few months on the job, and he wasn't used to scenes like this. But the Rose, a haven for prostitutes and local businessmen on their lunch hours, was a regular part of his world. That was why they were here. Book and his partner, Frank Harker, a thick, slow moving veteran of the vice division whose powerful body had been softened by years of eating on the run, keeping odd hours, and needing a drink or two before he could fall asleep most nights, could identify the bodies and maybe shed some light on what might have happened for the homicide crew. One thing was obvious to everyone, even the two vice cops. The nude body in the corner had once belonged to an expert killer. A professional.

"Jesus Christ," Harker said to no one in particular as Book entered the room behind him. He waved a meaty finger toward the nearly identical bullet wounds above the hearts of the three dead attackers. "Like paper targets."

From the punctured fabric on Donnie Cessic's jacket, Book could see that three bullets had struck within a circle about the size of a silver dollar, right above his heart. Book looked back to the man in the corner. His body was a gruesome mess of maybe two-dozen entrance and exit wounds, but he still held the gun in his hand. "Yeah," Book agreed with his partner, "but paper targets don't shoot back."

Book and Harker were there to make the second simple observation, the detail only they could see. They looked over Donnie Cessic, the familiar faces of his two friends, and the wilted bodies of the women on the floor. They knew all of them, and they knew what had happened right away. They also knew that someone was missing. A witness.

Chapter Five

Sara Jamison had been in Los Angeles for just under a year. She was nineteen years old and she had run away from a man. Her father, her boyfriend, her husband; from a vice cop's perspective it made little difference. Book was beginning to notice that all of the street stories eventually begin to blur into a single, consistent, cheerless narrative. Whatever hopeful plan she had brought with her was gone by the time Book first met her. The urgent need for food and shelter that surprises so many young girls coming to this city alone and without money had already led her to Donnie Cessic.

Book never chose the Vice Division. He had entered the force a frustrated hero, eager to serve, dedicated to fighting for whatever cause he could find. As a result, he made detective very young. Vice was his first assignment, so he took it with the idea that he'd make the best of it. But it was depressing work, policing sad people for doing ugly things that, for whatever reason, they just couldn't avoid doing.

Sara represented everything that gave Book hope for his new position. She was an opportunity for him to help someone who was too new to this life to be too far gone. She also represented everything he hated about his job. Few people he encountered on the street really wanted to be helped at all. Sara was no different. She just wanted to sink a little further each day, until maybe she couldn't come up for the next breath. Suicide without really having to think about it.

Frank Harker was an excellent partner, the kind that would bend a rule or look the other way out of his own sense of justice, and the kind that wouldn't hesitate to give good advice whether it was wanted or not. Frank viewed deep concern for tragic figures as a professional character flaw that could completely overwhelm any vice cop who couldn't develop a hard callous soon enough. He had warned Book about Sara before. Book's big-brotherly attitude was one of the quickest routes to burnout for a police officer. Though he was beginning to feel the strain, the wounds his profession inflicted on the heart had not yet hardened. Book still wanted to help.

Book and Harker found Sara Jamison in the first place they looked. She had fled the killing room at the Rose and gone straight back to Donnie Cessic's apartment. When they found her, she was alone and frightened half out of her mind. They also found James Ford's wallet, complete with his Wyoming driver's license, flopped open on Donnie's coffee table.

Harker noticed Book soften at the sight of her tears. Her weakness seemed to leave him vulnerable. Harker moved quickly, stepping in to test her sobriety, to see if she could be of any use. "Who was he, Sara?" He leaned in authoritatively, locking his eyes to hers, pushing her thoughts back to the killing room. "Did he say anything?"

Sara answered his question, whispering James Ford's last words as if afraid to speak them too loudly. The words she recounted meant nothing to Frank, but they brought an itch to the back of Book's skull. Harker watched as his partner's brow involuntarily tightened and his eyes rolled to the side as if searching for a memory in a dark corner of the room. *Nothing is true. All is permitted.*

"Mean anything to you?" Harker jokingly asked him.

Sara was obviously still high. She was babbling, making no sense.

For some reason that escaped both men, Book did not think his partner's tone was funny. He abruptly decided that Sara might be a better witness in a few hours and that it was best to get her off the street. They took her from Donnie Cessic's apartment and were headed to drop her in the tank on Wilcox, when the news came in over the radio in their car.

Shortly after midnight, police frequencies became flooded with cross talk, so many stunned and frantic voices at once, that Book and Harker couldn't get the straight story until they reached the desk sergeant at the Wilcox station. A United States Senator had been shot to death at the Ambassador Hotel in downtown Los Angeles. Robert Francis Kennedy had been the odds on favorite to be the next President of the United States.

Everything had suddenly changed.

Chapter Six

Book had not been afraid of anything in particular since he was a child. He was not afraid now, at least not of anything in particular. But it had been just as long since he could not sleep at night. There had been a time, when he was very young, when fear kept him awake long into the night. Fear of bad dreams.

Book was usually asleep by noon. But at three o'clock, his thoughts swirled over what he had seen and heard the night before. The gruesome scene at the Rose, the tragedy at the Ambassador, and maybe most of all, what they had learned about James Ford from Sara Jamison, all combined to leave Book staring at the ceiling above his bed.

Who was he, Sara? Frank had asked. *Did he say anything?*

The itch that had risen at the back of his skull remained, demanding and persistent, until he began to recall the last time he had felt it. Like some nightmare creature rising from a still pool, Book's father reached out to him from the past. His mind turned back to that time and place, and he remembered what it felt like to be afraid. Book recalled the first time he had heard James Ford's dying words. That was the last day before the bad dreams began.

***

Wendell Book's father led him by the hand along the sun-bleached wooden planks of the Santa Monica Pier. They moved within the afternoon crowd toward the end, where the boardwalk penetrated the ocean to within a few dozen yards of a precipitous undersea slope, where the shallows rapidly fall into the deep.

The old man no longer slept at night. By day he watched and listened, weary and anxious as a rabbit chased by hounds only he could see and hear. And they seemed to have caught up with him at last.

Though not truly very old, his father seemed aged before his time by the rigors of the hunt. Wendell had known nothing of madness before. It could have been the harsh thing his mother had shielded him from all along. But she was gone now, and he had come to know madness through the old man as a strange and frightening thing.

They stood with the clamor of the swirling carnival machines behind them, and an endless expanse of silver sunlight flashing on grey water just beyond the railing. Carl Book gently reached to the third finger of his left hand to touch the golden wedding ring, the symbol of his life-long bond, now broken by his wife's death, too suddenly, without justice, without mercy. She had been buried less than an hour ago. Father and son still wore their funeral clothes.

"Listen to me, boy," he said as he nervously scanned the crowd behind them. Though the old man's face appeared frightening, drawn with fatigue and his eyes red from the intense effort to remain alert, the boy tried to open his heart to listen, as if nothing had changed. Wendell felt rewarded and suddenly encouraged when his father began a familiar tale.

"A hungry tigress, heavy with her cub about to be born, fell upon a flock of sheep one day in a meadow."

A bedtime story. Wendell knew it by heart. He and his mother had play-acted the events nearly every evening throughout better times. Though he was too old for bedtime stories now, this was the first time he had ever heard his father tell the tale, and the boy wondered at that as he listened.

"But the fury of her attack upset the baby tiger in her belly. She brought her little one into the world in that moment, but hungry and weak as she was, the young mother tiger died from the effort."

Wendell took a short breath, though the story was very old to him, in this moment, the death of the mother carried more mystery, more pain. Tears came to Wendell's cheek, but he did not weep. He listened. "Now, when the flock returned to their meadow, they found a little tiger cub, alone, and crying out for his mother." His father paused at the sight of the quiet tears. He drew in a hard breath through his nose and forged ahead, rushing to complete the tale. "Being friendly sheep, they took the cub in to raise as one of their own. For one year he lived among them, wandering like a sheep, *bah-bahing* like a sheep, and grazing on grass and roots like a sheep. He learned all of their ways and believed with all his heart, since he had never known anything else, that he was a sheep."

Carl Book paused to look toward the crowd on the pier again, penetrating deep within it to see if anyone looked back.

"What about the other tiger?" Wendell spoke up, sensing that his father was drifting away from him, and wanting desperately to bring him back.

The old man turned back to his son. He softened a little at his child's pain, and found pride in the way he carried it. "One day a very great tiger, a powerful warrior with many battle scars in his fur, fell upon the flock for a meal. And standing over his dinner, he noticed a sickly young tiger hiding among the frightened sheep. 'You there,' the great tiger roared, 'what are you doing among those sheep?'"

Despite being too old, Wendell replied on cue, "Baahh." He did this for his father's sake, for the sake of the story.

His father returned a little nearer from the desolate place his mind took him, smiled, and dried his son's cheek with his thumb. "'Well, now,' said the great tiger, 'this won't do at all. Come here.'" The old man continued at an increasing pace. "Though he was very frightened, the little tiger thought he was a sheep, so he obeyed. The great tiger led him to a pond. They stood side by side on the edge and looked in. 'What do you see when the water is still?'"

"'A tiger!'" Wendell answered, happily wrapping himself in the familiar warmth of those better times. "'I look like you!'"

"'Yes,' the great tiger answered, 'like me, only skinny, sickly, and weak from eating grass and flowers all of your life.' The great tiger was angry. 'Who told you to live this way? Who told you that you were a sheep?'"

Wendell smiled as he spoke his part, a boy reunited, at least for the moment, with his father. "'No one told me. It's just all I can remember, all I have ever known.'"

As he looked deeper into his son's eyes, the manic glare seemed to fade even further, replaced by an anxious and aching joy. His mind burned to teach the boy what he knew he could not. Wendell was too young, still at peace within the walls of his ignorance, and utterly defenseless should the hounds catch his scent.

"I cannot tell you who and what you truly are, boy. That is something you can only find out for yourself. But I can tell you what you are not." The father's hand entwined with the son's hair, affectionate, loving, but too hard, and with too much need behind the gesture. Wendell remained quiet, listening. "You are not a sheep," the old man sputtered; close enough to tears to frighten the boy again, letting all the comfort of the familiar tiger tale slip away. "No matter what they might tell you."

The old man realized that his grip was hurting, and that the boy was either too brave or too frightened to tell him. He unclenched his hand, and smoothed the hair back down where he had mussed it.

"There is not much time," his father warned, returning sharply to the pier, where his darting eyes seemed to sense dangers lurking all around.

He lowered himself to the boy's height to better reach his heart. He showed Wendell the pale wedding band on his finger, an heirloom of his wife's family once worn by her grandfather, so that the child might *feel* something of the weight of time. "This is the *King's X*." His eyes pierced the boy now. "Do you see it?"

Wendell looked from his father's gaunt face to the ring and back again, puzzling over his words. *King's X* was a child's game. *King's X,* the most powerful rule of the playground, the rule that turns all other rules upside-down.

"Do you see it?" he demanded, rattling the silent child with one quick shake.

"Yes." Wendell knew the words, but he did not understand.

To claim "King's X" out loud during a game of Hide and Seek, Ghost in the Graveyard, or any other is to call upon inviolable protection from being "It." To merely cross your fingers in the sign of the *King's X* and then hold them hidden behind your back, places the invoker in a fantastic, invisible field wherein the weight of ethics vanishes and all rules are suddenly null and void. Any child who knows this sign can become free to lie, or make false promises. Wendell knew all this, but he also knew it was make-believe. The sign of the crossed fingers, or the power of the spoken words, *King's X*, were known to all on the playground, but it seemed very odd to hear the words coming from his father. Wendell wondered for the first time where the great rule really came from, how far back in time it might reach, and how many other adults might know it. But his father was saying something different now, that "King's X" was something real. Something you could touch. An old wedding ring.

"That's a game," Wendell protested, stating a fact, trying to stand on hard ground while his father moved in quicksand. "It's not real."

"I will tell you a secret, son. A very great secret." His father calmed and the glare faded for a moment from his eyes. "Nothing is *real*."

Wendell did not understand this either, nor would he ever forget it. He could see that, even if for only a moment, this was his father speaking and not the mad man.

"Nothing is *true*." His voice lowered further. "*All is permitted*. That knowledge is a weapon. Remember it, and one day it will make you strong enough to fight."

Wendell squinted as he tried to understand. "Fight?"

"One day a great tiger will come for you, Wendell. You will discover what you really are. You need only wait." He spoke the word once more like a command, before his eyes turned again to search the crowd. "Wait."

If he could have thought beyond the pain and fear of watching his father's disintegration, if he could have seen it for what it was instead of struggling with only a child's understanding to make sense of it, Wendell could have pointed out, *there is no one watching us!* He would have insisted that his mother had died just as the police had explained it, that an unlucky encounter with a desperate drifter had left her purse empty and too much of her blood on the sidewalk. But he could say none of those things.

The old man lifted his left hand between them again to let the child's attention linger for a few more heartbeats with the wedding ring and all it might mean to him. "When the dreams come to you... bad dreams..." His voice wavered and cracked as if from a deep pain. The boy looked away out of fear, closing his heart against it until his father reached out again and turned his head back, forcing him to see. "Remember what you see now."

A tingling sensation climbed like slow lightning up the boy's spine as he watched his father's right hand draw the small hunting knife from beneath his jacket. Wendell looked on in silent terror as the madness took control. The old man dropped from his crouch onto his knees, flattened his left hand against the pier, inhaled powerfully through his nose, and pushed the point of the blade through his third finger just behind the golden ring.

Wendell's eyes remained locked on the sight even as his muscles suddenly failed him. His face remained oddly unchanged by the horror he felt, while his legs gave way so quickly that he simply fell backward into a sitting position, only inches from the pooling blood. A woman gasped, and voices murmured and protested. Wendell remained transfixed as his father sawed the rest of the way through, detaching the ring along with the entire finger.

Breathing hard with the effort to remain conscious, Carl Book snatched the dead finger from the crimson pool, pulled the ring free of it, and rose to his full height. He turned to show the bloodied band one last time to his silent child, repeating, *"Remember what you see."*

Wendell quivered to his feet, watching as his father moved unsteadily to the rail. The old man hurled the ring far into the ocean. It tumbled and fell for several seconds, until it passed into the water through a sudden and silent rip at the surface. His father lingered over the spot where it had disappeared for a moment longer, then he turned back to study the crowd, to see who else might have been watching. Many watched them now, in a fearful and widening circle.

***

Book blinked at his ceiling. Beyond his drawn blinds, the sun was sinking fast. He had not slept, and it was time for work again.

Sitting upright at the edge of his bed, he wrapped his hands around his knee to warm some of the stiffness from it. His mind remained with his father, sixteen years ago, and at the same time it was with Sara Jamison, the last person to ever see James Ford alive. *Who was he Sara? Did he say anything?* The words were the same. *Nothing is true.* His father had called it a great secret. *All is permitted.* But his father had been a lunatic. Only hours after burying his wife, after those terrifying moments on the pier, he had wandered into their garage and shot himself in the head. That was when Wendell was left alone. That was the night the bad dreams started. That was when everything changed.

Book crossed slowly toward his desk. He studied the metal wastepaper basket for several seconds before finally nudging it over with his foot. A week's worth of magazines and papers spilled out on the floor. Among them was a thick envelope, heavily taped and yellowed with age, addressed in a hasty scrawl with one word, *Wendell.* It was the last thing he wanted to do, but he would have to do it. Book tore at the tape and opened the letter.

Inside he found a note with a few words in his father's jagged handwriting, and something heavy, wrapped in newspaper. The note was simple and sounded as insane as Book remembered the old man, but it did nothing to lessen the itch crawling up the back of his skull.

Wait for her. KX.

Book furrowed his brow at the note while he held the newspaper-wrapped object in his other hand. At least he could be certain this note came from the old man. His final command, *wait for her*, scribbled in the midst of his downward spiral, close to the very end, undoubtedly referred to some character from the terrifying fantasies that constantly competed for his hold on reality. Ultimately of course, the fantasies won out. And then, *KX*. Book lifted his disapproving eyes to the ceiling and tried to lick the smirk from his mouth. *King's X*. A child's game, a playground rule that his father believed was an old wedding ring. Now, apparently, he also believed it was a heavy object wrapped in newspaper.

He continued to stare at the ceiling as if asking it what he should do next, but the itch remained. *Who was he Sara? Did he say anything?* Book stared at the thin bundle of faded paper.

No boy can witness his father's cowardice and not be scarred. No child can see a father's insanity and not carry it with him forever. What cannot be forgotten takes great effort to suppress, and years of work can be easily undone in a single unguarded moment. Book knew the emotion that was creeping in like a poisoned tide to re-color his darkest memories, and he feared it almost as much as the images themselves. Book was beginning to feel hope. Unwarranted, foolish, empty, and possibly devastating hope that there could have been some reason, some cause, some purpose behind everything the old man had done and said.

Book acted quickly, before his better judgment could stop him. He tore at the newspapers, unraveling the bundle until the hard object slid out into the palm of his hand. *King's X*.

Book rolled it over in his hand once to look at both sides, and his returning smirk quickly grew into laughter. Taken from the munitions plant where his father had worked during the war, it was a thick disk of brass, much wider and thicker than a silver dollar, forged of scrap metal culled from the donated possessions of patriotic Californians. Once meant to be the firing cap of a 105 millimeter artillery shell, it was now a simple souvenir from a time of great and terrible deeds, and yet another unwanted reminder of a broken, crazy old man, sixteen years dead. Meaningless, valueless, it might as well have been a baseball or a shoe.

"Son of a bitch." Book smiled at the pain, forcing another laugh at how the old man could still reach him.

Chapter Seven

Virginia. November, 1968

At first, Molly could not recall the nightmares that left her fighting for consciousness and screaming in the dark. No images lingered of the terrors that brought her mother rushing to her bedside in the middle of the night, that saw Julie Reed arrive frightened and unrecognized, until she could cradle and soothe her daughter back to the light of her bedroom as she hadn't since Molly was a small child. In the summer, they came once or twice a month, infrequently enough that her mother could reasonably convince herself that they were a simple byproduct of hormones. But once school began in September, they came more often, sometimes more than once a week. Now, with only a week to go before the Thanksgiving recess, Molly knew she was losing her mind.

They came every night, grim phantoms relentlessly assaulting the girl until the images began to take shape in her conscious mind as well. There was pain; the burning torment of every muscle in her body cramped tight and torn loose all at once. She could not move even to draw a breath. Men stood all around her, vague shapes barely touched by weak and shifting firelight. They were indiscernible to both the fevered mind that saw them and to her waking mind that struggled to bring them into focus, yet they gave off an unmistakable odor of aged masculine sweat which blended with the stench of rot pervading her dream world. Each night the dream was of the same place, the same circumstance, and each night it grew clearer and the fear more acute. She was trapped, held fast and torn asunder all at once, fighting for a breath that could not come. Though she could not tell from where the knowledge came, this one thing she knew; the unbearable pain would not stop until she was dead.

Each encounter came with increased ferocity until Julie Reed rushed to her daughter's bedside again, pulled Molly tightly to her, and looked into her face only to see someone else's eyes looking back at her.

Molly had stopped screaming, held securely as she was in her mother's arms. Her next words came as an emotionless request, spoken by someone who had no more levels of pain to reach, no more will to endure, and who had suddenly looked up to find the sympathetic face of a woman looking down from above. "Kill me."

Julie could not understand, but she nevertheless knew in that instant; the person who spoke those words was not her daughter. The child in her arms continued in a leaden whisper, heavy with despair, "It is lost. It is lost." Julie waited in helpless silence for a moment, until Molly could come all the way back to her, until the child could return to bury her face in her mother's bosom, sobbing and crying, finally, without control.

The next day, Molly stayed home from school and Julie stayed home from work to be with her. The hysterics of the night had passed, and Molly was again calm and thoughtful. But Julie still sensed something different within her, and watched over her with poorly hidden concern.

Molly had spent the morning searching the house for books. Any books. She searched her own girlish bookshelf with growing frustration at the conglomeration of poetry, romance, and her own childhood fascination with horses and dolphins. She went through her mother's bookshelf and the boxed up text books from her parents' college days. Molly did not know what she was looking for; she only knew that she couldn't find it.

Seated at the kitchen table, Molly poured over the pages of the largely unused gift her Grandmother had presented on the occasion of her tenth birthday, a Bible. She had found nothing helpful in it yet, and the half-completed college application sat untouched on the table. Molly had planned to apply for early admission to Georgetown, to follow in her father's footsteps and go on to law school. Her mother thought working on her application might be a welcome distraction for her. Welcome or not, it failed to distract. College and the future, to Molly, now seemed pointless diversions. She rapidly turned pages, as if she operated under a deadline or expected to find a forgotten bookmark. At times she would pause over a few words standing out in mid-stream among thousands, as if her eye had been caught by a photograph.

She lingered with the mysteriously familiar tale of Daniel. Plagued by terrible dreams, the mighty King Nebuchadnezzar, his own sorcerers having failed him, had summoned the Hebrew to discern their hidden meaning. Her mother's voice faded into white noise behind her in the kitchen as she concentrated on the prophet's words.

And he changeth the times and the seasons: he removeth kings, and setteth up kings: he giveth wisdom unto the wise, and knowledge to them that know understanding...

For Julie, there was only the sense of slow-rising panic, not unlike what she had felt when she first began to suspect her husband would leave her and their daughter alone. She made toast.

"Mol? I talked to your father at his office this morning. He said he'd come over this weekend."

He revealeth the deep and secret things: he knoweth what is in the darkness, and the light dwelleth with him.

.

"I'm starting to see it when I'm awake," Molly offered quietly from the table.

Her panic threatened to boil over. Julie quietly gripped the kitchen counter at her hip to keep it suppressed. "Mol, I think maybe we should talk to a doctor."

Molly looked up at her mother. "It doesn't hurt. That's only in the dream. The dream is like real. This is only like..." She thought about it, not feeling the weight of her mother's pained and searching eyes, "...remembering. It doesn't hurt."

"It's okay, sweetheart." Julie touched her daughter's hair, soft and auburn like her own, but still long and straight like a little girl's. This is perfectly normal, she told herself behind a mask of a smile for Molly. It's hormones.

"I have to go." Molly's words were a simple statement of fact.

"To school?"

"No."

Molly searched but had nothing else to say. Her thoughts remained focused inward, to something forgotten that brought an itch to the back of her mind and tightness to her stomach. There was something that had been important. She tried to recall it for a moment, and as she looked up again into a patient and hopeful face, her mother felt different to her. Like a darkened lighthouse, or a silent bell now covered in a layer of dust, the connection that bound them, that bound all mothers to their children so firmly and forever, had suddenly come undone. Molly felt a sharp, sudden pain of loss with the impossible certainty. They were strangers to each other.

Looking up at her from the breakfast table where she had sat nearly every morning and evening of her life, Molly could not tell if her mother knew it too. She felt alone and responsible in some way just beyond her ability to understand. She quietly stood and left the table before her tears could come. And stranger still, even alone in her room, the tears did not come at all. As she sat at the edge of her bed and turned again to her Grandmother's gift, there was only the feeling that she didn't have much time left.

Chapter Eight

Sara watched the swift rise and fall of Wendell Book's chest where he lay exhausted beside her.

It had been six months since the night he found her in Donnie Cessic's apartment. There were times, before and since then, when Sara had craved an early exit from her life. For weeks she hated him for stopping the end from coming, and she let him know it with all the cruelty and venom she could find. It made no difference. Book was relentless. Within months she was off the street all together. With the help of a few people he had known in college, she now worked as a receptionist in a law office, in the safety of a concrete and steel tower well above the streets of Westwood. For the first time since she had left home, she was unafraid and beholden to no one, or at least no one who wanted anything from her. Sara was beginning to believe in her new life, to trust that it could stay, and her anger toward him had become something altogether different. In an unexpected moment, a kind word had led to a soft touch, her touch to his strong kiss, and suddenly everything had changed. She was in love with Wendell Book and she knew it.

She also knew that he did not share her feelings, at least not yet. And she was smart enough not to press him on it. Sara would let him come closer to her of his own mind, to let him feel the peace and ease of her bed, until he might find himself right where he was now, and realize it was where he had wanted to be all along.

Book watched the subtle orange of the setting sun bleed through a closed window shade. It was time to go to work. He stood slowly, found his clothes draped over a chair in the corner, and began pulling them on one article at a time.

Sara quietly luxuriated in the sight of him in the half-light. She studied him in the way a young woman does when she is wrapping her heart around a man. His close-cut hair of last summer had grown into unruly brown waves. He wore work boots beneath old jeans instead of shoes and slacks, a soft black T-shirt instead of a neck tie, and an old brown leather bomber jacket instead of a suit coat. Book had few poetic thoughts, and likely wouldn't recognize one if he did, but he occasionally showed an unusual fascination for the meaning of words. In one of their long talks together, Sara had asked what he liked about working Vice. The answer was odd and came in few words, but still provided more insight into him than Book would normally allow. The words "collar and tie," she surmised, meant a great deal to him. They seemed to speak of animals, beasts of burden with masters only vaguely known. Innately suspicious of uniforms, Book was never one to voluntarily stick his head into a yoke or fasten his own leash. Vice detectives worked streets where no one but a cop would ever wear a collar and tie. A vice detective never had to wear a suit or look the part of anyone's servant. That was the only thing Book liked about it.

Sara had told him that his suspicion of uniforms probably came from the fact that he was a very old soul who had once had good reason to distrust someone in uniform, maybe even a policeman or a soldier. Book showed little interest in her theory. Sara didn't mind at all. What he lacked in nuance or introspection, he made up for in power and presence. Book was a good and decent man.

Even as a little girl, Sara had never really felt particularly cherished or safe. But when Book walked with her along dark city streets in the time of night when imagination held sway, his presence filled her with a sense she had never felt before. It wasn't that there had been any great dangers lurking in the shadows, though she supposed there could have been. It was the way he made her not even need to think about it. Often, she would look up and catch him protecting her, his eyes penetrating each shaded corner, in his constant vigil to keep her from any possible harm. She never mentioned it, and he would have been embarrassed if she had. Still, she knew with a peculiar and unexpected certainty that, as long as she was with him, nothing bad could happen to her. Book was the strongest man she had ever met. An old soul, she was certain.

There had been a time when Book was simply a cop, and she had been just another runaway to him. But there was a common ground that brought them closer together than either would have thought possible before. Neither had ever let go of that June night in Hollywood. At first, Book would just check up on her to see that she was making an honest living, but their talks would last for hours. Book could listen to the details forever. And she had grown happy to tell him again and again as long as it would keep him near, about the Rose, about James Ford, and the strange thing he had said. *Nothing is true. All is permitted.* The words never made him happy. They never left him satisfied. For some dark reason he could hear them repeated endlessly. And, even more important than the things that happened in real life, Book was fascinated by the dreams that began for her soon after.

Her dreams were very strange, and Sara did not like to recall them. A presence moved within her sleeping mind. It seemed to stand beside her, whispering into her unprotected ear. She told this presence everything she saw. She had not dreamt of it in months. But she would take her waking mind back to go over it all as many times as Book asked, just in case there was anything he missed, anything new she might remember. But there never was.

"Book?" Sara had never begun to call him by his first name, and he had never asked her to. "Do you think..." She grew quiet for a moment, as if her question might be overheard. "Did it have something to do with Kennedy?"

Book watched her where she stretched on her side beneath the rumpled sheets of her bed, his face utterly non-committal. He could choose to laugh at the thought or enthusiastically agree, because he had wondered the same thing before, just enough to make him feel uncomfortable and foolish. "What do you mean?" he hedged.

"Well," she said thoughtfully, "President Kennedy, Martin Luther King, then Bobby Kennedy... it's like somebody just reached out and..." Her heart quickened. "It's like they can just reach out and take anybody they want."

"They?" The word escaped his lips before he could check it, before he could analyze it as a question.

She remained silent and their questions hung heavily between them for several moments. These had been frightening years for the country and the world. People everywhere were living scared. The men she named had represented the possibility of great change, a way out of the mindless cycle of war. All three had died at the hands of lone killers, who may very well have not been working so alone. And their deaths greatly undid all they had worked for. The death of JFK replaced hope with sorrow. The death of MLK transformed a vision of peace into rage. And the death of RFK, only two months later, curbed rage to despair.   The result was silence, the hopeless resignation and useless potential of a tiger in a cage, a different kind of peace altogether.

Book did not like to think about questions like who *they* might be, or what *they* might be up to if *they* existed.   It seemed ridiculous and frustratingly possible at the same time.   Book would much prefer to consider others who talked that way to be fools.   But he did not think Sara was foolish for asking.

He paused above her at the side of her bed on his way to the door. She raised subtly toward him, prompting him to wrap his hand behind the small of her back and lift her gently toward him.   She smiled as she allowed herself to become heavier in his hand, making him work to hold her there. She was selfish and greedy for warmth and comfort.   Something within Book liked the selfishness in her.   She liked the feeling of being held and wanted more of it.   Book pulled her close, pressing her body to his.   Her scent returned to him.   The clear depths of her eyes grew calm and forgetful.   Her lips parted, still swollen.   Her heart moved faster and her soft skin warmed him even through his clothes.   He did not speak again.

***

Book left Sara Jamison's building in the chilling wind churned by the November sunset, unaware of who watched him from across the street. The Shepherd stood unnoticed on the sidewalk, just beyond the circle of light made by a street lamp.   He monitored the young detective more closely now as the time approached.   Souls older and darker than his had told him to be ready.   If she was to come at all, she would come soon.   He would continue to wait and watch for as long as it might take.

He knew the girl.   Sara.   Though she had become important to Book, he knew she was not the one for whom he waited. He had visited her in her sleep. She had witnessed the death of an Assassin. But her voice in the world was unimportant and quiet to all but Book. He would return to Sara in the hours before dawn, to learn more about the things Book knew, and what questions he had asked. The time was approaching fast.

A startled young woman, passing along the sidewalk with a bag of groceries, gasped at the sudden emergence of a man from just beyond the light. She laughed at her own suddenly speeding heart, turning to watch as the Shepherd passed without a word. He was a striking figure; tall, stern, impeccably dressed in a black suit and tie of fine silk, cloaked beneath a long coat of black cashmere. A soft fall of silver hair hung at shoulder length beneath a black fedora. She wondered as she watched him go, how she could not have seen him just a moment before.

Chapter Nine

Molly awoke from the searing dream into the chill of a strange car just at the side of an unfamiliar road. Her cheek was cold and wet where it had been pressed against the vinyl seat. She gripped the wheel with both hands as she returned from the dream without her mother to guide her back to the real world. She checked the clock and tried to get her bearings. She had been asleep for one hour; it was early Sunday morning, still dark. The car rested at the edge of a dirt road, about a mile south of Interstate 40. She was in Texas.

Molly had set out before dawn two days before. Her movements were deliberate, decisive, and systematic. Taking the keys from the peg without really considering it, she traveled two hours West on Interstate 66 in her mother's Vista Cruiser station wagon before she was even missed. It wasn't until Arkansas that she realized how she could be tracked and found through the registered vehicle. After removing the license plates, she abandoned her mother's car at a junkyard with the keys in the ignition. It was unclear why or how any of this even occurred to her, but it seemed a safe bet that once discovered, the car would go unreported at least for a while, if ever. She returned on foot to a parking lot she had scouted before leaving the Vista Cruiser behind, entered an unlocked car, and somehow knew which of the handful of wires pulled from underneath the dashboard could be cut, grounded, and spliced in a way that would start the engine.

It only dimly occurred to her while she worked that her father had once scolded, then laughed at her after she had thrown out a transistor radio because the batteries had died. She had cried, not for his anger, but over her father's laughter for days after it had happened. She had carried the pain of his disapproval, that he thought she was too foolish to teach, for years. Yet now, the memory was more a curiosity. Now, she thought more about the radio.

At the side of this open-country road, Molly was alone except for the unwanted company, almost like the thoughts of another person altogether, which had carried her like a hostage nearly 2,000 miles from her home. No, it was not a captor who moved her, but more a guide, like the priests' devil on one shoulder, or maybe the angel on the other, whispering suggestions into innocent ears. She was losing herself to that voice, being overtaken by something she could not understand, something that brought with it such strength and urgency that it threatened to overwhelm her. She tried to fight it here, asking herself, what would Molly do in a situation like this? The answer was easy, Molly would cry until someone came to help her.

She thought of her mother, imagined the frantic call to her father, and the search happening right now at the homes of her friends and in the woods behind the school where they used to smoke cigarettes. She fought hard to keep these things in her mind. What she fought against she could not perceive. She sensed only the struggle was nowhere near an end, that she was just wasting time. She did not cry.

She glanced down at her Bible, face down on the passenger seat. She had read it all the way through once already, finding nothing to quiet the demanding voice in her thoughts. She turned away from the book to look out of the driver's side window toward the South, where the Texas autumn provided a deep black, unclouded view of heaven.

Molly became caught and soothed by the familiar beauty of the night sky. She could see Saturn rising through the constellation of Pisces. She followed the arc of Pisces to the South and West, calculating her position against the date and time as she went so that she was aware of passing through the vernal equinox, until she came at last to the water flowing from the Jar of Aquarius. She stared in familiar amazement at the grandeur and impossible symmetry of the great celestial gears until fear threatened to overtake her again. Molly knew nothing of these things, yet the courses of the stars flowed to her as if from a page. She forced her attention back to the steering wheel, suddenly desperate to see no more of the sky.

Thoughts of yesterday, the forty-eight hours of straight-through driving it took to get this far, and all things East of where she now rested, were fast fading into obscurity. She focused again on the road West and what was to come. She wanted to send a message to her mother, to ease her worries, but she would not know what to say. She knew that she would not see any of the people she had left behind, ever again. Still, no tears came to her.

When she had fallen asleep by the roadside, Molly felt only that she was headed in the right direction. But now, with new degrees of clarity filtering through to her with each passing day, she knew a little more. She touched the dangling wires and quickly bound them with a twist to start the engine, watched the gauge rise to a quarter-tank, and started back toward the interstate, toward the West, toward California.

Chapter Ten

For six months now Book had felt like a man standing at the edge of a high cliff in a thick fog. He could not see any particular danger, but he sensed it all around. Too many unanswered questions robbed him of too much sleep each day. Asking these same questions out loud was beginning to make waves in the department, attracting the attention of superiors and causing him to wonder if he was making enemies.

"They've got their man," Harker had warned him. "It's kind of embarrassing to lose a Kennedy on your watch, you know? But it's not so bad when you can wrap it up with a quick arrest and an easy conviction."

He watched the light flashing on his phone as he eased his knee under his desk. Frank had already told him who it was, announcing the call from across the squad room with a note of fatherly disappointment in his voice. Sara, calling him an hour before dawn because she knew he was about to get off work. Book scratched his head, debating whether or not to pick up. He had put himself in the position of savior, and she was repaying him with something he never wanted from her. Love, hero-worship, whatever it was, it was more than he could return, and he was starting to feel guilty about seeing her. It was either that, Book realized as his thoughts drifted to the welcoming haven of her bed, or his feelings for her were getting stronger. Maybe that was the more honest reason why he did not want to pick up. Either way, she was somehow the link in his mystery. He could not let her go, even if it would be best for both of them.

Book studied the flashing light of the telephone a moment longer.

Harker was right. If the LAPD wasn't interested in his questions, why should he be? Still, often as he stared at the ceiling above his own bed, deflecting and delaying the silences that had to come before he could sleep, his mind would reach for this odd puzzle. He would think of Laurie Ford, a shattered woman from Wyoming who had no idea why her husband of eleven years would suddenly run off to Los Angeles to die in a drug fueled gunfight. And he would think of a man in a maximum-security cell, on trial for the murder of a U.S. Senator in the midst of a campaign for the presidency.

The same night that James Ford died, Sirhan Bashira Sirhan had shot Robert Kennedy in the head in the middle of a room full of witnesses, and then claimed to have no memory of it at all. Book would think of the whispers, the unsubstantiated rumors of the CIA, the communists, conspiracies, brainwashing, hypnosis, and many more increasingly absurd scenarios surrounding that night in June.

More inexplicable still, Book and Harker had supplied the identity of a skilled killer found dead in a Hollywood motel just hours before the assassination. No one but Book seemed at all concerned about it. In fact, once they had handed Ford's wallet over to Homicide, it was as if it never existed. No follow up and no answers when Book asked. *It's like they can just reach out*, Sara had said, *and take anybody they want.*

Book felt very much like a man watching a magic act. He was perfectly willing to suspend disbelief and just enjoy the performance, but he could *see* the wires supporting the levitating lady. He just couldn't see who pulled them, and he couldn't understand why the LAPD would be so adamant that she really *was* floating out there on the stage.

The lady in this act was Sara. Book knew from the beginning that she was not in on the magician's secrets, although she had seen at least *some* of what had gone on backstage. Enough to tantalize, but not enough to understand. However naïve her intentions had been that night, Sara Jamison was still an accomplice to a robbery/homicide, caught with the victim's wallet in her possession. But she was never charged with anything. She was simply interrogated and released. Like the volunteer in the magician's act, she just returned to her seat in the crowd. The whole thing had been swept under the rug, as if someone did not want to draw any more attention to James Ford's death.

And now, six months later, Book still didn't know why. All he had was the useless testimony of the levitating lady. *Nothing is true. All is permitted.* He lifted the receiver to his ear, pressed the flashing plastic button, and grumbled, "Book."

"I had the dream again." Sara's voice was heavy with fear.

Book leaned forward in his chair and looked around the squad room as if expecting someone to be watching him. No one was.

"The same?"

"Yes. But different." Her voice climbed in pitch. "It was like someone was here. Asking questions."

"Questions about what?" Book asked with a calming voice.

"About you." He heard her rapid breathing. "It asked about you."

"It?"

Frank Harker hung up his own phone. "Hey, Book. That's the desk sergeant downstairs. Somebody broke into your apartment."

Book covered the mouthpiece with his hand and glanced over at his partner like he hadn't heard correctly. "*My* apartment?"

Harker waved a dismissive hand toward another flashing light on his phone. "Line two."

"Book," Sara whispered. "I'm really scared."

"It's okay, Sara." Book's mind raced. "Stay on the phone. I'll be right back."

He clicked the second flashing button. "Book."

"Beat cops caught a kid breaking and entering," the desk sergeant announced.

"*My* apartment?" Book said again, incredulous.

"That's what they tell me. They've got the kid over in the tank on Wilcox. No I.D. Won't cooperate. They want you to come down and see if you know her, or press charges so they can send her up to Juvie."

Book checked his watch. "I'll be there in an hour." He clicked the button back to Sara. She sounded closer to frantic, "Don't put me on hold again!"

"I'm sorry, Sara. Listen, everything is going to be fine…"

"No," she interrupted. "I think somebody was here."

Book wanted to dismiss the idea, but dark dreams were the deep thing he and Sara shared. He knew exactly what it felt like to wake up with the sense that someone had just been standing over your bed.

"I need you to come get me," she begged. "I'm frightened."

"Alright." Book pushed back his chair and climbed to his feet. "Just lock your door and try not to worry." He thought to add, *it's only a dream*, but decided not to. "I'm on my way."

Just as Book dropped the receiver in its cradle, his phone rang again. He paused, thinking not to answer, to let whatever it was wait. Instead, he reached for it, impatient and nervous. "Yeah."

"Detective Book?"

The shaky voice on the other end might have belonged to a woman, but it sounded to him more like a frightened kid. "Yeah. Who is this?"

"My name is..." She paused as if debating what to say, "...Molly. I'm under arrest, and they gave me one call. You've got to get me out of here, right now!"

It *was* a kid, and she sounded terrified. "Why are you calling *me*?"

"They're coming for me. Please, hurry."

Chapter Eleven

Book cast an annoyed glance at the sky. The cold and wet that passed for winter in Los Angeles seemed a little early. He lifted the collar of his jacket against the wind and rain as he climbed out of his Dodge Rambler in the parking lot behind the Wilcox station.

Book entered the fluorescent-lit lobby and looked over the unfamiliar desk sergeant working the day shift. "I'm Detective Book."

"Go on back." The desk sergeant flicked his finger toward the corridor that led to the holding cells.

Book had so many thoughts running at once, he couldn't form the right question. "What, uh...?"

"Your landlady spotted her climbing in through your balcony," the sergeant offered. "She broke through your sliding glass door with a potted plant. Around 4 A.M. The kid wanted in, I guess." He added, "No drugs on her. No weapons."

"Thanks." Book continued to work on this new puzzle as he headed down the short corridor. Why would someone bother to climb to a balcony on the second floor if all they were going to do was break a window to get in? Unless, of course, only that particular balcony would do.

He found the jailor on the phone behind a small desk just outside the door to the holding cells. He heard the rapid-fire voice of an angry woman, his wife or girlfriend, on the other end of the line. Book flashed his badge. The jailor nodded, rose slowly to fumble with the lock, dutifully keeping the woman pinned between his shoulder and ear.

As the guard re-locked the door behind him, Book saw her through the bars of her cell before she saw him. She rocked back and forth with her head and knees to her chest, so that she seemed to be looking at her feet through her legs. She looked exactly as he thought she would. A kid, a runaway, wearing the same jeans, t-shirt, and plaid flannel shirt she'd probably had on three or four days ago. They were alone, except for a drunk sleeping it off in a different cell.

"Molly." He said sternly, maybe a little rougher than he had intended.

Molly started at his voice, as if shaken from deep concentration. It took an instant before her fear caught up with the moment. "Who are you?"

"Detective Book."

Molly glanced furtively from cell to cell like a timid animal. Her eyes lingered on the snoring man in the other cell. When she was certain that they were alone, she stood and moved to the bars, closing the distance between them.

"I need to speak with Karl Buchner." She whispered.

It had been years since Book had heard that name. Buchner. It had been his family's name until shortly after he was born. In 1943 his parents left that name behind when they fled their home, escaping Germany for America. The name had remained unspoken, forgotten, for a while at least. It was also the name that had brought Carl Book's new life crashing down around him when the truth eventually came to light again. Wendell had been ten-years-old and about a week away from being orphaned. He didn't understand completely then, and had never really tried to understand since. He had handled it as any child might, by ignoring it until it went away, or at least until he could bury it so deep it might never be found.

The mere mention of that name, Buchner, came like a shocking invasion. Book bristled. "I'd like to talk to him too. But he's dead."

"Are you sure?"

On some level, Book realized that the fact this girl was asking him about this was astonishing, but she was also poking at a raw nerve he had thought long ago turned to scar. It took effort to keep his voice even. "Pretty sure, yeah."

For her part, Molly knew that asking a grown man if he was certain his father was really dead was a rude and ridiculous question, but she found it no easier to fight the impulses that had moved her this far. "You are his son?"

"Why do you want to know?"

Molly seemed to think about his question before ignoring it. "How did he die?"

"Look, kid..."

"Please tell me," she interrupted, not quite impatient, but demanding.

Beginning to feel a little insulted by a disrespectful child, Book decided to give a complete answer, curious to see what she might do with the information. "He stayed awake for more than a week. Sort of a long, slow nervous breakdown. My mother died right in the middle of it. That seemed to make him even crazier. We went for a walk by the ocean after her funeral. Then, after we got home, he walked out to the garage for a little privacy and shot himself in the head. Sixteen years ago. That help?"

Molly retreated again into her own thoughts, seemingly unimpressed. "How did your mother die?"

"Murdered. Killed on the street over a few bucks," Book continued, his annoyance clearly showing. "Look, kid..."

"You've got to get me out of here," she said with renewed urgency, as if his answers had confirmed some suspicion.

"Why should I do that?"

"I made a mistake by going to your apartment. They'll find me here!"

"Who? *Who* will find you?"

Book watched as she continued to search her thoughts, like she was trying to remember the combination to an old lock. He sensed that she was not worried about her parents coming for her. It was something more.

"I don't know."

Molly had stirred Book's worst memories of his father and brought them rushing to the surface again. He recognized the familiar look of anxiety mixed with exhaustion behind Molly's eyes. It was the look of a rabbit hearing hounds in the distance. He studied her arms where the flannel sleeves were rolled up to her elbows, looking for signs of needle use. Nothing. "You look tired," he said. "How long since you slept?"

"I don't sleep much any more."

"Why not?"

Molly drifted between Book and her own foggy thoughts. "I have bad dreams."

His father's long manic stare was so close now he could almost see it, leering at them both from over the girl's shoulder. Though it was only a specter of his own making, Book felt an impulse to protect her from it.

"Listen." She shifted suddenly from looking inward to directly at Book. Her eyes locked on his, and her voice became commanding.

He listened.

Molly stepped closer to him, leaving only inches and steel bars between them. "If you don't get me out of this jail, right now, they will find me."

Crazy or not, she was serious. But more than that, there was something about her voice, or her eyes, or both that seemed to work on Book from the inside out. He was aware of wanting to help her, wanting to do as she said, even as he remained aware that she was a runaway who had been arrested for throwing a potted ficus tree through his sliding glass door.

It seemed like he had to make an effort to keep his head about him. "What's your last name, Molly? We need to let your parents know where you are."

"I won't tell you that. They have nothing to do with this."

"With what?"

"Open the cell."

Her command carried such weight that Book caught himself swaying toward the bars, almost as if she were pulling him toward her with a hidden string. They paused in silence for a moment.

"Open the ce..."

"Shut up!" Book jammed his hand between the bars and caught Molly by the neck. He roughly yanked her into the cell door so that her chest hit with a hollow thud. He had no idea how or why this was happening, but Book had felt himself losing control and reacted instinctively with anger and brute force. He towered over her now, glaring down into her eyes through the bars that divided them.

Molly's confidence instantly scattered. Even as she tried to shrink away from him, he held her in place, pinned against the steel.

"Who are you?" he hissed down at her.

His grip on her neck and the pain it brought were so intense, she felt sure he would crush her. She tried to speak, but knew she had nothing to say. And finally, after they had abandoned her for so many days when she had most needed them, the tears came.   As she began to weep in frustration, loneliness, and sheer terror, she took little comfort from the fact that it was the first time in days she recognized an action as truly her own.

Book was shaking with anger, but slowly growing aware again that this was a girl, no older than sixteen, whose life had to have been bad enough before this moment, and he wasn't making it any better now. Still, he held her fast. "I'm trying to help you, Molly. Tell me who will find you."

She sobbed before him. The soft skin of her face was aflame and she sucked in her breaths in fits and starts, fueling the free flowing tears and running nose. "I don't know!" she screamed at him, too afraid and too alone to care who heard, letting the feelings she knew were hers flood out of her as though a gate had just been opened. "I don't know!"

Every instinct in his body demanded that he loosen his grip, that he turn suddenly gentle and wrap her in his arms even through the cell door, but he remained steady. "Bullshit, Molly. Tell me the truth. What were you looking for in my apartment?"

Molly quaked against the cold bars and under his hard breaths, searching for an answer but still finding nothing he would understand. *She* understood nothing. There was only the terrible urgency she had felt every moment since the dreams began, and the demanding whispers she heard within them. Molly looked up into his angry face and searching eyes. She offered him what she could. She spoke a thought aloud as it came to her, meaningless, yet strangely familiar. "Lost." It drifted past her lips and left her uncertain, ashamed, and without expectation. *"King's X."*

Every thought, impulse, and drive that had been in Book's head the instant before suddenly left him, like water draining from a broken vessel.

He released her, backed two full steps away, and stared.

"Everything alright, Detective?" the jailor called through the bars of the outer door.

Book watched her in the cell, holding her neck where he had nearly crushed her collarbone, sobbing like the child she was. "Open it up," he called to the man behind him, never taking his wide eyes off the girl. "Open it up."

"Be sure there's nothing vanishes in the universe; it does but vary and renew its form."

--Ovid

Chapter Twelve

City of Acre, 1291

The wind from the west carried the salt of the Mediterranean air to the top of the north wall, mingling the musky smell of the harbor with the black tar smoke that flowed from the Saracen siege engines on the plains below. Sebastien Broussard took in each scent with equal parts pleasure and melancholy, the warmth and peace of the sea and the acrid, slow burn of an impatient army gathering strength outside the city gates. He watched the growing shadow of night obscure the enemy encampments that stretched to the horizon. In these last moments of daylight, as the sky turned from warm gold to a soft, liquid crimson, he thought of blood.

Blood of armies and blood of innocents had stained and enriched this soil for thousands of years before his arrival. Faced with the knowledge that if these attackers were resolved Acre could not be held against them, Broussard's doubts began to coalesce. Perhaps the Christian army was not the armored hand of God as they had been told. And if they were doing God's work at all, then God's work merely delivered more blood to these arid fields. A young man, still, Broussard had known little more of life than war, and he remained unmoved by these new thoughts.

As he stood alone and calm on this wall, watching an exchange just to the West that had Saracen engineers scurrying in and out of their shallow mines and scrambling for cover under volleys of arrows from mercenary archers manning the rampart, he tried to pick out the spot beneath the imposing wall where they were digging. With the myriad directions their tunnels could be taking under the earth, he tried to guess which section would be the one to suddenly collapse and open a breach for the encamped soldiers to pour through. He settled on a looming turret near to the archers' overlook, six-hundred tons of stone that had taken many years and many lives to raise, and which, suddenly finding itself with no foundation, would need little urging to fall and take a large section of the wall with it.

That tower belonged to one of the many fortresses within a fortress that was Acre, a city built by soldiers in a land of perpetual war. Broussard lingered on that spot for a moment, calculating. He reached under his white tunic and absently fingered the iron crucifix at his throat. More blood was coming and his time in Palestine, one way or another, would soon end.

It had been 31 years, eight more than the length of Broussard's own life, since word had reached the Christian kingdoms of the death of the Great Khan. In the years leading up to that moment, his Mongol warriors had swept steadily westward from mysterious and exotic lands into the heart of Islam. The Great Khan's own brother, Hulagu, had been his emissary, riding the Golden Horde like a terrible beast of war into Baghdad, into Syria, destroying the city of Alleppo, seizing Damascus, and successfully laying siege to Alamut, the mysterious mountain fortress of the Assassin cult, once believed impenetrable by the Christian armies.

The eastern invaders had been the great hope for Christendom in the Holy Land. Christendom, whose lust for the land of its birth had waned steadily under the weight of the dead, whose hunger for empire had been all but drowned in the blood of nearly two centuries of gain and loss. Fear of the Mongol Horde had occupied the resources of the Sultans, giving false hope, tenuous comfort, and another chance for the Europeans to build foundation, to create permanence.

Such hopes and plans were soon abandoned when the Great Khan died in his far away land. Hulagu removed his armies and returned home, as a good general should in such times, to keep the peace. And with the threat of invasion gone back to the darkness from which it had come, the Egyptian Sultans returned, inspiring new armies with old stories of Saladin the Great, and the promise of a heaven won on the battlefield. Their armies swept through all of Palestine like yet another wave on an eternal beach, erasing hundreds of years of conquering and loss, conquering and loss, until all of the Holy Land became a virgin anew in the arms of Islam. All but the city of Acre. And now, at last, they were here.

Khali saw him for the first time from within her master's house. He stood alone very near the edge of the wall she had been told to stay clear of for fear of Saracen arrows. She approached with the humble footfalls of a servant, watching him, curious as she came. Though clothed in the white tunic of one of the Christian orders, though heavy in the rich chain armor and the fine cloak of a nobleman, he was not like the others now reveling at the table of her Genoese Lord. His hair was not shorn close nor his face clean-shaven. Nor was his beard long and full, but rather just unkempt and maverick, as though he had simply never developed the habits that the other brethren kept, or perhaps as though the grip of such habits was slipping.

Though her approach was silent, still he heard. His thoughtful gaze to the West suddenly turned to her. Khali froze. He was enormous, like many of the Europeans. As his eyes locked with hers, she became aware that she was alone with a soldier.

That men found her beautiful had long been a curse for Khali, living as she did in a land where men kill for what they desire and then ravish and waste what they have gained once the fighting ends. Khali quickly averted her eyes to the ground just beside his feet. She spoke his name slowly, trying hard to mimic the sound as it had been told to her, "Bruu-sard?"

He continued to watch her, giving no indication, at least, that this might not be his name.

She continued in broken but discernable French, a surprise that seemed to please him, "You are missed at Lord Ardenti's table."

Broussard supposed that one more Templar at the table might make the Order seem more interested in the rich merchant's business. But he had always held even less patience for such things than interest.

Khali kept her eyes averted, wanting only to return to the bright torchlight of the open and crowded hall. "May I tell them you are coming?"

Broussard was much happier out here. The machinations of the invading army beneath were more familiar and more comfortable than the maneuvering now taking place at that table. He looked down at the girl. "Do you know why I am here?" He asked in awkward Arabic, though he expected no answer from her.

Khali did not respond, careful to offer only the presence of a waiting messenger in the shadows.

It was nearly dark now. Broussard took a step to the side, so that the light from within Ardenti's house might better catch the girl's face. She turned the other way, forcing him to squint to see her.

"I am here," he said, speaking with contempt and mostly for his own benefit, "to see how much your master's safekeeping is worth to him. To learn how much land or Genoese bullion he might surrender in exchange for safe passage to Cyprus." Broussard waved his hand for effect, offering still more disdain for both Ardenti and the Order which commanded his presence at this fool's errand even as the city walls were being undermined. The girl took a nearly undetectable step back at his sudden move.

Noting the shift, he paused.   The fact that he had frightened her brought him to a sudden awareness of the danger he undoubtedly represented to her, and compelled him to gentleness. "You have love for your lord, of course."

Something about this man alarmed her. Something in his presence created a weight within her chest, as if her body itself was sending a warning, or merely demanding as her mother might, "pay attention Khali." She looked slowly up at him, seeing him clearly now in the flickering torchlight. Though hardened like other soldiers, he still had the look of a young man. And the small scars and lines etched in his face by the desert sun only made him seem more handsome. She did not fear him, but he was right to think she was frightened by what he said.

"What is your name, girl?"

She heard compassion in his voice. And compassion coming from a man such as him left her uneasy. "My name is Khalidah."

He stepped nearer and she looked down even harder at his feet. Broussard saw a slight shiver run through her body. He slowly continued around her, putting himself between her and the light.

"Khalidah." Broussard held her there by continuing to speak to her, knowing well he had no particular reason for doing so other than delaying his return to Ardenti's table. But her presence pleased him. "What will you do if the walls fall?" Ardenti was a glutton and a coward. Broussard knew he would do all in his power not to be here at the end, and that servants and concubines alike would be left with his private soldiers to hold this house alone. He wondered if she knew that.

She kept her back turned and her head low. "The women of this house have lived in this city during a time of peace. We will not welcome another invading army."

"You know what is coming, then?"

"Yes."

The girl seemed as afraid as she should be, but Broussard sensed courage in her as well. "Come here," he commanded as he crossed the rooftop to the opposite wall of Ardenti's house. Khali hesitated, then obeyed.

The home of Ardenti, as with many private homes of the very wealthy or powerful in Acre, was a fortress in and of itself. To the North, where Khali had first approached Broussard, it abutted the outer wall of the city, with Ardenti's men bearing some responsibility to guard that section from attack. To the South, the entrance to his home was fortified by another twenty-foot wall, which looked down onto an earth and stone street. To breach the outer wall of the city was one thing, but Broussard knew that the Saracens were due for a rude surprise once they entered the city and found themselves surrounded by castles on all sides. When Acre fell, it would fall slowly and painfully.

He kept his back to her, aware of the wisdom in her fear of soldiers. Together, they looked out over the city. She followed the movements of his hand and studied the places he pointed out as he spoke. He gestured across the grotto to an alley, just visible beyond Ardenti's walled courtyard. He spoke of how that alley would lead to another street, and beyond that street a harbor, and beyond that, the sea.

Khali wondered if he lied to test her. But if this was a trap, she saw no harm in stepping into it. "That alley does not lead to the sea," she said at last. "It leads to another wall."

It was as he suspected, this was no child of luxury bred to be the concubine to a fat merchant like Ardenti. Khalidah had come far through the streets of Acre to reach this rooftop and to deliver messages at dinner parties to nobles and knights. He turned and looked at last into her face, now caught in the oil lamps of the courtyard beneath them. He had intended to speak, but instead stared. Khalidah was beautiful. Her hair, straight and black, framed a face like none he had ever seen. Her flesh was soft and light like the color of the earth in Palestine, if not quite the people. But it was her eyes, framed as they were by that black hair, that shone a startling blue-gold. Not too unlike, he surmised, the blue of the milky skinned women of France or Briton. The beginning of her story was clear with just one look. She had been born of a Palestinian woman most likely ravaged by a marauding Crusader. Broussard had spent much of his life in lands far from his home, and he knew what it meant to look as an outsider. Yet he wondered, now confronted with this fragile and unlikely beauty, what it must be like to look like an invader in the land of your birth. Her ability to speak in broken, yet practical French hinted at skills more suited to surviving alone in Acre than entertaining Ardenti. Broussard could now be certain; she knew the streets of the city quite well. And sheathed in the delicate silks of a rich man's woman, adorned as she was with rings on her fingers, with thin chains of gold about her neck and bared waist, she likely felt very grateful to Ardenti for allowing her to forget her life among them. He determined in that moment not to speak ill of his host before her again.

"Perhaps you know the way better than I."

She met his eyes. "I know the way. But there is nothing in the harbor for me if the walls fall."

Certain the walls would fall, and guessing the plan of Ardenti's ladies should they find themselves abandoned in their master's burning house, Broussard averted his eyes. Khali headed dutifully back inside, and though he thought to study the streets below, Broussard found himself turning to watch the girl go.

Chapter Thirteen

The rain fell heavier now, clicking loudly in gathering puddles and creating a frosting of condensation on the glass door to the Wilcox station parking lot. Molly stood behind Book just inside the door, wrapped in and dwarfed by his bomber jacket. The sleeves reached far past her hands and the upturned collar covered half of her head. As Book studied the weather, she easily slipped her arm from the sleeve within the jacket to massage her neck and shoulder where his hand had been.

She stopped when Book turned back to her. As he tugged the jacket further above her head, arranging it like a tarpaulin to keep her dry, Molly again stood only inches beneath his face. She watched his chest rise and fall with agitated breaths beneath his faded black t-shirt. She had never seen a man like Book before. The boys she knew were thinner, with no hint that they might someday grow in this way, and the men she knew were more like her father, soft and more or less pear-shaped. Book was just the opposite. His body was widest at the shoulders, thick and heavy through the chest, appearing like a healthy tree above a dense and streamlined trunk. She recalled the terrible strength that had surged through his grip on her. She stole a glance upward at his face, stern and still angry. As coarse as it had looked on the outside, his jacket was warm and soft on the inside, and she liked the way it smelled. She wondered if he was always so angry. He glanced down at her and his penetrating brown eyes caught hers like a thief in a searchlight. She looked quickly down at his feet, embarrassed for some reason.

Book was completely soaked with cold rainwater by the time they crossed the parking lot to his car. He shoved Molly past the driver's side and dropped in after her.

They sat for a moment as water rapped on the roof and fell in swift, opaque cascades past all the windows. Molly watched him think, his eyes drilling a hole in the steering wheel.

Book, just coming to grips with the return of a feeling he hadn't felt since he was a small child, wanted to ask, to demand, "what the hell were you doing to me in that cell?" But he knew she would have no answer for him.

Molly noticed his barely perceptible shiver. "Do you want your coat back?"

"No." He concentrated on the steering wheel.

"Where are we going?"

He looked over at her, still stern, still angry. He silently debated two options. He was either losing his mind, or Molly had just told him she broke into his home looking for the firing cap of World War II era artillery shell. "What did you want in my apartment?"

She didn't want to tell him she didn't know. Again. "I was hoping I'd recognize it when I got there."

"Maybe we should go back and take a look, then."

"No." Fear flowed back to her, less urgent, but steady.

"Why not?"

"I told you. They know. They'll be waiting."

"*How*?"

She saw his anger rise again as he avoided repeating the more obvious questions. *Who* were they? And *what* could they possibly know? She had no good answer for him. She could just make him even angrier. Her tears came more easily this time, less an explosion and more familiar, more like Molly.

Book rolled his eyes in quiet frustration. "Would you cut it out?" He knew from experience that he had just made it worse. He was right.

Molly had not seen a sympathetic face or heard a word of reassurance since leaving her mother, and Book's anger only made her feel more alone. In an instant, she was sobbing again.

Book tried to dig up some sympathy for her, but couldn't quite find enough. "Goddammit," escaped under his breath before he could check it.

"I'm *sorry!*" she screamed, her pain turning to fury.

"Okay, okay." He backpedaled, now trying to fake compassion for her. "I know you don't know. But if you could guess, why are they looking for you?"

Molly managed to subdue her sobbing to a few occasional short bursts. "Your father."

"Okay." Book waited.

"I found you by looking up your father in the city records, downtown."

Even as he puzzled over the shreds of information as she revealed them, Book was quietly impressed with Molly. Whatever it was she'd been trying to do in his apartment, her method in finding it showed that she was smarter than she looked. "How can you *not know* why you're looking for my fa...?"

"I didn't even know I was coming to Los Angeles until yesterday! I don't know why I do *anything*! I just do it, that's all!"

They watched each other in silence for a moment, Molly sniffling and wiping her nose on his jacket sleeve, and Book thinking a little more about

James Ford and Sirhan Bashira Sirhan.

"You are Karl Buchner's last living relative in Los Angeles," she continued, calming a little. "If I could find you that easily... they've probably been watching you since he died."

Book burned with the impulse to again demand *who* and *why*, but his desire for her to stop crying was stronger. He arranged his words more carefully. "So, someone... *they*... have been watching me for sixteen years?"

"I guess." Molly saw an explosion building up in Book. She quickly continued, "I've been having bad dreams for a while now. But about two weeks ago, they starting getting worse. A lot worse. I stay awake. Sometimes for days until I can't stay awake anymore. Because I know they'll come again and I'm afraid."

Book's face contorted into a squint as she struck another nerve. "He used to say the same thing."

"Who?" Molly asked.

"My father. That's why he didn't sleep anymore. Bad Dreams."

Molly lingered on this news, realizing more clearly that she was several months into what Book had called a 'slow nervous breakdown' that had ended with a man killing himself.

Meanwhile, Book had turned his thoughts from his father to himself, to the days just after his parents' deaths, and the dreams his father warned him would come. He cautiously formed his next question, but the words still sounded crazy when he spoke them. "Do they ask you questions?"

Molly studied him for a long moment. This time it was Book who eventually looked away out of embarrassment, the absurdity of his question echoing in his head.

"No. It's not like that," she answered at last. "They tell me what to do."

Book wanted to inject sarcasm into his next question, but in the context of this conversation it seemed perfectly reasonable. "So, a dream told you to come to Los Angeles to find a man who's been dead for sixteen years. And once you realized that he was dead, you came after me, instead?"

"Something like that. I guess. Yeah."

Book turned back to the question he did not want to ask. "That thing you said in the cell..." He spoke as if he had never heard it before, but he was a bad liar and felt certain she could hear the deception in his voice. "*King's X?*"

"It's something we used to say as kids on the playground." Molly searched, and Book could tell that she knew this was not the real answer.

"I remember." Book held up two fingers, middle crossed over index.

Molly watched him, as if thinking through a dim memory. "But..." She worked hard to retrieve what she could not quite reach. "There's something else about it, too."

"What else?" Book felt suddenly close to the answer to a question he had never really asked before, but had always wanted to know. It was a question for his father. Instead, he asked the girl. "Why did you say that?"

"I don't know that, either." She continued with her private puzzle. "Do you?"

"Do I know why *you* said it?" Book snorted at another bizarre question and turned back to the wheel. "No. It's just that... It's something my father used to say."

Molly's attention suddenly focused. "What did *he* mean by it?"

"I don't know."

She knew that he just wanted to understand. She resolved to do her best to help, even if that meant digging up what she did not want to face.

"I swear to God, I don't know how I know the things I'm telling you. But there are people in the world who..."

Book saw her fighting for it, reaching deep for the rest of that thought. He saw that it took courage for her to try. He regretted making her cry before.

"They can do whatever they want," she gave what she could, "whenever they want, and to whoever they want to do it to."

"Do you have any idea what they want now?"

"They want me." She didn't have to reach for that. She was clear and certain. "And because I came to you... I'm sorry, but I think they will come after you now, too. And anybody who is close to you. To get to me."

"Anybody close to me?" In an unpleasant flash of insight, Book wondered at the fact that the only people he had ever loved were dead, and how hard he'd worked to keep others from getting too close to him. "What can they do to people?"

"I told you. Anything they want."

Book started the engine. Fear suddenly clawed at his gut. Someone had gotten too close to him. Sara was alone and waiting for him right now.

"Where are we going?" Molly asked.

Book switched on the windshield wipers. The blades instantly swept the cascade clean. Molly gasped a deep and urgent breath at the sight of a tall man with dark, angry eyes glistening in the headlights. He walked straight at them, not ten feet away and coming fast.

Book looked up from Molly, following her eyes to the man outside. Rain fell from his black fedora, and his black cashmere overcoat flared around his heels like a billow of smoke as he moved, closing in, heading for the passenger door. The shock of Molly's scream sent a surge of adrenalin through Book's body.

"*Run!*" Molly shrieked at him.

Book jammed the Rambler into reverse and stomped on the gas pedal. Molly became as small as she could in the seat, gripping the door with both hands as the car shuddered away from the Shepherd. They slammed into what must have been a parked car behind them. Book clanked the transmission into gear again, gunning the engine. He swerved past the man in black and bounced over the curb onto Wilcox Avenue.

Molly had just seen something she had expected and dreaded for these last several days. With each glance in the mirror as she drove mile after mile, with each corner she turned, and with every look in a new direction, she had expected to see someone coming for her. Now that moment was upon her. No longer imagined. No longer dismissible as a fevered dream. It had become real. She stayed low and silent beneath the window, sinking even more deeply into Book's jacket.

Chapter Fourteen

In the great dining hall of Ardenti's home, thick walls of blonde stone reached two stories up to the strong cedar beams supporting the roof. A carefully maintained fire provided a warm glow and a pleasant scent from a large cooking pot, where the tender-meated thigh bone of an ox protruded from a savory stew. Enormous silk tapestries hung along the other three walls, depicting the histories of other peoples which had little to do with the lord of the house. Rather, they spoke more of his ability to acquire enormous tapestries.

In the center of the hall stood Ardenti's great table. Ardenti, a slow moving man of appetites, prided himself on very few things. Among them he counted his impeccable eye for beauty, his skills as a host, and his steadfast belief that he was loved by all who knew him well. All of which made Ardenti's great table a point of unique interest, because it was by all accounts ugly, uncomfortable, and often compelled visitors to complain to his face and laugh behind his back. Personally commissioned by Ardenti himself, the great table was fashioned in nearly European design out of long planks of Palestinian cedar. It was set low however, in the Persian style, so that his guests sat upon plush cushions rather than chairs. He had hoped to create a pleasingly eccentric mix of European and local flavors, but the combination managed only to annoy guests from either region and please no one.

Once inside, it was clear why Broussard had been summoned from the roof. Their enemies had unexpectedly arrived. On one side of the great table, armored and adorned in the familiar black tunic with gold cross at the level of their hearts, sat seven stalwart examples of the Knights of St. John of Jerusalem, more known as the Knights Hospitaller.

When Broussard rejoined his comrades, he made a total of six dressed in the uniform white with crimson cross of the Templars, crushing their plush cushions to the floor with the weight of their mail. The great table resembled a chessboard, and the Hospitallers held the advantage. Sebastien took the open space beside his older brother, Vincent, who sat authoritatively in the center.

Vincent Broussard was their father's first son, and his mother had died in the effort to bring him into the world. This mischance had provoked within Vincent a burning and life-long need to prove his worth. The list of judges was rapidly shrinking, as he surely had surpassed outside expectations long ago in multiplying the breadth and value of their father's lands many times over. Still, the need festered like a painful, unhealed wound within him.

Vincent, nearly twice the age of Sebastien and certainly far wiser, often sought to foster greater interest within his younger brother for tests of manners and politicking. This, Sebastien knew, was the true reason why his presence was required at Ardenti's ridiculous party. He silently thanked God for the Hospitallers, whose arrival had suddenly made the evening more interesting.

To Vincent's right sat Durand and Leveque. Two men of a most fearsome and deserved reputation, and Vincent's oldest companions. Through campaign after campaign and battle after battle in service of the Order, they shared the kind of bond men gain when they face death shoulder to shoulder so many times that some episodes have been forgotten. With Durand as agile and quick as a snake, Leveque as brutal and strong as a bull, and Vincent, chief among them and as fearless as he was clever, these three were well-known as the fiercest and most lethal fighters in Palestine. Any thought of fighting which the Hospitallers might have carried to Ardenti's table surely dimmed when they realized who sat across from them.

To Sebastien's left sat two Templars closer to his own station. St. Ives was younger than Broussard, but in his twenty-first year, he was the oldest surviving son of a landed family whose wealth and eagerness for conflicts and tests of courage had seen him rise quickly, perhaps too quickly, to knighthood within the Order.

De Buci was a veteran of many such conflicts and tests. Now more well-fed than hardened, he was no longer eager, but always prepared for them nonetheless. De Buci was more likely to keep St. Ives and the younger Broussard out of trouble than help them to find it. De Buci, in particular, seemed most unhappy with the cushions, and he fidgeted often with his balance, offering frequent annoyed glances at his host, who had hoped for but received no compliments on his unusual decor.

Any merchant, especially one as cunning as Ardenti, knows that the surest way to get the best price for a service is to instill competition for his business. He knew well that if there was anything at hand for Templars and Hospitallers to contend over, they generally would. Even something as unimportant as ensuring the safe passage of a distasteful Genoan to Cyprus ahead of the impending Saracen onslaught. Ardenti was gambling that each Order would not find the other's unexpected presence so insulting that no fee would be enough recompense. It was a desperate chance to take.

All the knights at his table were dressed for battle, as a breach of the outer defenses could come at any time. All had removed their weapons, as a sign of peace in Ardenti's house, while leaving them within easy reach in the outer hall. The Templars may have been outnumbered here, but it was well known that theirs was the strongest single force in Acre, and their keep, the strongest fortress and safest haven in the city.

Equally obvious, as Ardenti quickly pointed out to end a silence that had gone on a little too long, The Knights Templar and Hospitaller would need to work side by side in defense of Acre just as they had in its conquest. They were enemies in times of peace. This war was not quite over.

Ardenti failed to realize, however, that none of the battle trained and hardened military minds of either order held much hope that Acre could be held against the army at their gates. The Hospitallers and the Templars merely wondered how desperate Ardenti was to leave. And as the evening wore on, promises of gold and boasts of influential friends prompted only silence and boredom from both groups. Most of the wealth of the Holy Land had long since been deposited in their coffers at home, and few, if any at all, were as influential in Europe as the great monastic military orders. All Ardenti could offer them was land. If the Templars and Hospitallers could not hold an empire abroad with their swords, they would gladly build a new one at home through such gifts. Sadly for Ardenti, he was not European gentry, and the only land he could offer them was already largely overrun by Islam. Once this fact was made clear, it became as obvious to everyone as it had been to Broussard all along, that despite his vast wealth, Ardenti had nothing to offer, and this exercise was a waste of time.

The feast was served by Ardenti's women, a dozen Acren beauties. None were more beautiful in the fullness and warmth of the lighted hall than Khalidah. Vincent was never one to miss a chance to hold something over his younger brother, as quick to tease and torment as he was to teach. When the younger Broussard saw Vincent studying him, he realized how closely he had been watching her. He had followed Khali with his eyes as she entered the hall, as she served meats and poured wine. He had also noted the attentions of both the Hospitallers and his fellow Templars, who easily recognized her as the jewel of Ardenti's collection. And he had seen how she gave no sign of pleasure or distaste at her role in this banquet. And once, as she slipped quickly out of the reach of Van Cuso, a giant in both stature and appetite among the Hospitallers, when he had thought to wrap his massive paw around her delicate middle but was instead left to scan the room to see if anyone had seen, Broussard even smiled. That was when Vincent took note.

"Remember your vows, Sebastien."

Vincent believed that all men maintained hidden agendas. Perhaps, the younger Broussard thought, because he had so many of his own. To Vincent, the idea that his brother had upheld the monastic vows he had taken upon entering the Order five years ago was either a naïve character flaw or part of some scheme he had not yet fully discovered.

Vincent had risen steadily through the Order over twenty years. He was an advisor to the Grand Master and his right hand in Palestine. He had learned many of the Order's secrets, secrets that young Sebastien burned far less to know. To Vincent every action was a means to an end. If a vow of chastity were necessary for the Order to receive the full backing of the Church in its mission, then a vow of chastity would be taken. But such a formality could not be expected to be adhered to except by those of lower station. For instance, the inevitability of an ignorant soldier ravaging a woman of a conquered heathen race, such as the act that had undoubtedly produced the lovely creature then casting her spell over his brother, could not, in Vincent's mind, have been the deed of a Templar footman. Templar soldiers were held to the most rigorous standard. Of that he could be certain and perhaps even proud. Vows, and the dedication to keep them, separated Templars of lower standing from the rest of the world. But Vincent had always held himself to a higher ideal. His true commitment was to bettering his position in life. Vows were merely tools for the task.

Van Cuso, however, given a moment to think it over, decided he had been spurned. He rose from the table with all the subtlety of a giant in chain mail. Vincent watched his brother tense. He studied Sebastien closely as the massive Hospitaller strode with purpose toward the back corridor where Ardenti's women had been emerging and disappearing.

Van Cuso's plan was clear enough, and when a muffled cry from the girl was heard from that doorway, to Vincent's surprise, he was forced to put a hand on his brother's arm to keep him from rising out of his seat. This was another of Sebastien's flaws, an odd and troublesome tendency to become unnaturally engaged in small matters.

The younger Broussard met his brother's stern glare, and relaxed somewhat in his seat. In a time and place like this, confronted as they were by Hospitallers and with 200,000 enemies outside the city, the Order must pick its fights carefully. Yet the younger Broussard had always cared little for the proper time and place of things.

With the sound of a silver tray hitting the floor beyond the door, all at the table looked toward the back room. All but Ardenti, who still nervously glanced about for a sign of an impending rescue from Acre. After a moment, Van Cuso returned to the hall, stained from a desperate defense with a bowl of sweet preserves. He bellowed at Ardenti until the entire hall,

Templars and Hospitallers alike were laughing at him. Appalled, Ardenti waddled to his guest as quickly as he could manage. "How?" the outraged host begged.

When Khali stepped ashamedly back into the hall in answer to her master's question, the laughter roared even louder.

"My Lord," Ardenti pleaded. "If she pleases you..."

"No." The word came from the frail girl bringing a third surge from the table. Laughter came from all but the half-brothers, Sebastien, who watched her closely, and Vincent, who studied his brother with equal curiosity. Even when Ardenti pulled back his fleshy hand and slapped the girl with the blow of a mannish woman, the younger Broussard did not move, but Vincent could sense his blood rising.

Broussard watched as tears flowed freely down her face, though she did not sob or cry out. He listened as she spoke, "I will not go with him." Ardenti reached back again, but this time Van Cuso caught his hand.

"You are a proud whore?" the giant asked with genuine curiosity.

Her tears flowed more freely as her indignation reached the surface in a burst of rapid Arabic. Through the laughter all around him at this spectacle, Broussard listened intently, straining for each word. "If you try to steal the master's dog, it will bite, his horse will kick, and his whore will fight you!" Khali, to the absolute horror of Ardenti, but to the delight of his guests, cuffed Van Cuso on the ear with all the strength her slender body could muster.

Both he and Ardenti looked confused, but Van Cuso's anger waned in the face of the girl's odd display. Soon, he was laughing along with his comrades. Broussard noted the breath escaping from Ardenti's open mouth, waiting for what was to come. Van Cuso would have to win here, on display as he was to his comrades.

"Give me the girl, Ardenti," he offered, maintaining his smile with some effort, "and I will teach her manners where you have failed her."

Ardenti, keenly aware that he would come out the worse for this bargain no matter what he did, put up no resistance. "Of course."

Vincent did not even reach for him a second time, but simply watched in amazement as his brother rose from the table and walked over to stand before Van Cuso with no discernable reason for doing so. He would have laughed out loud if this were not likely to turn into another unnecessary collision with the Hospitallers.

"I think you are missing the point, as usual, Van Cuso." Broussard calmly spoke in a vaguely diplomatic tone. "And, friend Ardenti, you are missing a business opportunity." Whatever he had in mind, Vincent knew his brother was not likely to talk his way through it. That kind of subtlety and patience was not in his nature. As they all listened, Vincent and the other Templars kept a close eye on Van Cuso's comrades, who were, in turn, watching them. All silently pondered how far away their weapons lay.

Khali watched him with equal suspicion as Broussard continued. "He asked us here to bargain. Ardenti seeks safe passage to Cyprus, and he is willing to offer anything he has to get it."

Van Cuso was no longer smiling, and Khali felt his anger through her wrist where he clutched it. She winced and pushed at his hand, afraid he would crush her bones, but he did not notice. Instead, he glowered down on Broussard as the two men stood only one stride apart.

"You seem to have settled on something of his that you want," the Templar continued, "are you prepared to meet his price?"

"The girl has insulted me."

"She has honored her master. *I* will insult you, Van Cuso. Answer. Will you meet his price?"

The giant released her wrist. The girl quickly backed away, clutching it in pain. Ardenti also backed away, sensing the end of his chance to escape Acre through the aide of the Hospitallers or Templars.

At the table, all Hospitallers and Templars rose to their feet. They paused as Van Cuso reached back and retrieved a hidden blade, sheathed under his cloak along his massive spine.

"I will meet no price. I will take what I want," Van Cuso hissed down at Broussard, "and you *have* insulted me."

Broussard had been unsure how a confrontation with this giant would have gone with neither of them armed, but now, he found himself reaching back toward the distant wall for a weapon, while unable to turn away from Van Cuso. Van Cuso swung the weapon in a wide arc for Broussard's throat. The Templar lurched backward, just dodging the flashing edge, nearly losing his balance, but still keeping his eyes locked with the giant's. The blade went up over Van Cuso's head to strike again. Suddenly Broussard found something very heavy, burning his backward reaching hand. He gripped it tight and swung more quickly than Van Cuso could. The sting of the boiling broth went into Van Cuso's eyes as the femur bone of an ox, slaughtered for this feast and only an instant removed from the steaming cauldron of stew above the fire, found its mark on his jaw. Broussard dropped the scalding weapon so fast, the bone hit the ground before Van Cuso did.

The Hospitallers started to advance in alarm, but the Templars were ready for them. Durand and Leveque each grabbed an oak leg from a nearby table, snapping it apart like a wishbone so that each suddenly wielded a long, heavy club. Yet, even as St. Ives leapt up on to the heavy table, ready to dive into the remaining Hospitallers, and as De Buci snatched up a heavy clay jar, Vincent put out a sensible, calming hand to their rivals.

"It was a fair fight." He offered.

Broussard looked back and saw the girl, now clutching at her other hand, which had been burned when she snatched the soup bone out of the fireplace cauldron quite some distance from where he stood.

Ardenti could barely contain his rage at her. But even as she backed away, an old crone burst from the doorway and fell upon her like an angry hen, shouting and slapping at Khali, pushing her out of the room even as the girl cowered before her.

Broussard saw how this had diffused whatever evil Ardenti had planned for her, and guessed that the old woman was being more friend than tormenter to the too-proud girl. He lingered on the portal where she had vanished with a rising sense of mystery. What force had driven him moments ago? What was she to him other than a girl?

The remaining Hospitallers, knowing that there would be more important battles to fight soon enough, gathered their weapons and their fallen comrade and made their way home.

Under the glare of another look of disbelief and dissatisfaction from Vincent, Broussard and his comrades returned to their Keep, abandoning Ardenti to agonize over his coming fate, or to devise another means of escape.

Chapter Fifteen

"Book?" Sara demanded into the telephone receiver after snatching it from its cradle beside the couch. "Where are you?"

"I'm on my way right now," Book answered, out of breath and shouting above the hammering rain and slow moving traffic outside the phone booth. As he spoke, he watched Molly between swipes of the windshield-wipers, patiently sitting in the passenger seat of his Rambler where it had skidded to a stop against the curb. Twenty minutes had passed since leaving the Wilcox station. Book's thoughts had stayed with Sara, with the fear in her voice as she told him about the returning presence in her dream, and Molly's horror at the sight of the silver haired man as he came for them. Now in Westwood, only minutes away, Book worried that he might not reach her in time. "I want you to leave your apartment."

His voice was tinged with an emotion Sara had never heard from him before. If she hadn't known better, she would have sworn he was afraid. "Leave? Why?"

"Something's going on. I'm not sure what, but I don't want you there alone."

She looked from where the couch was positioned in the center of the room to the door of her apartment. She had locked it the night before, and it remained locked now. "Book, this isn't funny!" She no longer heard the rain or the traffic. "Book?" The line was dead. "Book!"

"He'll be here as soon as he can, Sara." The Shepherd's voice was deep, smooth, and malevolent. Sara jerked her head around to see him moving toward her, reaching for her over the back of the couch. "You can rest now."

In her last thought before she lost consciousness, it occurred to her with lucidity through her horror that he had come from outside. She saw that water dripped unevenly from his black fedora, glistened on the black leather of fine calf-skin gloves, and beaded on the shoulders of the black cashmere overcoat that hung loosely about him and flared almost unnaturally as he moved like a billow of thick smoke.

***

Molly stood quietly on the landing between the fifth and sixth floors, out of sight but still able to listen as Book knocked on the door to Sara's apartment above her. He knocked three times, calling her name and pausing before each try. By the third attempt, he was pounding the door with his fist and shouting. Molly flinched when he finally kicked the door off its hinges. She peered timidly around the stairs above, but he was gone.

Book rushed to the couch in the center of the room. Sara lay still, sleeping.

"Sara?" She did not wake up. He shook her, patted her face with gentle slaps. She was unmarked, fully clothed, breathing, warm, alive, yet still deeply, unreachably asleep. He glanced around for any sign of what might have happened. A cup of tea remained unfinished and cold on the coffee table. The door had been bolted from within. No sign of invasion, no sign of robbery or attack. All seemed as it should be. "Sara."

Molly had stayed behind at his command, but she did not feel safe. No sound came from within the apartment except Book speaking the name of the woman he had come for. Molly began to inch her way slowly up the stairs.

Book spotted the phone on the floor where she had dropped it. He listened to the silence of the dead line for a moment, then placed it back in its cradle. Baffled, he began to make a more thorough search of the room. He noticed the wet carpet and the trail of rainwater that led to the sliding glass door of her balcony. He slid open the door. There was no one there now, and it seemed an unlikely means of entry to her sixth floor apartment.

Molly slowly peered through the open door, keeping her face against the wall so that only one eye could peek in, not wanting to make the detective any more angry at her, but wanting even more urgently not to be alone in the hallway. She saw him leaning over a couch in the middle of the room. He touched the bare feet of the woman, then studied his fingers to see if they were dirty or wet. She didn't notice him at first, but when her eyes became acclimated to the room, she saw the man in black, standing still and silent, just a few feet behind Book, watching him.

The Shepherd's eyes turned suddenly away from Book and locked on the girl just outside the door. Molly took a step back as he burst from his stillness and came for her. A thin gasp, priming a welling scream, escaped her lips. Book turned. Before he could even form a question in his mind about where he had come from, Book grabbed the man's shoulder and spun him around. He was about the same height as Book. His eyes flared with malice and controlled anger beneath the brim of his dark felt hat as they briefly locked with the detective's.

In the next instant, Book's own strength and momentum were unexpectedly turned against him. For the first time in his life, Book faced a man who seemed much stronger and moved far more quickly than he could. He was forced head down and stretched over the back of the couch so that his face was pushed hard against Sara's knee, and his right arm bent and held painfully behind him.   Book could do nothing to prevent the Shepherd from pulling the police issue .45 from the hip of his jeans. Looking about him for any means of escape, Book spotted the girl in the doorway, watching, seemingly paralyzed with fear.   Helpless, his only thought was that he didn't want her to see what was about to happen.

"Run, Molly! Get out!" He heard the metal on metal click as the hammer was pulled into position. Still unable to move though he pulled and strained, Book closed his eyes hard. After the silence that followed, the report from the weapon was almost deafening.

Book opened his eyes, still alive, unharmed but with a whistling ring burning in his right ear. He turned quickly to Sara. The bullet had passed through her forehead. The cushion underneath was wet and reddening. Book wanted to scream his confusion and despair, but managed only a muffled, choked cry.

He then felt the heat of the just-fired barrel of his own gun against the side of his head. He clinched his teeth as a new realization filtered into his mind. He understood why Sara had died. He understood something of what Molly had meant.

Molly understood only that if she could not move, Book would die. And the man would then come for her. She moved.

"Hey!" She called out as she climbed to an unsteady perch on the thin iron handrail of Sara's balcony.   She was careful to watch only her feet, trying to block out the swaying view of the blacktop parking lot sixty feet below.

"Stop!" The Shepherd commanded in a low, harsh voice as he rushed to catch her. Book could not see what Molly did to make it happen, but when he felt the pressure on his arm release and the gun pull away, he knew he would only have one chance. He snatched up the dead telephone by Sara's knee as he stood and swung it backwards in a wide arc. The heavy base struck skull like a cinder block falling from a ladder. A thick, smooth mane of silver hair, mingled with red from the wound Book had opened, spilled from under the fedora as the hat flew off. The man dropped to the floor.

"Molly!" Book shouted in a voice between panic and rage at the sight of the girl wobbling on the quaking rail. Molly fell back onto the concrete balcony, hitting hard on her elbows. Book snatched her arm and yanked the girl to her feet.

The Shepherd stirred, and Book did not even consider rushing over to retrieve the gun still clutched in his gloved hand.

They reached the hallway an instant later, descending past each landing in the stairwell in three steps or less. Book looked upward after each turn, peering quickly between the railings for a sign of pursuit. When they reached the second floor, he saw a gloved hand grab the railing four stories above, and then the furious, penetrating eyes, glaring down at them from within a wild tangle of silver.

At the fire exit at the bottom of the stairwell, Book crashed into the heavy steel door without pause. It burst open with enough force to crease around the handrail embedded in the concrete steps to the alley. Book heard the popping sound from his knee as he tumbled onto the pavement. He ignored the pain as it surged through his leg, scrambled quickly to his feet, and reached back for the girl. Book caught a glimpse of another face, an unruly salt and pepper afro above brittle grey-black skin hardened into the sheen of paper by age and exposure to the elements, before the two-by-four inch board this man swung like a baseball bat struck him in the side of the head.

Chapter Sixteen

In the hours just before dawn, in the even greater darkness beneath the earth, Saracen engineers watched the soil falling like a misting rain in torchlight from the roof of their tunnel. Somewhere beneath the great tower, the timbers bracing the earthen roof creaked under the strain. The diggers grew steadily more anxious with each impact of shovel or pick, willing to go further but still holding a hope that the engineers wanted to live as badly as they did.

The engineers were still calculating, always calculating. They had been digging this tunnel for six weeks. When the time was right, when it was wide enough, deep enough, and in proper alignment with the wall above, the tunnel would be emptied, the supports pulled out with ropes, and the wall, hopefully, would collapse into the vacuum they had created underneath. If their calculations proved true, the tower would topple, opening an enormous gap in the city's defenses. If they were short, only the tunnel would collapse, and they would need to start the entire process again. They could not afford to be frightened by creaking wood and falling dirt. The diggers pressed on.

***

Shahin lay awake next to Dalal as she slept, letting her soft rhythmic breathing lull his mind away from the darting thoughts that prevented rest. It had been two weeks since she began sharing his bed, and he had grown accustomed to the feel of her delicate hand on his chest. He had come to enjoy the way she entwined her leg with his each night before she could fall asleep, like a delightful, spoiled child luxuriating in all the warmth and comfort he could provide her. But still, Dalal was only real to him while his eyes were open. When he closed his eyes, he saw only Leila. He saw her now as she had been ten years in the past. And so she remained forever youthful, beautiful, and frightened, clinging to a vain and impossible promise that he would return to her.

This night, however, burdens far more real than mere memories held his eyes open. There was little time before the walls would be breached and less chance that the Christians would hold the city after that. There was still much to plan. He watched the stars, framed by the window, moving slowly across the sky, wishing for a moment that he was already at sea, out from under the weight of his responsibilities in Acre, obligations and duties which held him here so dangerously close to the end. The Christian flight before the returning Saracens would mean the loss of his livelihood in Acre, as new governments always tended to officially frown on those citizens who provided for the more sinful appetites. Shahin had no knowledge of the Egyptian Sultan at the gates or his generals. Even if he did, after five years of dealing with the Christian governors, he had no more bribes to offer.

Of course, there was a time for work and planning, and there was a time for resting. Knowing he would need all of his strength for the days to come, Shahin resolved to let Dalal soothe him into sleep. He looked down at her face, nuzzling against the hard flesh of his arm, at her body clinging to his, so peacefully convinced that she was safe as long as he was near. He pushed that thought away before it could fully form and turn painful in his mind. He concentrated on her breathing. The gentle rise and fall of her bosom beside him became like the familiar rhythm of a calm sea, until at last his eyes grew heavy enough to close without his will forcing them.

It was through the slow encroaching fog of sleep that he heard the heavy footfalls of soldiers in the street below. He waited until he was sure they were getting closer before he let his eyes open again. After another moment he rolled smoothly out of the sleeping girl's grasp and moved to the open window. In the starlight, he saw clearly the white tunics of two Templars headed for the darkened and locked door to his bordello.

Shahin snatched up his clothes and boots, heading for the chamber door.

Dalal stirred and delicately spoke his name. "Shahin?"

Below, the Templars shattered the silence in predictable fashion by knocking the heavy wooden door off its hinges. Dalal sat up sharply, frightened by the sound. She saw the clothes in his hand. "What is it?"

Shahin paused to look back. A bitter memory flashed in his burdened mind. He saw Leila in his bed. "Do not concern yourself with me, child. Get to Qayyum's ship. I will join you when I can."

He heard the heavy footsteps in the empty parlor below. The sooner they got to him, he realized, the safer his girls and his guests would be.

"Shahin?"

Dalal was quick to tears and he had no time at all for them now.

"Tell the others. Go together and just get to the ship," he quietly hissed, more cruelly than he intended. He closed the door behind him as he left.

Two Templar soldiers looked up at him from below, rudely demanding, "Where is...?"

"I am Shahin," he announced calmly as he walked down the steps to meet them, still naked with his clothes slung over his shoulder. Though he was certain everyone had heard the Templars enter, no other rooms were open, and but for the presence of these two dangerous men, all else seemed well enough. "It is very late. What do you want?"

"The Master has summoned you."

"I see." Shahin paused before the impatient Christians and poured a cup of wine from a jar left over from the evening's entertainment. "Can the Master wait until I get dressed?"

Chapter Seventeen

"What have you seen?" The voice echoed with power and malice in Book's thoughts, and he knew what it was. He remembered the voice from long ago. This was the voice of Sara's dreams as well. "What have you seen?" The presence demanded with the resonance of a hammer. Memories of recent events, of James Ford's gore-riddled corpse, of Sara's delicate touch, of Molly's desperate face, began to coalesce in his mind. Impossible as it seemed, Book knew what was happening to him. It was the same thing that had happened to him so many years ago. With the steady beat of the same question battering him, he looked for a way to fight it.

That way was still there, and not hard to find. Book turned to an image permanently scarred into his mind, which had dominated both the waking and sleeping thoughts of his life. The pooling blood on the pier, the lifeless finger, the wedding band hurled into the sea, and the old man commanding the child, *remember what you see here.*

Beyond the horror of what the old man had done, Book suddenly began to see it as something that had never occurred to him before. The memory was a weapon, a defense against this dream. As the voice pounded at his defenseless thoughts, Book clung to the shock of the amputation, the sight of the ring as it tumbled through the air before it slipped beneath the pulsing ocean surface, and the bizarre words of the old man. *This is the King's X.*

***

Book awoke to the scent of spent coffee grounds and rotting fruit on the air.   His first movement sent a searing pain through his skull, reminding him of the last thing he had seen; the paper-faced black man and the two-by-four swung like a baseball bat. He managed to roll onto his side to take the measure of his situation.   He was lying in a shallow puddle among overflowing garbage cans in an alley. The rain had stopped, but his T-shirt and jeans were soaked through. He shivered from the cold.

The details of his last waking moments filtered back to him. He sat up slowly and looked around. He was alone. Molly was gone. As he looked to the street beyond the alley, he also realized he was miles away from where he had been hit in the head. He was back in Hollywood.

The old pain of his destroyed knee surged again, registering its violent protest over his sprint down six flights of stairs. Book climbed unsteadily to his feet. He struggled for focus. His wallet was still in his back pocket. His gun was gone.

The last image of Sara, after the shot, flared brightly in his mind. Whatever clarity of thought he had regained left him again. He dropped to his good knee, not sure he would be able to stand again. They remained locked together, Book unable to move as Sara stung and punished his thoughts.

Gradually, after the futile insistence that none of this was truly happening had collapsed under the weight of what he had seen and how badly he had failed in the face of it, the pain gave way to a focused memory. The glimpse of understanding he had received in the instant following that single gunshot returned to him.   He had understood what Molly meant when she said these people could do anything they wanted, and to anybody. What they wanted was the girl.   He had been quickly and easily maneuvered to deliver Molly to Sara's apartment. Once there, he could be taken out of the picture with a simple illusion. A murder and a suicide. An equation, a matter of logic. Sara had been murdered simply to provide sound motivation for his own death. That insight was clear enough, but it offered no explanation for how or why he had awakened halfway across town. Home. Alive.

Book fell forward onto his hands and vomited onto the wet pavement. He hung his head until the urge to cry out could be crushed. The pain of loss and failure gave way to controlled fury as Book pictured Sara's murderer. Even as he imagined crushing that silver-maned head with his bare hands, he still wondered how the man could have been inside her small apartment without being seen. He thought of how easily he had been overpowered, and the malice he had seen in his eyes. He thought of the blood he had seen on the back of his head where the heavy phone had struck him. Book held on to that. Even if it meant he had to strike from behind, he could still draw blood. He could still win.

"Frank," Book said calmly into the payphone.

"Book! Where the hell are you?" Harker sounded relieved and alarmed. "Do you know we've got an APB out on you right now?"

Standing across the street from his two-story, bungalow style apartment building, Book watched the setting sun shine beneath the clouds from the west, bathing the cheap stucco facade in a warm glow. "What time is it?"

"Five-twenty. Book, listen to me. The LAPD is looking for you." Harker paused to search for a way to deliver bad news. "Sara Jamison is dead. She was murdered in..."

"I know." Book cut him off. "The guy you're looking for is about my height, maybe 50 years old, long silver hair and he's dressed kind of sophisticated, maybe European." While he talked, Book noticed a car parked just up the street. It stood out as an unusually expensive car to be parked on the street in this neighborhood. A slender, graceful Jaguar coupe. A rich man's car. A vain man's car. Deep black paint offsetting glistening chrome, windows blackened for privacy. "Black coat," Book continued, "like cashmere or..."

"Listen to me, Book, the guy they're looking for is *you*."

Book quickly scanned the streets as he listened, to see who might be coming for him, knowing that he could not stand out here much longer.

"They think you did it. Somebody saw you running out of her building."

"Just me?" Another thought crossed his mind, but he stifled the urge to bring it up to his partner. How could one of Sara's neighbors identify *him*, specifically, among the entire population of Los Angeles unless the interviewer had showed them his picture? That could only happen if someone expected the murder and expected Book to do it. He thought again of Sirhan Sirhan and of Molly's vague, fearful warnings. *They can do anything they want.*

"You need to get off the street and come in," Harker fretted. "Where are you?"

Nothing made sense to him, but there was enough for Book to form some decent questions. If it had been a good idea to kill him in Sara's apartment, then why was he still alive now? Why bring him back to his own neighborhood and dump him in the garbage? What value could he possibly have to these people?

"I'll be in soon, Frank. You got a trace on this number yet?"

Frank fell silent with embarrassment, surrounded as he was at his desk by their Captain and two homicide detectives, all hoping he could keep the conversation going while they waited for the trace to be completed. "Not quite."

"I'm still figuring this out, Frank. I'll be in touch." Book dropped the receiver and let it hang there, the line still open. He puzzled in vain to find the logic of his dilemma as he hurriedly limped across the street and up the familiar damp concrete stairs.

He unlocked the front door to his second floor apartment, and swung it slowly open to a sight that horrified and further enraged him, but did not quite surprise. The vertical blinds clicked together in the breeze where Molly had hurled his ficus tree through the sliding glass door earlier that morning. Every drawer had been opened, its contents spilled. Two uniformed police officers, who had come here in answer to the all-points-bulletin on Book, were already dead on the floor, riddled with bullet wounds. Their weapons were still holstered. Whatever had happened, they had not even seen it coming. Book's breathing grew faster and weaker as he stepped inside.

His thoughts continued to race, searching for a direction, a reason for any of this to happen. There was not enough information for a solid idea. The uncertainty bled into a palpable anxiety that lodged itself deep in his chest. With a trace to that payphone and a call to a patrol car, more officers could arrive at any moment. It would seem that Book was a cop killer, now, too. Still, he sought shreds of logic within the chain of facts, anything that could guide him.

The men in his living room were only recently dead. And a killer who is still killing is not satisfied. He must not have found what he has been looking for. Book crouched over a pile of debris from his overturned desk.

What had Molly been looking for? What could the killer hope to find here? As these questions slowly moved in his mind, a new thought turned his fear into a surge of adrenaline. He stood again and his eyes darted from corner to corner. Whatever they hoped to find, both Molly and her pursuer thought he could lead them to it. That was why he was still alive. Book knew he was not alone in this room.

He quickly drew the service revolver from the holster of the nearest fallen policeman. He waved it around the room, like a nervous hunter waiting for birds to flush from a field. He waited at the ready, with only the clicking of the blinds in the breeze obscuring the stillness.

That there could be a man in this room, waiting for his guard to drop, was impossible, he knew. Yet he pulled back the hammer of the .38, clicked it into firing position, and held the gun in front of him for what might have been several minutes.

The footsteps were faint against the concrete of the exposed stairwell leading up from the gate, growing louder as they neared. In moments, two uniformed policemen stood outside his open door, drawing their weapons at the sight of Book standing among the dead.

"Drop your weapon, Detective Book." There was a sense of relief for Book, at least no longer alone. He recognized the men at the door as Hollywood beat cops, one named Jack, the other Pete. He wasn't certain which was which. Yet the weight remained in his chest as he reset the hammer with his thumb and dropped the revolver to the floor.

He raised his hands slowly. "Keep your guns out, look sharp, and get me out of here."

The cops were scared at what they saw, and uncertain of Book's involvement. "What's going on, Book?" Jack or Pete asked. They backed into the partially covered hallway to let Book out into the heavy and wet night air.

"If you're arresting me, do it quicker." He looked at one, "Pete, right?"

"That's right. Put your hands behind your back, please."

"Do you have to do that?" Book asked, not eager to be cuffed. Pete looked again at the bodies of his friends inside the apartment.

Book complied and Jack moved behind him. The weight in his chest grew heavier, as the cuffs clicked together, fixing his hands in place behind his back.

Book watched, unable to take his next breath as Pete's face turned in an instant from confusion to shock and then to pure fear. The first shot produced a muffled choke from the young officer behind him. Book turned just in time to see the second shot, fired from within his apartment by the man in black, silver hair re-groomed and flowing from underneath his hat. He could hear the lead missile hum past his ear on its way to Pete's forehead. There were *four* dead policemen, now.

The Shepherd stood among the first bodies, Book's .45 smoking in his hand. Their eyes locked. It would be useless to run now.

"Where is the girl?" The Shepherd's voice carried an unnatural element of command beneath its malice. Book felt himself once again drawn forward as if pulled by an invisible string. As his mind struggled to process what was happening, Book hung onto to the revelation that Molly *had* escaped.

The Shepherd slowly closed the distance between them, moving to where Book stood frozen, just beyond the door on the concrete landing above the courtyard. His voice penetrated deeper each time he spoke. "You want to understand. You are confused and angry. I can remove the hurt from you, Detective." His voice soothed almost like a mother's might a frightened child, but more like that of a skilled liar who knows your deepest fears and fondest desires. Book leaned a little closer toward the sound. "Where is the girl?"

Rage boiled up in Book with the returning sensation of lost control. But anger was not enough to break the invisible string as it had with Molly at the Wilcox station. Not this time. He might have told this man anything he wished, if he only knew the answers.

The two men's eyes remained locked as the Shepherd stepped over the fresh bodies and past the doorway until they stood face to face.

The sirens of Pete and Jack's fast approaching back up drifted out of the distance both east and west of them. Book struggled to form a question.

"Why?" he finally managed.

The Shepherd casually tossed Book's gun back into the living room. He began to walk away. Book knew that this man wasn't just guessing that he did not have the information he sought. As he stood helpless outside of his open door, watching the Shepherd disappear around the corner, Book was aware that this man knew with certainty that if he'd had any information at all about Molly, he would have told him. The invisible string Book had felt pulling him this time had been that strong.

His choice now seemed simple enough. He could stay where he was and take his chances with his colleagues at the LAPD, or he could run. Instead, even as the approaching sirens grew louder, Book decided on a third option.

He rushed past the fallen cops, back into his apartment, back to his bedroom. Dropping awkwardly to the floor and turning his back so that his cuffed hands could dig, he sifted through the spilled contents of his dresser on the floor until his fingers touched what he sought. A thick disk of dimmed brass. For six months it had lain stashed away in a drawer alongside yellowed postcards, wrinkled photographs, and other weak links to old memories. He hadn't looked at the thing again since opening the envelope his father had sent it in. Yet here it was now in his hand; the secret rule that changed all rules, his father's final gift to him. *King's X.*

"For seeing they saw not, and hearing they understood not, but like shapes in a dream they wrought all the days of their lives in confusion."

--Prometheus

Chapter Eighteen

The creature stood before him at the foot of his bed, in the form of a man imperfectly cloaked in shadow. Broussard strained to move, but could not even lift an arm to defend himself. He could only focus on the face, illumined by starlight from his window and looking out at him from an obscure murk, as if bobbing at the surface of pond. The face had strange, unfamiliar features; thick flesh of yellow gold adorned with a thin and braided black beard, hooded eyes that shone with intelligence and malice.

"What have you found, Templar?" the golden man's voice stabbed at him from the murk. "What have you found?"

Broussard awoke to the sound of a fist hammering at his chamber door. He was alone, and it was still well before dawn outside his window. He rose from his bed with some difficulty as consciousness sluggishly flowed back to him. He yanked open the chamber door to find St. Ives, also looking like he had been recently roused from sleep.

"The Master has summoned us."

***

Broussard stood in the pre-dawn chill of the cavernous meeting hall alongside St. Ives and De Buci before the Master of his order, Guillaume de Beaujeu, a drained and haggard-looking man in his nightshirt. His nephew, Garvin, worked quietly at Beaujeu's side. Garvin was a young squire of sixteen years and a gentle soul unsuited for soldiering, though so fiercely loyal he could always be found at his Uncle's side even on the battlefield. He had brought the Master his bread and had begun girding him in his tunic as the three just-arrived Templars waited.

Just at the edge of the dim circle of light cast by the oil lamp, Vincent Broussard studied the proceeding from a heavy wooden chair. It was not odd for him to be in this chamber, as he was a powerful Templar, initiated into many of the Order's greatest secrets, and he had held the ear of the Master for sometime. But he did not speak when they had come in, or even acknowledge his half-brother. He merely leaned forward, watched, and calculated.

As Garvin tugged at his tunic to straighten the insignia, Beaujeu spoke haltingly, as if too fatigued to hold each thought for too long. "The time is coming, my brothers, when the Order will quit the Holy Land."

"We are prepared to hold the Keep," St. Ives spoke up out of turn. Broussard saw De Buci glare at him with a veteran's unspoken rebuke. He sensed as well that matters which could concern Guillaume de Beaujeu to distraction were likely greater than mere sieges.

The Master continued as if St. Ives had not spoken at all. "I have been approached in the night by a stranger and asked many questions."

A thought flashed to Broussard, the eerie image of the golden man in his dream. He studied his leader, thinking he looked like a man whose nights taxed him more than his days.

"All we have worked for is near compromise." The Master had wandered over to a table and held a stick of sealing wax to a candle until it formed a puddle of red on an envelope.

"De Buci, young Broussard, and St. Ives. You have a long journey ahead of you. You will leave Acre this morning."

Broussard was stunned. His mind raced with thoughts of what was to come, when one hundred Templar Knights in command of a few thousand soldiers would face two hundred thousand enemies in Acre.   Every sword would matter, and now they were to leave the battle behind?

Beaujeu carefully stamped the wax with his signet ring and held up the letter. "When you arrive, present these orders to those you find there, take what they give you, and return with your cargo to Cyprus."

Broussard knew he spoke beyond his position, but the words rose faster than his will to stop them. "Surely there is someone else qualified to be a courier, Master. Are we not needed here?"

"Acre will fall just as well without the three of you to prop it up a little longer."

Broussard and St. Ives watched as the Master approached De Buci and held the sealed letter to him.

"De Buci," Beaujeu spoke his name as if addressing an old friend, "I am entrusting this to your experience and wisdom." He then looked to the younger knights. "And I am entrusting De Buci, in turn, to you, St. Ives and Broussard. You will escort this old fox at Godspeed and at all costs."

All three Templars stood confused before Beaujeu. His words were, as usual, sparse and enigmatic, but De Buci had heard the grave tone in his voice only seldom before. St. Ives' mouth fell open again as if to speak, but De Buci kept him silent with a wave of his massive hand.

Broussard found himself looking over to Vincent. This was all very suspicious and had the print of his brother's hand on it. Perhaps it was part of a scheme he had yet to discover, but it felt very much like he was being removed from an obvious danger, so that others might die in his place. At last, Broussard could stomach the mystery no longer and voiced what the others were thinking. "Escort him to where, Master?"

Even as he spoke, the doors to the chamber opened. Two Templar guards entered with a disheveled and rather annoyed looking Moor. "Brothers," Beaujeu offered almost politely, "this man will be your guide. He calls himself Shahin, 'The Hawk.'"

"I call myself Shahin," the Moor corrected him, less politely. "Guide to where?"

Beaujeu looked past Shahin to the guards. "Leave us."

Once released, Shahin took a cautious step deeper into the chamber to watch Beaujeu seal another envelope with wax, this time neglecting to stamp it with his seal. Shahin had been in enough meetings this secretive to know that little good could come of this one.

When the doors closed behind the guards, Beaujeu spoke again. "Captain Shahin, you will take these three men in your fastest ship." He held the envelope out for the Captain. "Here is your destination. You may open it once you are at sea." Shahin made no move to take it. "Furthermore," Beaujeu continued, still holding the envelope, "once their task is complete, you will return these men and their cargo to Cyprus."

"I will?" The Moor's tone was a challenge.

St. Ives managed one menacing step forward before De Buci clamped a firm grip on the back of his neck. Broussard studied the Captain. Shahin had noted and understood St. Ives' youth and volatility, and also De Buci's power over him. Broussard wondered with growing disappointment how important a letter could be that it might be entrusted to three men who would so quickly reveal so much about their temperament, weakness, inexperience, and chain of command to a merely insolent Moor.

Beaujeu also noted Shahin's tone. He dropped the letter at his feet and stepped closer, letting the Moor know he had the full attention of the Templar Master.

"There is a ship anchored in our harbor. It belongs to you."

"I have quite a few ships."

"This one is special to you.   Under cover of darkness in the past several nights, you have loaded it down with gold and jewels paid to you by the wealthiest noble women of Acre in exchange for their safe passage to Cyprus."

Broussard detected the slightest hint of disappointment from Shahin, as a man who thought his secrets were better kept.

"It seems likely to me," Beaujeu continued, "that such a ship, burdened as it must be and with the city in such turmoil, will likely never make it out of the harbor."

"And if I do as you ask?"

"Since you will be preoccupied and unable to captain that vessel, I believe it would be fair and proper for the Order to provide for its protection. An escort of two Templar warships should be sufficient to see your cargo safely to Cyprus."

"And safely into the Order's coffers."   Shahin did not feign pleasantries, something Broussard could appreciate. But he was surprised to see how impervious to intimidation a Moor, alone in the heart of the Templar keep, could be.   He wondered which parts of this man were substantial and which were mere bluster. The whole idea of leaving Acre on the eve of a siege, Beaujeu's secrecy, and his entrusting of this mission not only to their youth, but now to an infamous criminal, and a Muslim criminal at that, was vexing.   "I see no reason to help you," Shahin concluded.

"You have a choice, of course," Beaujeu countered, turning to walk back to the table. Standing with his back to Shahin, he gazed into the candle flame. "Undoubtedly you realize that we will not hold this city for long. However, we can hold you. We will hold you in our cells until the Sultans find you. And when they find you, I will ensure that they will know who you are."

Broussard detected another flash across Shahin's cool demeanor. He knew this man by reputation, of course, as a smuggler, pirate, and a shrewd purveyor of mischief, known throughout the Mediterranean by Christians as "The Hawk." Though a popular figure in the largely ungoverned environs of war-ravaged Acre, Shahin was pariah in many ports throughout both Christendom and Islam. Broussard had wondered which culture hated him more, and in whose hands the pirate would least like to fall. Beaujeu seemed to know the answer.

Shahin pushed heavy black curls from his face, further revealing a man who was older than Broussard had expected. He scratched at his beard thoughtfully for a moment. He stepped up toward the Templars, looking at St. Ives in particular, as if testing De Buci's hold on the young man. For a moment, his eyes locked with Broussard, and the Templar discerned that many thoughts ran through the Captain's head at once. Finally, he addressed the Master again without taking his eyes off Broussard.

"Make a deal."

"Refuse me and your ship will be taken, her crew killed, and you will be left to die in this tower," Beaujeu offered without turning. "Succeed in your task, complete the return voyage to Cyprus, and you will be restored your ship, her crew, and her cargo. And freed, of course."

"Of course." It was clear to everyone that Shahin placed no faith in Beaujeu. Somewhat to his surprise and disappointment, Broussard was unsure of what to believe as well.

It was only minutes before dawn, and as the Templars watched Shahin calculate in silence, the slow steady report of a warning klaxon sounded from the north end of the city. Only a moment later, the bell was smothered by a terrible rumble, like a distant earthquake. Time had run out. Vincent rose from his chair in the half shadow and moved with Beaujeu to the overlook. The attack had begun.

"Decide." Beaujeu commanded.

Shahin understood. There was no real choice, and no point in waiting. He turned decisively to the three knights and spoke like a man accustomed to issuing orders.

"In the harbor you will find a small ship called the *Gull*, single mast, white sail. Leave behind all signs of rank and Templar insignia."

Shahin then turned to Beaujeu, already lost in new thoughts and searching to the north from the overlook. A once great tower along the north wall was gone, replaced by a plume of dust barely visible in the first hint of the approaching dawn.

"That ship sails with the tide." Shahin announced to Beaujeu's back. "See to it your *escort* is informed of our bargain."

"Your vessel will reach Cyprus. Your people will be waiting for your return."

Shahin spun quickly around and scooped up the letter from the floor as he hurried out.

In the corridor, Broussard caught the Moor by the arm. "I have a passenger for that ship bound for Cyprus."

"There is no room."

"Make room."

Shahin liked this deal less and less by the moment. He trusted no Templars. However, if this one wanted to get a passenger on that ship, perhaps it was a sign of confidence that Beaujeu was sincere. Or perhaps he wanted this person drowned. Shahin played this over in his mind in an instant before realizing it made little difference what he thought.

"The ship is the *Leila*. She sails at her captain's will, now. I cannot stop it."

Broussard turned and announced quietly to De Buci, "I will come to the *Gull* from the north." De Buci watched Broussard head quickly into the darkness of the corridor with a frown. He also snatched Shahin by the arm as he tried to pass and turned to St. Ives, speaking with some weight behind his words, "See the Captain to his ship." For his part, Shahin was growing tired of being handled by these Templars, but he chose to wait for a more opportune moment to express his displeasure.

Within Beaujeu's chamber, the Master, young Garvin, and Vincent Broussard watched and listened as the city awakened in terror beneath them.

"This is foolish, Master," Vincent quietly announced as Beaujeu continued to study the city. "De Buci is no leader of men. And my brother..." Vincent cut his words short, reigning in his anger until it again felt righteous and no longer like disappointment. "Even now he goes to jeopardize the trust you've put in him." Vincent continued with an element of concern in his voice that he could not overpower. "He is naive and *noble*."

Within his silence, Beaujeu recalled the golden face that had peered out to him from a dream. He remembered his struggle to hold his tongue and keep his secrets. For of all Templars in Acre, only Beaujeu knew the answers to the golden man's questions. *What have you found, Templar?* Even Vincent Broussard's keen mind and thirst for knowledge had led him only to the first hints of the dark truths Beaujeu held. *What have you found?* Beaujeu would not risk sleep again.

As he watched the light of a growing fire at the breach of the city's North wall begin to compete with the slowly arriving sun, Beaujeu knew in his exhaustion that it had taken nearly all of his strength to turn that dream away unanswered. More than this he did not know, but to choose a man as wise and comprehending as Vincent Broussard would be to send him to certain failure and death. He thought of De Buci, capable and unimaginative, an unshakable foundation, happy with his place in the world and harboring no designs on further growth. St. Ives, fiercely committed to causes he does not as yet understand. And the younger Broussard, whose naiveté could save him, and whose nobility could possibly save them all. "It is thought the Fool journeys under God's protection. Your brother must do as his nature drives him."

"So must we all." Vincent Broussard's boots echoed off the stone floor as he left the chamber to prepare for the coming battle.

Beaujeu lowered his head and closed his eyes, weighed down by many secrets, great and terrible.

***

The tower had come alive with soldiers before Sebastien Broussard reached the stables. He had discarded his white tunic in favor of the loose cloth shirt underneath, and he felt the freedom of being unarmored. He leapt to the back of his horse, hammered heel to flank, and held tight to the reins as the animal burst from the stalls into the streets of Acre.

It had been two years since he had ridden a horse so hard and so fast.

The fields of his father's home encroached for a moment on his concentration as his horse clattered and careened through the winding city streets. But just as there was no time to spare for him to be thrown, or for his horse to go down due to his recklessness, neither was there time to take care. What he did now, he did for honor's sake. Yet a persistent voice in his head, one that sounded suspiciously like Vincent's, also knew that there was more to it than that. With effort, he banished all voices from his head, even his own, as he struggled to match his thoughts with the horse on this frantic ride, urging the beast on toward the North. Already, he could smell the smoke.

"Do not arouse the wrath of the great and powerful Oz.
I said come back tomorrow."

--The Wizard

Chapter Nineteen

Book shuffled and limped down the concrete steps, trying to keep his balance with his hands pinned behind him. He threw his hip into the locked gate to the sidewalk. The impact warped the steel where the bolt fit, and the gate clattered into the stucco façade. The distant wail of a police siren burst into a scream as the cruiser fishtailed around the corner in front of the building. He saw the wide eyes and pointing finger of the policeman in the passenger seat. Book turned back into the alley beside his building, pain from his knee stabbing at him as he hobbled into the best sprint he could.

The patrol car, still a few moments ahead of more approaching sirens, bounced into the alley in pursuit.

"Book!" a voice called to him over the car's loudspeaker. "Stop!"

The alley was long, the concrete walls on either side too high to scale. Book limped to a stop near the trash cans where he had awoken earlier. He hung his head as he pulled in breath after breath.

The car stopped, the doors opened, and the officers approached him on foot.

"Don't move a muscle, Detective," one cop said.

"What's going on here?" asked the other.

"They're dead," Book responded, searching for words that made sense.

"Who?" the second voice demanded. "Who's dead?"

Book gave them the truth as he saw it, his voice leaden with despair.

"Everybody."

As he listened to the sound of the two officers' shoes cautiously move up behind him, knowing their weapons were pointed at his back, a second sound emerged from ahead of them. The rattling roar of an old engine and the protest of thinning tires being worked too hard became clear as a faded black Lincoln Continental lurched into view and accelerated into the alley from the far end.

The revving engine became the urgent chug of a locomotive as the car bore down on them. Behind the wheel, Book saw a familiar but decidedly unfriendly face staring straight into him. The driver was a sinewy black man with an unruly salt and pepper afro, and a face of brittle, weathered flesh. Book had seen this man for a split second, swinging a two-by-four outside Sara's apartment building. It was his last memory before waking up in this alley.

The car wasn't going to stop. Book and the two cops reacted the only way they could, scattering to either side and tumbling into the metal cans and rain-soaked garbage lining the alley. The Lincoln skidded to a stop just in front of the empty patrol car. Book looked up from the toxic puddle he had rolled into to see the brittle-faced man step out of his car, wielding the same two-by-four inch board.

The first cop reached for the gun he had dropped. The board came down on his extended arm, breaking his wrist. As he cried out in pain, his partner leveled his own weapon at the attacker.

"Freeze!"

Book watched helplessly as the man moved with the cold grace of a machine. He lifted the wounded cop by a handful of hair and swung his body into place as a shield an instant ahead of the shot from his partner's gun. The single report echoed off the surrounding buildings. The young officer's mouth hung open in mute shock as the wound he had just opened in his partner's chest begin to color his uniform.

At the speed of reflex, the interloper snatched the dead man's gun hand, and forced the lifeless finger to pull the trigger. He put three bullets into the dumbstruck cop before his body hit the ground.

"No!" Book could only shout from the wet ground. It had taken an instant. Both of the young policemen were dead.

The paper faced man paused in the aftermath of the kill, as though just realizing what had happened. He let the limp body in his hands gently to the ground and then rose to his full height.

"I'm sorry," he said in a voice honed on cigarettes and the diesel air of Los Angeles. "They would have killed you."

Book fought against this incomprehensible moment.

"They were cops."

"Book," the killer called him by name, "if they catch you now, they will kill you. Here, in jail, anywhere. You're a dead man."

"Who the hell are you?" Book climbed awkwardly to his feet. One good look at this man made it clear that he had nothing to do with the vain and elegant murderer who had just left him in his apartment moments before. His clothes were as soiled and unwashed as the rest of him. The word for such a destitute drifter would have been "hobo." But that word did not seem to fit. In the distance, they heard the approach of police sirens, more back up for the dead men in Book's apartment.

The man continued to study the bodies near his feet. Regret and sorrow crept into the gravel baritone as he answered Book. "I am a killer. Murderer. Assassin." The moment passed and his yellowed eyes flashed up at Book's again, as emotionless and determined as before. "Get in the car," he commanded.

Book's confusion and despair gave way to rage. Even with his hands cuffed behind his back, he charged like an attack dog on a broken leash. He planted a sudden and heavy work boot in his chest and the man fell backwards against the Lincoln's thick fender. He glared up at Book as if not expecting any resistance.

"More cops are coming. There's no time for this." The man spat dismissively as he climbed to his feet and came at Book, driving the two-by-four like a battering ram into the detective's stomach. The air blasted from Book's lungs, taking his strength with it. He doubled over, ready to fall when a powerful hand yanked his head up by the hair. His attacker's eyes bore into his. "We have the girl." He turned back to his car, dragging the detective, stumbling and fighting for a breath. He opened the back door and shoved Book inside. "Keep your head down and your mouth shut if you want to live."

Book pulled in a breath at last, as he lay across the worn vinyl of the back seat. Any thought of fighting vanished with that one spoken revelation and the myriad of implied threats it carried. The girl. Molly.

He felt the car rock when the paper-faced man fell in behind the wheel. As the deep chugging engine pulled the Lincoln toward the far end of the alley, he could hear the sirens and shrieking tires of police cars arriving in the distance behind them on his street. His mind struggled to penetrate the mystery, but he was certain of nothing beyond all the dead bodies in his wake.

Chapter Twenty

While the other women wondered at the klaxon in fearful, rising tones, Khali dressed hurriedly and rushed from the room to find Baseema. Since the death of her mother, Baseema had cared for her. It was kindly old Baseema who had seen Khali hunting for bread in the marketplace and, moved by the beauty hidden beneath the city's soil on her face, had taken her to the house of Ardenti to start a new life. It was Baseema who had delivered her from his wrath in the dining hall. And now, as the long dreaded attack arrived at last, it was the kindly old woman the girl sought.

As Khali hurried through the dark corridor, Ardenti's home began to shift, filling the air with the deafening rumble of shuddering earth and cracking stone. The event was so loud and so violent, she clutched at the stone walls of the corridor with both hands and still could not keep her feet. Before the unnatural quake ended, it grew louder. She felt its force through the walls. The awful grinding was far louder than any sound she had ever heard before. It overwhelmed so completely that she could only close her eyes tightly against the welling terror.

When the house again became still, the voices of Ardenti's panicking men and the shrill calls of the other women trying to find each other in the dark filtered past her ringing ears. Khali opened her eyes and rose unsteadily to her feet. She rushed on toward Baseema's door, but found the way blocked by stone and timber where the north side of the hallway and the floor directly above had collapsed. Khali's eyes lingered for a moment where dust drifted in through the hole to the outside, and an enormous fissure opened across the length of the wall. A new fear piled onto the others.

She ran back the way she had come until she reached the portal to the rooftop overlook, where she had first seen the young soldier standing alone the previous night. She thought of the mighty fissure in the hall, and tightness came to her chest. She stepped through the doorway to the rooftop.

Once outside, intuition grew to understanding. The air was blood-red, filled with rock dust, thick as fog and lit by the just rising sun. The mighty tower to the west had fallen, taking with it a massive section of the city wall, and any chance at defense for Ardenti's home. Khali saw the pile of debris that had been part of this house, now collapsed into the street below. Saracen soldiers howled their battle cries and streamed through the breach into the street like wine through a punctured cask. Through the thickening haze of dust, she could see several of them climbing through the rubble toward her. Ardenti's guards would not be able to stop them. Khali darted back inside, knowing the house was doomed.

As she dashed through the dim hallways, she thought of the plan decided on by the women of Ardenti's house. So much had happened to all of them at the hand of war, so much loss, so much injustice, so much pain; they would all die together before they each would fall alone into the hands of yet another conquering army.

Khali's mind began to race like that of a mouse caught under the shadow of a hawk. Cut off from where she knew Baseema to be, with a growing fever she began to seek the old woman everywhere else. She came to the door of her Lord and Master's bedchamber. Cunning, but weak and fearful, Ardenti seemed to feel that the invading Saracens would take him for a criminal. If there were a way to escape, Ardenti's fear, as sure as another man's courage, would help him to find it. She opened the door.

The woman in his bed appeared lifeless, and fat Ardenti's eyes were glazed with a yellow film as he looked upon Khali from her side. "Come, child," he gently offered, raising the cup in his hand. "It will not hurt you. It is wine." He weakened, spilling a little of the poison before steadying his hand again. Khali bolted from the sight and ran back the way she had come.

Sounds of fighting, steel crashing on steel and men dying in pain now filled the house. Khali shrank into the shadows near the portal as the soldiers entered Ardenti's home from the roof. She stood perfectly still.

There was death behind her in Ardenti's cup if she wanted it. And there was surely death before her in the hallway if she could not stay hidden. Once the soldiers had passed and the corridor grew quiet, Khali dashed across the opening from the roof, plunged into the gloom of the corridor beyond, and returned to the pile of stones within a few feet of Baseema's chamber.

As she began to move stones from the pile, more fell to replace them from the floor above. The stone bruised her hands, grown soft in her time with Ardenti, but still she moved them. Khali thought only of Baseema, as if the old woman were waiting for her on the other side. She knew that the stones were making enough noise to draw the attention of the next soldier who entered the dark corridor behind her. When her mother's face came to her thoughts again, Khali wept. She pulled at the stones and shattered pieces of timber until her hands bled.

Khali pounded the stones where she could not move them, and through the fever of her occupation, she could smell the smoke on the air.

Another dim recognition set in. The house was on fire. She kept at the futile dig until the rough hand that she knew would come, came at last. She was yanked from the pile and forced to face the invading soldier.

He was ugly, and dirty from the assault. Through the hanging dust in the air and the dim light, his face curled into a snaggle-toothed grin at the sight of her. She understood, as Baseema had taught her, that her beauty could lead men to smile when they first looked upon her. It was up to her to determine what would happen next. To react with fear, anger, or disdain, could bring her fears into reality the fastest. But to return the smile could dull his wits and soften his lust, for at least a moment.

Khali summoned all of her strength to crush her terror, met the young man's eyes, and smiled at him.

As she felt the grip on her wrist soften a bit, Khali held his gaze, aware now of more footsteps approaching. The soldier turned and held his prize behind him as the second Saracen approached. These were like the men she had known in her other life among the city's streets, ever hungry for the moments of life that were not toil, not at all like the wealthy men, Saracen and Christian alike, she had entertained for Ardenti. The grip again tightened around her wrist.

Faced now with a more familiar danger, Khali felt her fear ebbing. She knew these men and what they wanted. Aware that tears could make her appear ugly, she quickly cleared her face with her free hand as the man holding her wrist postured himself to defend her. The newcomer was larger, stronger, and appeared unmoved by the smaller man's display. He looked beyond to the girl trapped behind, and Khali met his eyes as well. Subtle enough to convince, but strong enough to convey her message, she smiled.

For just an instant, she thought they would fight like starving dogs over a scrap. But the instant passed, the camaraderie of a conquering army prevailing. These two would share their find. As their hands began to compete for her, the larger of the two nudged the first to the side. Khali tried not to shrink from him, knowing that if she pleased them, she might live past this day to a time when smiling for a more powerful man might see them both put to death. She turned away from the larger man's hot and foul breath. Her heart sank further at the sight of yet another soldier fast approaching. She watched his silhouette grow through the gloom created by thin beams of sunlight filtering through cracked walls and hanging dust. She heard the rising sounds of his breathing, heavy and labored from the fighting outside.

Khali was struggling to close her mind to her failing hopes and to what was about to come, when she saw a flash of steel in the weak light, heard a soft groan from the smaller soldier, and a sound like water hitting the floor. The man who held her heard it, too, and spun quickly around. Khali stepped back toward the fallen rocks as the hilt of a heavy sword came down on the soldier's head with a sickening, hollow crack. She flinched as something warm and slick tapped against her cheek.

The body fell between them. The third soldier's eyes flashed down at her, still wild and dangerous with the look of the kill. Khali lost her feet and fell against the collapsed wall, looking up at him in mute amazement. Wearing no armor, no white tunic and crimson cross, the face that had seemed almost gentle in the night air now glared fearsome and grim. Broussard.

Chapter Twenty-One

Molly sat at the edge of the tautly made-up cot, knees together and feet apart, trying not to think. She stared at a spot in the worn carpet between her shoes. The grey man, speaking in a peculiar accent that made her think of villains from old black and white movies about the wars in Europe, had told her that she would be safe here. When she protested, he offered that she was free to leave whenever she wanted, yet didn't hesitate to point out, "but where would you go?"

She was on the second floor of a two story building in the back room of a drafty and sunless three bedroom apartment. Connected by a wooden staircase to an old book shop on the ground floor, the apartment was quiet enough that she could hear the voices if not the words of conversations, or the creak of footsteps on old wooden floors in the shop below.

The grey man had brought Molly to this back room, as over-ripe with a musty odor as the rest of the shop. She remembered what she had seen below. All of the books were old, odd-sized, many were bound in cracked leather, and none offered any color outside of black or brown. Even the dark corridors of bookcases in the storefront were bent with age as if they were made of ancient trees. No customers had entered during the entire time she had been listening, though she had seen, when first led inside, a sign on the front door that proclaimed, "We're Open! Come on in!"

The only other people in this dusty old place were the grey man who carried a pipe even when he wasn't smoking it, and his wife, a heavy woman in a brown and green flowered dress. The woman, who had introduced

herself with a gentle smile as "Trudie," reminded Molly of her
Grandmother, except that her Grandmother seemed softer where Trudie
was quite solid.   When Molly first arrived, Trudie appeared angry at her
fatigued and disheveled condition.   She had saved most of her more
scolding tones on this matter for her husband, as if he were somehow to
blame for it, but she still directed a frown or two at Molly. She had quickly
suggested a bath and brought a choice of clean clothes, all of which, in
keeping with everything else in the place, seemed well worn and dimmed
with age. Molly refused the bath, then ignored the short flowered dress, the
boys' jeans, and the sweater, even after Trudie had left her alone, choosing
instead to silently study the spot between her feet.

Trudie had made her a sandwich out of the leftover turkey from their
Thanksgiving dinner. The only things Molly had eaten in the last two days
were the two slices of Wonder Bread she had pilfered from Detective Book's
refrigerator earlier that morning. Thanksgiving must have come and gone
and she hadn't even noticed. She wondered now what her mother had done
for the holiday without her. She had forgotten her own hunger until she
smelled the inviting sour scent of the pickle and the chips and the yellow
mustard under the bread. She debated the dangers of taking food from a
stranger for as long as she could, feeling a lot like a little girl in a fairy tale
when the witch was trying to fatten her up to make the best possible meal
out of her later. A few minutes after Trudie left her again, she devoured the
gift completely.

The old couple had left her alone since then, hoping she would try to
sleep. They seemed to think her sleeping was important. Molly found
herself fighting the impulse to sink into the cot and surrender to her
exhaustion. But she feared what might happen to her at the hands of these

strange people in this strange place, nearly as much as she feared the voice that would still be waiting for her the next time she slept.

She remained seated on the edge of the cot, continuing to weaken until she decided to change her approach. She tried to think through the spinning haze of her mind, fatigued beyond reasoning, reaching out for anything that might keep her from rest. Against her will her thoughts turned to the man in black and the wicked gleam she had seen in his eyes as he came for her. She remembered what he had done to the woman lying on that couch, just out of her sight. She had been alive, and now she was dead. She remembered Detective Book and the choking sound that had escaped his lips after the shattering explosion from the gun. Her tears came again, warmly streaking her cheeks before cooling and becoming uncomfortable in the stale air.

Molly absently wiped her face with the sleeve of Book's jacket. She cried for that woman, and for the sad sound he had made. Though she wasn't sure why, Molly wished that Book were here with her now.

Chapter Twenty-Two

Blood, still wet, stained Broussard's chest and hands, and still more coated the obscene blade he held at his side. From the prickling hairs of her neck to the leaden weight she bore deep in her chest, Khali's body seemed to shout warnings to her. Her courage failed her. She withered before him, turning weakly to remove more rocks from the collapsed corridor that kept her from Baseema, as if the soldier weren't there.

Broussard snatched at her arm and roughly spun her.

"Come with me." He demanded.

Khali was lost. Suddenly it was the child, alone again on the streets of Acre, who shrieked at this menace in the darkness and bit his hand like a cornered animal. Startled by her reaction, Broussard released her and she returned to the stones. He quickly regained his senses, realizing that she might have already lost hers. Broussard had traveled and fought among enough invading armies to know that her panicked scream would attract more like the men at his feet. It had never occurred to him that the girl might reject his help.

As he turned to scan the shadows and to listen for approaching footfalls, he allowed himself to wonder at the unseen force that had compelled him to this moment. He saw his mad ride and the trail of Saracen bodies from the streets below to this hallway with more sober eyes. He saw that what had guided him was indeed a fever of his mind. What had he expected to find here? And why could he not stay away?

"This house is burning," he said in nearly even tones. He grabbed for the sobbing girl again, dragging her as she stumbled in his wake, back the way he had come.

Broussard paused in the corridor where shafts of sunlight thickened in the dust before the entrance to the roof. Khalidah felt his entire body tense. His grip tightened around her wrist so painfully that she cried out again. Even as she pounded weakly at his left hand, she saw the massive blade he held in the other flash in the half-light. She saw it hack deeply near the steel cross of its hilt into the throat of another Saracen soldier, a slender and suddenly terrified young man who had just stepped inside from the roof and into the rising arc of Broussard's weapon. Her eyes widened in horror as Broussard quickly dragged the length of the blade across the man's throat as if pulling it from a sheath. He fell, unable to cry out as his life spilled on the cold stone floor at her feet. The Templar's grip tightened further around her wrist.

"Do not make another sound if you want to live." He glared at her, the look of the kill burning in his eyes, before easing his painful hold on her.

Though the sun was now above the horizon, Broussard could not penetrate the gloom of earthen dust raised by the collapsed wall. Yet where there was one prowling soldier, he knew there were likely many more. He chose to return the way he had come, straight through the bowels of the dying house to the main gate, which opened to the street further from the breach now filling the roof with enemies.

Khali, who had grown accustomed to many fearful sights and outrageous injustices, had never seen death run as free and unchecked as it did in her master's house this morning. The lifeless bodies of Ardenti's personal guards lay all around them as Broussard led her through the corridors and open halls. The horror of their last thoughts as life was blasted from them by crushing blow or ripping blade remained permanently emblazoned on their faces. Khali had learned from her mother, from her courage and gentleness at the time of her leaving, that where life meets death is a sacred moment, a transaction with eternity. Though her head spun and her vision fogged at its edges as her heart pounded too fast and too hard, she remained aware that a terrible blasphemy had occurred. Something holy was being perverted here.

Smoke from Ardenti's amassed wealth, now in conflagration, filled the halls. Khali tried to look only into Broussard's massive back as he led her without hesitation past the dead, and silently past broken doors that did nothing to hide the sounds of the other surviving women. Those who had been unable or unwilling to take the escape they had all decided on were now paying the price at the hands of the invaders.

Retracing the circuitous route through Ardenti's home he had used to find the girl, Broussard managed to reach a guard's overlook above the enclosed courtyard and only about three times his height from the ground. From this vantage he could see that the invaders now held the fortified house unopposed and had opened the front gate to the street. As he watched a Saracen soldier leading the winded horse he had left behind only minutes before toward Ardenti's stable, he realized that he had no plan. He had not put much thought into finding her, and even less, it was now clear, into their escape.

Broussard glanced back at Khali, still held fast in his left hand. She no longer seemed about to cry out or attack him. She seemed more stunned, as if she had been struck in the head.

"Can you reach that gate if we have to run through this courtyard?"

Though harsh and demanding, his voice again seemed to carry

unexpected compassion, as it did the night before. Khali saw his face and heard his voice as if within a dream. Though she knew better, she felt a growing desire to give herself over to him in this moment, to either lead her to safety or to death, as long it was to somewhere else. She was finished struggling. After a moment's search, she found her voice again.

"Yes."

Broussard's plan, such as it was, amounted to a dash for the man leading his horse away, so he could reclaim the animal. From there, he hoped to ride through whatever awaited beyond the gates. The fact that there were only a few soldiers about led him to believe they were mere stragglers, intent on avoiding the real fighting that raged to the West, where a strong force of mercenary soldiers still protected the breach.

He silently cursed himself and Khalidah as he timed his attack. It was unlikely a scheme so reckless and ill conceived could have worked even if he wasn't dragging the girl behind him. He glanced back at her once again and saw that she was fading, like she might faint.

"Khali..." His voice cut through the fog and pulled her part way back. This time, Broussard forced his way into her eyes, afraid he might lose her if he could not hold her there. "I am going to leave you here for a moment. But I will be back. You can run from me, back into this house, or..." He paused for a moment, suddenly burning with a fear that she would run, and still wondering why he should care if she did. "...or you can come with me. You will have to jump from here when I tell you." His hard tone trailed into more request than command.

Khali met his eyes, using the strength behind them to draw herself back from the dream state, back toward alertness. She thought to ask why he had come for her, but managed only, "I will come."

The soldier just had time to unsheathe his sword before Broussard was upon him. Khali turned away, and when she didn't hear the expected clash of metal on metal, she looked back. The young soldier was dead and the Templar was already rushing the horse toward her, pulling it by the reins, looking away all the while, distracted by something on the roof she could not see.

Khali climbed to her feet and looked down for the first time at the jump he had asked her to make. She swung her legs over without hesitation, and remained perched on the ledge, waiting for his command.

Broussard followed the arrow's long flight and easily side-stepped it. The bowman was alone on the roof and calling out for help. Broussard arrived beneath Khali, waited to dodge the second arrow, and then beckoned to her while the archer notched a third.

"Jump, Khali!" He reached toward her, expecting that she would need coaxing, and knowing that any delay might prove fatal to them both. Khali leaped without pause, falling lightly into his arms. He set her on her feet, his body between her and the archer, and quickly shuttled her behind the stamping horse.

He began to hurry the animal toward the gate, using its massive body as a shield for them both. The archer was not deterred by the thought of damaging captured property, as he had hoped. The horse screamed when an arrow pierced its flank. Broussard held fast to the bridle to keep it from bolting. Khalidah gripped his arm as the animal tried to rear above them.

Broussard steadied the animal and kept them moving toward the gate. His heart sank further, and his plan seemed more futile, at the rising sounds of combat on the street beyond. The fighting was spilling eastward from the breach.

Broussard's mind raced with hopeless strategies and unacceptable options. Reaching the street with the girl but without a horse would see them overwhelmed by the first wave of invaders. To remain would be worse. Even if they could make it back to the house, they would only be further from safety.

A second arrow lodged in the horse's chest. A guttural moan sent a blast of hot breath past Broussard's face. The animal staggered, its wounds clearly fatal. Even as he thought to make a run with Khali for the street, a ragged wave of Saracen soldiers spilled through the gate into the courtyard ahead.

Broussard pulled the dying beast to the ground, pushing the girl down beside it, hoping its body would shield her. Khali understood and looked on from where she lay, partially hidden. The horse labored to breathe. The animal was frightened, and Khali instinctively placed a gentle hand on the soft hair of its neck. Still, her eyes remained locked on the Christian who, for some reason she could not grasp, was about to give his life in her defense.

Ten invaders advanced on the Templar. Broussard watched them, menacing sword in hand. So strong was his conviction to stand his ground, she thought they would turn and run. They did not. They only smiled at the realization that he was not quite so alone as he looked.

"The Archer!" Khali called.

Broussard again side-stepped the arcing missile, giving the soldiers an opening. All at once, they rushed him.

Khali saw only a glimpse of unimaginable ferocity as Broussard seemed resolved to die with as much of his enemies' blood on his hands as he could spill. She turned away in fear, looked again to the archer on the roof, and saw that he no longer stood upright. He hunched over like an old beggar. She saw the outline of a crossbow's short bolt embedded in the man's hip. The archer dropped to a knee, and then out of sight altogether.

When she looked back to Broussard, five men lay dead or dying at his feet. The Templar sucked air hard. She saw that some of the blood on his clothes was his own. The remaining Saracen soldiers had stepped back to re-evaluate their attack.

Broussard's wounds screamed pain at him, but he did not acknowledge them. The men he faced were ill-trained, the lowest of foot soldiers, the first wave of an assault, and expendable. Had he worn the crimson cross of his Order, they likely would not have attacked him in the first place. Even as blood ran steadily from a searing gash in his thigh, and as a deep puncture at the left side of his ribs made breathing difficult, Broussard showed no weakness that might give them hope. He glanced at the empty perch where the archer had been. He looked longer and realized; not gone, the archer was dead.

The noise from the streets grew louder, suddenly sounding less like a frenzied sacking and more like a fight. Broussard realized they had allies outside this courtyard if they could reach them.

"Come!" he called to Khali, extending his hand backward to her as he glared at the remaining soldiers before him.

Khali obeyed and rushed to him, gripping his blood-streaked hand.

The five remaining Saracens seemed unsure if they should fight, if they could win, or if the Christian might simply drop dead where he stood if they waited long enough.

The girl was a prize worth fighting for, but the Christian behaved like a wounded bull lion defending a pride of one. His chest still rose and fell with heavy strength as he advanced. And even as his heart pumped more blood from the gash across his thigh, soaking the soft linen in crimson, the Saracens looked at their dead friends. They gave ground, opening a path to the gate.

As Broussard led her slowly and steadily toward the street, Khali offered them only the same grave expression they found on the Christian's face.

For a moment, Khali thought they would make it to the gate. But as quickly as that sense had come, the expressions of the watching soldiers changed, and Broussard was pushing her quickly backward from the gate. When she peered around him, her heart fell again. A large crowd of Saracen soldiers had spilled suddenly through the gate, blocking the street. Not even the Templar could stand against so many.

Broussard watched them enter the courtyard backward, driven in by an outside force. He knew there was still hope outside if they could reach it. Though most of the men before them focused on the commotion at the gate, Broussard locked eyes with the five he had fought before, and steeled himself again.

Khali reached up to his raised arm. Her light touch made his weapon feel heavy, and he lowered it, as though his rage were being drained, until the sword point touched the ground. Broussard turned for a moment, compelled to look down at her again. She stood boldly at his side. He saw the softness of her silk clothing and the sheen of perspiration on her skin. He saw the blood of men staining her delicate cheek and rising bosom. He saw a humble conviction in her eye that gentled his fierce glare. It was only the briefest exchange, but it was enough that he understood and was even somewhat ashamed. Whether they lived or died in the next moments, she had seen too much of his world this day.

The defense at the gate was broken by horses. Four riders in armor and Templar whites hammered into the makeshift line. Broussard recognized two of them as Durand and Leveque, forcing through to the courtyard, scattering and slaughtering the footmen with wheeling sword and axe.

At the height of this new chaos, Khali took an involuntary step back at the sight of a fifth rider charging through at a gallop, face obscured beneath his helmet, his cloak followed him like white smoke from a holocaust, framing yet more blood splayed across the crimson cross over white at his chest. She could not see his eyes, but she nevertheless felt them burn through her as he came straight for them.

Panicked foot soldiers fled to either side as he came. Finally, he ripped the helmet from his head as he reined his horse back hard, hurling the heavy object with disdain at the back of a fleeing enemy. Vincent Broussard glared down at his half-brother with such fury that Sebastien took Khali by the arm and moved her behind him. Vincent dismounted the stamping horse, heavy heels bruising the earth where he landed, and stepped toward his brother. Vincent removed his gauntlet. Only Khali flinched when he slapped his brother's face with the hard-knuckled back of his hand. Sebastien stood still, met his brother's eyes, and said nothing.

"Take my horse. Get to your ship. Ride!" There was an importance beyond mere fury in the elder Broussard's voice. Khali felt it as well when her protector pulled her quickly to his brother's horse. He tossed her into the saddle and leapt on behind her, wheeling the massive animal around with such control that she did not fear it. She watched Vincent as he glared contemptuously at her and then again at his brother, before raising his sword and falling upon the scrambling invaders now trapped by the walls of Ardenti's home with a fearsome rage.

Broussard dug in his heels and the animal bolted through the open gate. He leaned forward, low above the girl, hardly taking notice as they fled past dozens more armored and mounted Templars now holding the street clear for their escape. Southward, away from the breach they rode until Broussard felt confident they could safely turn again to the West and head for the harbor.

Khali had never been on a horse before. Even as she clutched the thick jet mane of the mighty animal until her hands turned white, an altogether new sense of exhilaration rushed through her as streets she had not seen in over a year, but once could have walked under a blindfold, flashed past at a dizzying speed.

The sun shone brightly, free of the dust raised by the collapsing tower, and the high tide had already passed when they finally burst into view of the harbor. Only then, as they forced their way through the teeming crowd of hopeful and hopeless refugees, only when he spotted the familiar flags of the two Templar warships flanking the *Leila* as she headed to sea, halfway already to the horizon, did Broussard let the shame of his failure wash over him. If he had not believed in the importance of Beaujeu's plans for him before, after his rescue at the hands of Vincent, he understood now. What had been for him a flight of fancy or a fit of madness had brought the body of the Order's elite away from the defense of the keep and needlessly into harm's way.

As the girl craned her neck to look back into his face, no doubt to see why they had stopped and what madness would come next, he told himself that he was merely repaying a debt from the night before. Her life for his.

An escape from a burning house for a scalding femur bone plucked from a kettle. Yet, as the scent from her hair rose to him, he filled his lungs with her again and he knew there was something more.

"That was to be your ship." He looked past her and Khali followed his eyes to the grey sails of three ships heading to sea. "The city is doomed," he said with greater effort. "The Christians cannot hold it."

Khali watched the refugees, most of them Europeans with desperation on their faces, as other ships in the harbor repelled boarders from the wretched souls still without passage. She considered his words and wondered at them. What was it to her whether Christian or Muslim occupied her home? Victory for either would be won through the blood of both, and neither would have a place for her in their city. She looked again at the *Leila*, grey sails now full, and wondered at what treasures she carried to warrant the escort of two mighty warships.

Khali knew little of the ways of war, but neither was she a fool. She had understood the words of the terrible rider whose horse had brought her to the harbor. She understood that the mounted knights had come only to create *their* escape. Had they come for her? Or had they come for the young soldier who had led her out of Ardenti's house? She wondered what sort of treasure she could be considered, and for whom she was destined, for these dangerous men to go to the lengths they had to put her on board that departed ship.

"Why have you done this?" she demanded at last, the painful confusion of sudden loss catching up to her where the horse rested.

Broussard considered an explanation, that Van Cuso surely would have killed him if not for her aid, but quickly realized that it was absurd. She would think him every bit the fool he was if he spoke of it now. "I must get to my ship," he said before his voice faltered. "Single mast, white sail."

Khali heard his strength ebb as he spoke. She looked down to the blood still flowing from the long opening in his thigh. She understood. The Templar might be no stronger than she at this moment. She wanted to fear him. Yet true horror would not come. She felt only a fear, curious and unexpected, like sensing a snare about to spring.

In an instant, feeling the warmth of his body behind hers in the saddle, and his shallow breath near her ear, Khali was overwhelmed by the need to escape him. She grabbed the tapering and hard muscled neck of the dark horse and slipped around it in a sudden movement that saw her safely to the ground. He was too weak to even try to stop her. She backed away from the horse, watching its rider sway in the saddle. She was free of him now.

She stood still within the chaos of refugees moving around and past her, like a fixed stone at the surface of a moving stream, watching him as he faded. Perhaps it was simply knowing that she could escape him now, if she wished. She might disappear, like that stone come loose, swept away with this current. But the moment of panic that had helped free her was giving way to another thought.

Broussard was dying.

Chapter Twenty-Three

"I want to see her." Book's voice carried a threat as he glared down at the angular grey man leading him into the dusty shop from the back alley. He knew it was ridiculous to try to appear menacing now, standing with his hands still cuffed behind his back in what seemed to be the old man's bookstore with the skillful and almost casually murderous drifter just behind him. Book was determined to handle each incomprehensible situation as well as he could. In this case, it was as a prodded and enraged bull. Even as he spoke, Book plotted the demolition of his captors and their shop with only his shoulders and his boots.

"You are in no position to make demands, Detective Book."

"Where is she?" he demanded anyway, a more colorful threat sputtering in his head before he could speak it.

The old man turned a disapproving eye toward Book's captor. "You should not have brought him here."

The paper-faced drifter offered no argument or sign of regret. He simply placed his board on a table and sat down.

"There's a new dent in your car. Sorry about that."

The old man looked again to Book in worried frustration.

"Well, you are here now, obviously, so we'll have to make due. Molly is sleeping."

"Show me," Book demanded again.

The grey man thought it through for a moment, annoyed.

"Alright, but please don't wake her."

Book had a thousand questions rushing through his mind, but they could wait. Maybe it was the sense of terror and failure he felt at what had happened to Sara, but he needed to see Molly. He needed to know that she was unhurt, that he had not failed her, too.

The grey man paused while winding through the brief maze of oak bookshelves long enough to impress upon the massive detective just how heavy his steps were as they approached the back stairs. Book stepped more carefully, puzzling over the oddest kidnappers he could have imagined treating the captive girl as if she were visiting royalty.

He stood in the open doorway and saw her. Molly slept, curled up within his weathered bomber jacket on a cot in the otherwise empty room. He stepped closer to her and lingered long enough to watch her breathe in and out in a sleeper's slow rhythm.

"You see?" The grey man whispered from the doorway. "She is safe here."

In the old bookshop on the first floor, Book sat at the edge of the heavy, high-backed leather chair he had been led to, waiting for whatever would come next, ready to implement his shoulder and boot demolition plan if the need arose.

"I'm quite certain," the grey man said in a calm voice tinged with an accent Book knew well, the kind of accent only developed in America after too long away from central Europe, "that you could tear this building apart with your bare hands if you wished." He leaned forward with a squeak of old leather from his own high-backed chair and offered a sly smile. "But I'm willing to risk that you won't."

The drifter moved behind Book and tapped his shoulder. Book tensed.

"Lean forward," the man instructed as his chafed hands straightened the loops of a paper clip.

Book complied, still half-expecting a knife at his throat at any moment. Instead, the same man who had nearly bashed in his skull with a two-by-four went quickly to work on the first handcuff lock with the thin strip of metal.

Though he had seldom felt as powerless, Book still managed to project a fearsome strength as he surveyed his surroundings. The grey man sat across from him, a low and heavy oak table between them. The rest of the room was entirely filled with books. Books were packed into shelves and stacked on tables where they overflowed, all very old, some leather bound, and none displayed as if they might sell. It seemed more like an oversized and cluttered office than a business.

"Who are you people?" Book asked at last.

"My name," offered the grey man, "is Jacob."

"That's it? Just *Jacob*?" Book watched him until it was clear that no further identification would follow.

"And this is our friend, John."

Book looked over his shoulder toward the paper-faced man with the blood of two young policemen on his hands, working the handcuffs like a pro. A gruesome parade of violent impulses coursed through him, but Book swallowed them all for the chance to gather even a little bit of information about what was happening to him. "Just *John*?"

"He has come to visit my shop many times over the years, but that is the only name he has ever given to me." Jacob hesitated. "We both agree that this is a wise precaution."

The binding on his right wrist clicked open. Book shifted his stiffening arms in front of him. He massaged the ache in his constricted muscles without taking his eyes off Jacob.

"More than that becomes a long story. How about an easier question?" Jacob suggested.

Book continued to study his face, looking for signs of truth and lies. John went to work on his left wrist with his paperclip.

"What do you want with the girl?" Book quietly demanded. "Who is that guy who...?" Even as he maintained his threatening demeanor, Book unexpectedly choked on his words as the image of Sara punished his mind.

"You have a lot of questions, I know," Jacob mercifully interjected. "It is likely we will not have all the answers you want."

Book found his voice again. "Start somewhere."

Jacob leaned back in his chair and brought his skeletal fingers together at the tips in a thoughtful pose. "Concerning the girl, I cannot say much until I have learned more about her. But the man who pursues her, who now pursues *you*... his kind has been known by many peoples in the past and by many names, but to us he is known as a *Shepherd*."

Book puzzled over that only briefly before asking, "Why?"

"Because," John spat out definitively, as if it were completely obvious, "they herd sheep with big sticks and packs of dogs."

"I learned of his existence, and others like him, 26 years ago," Jacob continued before Book could question John any further. "I followed him from Europe to this city at the height of the second World War. And for all that time I have watched him in secret from the safety of my store."

"*You* followed *him*? Why?"

Jacob's attention seemed to drift. "You have seen what he can do."

Buried deep within the grey man's voice, Book sensed old pain, lingering sadness, and embers of anger still warm enough to ignite. In his mind, Book watched Sara's blood spreading from her hair onto the fabric of her couch. "He killed someone. Someone close to you?"

"My child." The old man offered no more.

Book realized that Jacob was suddenly less eager to talk. "But who is he? Who does he work for?"

"Shepherds are powerful agents of the Enemy. Their sole occupation in life, as far as I have gathered, is to keep a secret within a secret." Jacob came back to the present with a slight, self-important smile that invited further questioning.

"So that's..." Book just managed not to roll his eyes. "...two secrets, then?"

"Two very great secrets."

"Right. And you know all about them, of course."

"No. I'm afraid that, after many years of searching, I know little more about the second, deeper secret than you do at this moment. The first secret, you've already discovered for yourself."

"What have I discovered, exactly?"

"That they exist."

Book could not dispute that. "Who are they?"

"The Enemy." The words came out leaden, like a heavy burden.

"That's it? Just the *Enemy*?"

"They have had many names throughout history that would mean very little to you now, whispers of the wise dead, men and women of forgotten times who once tried to warn us. But any words ever spoken of them come to the same thing. They are the enemy of all men."

Book squinted in frustration, his eyes darting between Jacob and

John as if one of them might suddenly become sane and offer some real help with his dilemma.

"I first heard about them," Jacob continued, "from someone who did seem to know a great deal more than I can tell you now. But of course, like you, I did not take any of this seriously until it was too late."

Book felt the regret in Jacob. Echoes of Sara's apartment still resonated. Book nodded with a peculiar sense of solidarity that made him even less comfortable. "He let me go."

"Because we have the girl." Jacob's words bounced in a leading manner, transparently letting Book know that there was more to each new revelation. Book always distrusted people who enjoyed answering questions as much as Jacob did. "He was only moments behind you when we..."

"Hit me in the head with a two-by-four?"

"You must understand," Jacob apologized as if he had merely forgotten to return a phone call. "We had no choice but to leave you behind."

"Sure." Book nodded. "I understand."

"It was the Shepherd who returned you safely to your home."

Book ignored the chill that passed through his body. "Why?" he asked as soon as he could.

The old man paused to consider the question. "Well," he began after a long moment spent studying the young detective, "whatever the reason, I can assure you it is logical. You simply must be of more value to him alive or you would certainly be dead."

Book's thoughts took him back to his apartment, to the Shepherd's voice, and the iron hold of the unseen thread as he probed, *where is the girl?* "Why did you come back for me?"

"It was John who returned for you, Detective. He has his own reasons for doing so."

Book glanced again at the paper-faced street dweller, but received no further indication as to why he decided to attack and kill two cops in that alley and bring Book to this store. John concentrated unwaveringly on the cuff around his left wrist.

Jacob moved to a more urgent subject. "Though you are obviously still alive, I should warn you. In order to walk among us as they do, Shepherds guard their own secrets very carefully. They rarely come into the light, and they never kill without leaving someone behind to hang for the crime. This one has killed several times today."

"With my gun."

"This is the first thing you must realize. You still live, but your life as you knew it is over."

"He set me up." Book focused on the puzzle.

"Irreparably, I'm afraid. There will be no recovery from this."

"I'm a cop," Book protested instinctively. The words sounded hollow even to him. "I have friends... they know..."

"The facts are clear enough, Detective Book. They will tell your friends what to believe."

"But none of it is true. I..." Book stopped.

"Yes." Jacob nodded, as if familiar with the frustration Book felt. "Unfortunately, what is *true* is of little consequence to most people. Our species is far more interested in being *comforted* by what is believable than in being *afraid* of what is true."

John clicked open the remaining lock.

"It is easier for the world," the old man continued gently, "that you are simply a mad man. A killer. The world will know what to do with you now, Detective."

The cuff slipped from his wrist unnoticed as Book waited for Jacob's next words.

"You may find, if you live long enough, that very little of what goes on out there is *true*. Perhaps nothing at all."

John tossed the steel bindings onto the oak table. Book flinched at the sudden loud clatter of chains.

Chapter Twenty-Four

Broussard awoke to the cool smoothness of dry sand hours out of the sun and into the night. He lay on his back staring at the sky. He could hear the ocean pawing the shore somewhere just over his shoulder, but he could not turn to look at it. He could not move at all.

Pale light from the moon bled through a low sky of dark, fast-moving clouds like a bright lantern behind a heavy tapestry. He watched the light, unable to turn away until the marching clouds at last opened above him like the lid of a great eye. The golden orb in the sky appeared as a living thing, as if a great hunting beast had suddenly caught sight of him where he lay helpless on the open ground.

Broussard thought to reach to his side for a weapon, but a great weight in his chest threatened to crush him, and he could not move. Instead he spent what might have been the last of his strength trying to draw a breath that would not come. The voice may have come from the stalking beast bearing down on him from the clouds, as it seemed to roll like a deep thunder. Broussard might have thought it was the voice of God had he not known better. He had heard its enigmatic question once before.

"What have you found, Templar?"

***

Broussard burst into the harshness of a high sun in blue sky, and the searing pain of his own flesh burning under hot metal.

"Easy, boy." De Buci said. · His voice carried a familiar calm as he held the smoking hot blade against the wound on Broussard's thigh. "Keep him still."

Broussard had cried out as he surged into consciousness and thrashed at the suddenness of the pain, but he calmed at the touch of soft hands at his face. He looked back to see the girl, raven hair framed by the disc of the Sun, leaning over him as she cradled his head in her lap.

Khali held him still and whispered softly to him in Arabic. De Buci waited until he stopped moving, then pressed the blade again to the wound.

"He'll live," Broussard heard him say at last. Then he heard no more.

***

The Gull was a small enough craft that she could be handled by one man if necessary. Shahin took comfort in that fact as he studied his passengers from his position at the tiller. The dead calm sea and the wilted sail gave him little to occupy his mind but strategy. He concentrated on the many dangers involved in having three Templars aboard. But of all the mysteries surrounding this voyage, Shahin found his attention pulled consistently toward the girl whose gentle and uncommon beauty was as out of place among a ship of soldiers, as it likely had been among the people of Acre.

Khali stood alone in the soft night air, watching the water from the low rail of the modest vessel. She had spent every day and night of life inside a city of walls. Here, on the ocean, the world was boundless.

The rich blues of water and sky had long ago turned to black with the coming of night. The subtle undulations of the dead-calm reflected the stars like a throbbing black mirror, making them appear to be both above and below at once. It seemed as if all she needed to do was step over the rail to find herself floating in the heavens.

The water proved colder than she had hoped as she watched a slow wake diverge where her hand entered it. But the steadily pulsing sea seemed alive with its own heartbeat, its own slow breathing, and it compelled her. The slick surface seemed like a barrier to still another world. Khali wondered what she might find if she surrendered to it. As safe as she had been with Ardenti before the walls fell, it had been a long time since she had seen so clearly the true distance between life and death. One slip, or one choice.

The voices of the men at the back of the boat drifted through the still air. They were arguing. The Moor, who seemed to be in charge of sailing the boat, sounded displeased, even more so than he had been earlier. The other two, whom she recognized as friends to Broussard, the young quiet one barely out of his boyhood, and the older, fatter man who had closed Broussard's wounds, both seemed equally resolute in opposition to him. She had heard once before that sailors believed women on ships to be bad luck, and wondered if they argued about her. She decided it was best to stay where she was, close to the sleeping Broussard.

The other Templars did not look on her as other soldiers might, certainly not as the men who had found her in the corridor near Baseema's bedchamber. These men seemed to follow an entirely different set of rules that came with an entirely different array of desires. Yet, she felt the danger she was in. It seemed to come from no place in particular, from all around her at once. She felt it as a weight pressing just above her stomach and just beneath her heart.

The Captain, his manner rough and rude, his appearance somewhat disheveled, seemed angry and dangerous, as a lone Muslim among these men well might. Yet Khali had sensed a depth within him as he met her eyes upon her boarding. There was a pain of *loss* which, whether recent or far in his past, he still carried very near to the surface. Shahin was not a particularly handsome man, but Khali knew, from that first shared look and again in this moment, in hearing the strength of his tone while confronting the Christians, that he was the sort of man whose attention women vied for, and the kind of man that many women might hold in their thoughts while drifting to sleep. She knew that pretty girls were not a novelty to Shahin. That thought alone made her feel somewhat safe around him.

Khali looked down again to where Broussard rested on stiff padding made of woven straw under the soft light of a oil lamp, no longer wanting to guess at the fate awaiting her when he awoke.

He would live. She had seen to that. It was only later, after she had found herself at the mercy of three other men, that she questioned why she had done it. She leaned over him now, moved the weak lamp closer, and returned to cleaning the dried blood around the openings his companion had burned shut with his knife. While delicately clearing the dead skin from the hastily patched gash in his side with a wet cloth, she took a moment to press her ear to his chest. His heart beat stronger now and his breath was no longer fearfully shallow as it had been at its worst. Khali smiled to herself over this. Knowing that he might not allow it when awake, she decided to clean the dried blood of his enemies from his body as well. She wrung the cloth over the railing, wet it again with more fresh water from the sheepskin sack the Captain had given her, and she set to work.

She had hoped to quell the questions brewing in her mind by keeping her hands busy. Yet, as she worked to remove the stains from his flesh, Khali was able to study his sleeping face without turning away, and the need to know only grew more urgent. Why had he come? When she could have fled, why had she stayed?

Khali knew it was foolish vanity to believe that she might have some special value as a slave. Moreover, she remembered the furious glare of the other Templar. And she felt the urgency Broussard had known when he pulled her roughly behind him at the rider's approach. The rescue by those mounted Templars had nothing to do with her and everything to do with the young man sleeping before her. *Why had he come for her?*

Khali had seen the bodies of men before. Whether fat or thin, the men she had known tended to be clean and soft, with skin that seemed to hang from their bones. Broussard was not like that. Her eyes lingered over him as she removed the crusted patches of dried blood. His soldier's body was hard and sinewy, like that of the horse she had clung to as they raced through the city. She discovered many old scars beneath his clothes, and traced her finger along a particular one she found on his arm to see what it felt like. The flesh above the old wound was hard and very smooth, like the glaze on a wine jar. Only a few years her elder, Khali wondered at the life he had led, and how many days like this one he had already seen.

She started and took a quick breath when a glance to his face found him awake and watching her. She thought to look away, but did not. Instead, they held each other in a silent gaze within the lamplight. Khali again felt as she had on their first meeting. Trapped by him, yet not trapped. The fear she had felt at Ardenti's house, and again on the docks when she leapt from the horse, was fading. In its place grew the realization that she had nowhere else to go, and nowhere else she should be, but here at his side where she was needed.

"Girl," De Buci's bass voice rumbled awkwardly to her from behind, almost but not quite demanding as the heavy Templar approached. "He'll need food and water now."

She lingered a moment longer on his eyes and smiled reassuringly before rising to gather a meal for him.

De Buci looked down at him with disapproval, and a faint smile.

"How?" Broussard managed to ask as he struggled to sit upright.

"I could ask you the same. We were ready to leave without you, when we saw that child leading your brother's horse through a mob of refugees." De Buci laid Broussard's sword next to the mat. "She tried to kill poor St. Ives with this when he got too close."

Broussard smiled, picturing the scene.

"Why did you take her on board?"

"Take her? We couldn't get rid of her. You've been asleep for half a day. She has watched over you like a mother wolf. We've been keeping to the other side of the boat to avoid getting stabbed." De Buci's infectious cheer sparked a wincing laugh from Broussard, but the pain shooting through his healing left side suddenly made it all seem less funny. "You almost bled to death, young Broussard. We've likely got two more days on this boat, then it's going to get difficult. Use the time to heal."

Khali returned silently with a small wooden bowl of hard bread and dried meat from the ship's rations. De Buci headed back to the other side of the ship, "We have much to talk about."

Chapter Twenty-Five

Book remained uneasy within the quiet of the bookshop. Despite the many questions he still had for the old man seated across the low table, he had no faith in his answers. His head throbbed where John had struck him in the alley behind Sara's apartment. His knee emanated a punishing shock with each movement and grew more rigid and swollen by the minute. He felt trapped and wanted to run, but he knew there was nowhere to go, at least not until he understood what was happening to him.

He turned to John, finding the drifter's disconcerting stare waiting for him. "Why did you bring me here?"

John paused as if mulling a deeper response than the one he would ultimately offer.

"So you can ask questions." He waved the back of his hand at the thousands of books surrounding them on creaking shelves. "Ask Jacob. He knows a lot."

Reluctant to engage the crazy old man any further, Book could not deny the link between the man he had called a Shepherd and the questions he had been trying to answer since June. "Six months ago," Book eventually announced to Jacob, "a branch manager from a Wyoming bank with a wife and two kids died in a gun fight in a Hollywood motel. His wife told me he didn't even own a gun, but he used the one we found still in his hand like a professional killer." Book glared at the grey man. "Who was he really, and what was he doing here?"

"He was a banker from Wyoming," Jacob said flatly.

"Bullshit." Book knew that Jacob was withholding information. He just didn't know how or why he could be so sure of it.

"James Ford has very little to do with what is happening to you right now, Detective. And I'm afraid you wouldn't believe the whole truth anyway."

Book sank back into his chair with a creak of leather, dragging the back of his hand across the forced smirk on his mouth. The crime had been hushed by the LAPD, but Jacob had called Ford by name. How, Book wondered, would he know that? "Give it your best shot. You think James Ford was in town to kill Kennedy?" It was a test. What else could this old man know about a quiet, six-month-old murder?

"Perhaps," Jacob responded slowly. "The function of a Shepherd is to keep the Enemy's secrets."

"You're saying that this 'Shepherd' killed Senator Kennedy?" Book folded his arms in a defiant posture.

"Not personally. No. But he was as responsible as any General for the death of an enemy killed in battle by one of his foot soldiers."

"Why?" Book spoke with unmistakable sarcasm. "Why would the 'Enemy' of all men' care about an American senator?"

"I don't know, specifically. But from time to time, some among us certainly do begin to see beyond the shrouding veil of illusion - a scientist on the verge of discovery, a prophet whose eyes have been opened, or a great leader who speaks of brotherhood rather than the pressing need for hatred and war. You can get too close to the truth, and they will kill you for it. This sort of thing goes on all the time, all around the world. For some reason, people tend to think of them as 'assassinations' only when the victim just happens to be famous." Jacob watched the young detective as he spoke. "A Shepherd has many tools at his disposal to remove disruptive children from the playground. Mr. Ford was simply one of many such tools. He was a redundancy within a larger plan, who apparently got caught up in a random crime and was killed before he could complete his assignment. But as we all saw, if Senator Kennedy really was his target, the larger scheme was carried out anyway, without him."

"Assignment? Scheme?" Book pressed, singling out the most leading words. "Redundancy?"

"Of course. If the first killer had failed that night for whatever reason, there were others in place. There might have been many more Assassins in that ballroom. You see?"

Jacob was a certain type of lunatic. He was a conspiracy theorist, the type of lunatic that always gave Book a headache. "No. I don't see." Book still clung to something solid, the fact of James Ford's bullet-riddled body in a hotel room. "What possible motivation would Ford have to kill anyone? What about his wife and family? What about...?"

"We all make promises," Jacob said as if it were obvious. "Promises made long ago can come back to haunt you even when you could not possibly expect them to."

Book looked for something useful among Jacob's dancing theories. His mind clicked through the old list of possibilities from blackmail to brainwashing, wondering if Jacob really knew anything at all, or if, like so many other nimble-minded crackpots, he was just plugging in facts and adjusting a malleable, foundationless theory until each new square peg could be jammed into a round slot. "Why do something so elaborate? If they are so powerful, why not just shoot him?"

"Kennedy? They *did* just shoot him," Jacob calmly pointed out.

Book was disappointed. He could see that, between John's obvious insanity and Jacob's slightly more subtle variety, there was less to learn here than he hoped. His mind moved back to Molly, and stayed with her until John spoke.

Realizing that Book had drifted, John broke the hanging silence. "Don't stop asking questions now, man." Once he started talking, a manic turmoil quickly rose within him. *"Who killed them?"* He demanded.

"Them?"

"RFK, JFK, MLK?" John implored, until he saw that Book was unmoved. "Mahatma Gandhi, Abraham Lincoln..." John's voice grew louder, and the next name on his list came out with a level of sarcasm bordering on rage, like a teacher trying to get through to his worst student and having a nervous breakdown from the effort. *"Jesus Christ?"*

Book raised an eyebrow at him. "They killed Abraham Lincoln and Jesus Christ?"

"Asshole!" John spat out dismissively. "They can do any *thing*, to any *body*! Any *time*! Killing is easy." John suddenly leapt to his feet. Out of the corner of his eye, Book saw Jacob flinch and shrink back into his chair. The old man could be frightened by his "friend." John loomed for a moment only a few feet from the seated detective.

Book felt the threat, the deaths of two police officers in the alley behind his apartment still very fresh in his thoughts. He played the scene over again, wanting to feel enough rage to pull himself out of this chair and risk a fight, even with the use of only one leg. But in his mind, he still saw the deaths of the two men in the alley the same way. Whatever else his intentions were, John had not come there to kill. In the moments of their deaths, he was defending himself.

John seemed to have reached the limit of his anger. His voice lowered, and he turned his stare away. "Don't stop asking questions now, man."

Book turned to Jacob again for one more attempt at clarity. *"They?"*

"Yes, Detective, *they*." For the first time, Book saw that Jacob could also grow annoyed. "It is the 'they' referred to in hushed whispers throughout all of history. As in "Shhh... *they* are listening...' or '*they*' will get you for that." Book squinted at the old man as the tingling heat of dark memories climbing for the surface grew stronger at the back of his neck. "They *do* watch. They *do* see. And from time to time, they *do* reach out their hand and kill."

"*Who*," Book let his anger rise, demanding in slow, single syllables, "*are they?*

Jacob seemed to think his next words all the way through before speaking them.

"The way of the world we see is war, murder, jealousy, greed, and sin after sin. As far as we know, it has always been this way, and we willingly do our part to pitch in, to try to make the best of it. We try to identify the world's problems, and then continue the long hard work of fixing them, one at a time. You as a policeman, another as a nurse, a priest, a soldier; like children on a playground, we choose a role and a side to fight for, call ourselves 'good,' and the other side 'evil' and then both sides have it. It seems so normal that very few can see that it is, in fact, quite insane. On the playground, the children know deep down that their foes are really just their classmates. You, on the other hand, have forgotten the game, and the fantasy seems real enough to kill for."

"Fantasy?"

"That is the first secret. The magician King and his courtiers *exist*, and they maintain the sad state of affairs we call the world by means of illusion." Jacob shrugged. "I don't know who they are beyond that."

"*King*?" Book asked, incredulous. "Of the *world*?"

"That is one way of looking at it. The Christians' Bible tells us, 'the god of this world hath blinded the minds of them which believe not.'"

"The god of this world? You mean the *King*? Okay, then who is he?"

"That particular verse refers to Lucifer, Detective Book. Satan. The Father of Lies. The meaning of *sin*, in the religions which use his name, is merely *to chase the illusions of the devil*. And so it is that, since the fall from the Garden of Eden, we have all lived in perpetual sin."

Book frowned and licked the front of his teeth in frustration. "Are you telling me that six cops and one woman were just murdered in front of me by a 'powerful agent' of Satan?"

Jacob shrugged again. "Possibly. If that name makes you uncomfortable, we can call them something else. I prefer the Enemy."

"Are you trying to be funny?" Book drew strength from the rush of anger.

"No." Jacob remained calm. "I am trying to tell what I know. *Stories*, Detective. Myths, legends, and fictions that still resonate with the truth handed down through the ages. That's all we have left to guide us."

Book let the tingling at his neck fester for a moment. Then, he reached for the easy comfort of indignation and disbelief.

Jacob watched Book silently work his thoughts back to steady ground.

"I told you that you would not believe the truth."

"I haven't heard any truth yet." Book countered. "You sound like the kid."

Jacob suddenly leaned forward in his seat.

"What has she said to you?"

Jacob's intense interest in Molly filled Book with a sense of impending danger. He thought to ask, to demand to know what they wanted with her, but another slowly rising fear compelled him not to. He would keep her safe, even if that meant keeping her out of the discussion.

"Tell me something real, Jacob. Who was James Ford?"

Jacob sighed with the sadness of a man whose wisdom is too much and not enough at once.

"Nothing you know is 'real,' Book. Nothing is true..."

"*All is permitted*," Book completed the verse, or whatever it was, showing Jacob that he was not completely removed from the world through which these men walked. "Tell me."

Chapter Twenty-Six

Atop the walls of the Templar keep, Vincent Broussard killed like a terrible storm, hacking and rending flesh with a gluttonous sword that flowed red and black from an unholy solution of blood and the tar smoke of a burning city. Where his blade missed, he cracked bones with armored fists and heavy boots. Great stone missiles covered with enflamed tar soared just over the heads of the defenders on the wall to fall upon the buildings and soldiers below. Saracen attackers rushed up ladders to breach the ramparts. Joined in common defense by the Hospitallers, Vincent and his brethren killed as quickly as they could, though they all knew it would not be enough this day.

Outside the wall, Vincent heard a triumphant roar of soldiers from the street below. He rushed to the edge and looked down. Though it should have been impossible for quite some time, Saracens poured through the open portal into the courtyard by the dozens.

"The gate!" Vincent shouted. He turned back to see as Templar footmen, attempting to hold their ground, began to fail against the unabated surge. Someone had raised the iron gate from within.

Charging down the stone steps toward the courtyard, Vincent paused at a strange sight. Durand stood by the lever to the gate. He seemed to wait in idle calm while the battle seethed around him. There was no time to puzzle over what could have driven his old friend. The consequences of his action were too immediate and too devastating. Durand had raised the gate.

"Durand!" Vincent shouted, but the din of the battle dominated.

Durand did not move. He seemed to be waiting, studying a spot on the ground as if trying to remember something he had forgotten, even as Templars, Hospitallers, and Saracens fought all around.

Having paused this long in the fight, Vincent began to notice more like Durand. He saw Hospitaller knights, dismounted and wandering within the melee as if confused or lost, then Templars, both nobles and footmen, doing the same. Perhaps two-dozen fighters, some Christian, some Saracen, had simply stopped defending themselves, as if stunned, asleep on their feet. He watched a young foot soldier, his axe held limply at his side, stand perfectly still as an invader came at him in the full and natural fury of the fight and took the sleepwalker's head.

Eventually, Vincent's searching eyes fell on Beaujeu. The Templar Master fought the wave still pouring through the gate with six knights at his side, all wielding axe and sword like some great threshing engine. Vincent leapt from the stairs and into the fray, killing like an indiscriminate wind as he worked his way toward Beaujeu.

"Master!" Vincent cried out to him as he neared. "We are betrayed!"

Beaujeu, his uniform whites sodden in blood, paused where he stood to acknowledge Vincent's words. He nodded in agreement, even as the youth Garvin looked up from the spot on the ground he seemed to study. Vincent watched in mute amazement as the boy's dead eyes suddenly came to life, locking in sharp focus onto the back of his uncle, mentor and protector, Beaujeu. In three quick strides the boy was on him, plunging a short blade just below the pit of the arm, where the armor does not protect, and into Beaujeu's chest. A look of surprise flashed across the Master's face as he stumbled forward toward Vincent.

"It is the dreams, Vincent. We are defeated." Beaujeu dropped to his knees in the mud. Still watching in silent amazement at the inexplicable betrayal, Vincent thought Beaujeu looked very much like a man about to fall asleep. "I do not flee, my friend. I am undone. Look..." Beaujeu raised his arm to show the blood spilling from the wound. "...here is the wound."

The six who had fought with him stared at young Garvin. The boy, the gentle soul his uncle had always tried to keep from combat, faced them all with the same, icy focus. Vincent approached slowly as the first Templar screamed in rage and came at the boy with a wild swing of his sword. Garvin calmly stepped inside the arc and killed the much larger man with a single, deft stroke. A second Templar attacked and fell. Then a third.

Vincent watched as other dead-eyed wanderers joined Garvin. Two dozen men, Templar, Hospitaller, and Saracen, stood side by side, as if a third front had suddenly been opened. Vincent found himself under attack by enemies and allies on all sides.

Vincent and the remaining Templars who had not gone suddenly insane stood back to back in a circle. Outnumbered, they would not stand for long. As Vincent parried swift and relentless attacks from Garvin, the Hospitaller giant, Van Cuso, attacked unseen. He knocked Vincent off his feet with a heavy boot.

Pulling himself quickly into a defensive posture, Vincent came face to face with an old friend. "Leveque!" Vincent shouted in confusion bordering on despair. "Do you not know me?" Leveque studied him as a hunter watches a deer, raised his sword and brought it down with fierce and deadly intent at Vincent's unprotected skull. Vincent parried the blow but did not return it. He hesitated, unable to strike at his friend when the opening presented itself. In that moment Durand's sword, attacking quick like a snake from his blindside, slashed and bit into his side, breaching his armor and cracking a rib while cutting an inch deep into his chest.

Vincent turned in amazement, meeting his friend's emotionless eyes as Durand jerked the blade free. "Why have you done this?" Vincent gasped, so thoroughly bewildered by this impossible moment, he felt no anger as he fell to the ground.

Van Cuso approached again, saying nothing even as he raised his sword high above his head for the killing blow. As if in answer to his question, Vincent heard a familiar voice shout a command.

"Stop."

The treasonous attackers all suddenly stopped fighting, and the battlefield grew eerily quiet.

From where he lay in the mud, Vincent looked around at the bodies of the dead, hundreds of Christian and Muslim fighters strewn across the courtyard. The battle was over. Walking toward him through the aftermath, the familiar face that matched the voice approached. Out of place within this particular war, the jet-black mane of a golden-skinned Mongol whipped the wind like a tattered flag. Vincent's brow tightened at the impossible realization. This golden face had first appeared to him in a dream, as he slept.

With little hope of living past the next few moments, Vincent determined to keep his calm, to show no fear, and to learn something of the mystifying circumstance that had seen him so suddenly and thoroughly defeated.

"Who are you?"

"Some now call me Shepherd, though I have had many names in the past." The golden man stood above Vincent, then crouched closer, impressed with the cornered man's composure. "Once I was known to your order as the Old Man of the Mountain."

The Mongol spoke perfect French, as he had in the dream.

Vincent cocked a doubtful eye at the man, who appeared no older than himself, yet spoke of Templar lore from his grandfather's time.

"I first took the fortress at Aluh Amut over 100 years ago." The Mongol rose again to his full height above Vincent. "Then, in the year of your Lord 1272, I returned with the Golden Horde of Hulagu to take it a second time. It was then, still little more than a boy, when I began to awaken once more."

The Mongol slapped a hand on the shoulder of Leveque, and the deadly Templar did not move or alter his grim expression.

"Since I left them so long ago, my disciples have waited." He pointed with pride to Garvin, who still watched Vincent with intense, expressionless eyes. "Some have stood right beside their targets as pupil to mentor, nephew to uncle." He waved a hand toward Durand. "Some as dear old friends."

The Mongol returned his attention to Vincent.

"Through every triumph and defeat, they stood with their future victims as in a dream, until they might someday awaken to the sound of my voice and receive my commands once more."

"The Old Man," Vincent quietly insisted, "died long ago. His mountain is empty and his disciples are dust. Unless he and his Assassins have risen from the dead, there is no truth in what you say."

"So they have risen." The Mongol gave a derisive smile, as if particularly pleased by the sight of a Templar knight at his mercy, prostrate in the mud. "As have I." The Mongol's smile vanished. "I will tell you a secret, Christian. Nothing is true. All is permitted."

Vincent squinted at his friends, Durand and Leveque. He could not fully understand the Mongol's claim, but he could see in their dulled eyes that the men he knew were gone. Through some unknown craft, this Mongol witch had made them strangers to him. He reached out for the hilt of his sword where he had dropped it, but the Mongol quickly stood upon the blade.

"Now, Templar..." As the Mongol spoke, Vincent's anger suddenly dulled and he found himself leaning toward the voice, as if pulled by an unseen thread. "...I have many questions."

Chapter Twenty-Seven

"There is an old saying, Detective. 'One should not seek illumination unless one seeks it as a man whose hair is on fire seeks a pond.'"

"Why is that?" Book still awaited a response to his last question, the true identity of James Ford or, at least, what Jacob believed it to be. The old man was stalling.

"Because the path to knowledge is perilous. It is to walk a razor's edge, and the fall to either side is a great and terrible drop. It takes great courage and uncommon ability to travel that path. The Enemy watches for such men."

"Why?" Book searched for connections.

"Because they require servants." The old man carefully measured his words. "You know the tale in allegory. Christ's forty days in the desert and the temptation of the devil, offering riches and power over the earth if he would only bow down. Great men often *become* great in the first place through their intense hunger for knowledge, their thirst for power. Of such ambition, Shepherds are sometimes born. Some can resist temptation. Some cannot."

"The Quran warns mankind," John offered quietly from some dark place in his mind, "*Shaitan al Khadhulu.*"

Jacob could see that Book did not understand. "*Satan is the Abandoner. The Forsaker.* Give in to that temptation in the desert, and power over the earth and all that's in it will indeed be yours, but know that you will be forsaken. The price is your soul."

Book disliked teachers. He resented Jacob and his bookshop more by the minute. "I don't believe in the devil, and I don't believe in Jesus in the desert."

"These stories are not meant for you to *believe*, Detective. They are there for you to *understand*, to see through the story to the meaning. Buddha sat under the tree of temptation, too. Odysseus lost his ship to the call of the Sirens."

"You're talking about fairy tales." Book smirked to hide the fact that the pain of his swelling knee was dragging his anger closer to the surface.

"I can only tell you what I know. But in the years since I became aware of the first secret, of the existence of the Enemy, I have learned a bit of history to go along with the fairy tales."

Book remained steady, unmoved, waiting.

"Very well, Detective. The truth." Jacob inhaled deeply through his nose as he considered his next words. "James Ford was a member of a very old and long-dead cult of forsaken souls who now serve as weapons of the Enemy."

The words were nonsense. This was the moment for Book to laugh out loud. It was the presence of the killer in the room with them that snuffed the impulse. His smirk disappeared and he took the ridiculous information like Jacob was an informant with a name and a street address. "Okay. What was a member of 'long-dead' cult doing in Los Angeles?"

"Their unreachable fortress was finally captured and destroyed in 1272 by Mongol invaders. The battle was to the death, to the last man. No survivors. The *cult* has been dead for 696 years."

"Okay," Book saw no choice but to take the bait. "Then what was James Ford, really? A copycat? Just some nut obsessed with an old religion?"

"No, Detective.   He was an original member, likely born in the Caucasus Mountains, perhaps 800 years ago."

Book sat frozen. The old man was not even trying to hide his insanity now.

Jacob pressed ahead. Once his answer had begun, he was determined to give Book all he knew.   "The cult known to the Europeans as the *Assassins* was created by a man named Hassan ibn Sabbah. A warrior, an alchemist, a mystic, and a true genius who had studied an esoteric, mystical form of Islam at the prestigious Abode of Learning in Egypt. There it was said that he achieved the ninth degree of initiation, supposedly the highest level of wisdom attainable by mankind."

"Okay. What's the ninth degree of...?"

"I don't know, Book, it's obviously a secret. However, he was famous for basing all of his actions after leaving the Abode on a simple and astonishing philosophy, which he summed up in his own words. *Nothing is true, all is permitted.*"

Book nodded as he allowed himself to recall part of his father's final advice, what he called 'a very great secret.' *Nothing is true, all is permitted. That knowledge is a weapon. One day it will make you strong enough to fight.*

"He established a stronghold for his movement at Alamut," Jacob continued, "a fortress built on top of a mountain near the Caspian Sea. There, he created a small army of the most feared warriors of the Middle Ages. The *Fedeyeen*, the 'Faithful unto Death.'"

"Created?" Book asked.

"It was the height of the Crusades, religious wars fueled by hatred, greed, and zealotry. Islam needed a weapon, a counter to the great and powerful Christian military orders of the Europeans, the Teutonic Knights, The Order of St. John, the Knights Templar, etcetera. Sabbah provided that counter. A military order of his own, as fanatical and deadly as any of the Christians. In many ways, his Assassins were much more so.

"He took young men in their sleep, carried them to his mountain fortress, and showed them his vision of Paradise, a 'Garden of Earthly Delights.' There, the young men were overwhelmed with every form of pleasure imaginable, plied with wine, incense and perfumes, dozens of beautiful young women highly skilled in the arts of love, and of course, copious amounts of poppy plants. Hashish. These young men would exist in this blissful haze of narcotics and sex for months or even years until they were needed."

Despite his frustration with Jacob, Book's thoughts drifted back to that room in the Hollywood Rose Motel, where he stood among drugs, hookers, and dead bodies shot up like paper targets. "Needed for what?"

"For killing, Book. This is where the word *assassination* comes from. Sabbah would pluck them from the pleasure garden and tell them, 'go out into the world and kill.' If they succeeded in their mission, they were promised a return to that paradise. Failure meant banishment, a return to the torment and toil of the outside world, eternally cut off from the bliss they had known. Death, after success, of course, would make their paradise last forever."

"Jesus." The word escaped his mouth softly. Book watched John drift to the other side of the room, as if suddenly uncomfortable with the conversation.

"Sabbah brought dark secrets to light within his mountain, Book.

Dark secrets helped to create them, dark secrets helped to control them. Never more than a thousand existed at one time, but they terrified the Kings of Europe, the Caliphs of Islam, whoever Sabbah chose to target. He taught his Fedeyeen to speak multiple languages with flawless attention to detail down to regional dialects, to dress and act as soldiers, priests, and merchants, to mimic the beliefs and attitudes of any religion or country from Persia to the Mediterranean. These men moved freely and openly among their enemies, like invisible wolves among the sheep. Just one of them could defeat an entire army by entering their camp at will to murder generals, ambassadors, or even kings in their own beds. Their method was to simply wait nearby in the open, unsuspected, for as long as it might take for the right time to strike. They killed in daylight, in guarded camps or homes, when their victims were alone or even addressing their own troops. Escape was not a factor. All they needed to do in order to return to paradise was make the kill."

"And all that takes," Book said aloud, but mostly to himself, "is skill, and an opportunity." He thought of James Ford's skill, and Sirhan Sirhan's use of an opportunity. Jacob's description of this long extinct cult seemed to explain a United States Senator's death in Los Angeles perfectly well.

"But what does this have to do with a man from Wyoming?"

"*Fedeyeen* means 'Faithful until death,'" Jacob instructed patiently. "And so they were. His Assassins swore allegiance to Sabbah until the moment of their death. But they were tricked."

"Tricked? How?"

"Dark secrets, Book." Jacob continued to weigh the Detective's willingness to hear as he searched for the right words. "As it turns out, they cannot die."

"They can't... what?" Book maintained an even expression.

"The Assassins remain trapped to this day, forsaken by their master, the man who made the bargain."

"What bargain?" Book felt torn between frustration and curiosity.

"Hassan ibn Sabbah, the Old Man of the Mountain, walked that razor's edge I spoke of. He was a brilliant seeker of knowledge and power. When the Enemy came to him with the temptation of more knowledge and power than even he had ever dreamed of, he fell. That's all."

"He fell?" Book squinted at the old man.

"Like an angel. One more Shepherd was born. And his army of Assassins became enslaved forever, deadly tools in the service of their master's new hidden masters, weapons for all Shepherds to use, including the one who hunts the sleeping girl upstairs."

Book leaned forward in the creaking chair to put the question as directly as he could. "Because they can't die?"

"Only their bodies die."

"You mean...?" Book scowled again.

"Souls do not die," Jacob confirmed.

"Yeah. I guess I'm just not a religious man. Sorry, but I don't believe..."

"It doesn't matter if you believe it or not, Detective." Jacob stopped his protest with a wave of his hand. "Every human life is like a slowly unfolding car wreck. In the end, the vehicle is destroyed, but the driver always walks away. Religion has nothing to do with it at all."

Another silence hung between them while Book assessed the lack of mania in the old man's demeanor.

"So, these Assassins, then. You're saying they're still around?"

"The yoke Sabbah put on them was on the soul-level. When he fell to the Enemy, he brought his army down with him. From lifetime to lifetime, they serve. Enslaved before they were even born, they have no idea of the bargain they made. When they are called, they have no choice, no will to question or refuse."

"They come in through your head." The voice belonged to John, speaking from the corner of the room and from an even darker corner of his own thoughts. "When you are asleep. They call you."

Book watched John. His pain was visible, and as crazy as his words sounded, Book knew that he was relaying something that was as least true in his own mind. He recalled the words John had spoken in the alley as he stood over the bodies of two dead cops. *I am a killer. Murderer. Assassin.*

Book frowned and sank deeper into his chair, slowly exhaling while weighing the odds of solving any of his mounting problems by taking his chances on the street. He was in the company of madmen. He couldn't go home, couldn't go to work, and it would obviously take more than a phone call to Frank to get him out of trouble. But stronger still, he couldn't risk taking the girl with him, and he certainly could not leave her here, alone. He resolved to continue to connect the incoherent dots until some picture might form.

"You still don't believe?" Jacob's voice was quite sympathetic.

"No."

"John had a family once," Jacob continued in a gentle tone. "And, like James Ford, he woke up one day many years ago and came to Los Angeles. Alone. He didn't *decide* to do that, didn't think about it. He just did it. Do you understand?"

Book thought again of James Ford, of his wife, Laurie, who didn't understand. Despite his resistance, the creeping anxiety continued along the back of his neck until he quietly relented enough to ask, "Why did he come to Los Angeles?"

"To kill a woman he had never met before. On the sidewalk, on her way home from the grocery store."

The anxiety burned his scalp. His composure came with great effort. "Why would he do that?"

"Because they told him to." Jacob spoke with patience and compassion

Jacob was doing this on purpose, he knew. The tale of John's life was too familiar, fit too symmetrically into a story held tightly within the dark spaces of his own memory. Now, for some reason he could not fathom, Jacob seemed intent to use those dark spaces against him. Still, an old fear buried long ago reached for the light of his waking thoughts. *They.* He fought it with reason.

"I thought you said there was no escape from them? What is he still doing here?"

"He was shot by the police. He fell from the Santa Monica Pier into the ocean at night. They did not recover a body, but believed him to be dead. "

Book's mind furiously processed the elements of this story as if he knew he were the butt of a joke. A drifter, a senseless murder, and a police chase that ended in death at the Santa Monica Pier. Jacob could easily have read about it in the newspaper. There was nothing secret here.

Yet Book's voice trembled as he asked, "Sixteen years ago?"

"Sixteen years ago," Jacob gently confirmed. "They never found a body, because there was none. I found John first. When the Enemy thought him dead, they simply forgot about him. Like spent ammunition on a battlefield. He was unimportant in the grand scheme. He has spent his time since then, all of it, trying to understand what happened to him. And trying to make amends."

The pain Book struggled to hide became too great. There was no action he could take at this moment to help himself, to help the girl sleeping upstairs.

Jacob studied the rigidity of Book's right leg, watching him hold his knee in both palms to keep it stable. "Would you like ice for your knee?"

"There's nothing wrong with my knee." Book lied as casually as he could, instinctively hiding weakness. He knew how ridiculous he sounded.

"Two ligaments were severed and then surgically re-attached." Jacob saw the look of alarm flash across the young man's face, and continued. "It looks like you may have re-injured yourself."

"How do you know that?"

"I think you will be here for some time. You'll need to eat and sleep." Jacob leaned to his side and called quietly toward the back of the store, "Trudie?"

Book followed the direction of his eyes and saw a thickly built woman coming down a staircase, making exaggeratedly soft steps on the creaking wood, and scowling at the grey man for creating so much noise.

Jacob spoke even more softly. "We must see to his injury."

The woman glared at Book with residual anger, but her eyes softened a little before she made her way back up the stairs.

"I asked you a question. How do you know about...?"

"I know many things about you, Detective. I have been watching you for a long time. Since you were a child. Since before your father died."

Book's blood went cold, stinging an inch deep from flesh to bone. The fear of what awaited in the silences pushed through to his mind in an instant, and he suddenly found himself back on that pier watching a growing pool of his father's blood.

Chapter Twenty-Eight

After he had adjusted the ropes of the *Gull's* tiller, holding her prow in place against the southern stars and with what little breeze there was in her sail, Shahin looked again to the horizon behind them. He saw nothing but starshine and the waning half-moon that streaked the black ocean. They were making what progress they could, alone on a flat sea, but he still liked this situation less and less by the moment. It took effort to push away thoughts of his own people, left in Acre to fend for themselves during the siege, and those aboard the *Leila* now heading to an uncertain captivity in Cyprus. Instead, he tried to deflect those fears with the matters at hand. He was captaining a ship toward Sinai, into the heart of the Egyptian Sultanate, and the land bridge that supplied armies in Palestine with Saracen and Mamluk soldiers. Few things could make that situation more dangerous for a man such as he, but being forced to travel with Crusaders was one of them. To make matters worse, his passengers were Templars, the worst kind of Crusaders. If there were any who had more reason than he to dislike Templars, it would be the Sultan's soldiers. And finally, he thought as he headed toward where they gathered at the bow, of all the available Templars in the world, for all of their purported wisdom and great military skill, he seemed to be working with the least of them. The leader of this expedition had little idea of where they were going, other than to take the most ill advised and dangerous route imaginable, and part of his charge had arrived that morning half dead already, brought to them by a young girl who seemed as in charge of the crew as anyone.

Shahin studied her as he approached the group gathered around the wounded Templar. She silently watched the young man, now sitting up, alert, conversant, and regaling his comrades with the rather ridiculous and likely fictional account of his morning, and how he and the girl eventually came to the *Gull*. She was a rich man's servant from her dress, but her bearing and lack of real fear showed her to be something more. Indeed, he had seen how, regardless of the specific facts, the young Templar had reached this ship through the sheer force of her will. As for the young storyteller, he didn't seem like much now, in his weakened state, but even under the dim light, Shahin saw the same look in his eye he had spotted at their first meeting in the chamber of Guillaume de Beaujeu.

Shahin had already lived many years longer than he should have, in part based on his ability to quickly find clues to the character of a man in his face. De Buci was loyal, no doubt cheerful by the campfire as he was now in the stillness of the evening on deck, and as with all Templars in Palestine, a veteran of more battles than Shahin cared to imagine and no doubt worth at least three good men in a fight. Most men he knew would suggest a Templar of his stature was worth as many as ten, but most men he knew also tended to exaggerate. De Buci seemed to be their leader, but as with any man who lacked the necessary ambition, he did not impress Shahin as much of one. Young St. Ives was a simple sword, a powerful man just beyond youth, with all the endurance needed for a long journey, all the courage needed for fighting, and none of the wisdom needed to question the reasons behind either. These first two were easy, and Shahin expected few if any surprises from them.

Whether the quality he sensed within Broussard was courage, wisdom, or profound foolhardiness brought on by the ignorance of his race, he felt that, in a way he could not yet see, the fate of this voyage, and therefore his own, centered on him. He wondered if Guillaume de Beaujeu had felt all this as well. Or perhaps it was the girl who triggered this moment of intuition, and whose own close orbit around the injured Templar made him seem more important than he actually was. Few things irritated Shahin more than the feeling that his own destiny was in any way out of his hands, and he found himself quickly resolved to dislike this particular Christian, Broussard, even more than the others.

Shahin stood just beyond their circle, his attention divided between Broussard's story and more long steady gazes at the dark horizon behind them. At last the tale reached the part Shahin enjoyed the most, when the Templar was unconscious and near death. De Buci attempted to incite the girl to tell the tale of the docks, as if she were a comrade in arms fresh from the field, but she demurred and stayed small and quiet in the dark.

Shahin recognized her caution, watched her move subtly closer to Broussard, and when he thought De Buci about to clap her on the back as if they had just hacked their way together through a siege, he decided it was time to speak.

"We are two days from Sinai," he offered from the near blackness, "less if we get any wind at all." The girl took advantage of the sudden lack of focus on her to quietly move to the now unoccupied stern. Shahin pretended not to notice her as he continued. "It is time I learned where I am taking you."

Shahin was greeted by silence as the Templars each seemed to be waiting for someone else to speak up. It had only been a few hours since he had opened Beaujeu's order, read the bizarre message, and showed it to De Buci. At that time, the Templar had seemed surprised and even confused before giving the simple instruction, "Make your course for the Sinai."

"What do my orders mean?"

Though he could not see the Moor's face with the moon behind him, De Buci knew he was looking directly at him.

Broussard spoke up first, making Shahin even further annoyed with De Buci.

"What *are* your orders?" "*King's X.*" Shahin spoke flatly. The words had no meaning to him at all.

Broussard puzzled over the message.

"Is that all it said?"

"That's all." Shahin recalled the rushed scrawl of the message, as if Beaujeu had issued the bizarre command while drunk or half-asleep. "Surely one of you must know what it means."

Broussard reflected with some irritation of his own over the enigmatic methods of Beaujeu, and indeed the Order of the Temple itself. Why must everything be a puzzle?

In the near silence that followed Shahin's query, the steady scraping of St. Ives' whetstone provided the only sound, slowly grinding the edge into his sword in the darkness.

Gathering his own thoughts on the mystery of their destination, Broussard reflected on a time, not so long ago, when Vincent held somewhat higher hopes for his younger brother's future. Sebastien Broussard had followed his brother into the Order of the Temple, searching for adventure outside their father's land. Vincent had sought to quickly move him through the ranks to a position of prominence befitting his own blood relative. Shortly after Sebastien began his initiation into the first few levels of Templar secrets, Vincent discovered with great disappointment that his half-brother was less than eager to learn. Sebastien had tried to convince the elder Broussard that he was simply not interested in dusty old secrets and grown men playing games with blindfolds and passwords. Vincent would go so far as to admit that Sebastien was not yet old enough, unwilling as he was to believe that anyone, especially anyone bearing his family name, could be disinterested in the hidden truths of the Templars, even at the lowest levels of initiation.

"The Order is a gateway," Vincent had once offered as advice to his faltering brother, "a hidden entrance to a secret world undreamt by the vast body of humanity." Sebastien remembered the words to this day, though he understood them no better. "Those who walk in that secret world become the mind of humanity, the engagers and directors of the body. Do you understand? The world is starved of the Wise and overflowing with the Ignorant. Yet it is ever that great mass who serve as the hands and feet of the few. There is so much to learn, Sebastien. So much more that you do not yet see."

Long ago his brother's deeds-piled-upon-deeds had justified his mother's sacrifice to their father, to Sebastien, and to anyone else who could possibly question or measure such things. All that was left, the younger Broussard occasionally mused when his brother proved beyond his understanding, was for Vincent to know his debt had been paid.

Sebastien, meanwhile, had found the adventure he craved. He had seen much of the world, without ever learning a great many of those secrets, and with no sense that he had passed through any "gateway." There were, it seemed, secrets to this world meant only for men like his half-brother, men whose desire to know what others did not remained forever unquenchable. Still, there was an education to be gleaned from passing through even the basest levels of the brotherhood.

Broussard pondered the tiny morsels of seemingly random information he had been fed while moving through the sub-levels of initiation. At the time they had seemed mere distraction, often barely intelligible nonsense. Now, almost for the first time as he saw the chain of hidden knowledge in action, he wondered how many links that chain might contain, and how far back in time or where on earth it might reach. Yet, within his collection of Templar secrets, there was no mention of *King's X*.

As little as Broussard knew, St. Ives knew even less. Broussard watched the monotonous honing of his weapon in the starlight. He could not see St. Ives' face in the darkness, and the young man's voice was silent. Still, he knew that his lips moved as he mutedly chanted his devotion in the manner in which they had been trained together. Fourteen *Pater Nosters* for the hours of daylight, and fourteen more for the Blessed Virgin, spoken in rapid fluidity so that the words might blend together, and the first prayer might flow from the twenty-eighth to create an endless loop of meditation. St. Ives had long ago found his calling. He remained wedded to the Church and kept his sword as his mistress. Broussard knew that when St. Ives slid his stone across the grim blade in the evening, it was an expression of love. And he was lost in it.

Broussard turned his attention to the standing shadow of De Buci, looming nearby in the darkness. Recognizing that the morsels of information he carried in his head amounted to nothing, or at best a half-constructed bridge between history and legend that reached neither shore, he wondered now how many Templar secrets De Buci held in his mind. And imagining that, how much further Vincent's knowledge might stretch. And beyond Vincent, there was still Beaujeu, the man who had given the enigmatic command and formed this unlikely band in the first place. As he watched De Buci slowly approaching a decision, Broussard wondered why he should be on this boat and not his brother, why armored Templars had been sent unnecessarily into the breach at Acre to ensure that he could be here now, to puzzle over a mystery beyond his capacity to solve.

Shahin was well aware that Templars were more likely to *know* when they said they did not, and *not* know anything at all when they acted like they did. Therefore, the silence of these men indicated a hidden treasure of knowledge steadfastly guarded.

"Christian," he spoke to De Buci again, stiffly reining in his anger, "I do not care about your secrets. I have enough secrets of my own to worry about. I did not wish to join your expedition, but I wish to die on it even less. If it is even possible to pass the Sinai alive, at least give me a fighting chance to find the route. I must know where you want to go if I am to guide you."

Broussard sensed St. Ives bristling at the Muslim's tone.

De Buci remained silent, but Broussard knew that was simply his manner while his steady but unspectacular mind weighed his response. For his part, Broussard did not care for Shahin's tone either, but he could not argue with his logic.

As he stood, oblivious to the weight of the Captain's expectant stare, De Buci mulled his own secrets, struggling to put them in order. He wondered now, as he sometimes had in the past, about the true nature of the Order's presence in Jerusalem.

Nearly 200 years ago, nine warrior pilgrims arrived in the Holy City at the spear-point of the first Crusade. Founders of the Order. Protectors of the Temple. The rock upon which Solomon had built his temple was said to be the foundation stone of the world, the center of creation, the *axis mundi*, where God's power, when He so chooses, directly flows into the world of men. There, the pilgrims dug in the darkness. Beneath ancient and holy ruins, they probed the sacred spot with blasphemous courage born of the most lusting piety. He pondered again the mysteries of his initiation; Solomon the Wise, keeper of the Holy of Holies, wearer of God's own Seal, the signet ring of Heaven, through which the prophet King summoned angels and demons by name and yoked them to his will. Solomon the Great. Solomon the Sorcerer.

It had never been for De Buci to comprehend the meaning of these stories, and it had never occurred to him before that any of them might in fact be true. In dealing with the secrets of the Order, any attempt to discern facts from among the great tangle of direction and misdirection generally gave him an aching head.

The confused path of De Buci's thoughts eventually led back to where he stood, and the command he had been charged with. He recalled the tale of a messenger, a dark-skinned Prince, emerging from an unmapped world like a herald from another time who came to the brotherhood in the Holy City with news unknown in Christendom. He brought them an ancient story of Solomon's child, a strong and noble son whom the great Ethiopian Queen had birthed in secret. And he revealed still greater secrets, passed from father to son, concerning what treasures Solomon had hidden beneath his Temple, and what treasures he had not. Some of the wise King's secrets, it seemed, were too great and too dangerous to merely bury.

Just as the letter he now carried was sealed with the mark of the Templar Master, his personal sign imprinted in wax by the unique seal on his ring, the order read by Shahin spoke of another seal.

According to the legend, Solomon's ring was brought to him by an angel as a gift from Heaven. And before that, presumably it had belonged to God himself. The first Templars, for their own enigmatic reasons, had a secret name for this object to keep its true name unspoken among the Order.

De Buci's furrowed brow was hidden in the dark as he reflected on the meaning of Beaujeu's brief instructions. They now sought what could not be found beneath Solomon's Temple. They sought the mark of the King, the signet ring of Solomon himself, what the original Nine had dubbed *King's X.*

Ancient truths, ancient secrets. Of these, De Buci knew little and believed less. But, for Beaujeu's purposes, he apparently knew enough. His task, as the simple order plainly set for him, was merely to recall the way, the hidden path walked by the first knights of the Order and known only to a very few. As his thoughts returned to the present, a weight began to form within his chest. Beaujeu had put great faith in him as a guide for the letter he carried. Desperate faith. But that was a puzzle for another time. The task at hand was to reach the end of the journey alive.

At last the old soldier breathed deep, cocked his head toward the waiting Captain.

"We must pass the desert to Qalzum on the edge of the Reed Sea."

After a moment or two of hesitation in which he seemed about to go into greater detail, De Buci turned on his heel and found a spot against the bulkhead to sleep. "Keep your course for the Sinai."

Chapter Twenty-Nine

The sturdy woman who had briefly appeared on the stairs returned with a hot water bottle filled with ice and a glass of water. "My wife," Jacob introduced her with more polite decorum, "Trudie."

Trudie knelt before Book, reaching for his knee with the ice. He stopped her short with a silent glare, seething in a toxic combination of pain and anger. As he watched Trudie back away to set the ice and the water on the coffee table in front of him, Book determined to ignore the old man, to take no more bait. Instead, he allowed everything that had gone wrong in his entire lifetime to crystallize into one hateful, malignant image.

"You know his name. The Shepherd. Tell me who he is."

"I can't do that."

"Why not?"

"Because," Jacob said somberly, "you would try to find him. If you did that, he would find the girl through what you know, find and kill all of us. In short, all would be lost."

Book paused to digest that thought, recalling his conversation with the Shepherd among the bodies of murdered policemen in his apartment.

"Look..." He tried to project his indignation, but it proved a poor mask for his growing unsteadiness. "I don't believe you. I don't know what you are talking about, and I don't care. Understand? As soon as I figure out a plan, I'm taking Molly and..."

"Yes." Jacob cut him off again, pieces fitting into the private puzzle in his mind as he continued to evaluate Book. "The girl." He seemed pleased for some reason that only unnerved Book more. "She came straight to you."

"I don't even know who she is." Book felt accused of a crime not adequately explained to him.

"You freed her from jail," Jacob said, "only minutes before the Shepherd arrived."

Book thought of the panic he had seen in Molly and the urgency he had felt in his own heart when he finally called for her cell to be opened. That man had been coming all along, just as she feared. He recalled his first brief flash of John's brittle-skinned face, realizing that he had saved Molly outside Sara's building, nearly bashing Book's head in with a two-by-four just to get her quickly out of harm's way. The echo of Jacob's words about the menacing and murderous drifter returned to him, *trying to make amends.*

Book looked up from his knee with a jerk of his head.

"How did you know we would be at her apartment? How did you know about Sara?"

Jacob watched him with pity as Book absently worked the swollen joint with his hands.

"I told you, Wendell. We have been watching you very closely for most of your life. Just as he has."

Book's mind struggled with more information than he was prepared to hear, and too little information to adequately understand it, all coming at once. Molly had said the same thing. *He's been watching....*

Book snatched the glass of water from the table as if it was going to solve all his problems, and drank it down. Breathless after draining the entire glass, he nevertheless demanded, "Why? *Why* watch *me?*"

"I don't know for certain. But since your father's death, the Shepherd has watched you. And therefore, so have I. I believe we've all been waiting for today. We've been waiting for Molly to try to find you."

"She said the same thing," Book wondered at the growing sensation of his heart beating too fast in his chest.

Jacob continued to study the young policeman.

"You have stood face to face with a Shepherd, spoken to him, and even fought with him. And you are still alive." Emotion had crept again into Jacob's voice. Book thought it sounded like admiration, which made him more uncomfortable. He pushed the feeling away, trying to continue his first reflections on the last twenty-four hours. His thoughts quickly fell back to one centering thought. Molly.

From the moment he'd first seen her in the jail cell, she had superseded everything else. Her safety was more important than his own, more important than his life, and more important even than Sara. That thought stung him and he shoved it aside. Still, forcing Sara from his mind only brought him right back to Molly. As impossible as it seemed, even in this moment, he also knew there was a reason for it. There must be a *how*, and a *why*, above the senselessness of it all. His father's last words attacked once more, *wait for her*. Book forced his thoughts outward again with greater effort, and found Jacob's eyes still waiting for him.

"Who is she?" he asked again.

As Jacob answered, Book noticed the manic quality creeping back into to his voice. There was also a familiar look in his eye that summoned an unpleasant memory of his father's militant fanaticism. Most disturbing of all, Jacob's eyes strayed briefly to the stairs, toward where Molly lay sleeping, hidden away in a back room. He looked, to Book, like a man with something to hide. For the first time, Jacob looked dangerous.

"Do you believe in Fate, Detective?"

"No."

"Neither do I." The old man smiled. "But I do believe, as did your father..."

"What makes you think," Sudden rage at the continued invoking of his father spilled out before he could check it, "I would give a damn what my father believed? He was a lunatic."

"No, Book. He was more sane than most."

"What do you know about it?" Book asked, not really wanting an answer.

"Tell me if this sounds familiar to you," Jacob said evenly. "A day will come when a savior will return from the dead, with the power to..." the old man's lips tightened over his teeth while he fished for the right phrase, then opened to release a wide tobacco-grey smile, "...lift a veil of shadow from the world, to lead men from darkness, to free humanity from bondage..."

"Stop."

"Mighty Pharaoh, let my people go!" Jacob chuckled.

Book was hearing his father. He glared bitterly at the old man, who sat across the oaken table like some impossible ghost returned to torment him anew.

"I do not believe in fate, Wendell." Jacob's smile vanished. "But I do believe we can choose to fulfill a purpose. Molly came looking for your father. Instead she found his son. She would not have survived this day if not for you. Perhaps that was it. It could be that this day has been the purpose of your life."

"You mean that my family, and everybody I ever..." Book swallowed the word 'loved.' He held tight to his anger and pushed ahead, "my scholarship, my goddamn knee...." His anger flowed easily.   "...everything I've lost, that ever happened to me in my life... was just to kill time so I could be around this morning when that *girl* showed up?"

"Maybe. Perhaps it's something more."

The words that came next were nonsensical, he knew. They came like the thoughts of a man clinging to outrage at his predicament because he knew that to deny it would be pointless. He also knew that, in this moment, he was talking to his father.

"Fuck you."

"The point is, Detective, you are here. Now. For her."

Book could not argue that. He was here for Molly. That much he already felt. He thought again of the invisible thread, and wondered if it wasn't still holding him. "Who is she?" He quietly demanded again, knowing that if he had to ask once more he would beg.

"She is Jesus," Book's father seemed to smile at him now through Jacob's stained teeth. "She is Siddhartha. The Savior of the world is asleep upstairs, Book. And she is about to awaken."

Jacob's words echoed in Book's thoughts as his breathing lost pace with his heartbeat. A new, more immediate danger occurred only dimly. He let his eyes fall to the poisoned water glass in his hand. It fell to the floor. Finally, only half way out of the chair, he watched the wooden floor rush up to meet him, and saw no more.

Chapter Thirty

Broussard studied the black water behind them to the northern horizon. Dawn was still some time away, and the waning half-crescent of the moon projected a jagged slash of pale gold across the surface to the *Gull*. This was the second night since they had set out. Broussard felt stronger, closer to his old self, though he still held his left arm in the makeshift sling Khali had insisted upon to keep him from reopening his side before the new scar could properly form over the wound.

Unable to sleep, he had finally convinced St. Ives to rest for the coming day, which would see them at last to the Sinai. St. Ives had insisted that a watch be kept, lest Captain Shahin slit their throats as they slept. Broussard knew Shahin posed no danger, at least not yet. He would not be with them at all if Beaujeu's threat did not carry tremendous weight with him. He wondered for a moment at the riches that must be aboard Shahin's ship, bound now for Cyprus, and at the unseen facets of Beaujeu's bizarre plot that saw their lives and their mission entrusted to a rogue as infamous as "The Hawk."

Still, during the entire time he had stood here, alone, the only waking soul on board, his thoughts could not stay long over these matters. He could not sleep because of the gnawing within, a vague pain that felt like hunger or thirst. His thoughts were of Khalidah. He thought of the strange power she had over him, as if he were in some way trapped, yet never held by her. He thought again of how he had risked both the wrath of his brother and the failure of his mission. He could not explain. He only knew that the spell she cast over him was real.

When he was a boy of sixteen summers, Vincent had taken him to the home of a servant-woman who had many daughters living on their father's land. Sebastien had learned about women there and had done his best to have his fill of them before his eighteenth year, when he was to join the Order. Upon his initiation, he had made a vow to serve Christ with his sword, in exchange for the adventure his restless spirit craved.

In five years of service to God, fighting His wars in the Holy Land, Broussard had not known a woman again. So often, when women of conquered races, cities, or nations were there for the taking in the aftermath of conflict, when simply to lay with one for a short while might have soothed his rage and stilled the armored fist that brought his sword down against their husbands and brothers, remembrance of his oath to Christ protected them and fueled his hatred of the infidels anew. He detested the practice of conquering armies ravaging the women of the conquered, as it had been explained to him that theirs was a holy cause, and the blood they spilled was a sanctification of the land, not to be defiled. Of course, his brotherhood of knights was only a small number among the Christians fighting to take Palestine.

Now, none of what he had thought then made any difference at all. The Palestinian conquest, what was once a certitude, what had once been pursued through incalculable loss and at the demand of Heaven itself, now seemed like a passing fancy. With Acre burning and the tide turned irrevocably in the favor of another God to bring the Holy Land securely again to the grip of Islam, Broussard wondered at the cost. After two hundred years of gain and loss, the maps would look roughly as they had before. He wondered at the cost to Christian and infidel alike, in men and in women, and he wondered what it should all be to either God. There was much in his mind that proved confusing given the silence, the peace to reflect, and the thirst arising with each thought of Khalidah.

Vincent had laughed openly at Sebastien's grip on his vows for some time now. Mistresses awaited Vincent's return in many lands. Sebastien knew of them, although his brother, as with most things, did not speak openly about them.

Broussard found little sign of God in the work of reclaiming the Holy Land. His sense of honor in his own deeds was fragile, and did not endure. There was only duty, promises made and kept. He thought of God, the promises of His heaven and the promises of His hell. He wondered now what secrets Vincent could know that he did not desire the one nor fear the other. He had assumed long ago that his older brother had always been that way. Now, though he thought that could still be true, Sebastien also began to realize that the differences between 16, and 18, and now 23 summers passing, could mean a great deal to any man. Vincent was nearly twice his age and infinitely more curious.

Lost in his thoughts, the darkness all around helping to place him back in the land of his youth as if in a dream, Broussard turned to the setting moon. It no longer resembled the eye of a hunting beast, no longer beamed a malevolent intelligence at him as it had during his fever, but rather reminded him of stories heard as a child. The peasants who worked his father's fields knew that the magic of the moon was like the magic of a woman. That its monthly emergence from darkness was like a rebirth after death meant to reassure the simple folk. After the death of the harvest, the procession of the seasons would bring new life to their fields, always and without fail, so that winter need never be feared. The message of the moon spoke loudly of life, an echo of the mystery that only women can know. Broussard glared sternly at the thin finger of light pointing to him across the water. His thoughts had circled their cage and returned to her. Trapped.

The scent of her hair, once breathed in at the city's docks, came to him. He had heard her nearly silent footfalls and knew she stood behind him now. He thought again of his vows, of Christ on the cross, the blood on his own hands spilled in His name, and the fires of hell that surely await the unfaithful. He thought of all these things so easily overpowered by this small, fragile girl. He remembered the touch on his arm that had lowered his sword in the courtyard and quelled his rage as the promises of Christ never had. He remembered his shame over what he had shown her that day, and he remembered what she had shown him through her eyes in that moment, the briefest glimpse of peace. She had stirred within him a mysterious longing, a desire that went beyond all talk of God, of battles won, of promises made, and kept. He knew that the dark, earthen magic of a woman was already killing the life he had known, and as surely as the changing of the seasons, whether he wished it or not, would bring for him a rebirth into something altogether new. He did not need to make any vow or swear any oath to know, no form of damnation could sway him from satisfying this fast growing thirst.

Shahin watched them from where he lay beneath the *Gull's* tiller. He dozed lightly there, waking occasionally to gauge the disposition of the sea beneath them and to check their position against the field of stars above the mast. The young Christian stood nearby, watching the sea to the north, and the girl approached softly from behind. Her movements were quiet, like a street mouse ever wary of prowling cats, and he wondered for a moment, as he watched unseen from the straw mat where he made his bed, if the young man was even aware of her.

"You should not have come." Broussard did not turn.

Shahin could not see his face clearly, but he thought the young man's voice seemed tainted by an odd pain. A silence hung between them for so long that Shahin was amazed the Christian could be so certain that she was there, without at least turning to look.

Khali stood a single stride behind him. She wished he would turn so she could see if it was anger she heard in his voice, or something else. Nevertheless, she knew there was no point in regretting what was done.

"Where would you be if I had not?"

Shahin nodded approvingly from his mat.

"The city will fall slowly." Broussard remained still. "There would be other benefactors to find, other chances to leave. It would be better for you in Acre. This will be a hard road."

"The others want you to leave me in Sinai?" She asked, though she already knew the answer.

"Traveling with soldiers is no place for a girl."

"I do not want to be left alone in Sinai."

Shahin heard the muted fear in her voice.

Broussard still did not turn to face her. He focused on his failure, and on the trust that had been put in him by Beaujeu and his brother. To what end, he still could not guess. He knew that Khali could destroy his ability to think clearly when he was obviously needed by his comrades. He let play a scenario in his mind where he might leave her behind in safe company, if such company could be found upon landing, and perhaps come back for her on the return voyage. He, too, had heard the fear in her voice, and he knew that he could not look at her face when he spoke.

"You will not be left behind, girl," Shahin spoke up at last, climbing slow and stiff to his feet in the starlight. He glanced with annoyance briefly at the Christian, before turning a gentler eye to the girl. "Shahin will watch over you. You will be safe as long as it is in my power."

At last Broussard turned, but only far enough to face Shahin.

"She does not need your help."

"I have many friends in many ports, Christian," Shahin retorted with cool, but rising venom, "and I would not leave a girl like this one with any of them. Therefore she goes where we go. I will watch over her." He looked again toward Khali. Caught then in her stare, the poison easily left his voice. "I will watch over you."

Still unsure what drove him at this moment, Broussard took an involuntary step toward the Muslim.

A soft, convulsive sob escaped Khali's lips before she could catch it, and she fled silently to the front of the boat.

Both men watched her go before Broussard took another step toward the steady Captain. As Shahin turned to focus on the dangerous young man, his eye caught a dark shape over the Broussard's shoulder, illumined by the dying moonlight and coming out of the northwest horizon.

Broussard opened his mouth to speak but the Muslim silenced him with a commanding gesture of his hand.

"Are you expecting to be followed on this voyage?"

Broussard turned slowly to follow Shahin's eyes until he picked up the shape in the distance. A sail.

"They are riding a better wind," said the Captain. "They will catch us tomorrow if that is their aim."

"We wrestle not against flesh and blood, but against principalities, against powers, against the rulers of darkness of this world, against spiritual wickedness in high places."

--Ephesians 6:12

Chapter Thirty-One

"Pull!" Shahin shouted again, his voice hoarse with fatigue. The Christians had strong backs and were not averse to hard work. They made decent enough oarsmen. All of the men were no doubt burning in their lungs by this time, as he was, but none complained or asked for respite.

Shahin kept a count to keep the pace steady between the two oars. He divided the rest of his attention between the girl, Broussard, and the dark sail still coming hard out of the Northwest through the morning sunlight. He watched the girl as she controlled the *Gull* at the rudder, to see that she was not losing sight of the navigation points he had given her when the Sinai had finally crested the horizon.

He watched Broussard, who had stood for hours now at his side, pulling his share of this oar, to see that the healing gash in his chest was not reopening. The Christian was not bleeding badly enough to stop, as the salve Shahin had retrieved from below deck seemed to be holding his flesh together passably well. Yet, even unable to make a close study of the young man's wounds, Shahin could see that it was the long shallow slash across the top of his leg that would eventually kill Broussard if this journey proved a long one. It had only just to begun to discolor around the opening which De Buci had seared closed with his knife. Shahin had seen such wounds before. It would begin to fester. The festering would spread.

The light of day revealed the pursuing vessel to be a warship of European design. Shahin found himself silently blessing the weak winds he had been cursing these last two days. Even under full sail, the heavy warship had only managed to close half the distance between them since they'd first spotted her and begun their prolonged sprint for shore. The *Gull* had at last caught the onshore current, and was picking up speed. They would have the better part of an hour or more upon landing before the gap would be fully closed. Shahin kept the rhythm of each stroke steady. "Pull!"

***

Nadeem held the thinning net in his weathered and sea-hardened hands. He had spread it along the red sand of the cove to assess whether or not he should even bother to take it on board his tiny craft. There were holes, he thought, torn into the knotted weave large enough for all but a whale to pass through. He would take it along anyway. He smiled as he began to roll the ancient equipment like a carpet beside his beached boat. After all, the sea had always been kind enough to provide in the past. Who should say he couldn't bring home a whale? He laughed out loud as he worked, an image of Fadia playing through his thoughts, ladle in hand, standing by her cooking fire, stricken by the sight of his whale.

His name drifted to him on a warm wind over hot sand. "Nadeem!" a boy's voice called in agitated excitement. "Nadeem!"

Nadeem paused in his work and looked over his shoulder at the boy running toward him from the line of palms that shielded the village from the sea. Nadeem was old enough to carry some wisdom, and young enough to make use of it. Because of these qualities, he had inadvertently fallen into a position of leadership within the village since his arrival here many years earlier. His position was unofficial, but it came with a certain degree of respect and deference that made life easier for Fadia and their children. And making his life easier, of course, was why he had settled in this little cove by the sea in the first place.

Hamal was the son of the village tanner, fast approaching manhood, and, as it often occurred to Nadeem in moments like this one, so bored with the tranquil peace of his surroundings, that he too often sought intrigue where it did not exist. Hamal was the unofficial herald of the village, always anxious to sail, always the first to ride out to a passing caravan to gather news or make a trade. Hamal, more often than not, ran at a full sprint, though he seldom had any place of importance to go or any truly pressing need to get there.

Hamal sprinted toward him from the tree line, pointing out to sea. "Nadeem!"

The fisherman turned toward where the boy pointed, and then he cursed the sea aloud. As Hamal arrived at his side, Nadeem was already issuing commands. "Go back to the village and spread the word from house to house... 'if you have one, hide your camel or your horse. If you have any wealth to speak of, bury it.' Tell my wife to gather sea rations. That's probably all he wants."

"Who, Nadeem!"

He spoke with more annoyance than fear. "Tell her it's an old friend of mine. Then run before she brains you for lack of me."

"But what about the other ship?"

Nadeem's annoyance flashed quickly to concern. "What other ship?"

The boy scanned the sea but the view was obscured by the rocky projections of the cove. "You can see it from the trees."

Nadeem turned again to study the *Gull* as she approached. She was a pitiful little boat, and the single oars straining on either side looked almost comical, but the Hawk was still coming fast. "Show me," he demanded at last.

***

Nadeem trudged across the beach to meet them alone as the oarsmen rammed the *Gull* into the pebbled sand just short of shore. He kept his hand on the hilt of the old saber he had strapped on before returning, and which he kept sharp for just such an occasion. Shahin slide over the side first, stood in water up to his knees, and smiled at Nadeem with that same, familiar, unreadable sly curving of his lips. "Allah be praised!" the Hawk offered to Nadeem in exhausted, breathless gratitude. "A friendly face!"

Nadeem reflected no friendship in return. Instead, he strode angrily forward into a lapping wave, knowing that he would tower menacingly over the smaller pirate when he reached him. He loosened his blade an inch or two from its sheath. "What plague have you brought down upon me now?" Before he could even fully convey his outrage Nadeem saw two enormous Europeans leap from either side of the *Gull's* bow, swords flashing to hands. St. Ives and Broussard suddenly flanked their guide in an aggressive stance.

"Whoa, whoa!" Shahin called out, blocking the path of the Templars. "This is my great friend!" He turned toward Nadeem, whispering, "Act like my friend."

Nadeem quickly nodded, and tucked his saber back into its sheath. "Vikings?" He asked as St. Ives and Broussard slowly returned their weapons to their scabbards.

"Worse," Shahin quietly lamented.

As De Buci handed Khalidah down to Broussard, Shahin watched his old shipmate's eyes settle easily upon her, and remain there. Khali's beauty ran very deep, and Shahin saw in Nadeem's face that she could capture even the hardest men just by stepping off of a boat.

"I hoped you would still be here. I need your help, Nadeem."

"When have I ever seen you when you did not?" Nadeem demanded, without looking over.

"How is Fadia?" Shahin asked, weakly trying to re-ingratiate himself, to reestablish old ties.

Nadeem broke away from the sight of the girl standing in the low, tranquil surf, and returned to his old Captain. "Better now than she will be once I've brought you into our home. You are an ill wind, Shahin. This is a peaceful place. What does that warship want with you, that you would bring it to us on your heels?"

"I do not know. The Christians have taken Quyyum's ship." As Shahin spoke, Nadeem watched the sea beyond the waiting white men, expecting the black sail of the coming warship to glide into view at any moment. "Her cargo was my *people*, Nadeem. I am to get these men across the Sinai and back before they will be freed."

"I am not one of your people any longer, Shahin. I am a fisherman." What Nadeem hoped would sound like impenetrable determination rang weakly, he knew. And though what he said next was true, and he sought to speak it from a position of strength, it sounded more like a plea for mercy. "My debts to you are paid."

"Many times over," Shahin conceded in an unexpected turn, twisting the full force of his charm to a tone that had always seemed to Nadeem unfair. As it always had been for any who sought to deny Shahin, he knew he was overmatched.

Nadeem thought of Fadia and the children. He considered the deeply satisfying peace of a paltry catch in his thinning nets. "You are not welcome here any more."

Shahin did not speak in return. The three soldiers, for though they wore no uniforms it was clear to Nadeem what they were, stood like the last survivors of a battle-atrophied phalanx, with the promise of violence clearly written in their eyes.

The girl seemed out of place to Nadeem. He wondered for a moment what manner of cargo she could be to them, as she waited just behind the one whose shirt clung fast to a streak of blood at his side. "You trust these Christians?" Nadeem asked at last, aware that he was losing an argument to a man who was hardly speaking.

"No." In that one word, Shahin's voice took on a quality Nadeem had never heard in it before. It still held that always present essence of defiance of a man who was often too foolish to know the undefiable when he saw it, but it also carried with it a tone somewhat akin to despair.

"Quyyum is a good man," Nadeem conceded.

"We need provisions for four men and the girl, and camels to get us to Qulzum. And we need a head start."

Broussard, his face etched in concentration as he watched the two Saracens talk, wondered once again at the depth of Beaujeu's plan for their voyage. So many seemingly random elements, three Templars with little to no knowledge of their purpose or even their destination and their unlikely guide, might come together unexpectedly well. Like a spider's web, Beaujeu's plans could often seem aimless and insubstantial from one perspective, but they always held a sublime logic of form when you were caught in the middle of one. He was beginning to believe that Shahin might get them through this hostile land more successfully than if they rode at the head of an entire army.

Khali watched Shahin beckon them with an odd, non-committal

glance as he and the heavy, dark skinned Muslim headed off toward the line of palms. She fell into step just behind Broussard as they stepped out of the water and onto the red grains of Sinai. It occurred to Khalidah that she walked for the first time into a new land. She had left the only home she had ever known behind her now, forever. The warm wind of this new place carried a scent, as it swirled from the sea to the palms and back to her, that both soothed and excited her at once. She breathed it in deeply even as she broke into a half-run to keep pace with the long-striding men.

It was not until they had stepped through the thin line of palm trees, however, that she understood what the warm sensation of that scent on the air truly represented. Before her, just beyond the humble fishing village they now entered from the rise of the tree line, the desert reached out to the deep blue sky at the horizon like a second ocean of red sand, filling the wind with the essence of an exotic spice. With her journey aboard the *Gull* being the first, her arrival in Sinai was the second time she had seen a world without walls to shape and contain it. Here there were only the mighty dunes, drifts of red suspended like sculpted waves that seemed to hold the world of sand back from a collision with the world of water now behind her. Beyond this meeting of earth and sea, however, the desert appeared without limit.

Far to the Southeast, dust plumed like smoke. A billowing cloud spread toward the West, focusing to a fine point in the East. The Christians saw it, too. "Bedouins," De Buci explained to St. Ives and Broussard, "traveling along the Mamluk army's trail in the direction of Palestine."

Fadia, having swept her daughters out of her husband's house like a fussing hen, eyed Shahin as he entered with a suspicion that bordered on anger. "Why does she look upon you like that?" Broussard quietly asked him.

Nadeem answered before Shahin could. "Because she knows him."

"She used to work for me," Shahin responded sheepishly. "As I recall, I kept her in fine silks and perfumes before Nadeem showed her a better life."

"It is not her old life with you she begrudges, Shahin." Nadeem met his eyes firmly. "It is the threat you represent to the one she has now that she fears." He turned to De Buci. "Christian, that ship will be here within the hour. Who is aboard her?"

"I swear to you," De Buci answered, "we do not know. But if it is us they want, we can lead them from your home and into the desert as quickly as we brought them."

Shahin watched his old friend as he read the faces of the three Christians, and he quickly added. "All of Palestine is in the hands of Islam now, Nadeem. The wars are over. These men are not here to fight. They are refugees."

Nadeem cared little whose hands were currently around the throat of Palestine. He had long ago sought to leave behind the concerns of wars. Now, his only thoughts were of making these refugees someone else's problem.

"I could ask a high price for that girl," Nadeem scowled. "I could hand you and these men over to that ship and not think twice about it tomorrow." Khali pressed into Broussard's hand until he wrapped his fingers around hers. Fadia held her breath as all three Templars moved hand to hilt in subtle unison. Shahin made no move, and he said nothing. Finally, Nadeem gave in to what he had known he must concede since first spotting the *Gull's* creaking mast. "If it were anybody but you," he spit out at last. "We must hurry, now." Nadeem ushered Shahin's charges outside, turning at last to his wife from the door. "If anyone should enter this house..."

"You are out fishing." She rendered her husband what he needed in that moment without looking up from her cooking fire, her anger only a thin mask for her fear.

Broussard watched alone, hidden among the palms as the shore boats approached from the warship anchored in the deeper waters of the cove. The others hurriedly prepared for the next leg of their journey as Shahin's friend, who seemed to carry a great deal of weight within the village, quickly gathered camels from among the fifty or so families living here. Even as Broussard had headed off to scout the mysterious ship, hoping to determine their strength and purpose, he was amazed to find over a dozen camels at the village well and more on the way.

He squinted against the white sunlight reflected from the blue sea as two shore boats, loaded down with men pulling toward the beach. It was not until the boats reached the shore that Broussard could confirm the inexplicable sight. Several black tunics adorned with gold crosses of the Knights Hospitaller and several white tunics with the red crosses of the Templars, mingled together with just as many Saracen soldiers. Blood enemies only three days removed from Acre worked side by side in the long boats. Looking deeper as the men began to disembark, Broussard began to recognize faces. Leveque and Durand sat beside the giant Hospitaller Van Cuso.

Confused and anxious to tell the others, Broussard had started to back away from the rise that separated the village from the beach when something caught his eye and he froze. A man stood at the prow of the lead shore boat, long black hair tangling in the wind, cloaked in black, wearing no uniform or insignia.

When he stepped over the side of the boat onto the sand, however, the wind shifted as it had when they first arrived, swirling off the barrier of palms back to the sea. The mane drifted away from his face, revealing his golden-hued flesh and dark, hooded eyes. Broussard had seen this strange golden man before.

"They know not, neither will they understand; they
walk on in darkness:
all the foundations of the earth are out of course."

- Psalm 82: 5

Chapter Thirty-Two

Book burst into consciousness, the sound of a woman's scream resonating in his ears. The high pitch of a woman in distress had always created within Wendell Book an immediate need to act, to find the problem and solve it.

He rolled reflexively in the dark toward the sound. A surge of pain shot from his swollen knee through his entire leg the instant he touched the floor beside the bed. A cold sweat surged to his face as he forced himself to stand, clutching at his rigid knee to brace it. His eyes focused and the room grew clearer. A hard cot in the corner. A wool blanket. He remembered. The drugged water glass. The old man. The bookshop. The girl.

Molly's second scream overruled his pain. Stumbling in the darkness like a drunk, limping on a leg that would no longer bend properly, he rushed from the room into a hallway lit by a bare white bulb. He could see the closed door that led to where Molly was screaming. Standing just in front of it, the old man was pointing a gun at him.

"I'm sorry, Detective." Jacob said, sorrow and embarrassment in his voice. "It is important that she sleep."

Book thought, for the briefest moment, to ask the old man if he had completely lost his mind, but he could hear the girl, tormented and terrified just beyond the guarded door. He limped with a single concern and without pause through the old man's warning, through his stare, and past his gun.

"Molly!" Book shouted into the dark room as he swung open the door. His sweeping hand struck the light-switch and he suddenly saw her on the floor, squeezed into a corner of the small room. She had crawled there in the darkness, as if trying to escape or hide from something that had come to her bed. She stared right through him.

Even as he hobbled to her, Book knew she did not recognize him. She pulled even more tightly into herself, trying to scream between choked breaths, clearly still somewhere else.

Book dropped stiffly beside her, taking her hard into his arms. "Molly. It's alright," he said, trying to bring her back to the room. "It was just a dream."

Molly had dreamt of the moment of her death once again, and was still seeing it even as he held her. This time, however, there were no faces obscured in moving shadows or weak firelight. Instead, she had been bleeding from a hot and pulsing wound in her chest that made breathing nearly impossible. What air she could take in was fouled by the stench of decaying flesh and the searing scent of lye. She could only stare up at the bright morning sky from where she lay in a trench atop the cooling bodies of the dead. In her horror and indignation, even as more shots rang out from somewhere above her, as fresh bodies, suddenly lifeless as dolls, fell into the trench all around her, she tried to cry out but had no force left in her ruined right lung to power her voice. Her final thought as death at last overtook her was the memory of her killer's uniform behind the plume of smoke rising from his rifle.

She felt powerful hands threatening to crush her arms into her rib cage, and heard a voice rising in her ears as it forced its way through the fog of her mind. Through vision blurred by free-flowing tears she found herself in a small, nearly familiar room. Turning slowly toward that voice, she found Detective Book at her side. She hadn't even realized that she was screaming until she recognized him, and felt him holding her.

"It's alright now," Book said again, grateful that he could hold her eye in his at last.

She stayed silent for just a moment, before full recognition of where she was and who was holding her caught up to her all at once. Then she began to merely cry.

Grabbing her to make her stop shrieking like a lunatic had been an obvious choice. But now she had become simply a crying girl. An uncommunicative grunt of uncertainty escaped his lips when she buried her head in his chest and stayed there. Molly sobbed convulsively, struck all at once by a wave of fear, sorrow, and loneliness.

As smoothly as he could without releasing the girl, Book started a slow and excruciating process to slide his knee out from the awkward position he had fallen into, privately enduring a pain that threatened to make him black out.

"What happened?" Trudie demanded as she arrived breathless at the door. Book, still focused on re-positioning his knee, glanced up long enough to note the anger on her face and the shame on the old man's as he meekly hid the gun in his pocket. Trudie squeezed by him and scurried toward Molly, still tying down her swirling, flowered robe.

"Bad dream," Book reported, suddenly grateful to give way to the whirlwind of maternal nurturing.

"Oh, child," she offered in a voice that seemed to understand and accept any and all pain at once. She knelt before Molly on legs that seemed fat and hard-muscled at the same time. "Let's get you warm again," she decided, clearly appalled to find Molly on the cold floor instead of underneath a warm blanket. Molly thought to resist and hold onto Book, but gave way without much struggle.

Book remained on the floor, ignored as Molly was helped to her feet and shuttled to the cot. He stared at his knee, his jeans stretched at the seams over the badly swollen joint. He hadn't seen it this bad since the surgery. He took a deep breath, and tried to bend his right leg. A second wave of cold sweat. The leg started to shake, but he could not bend it. The doctors had explained to him years ago, after the original injury, that the ligaments had been torn loose completely. Where they were reattached had long since turned to inflexible scar tissue. He knew that one or more of the ruined ligaments could be torn again right now. Or maybe not. He had just never had it swell up this bad before.

"Detective," Jacob said from the doorway and Book realized he had been watching his quiet struggle. "Perhaps we should leave the women alone."

Book stared at the old man, a merciless stare after calling the bluff of a man with a gun. But his own thoughts still churned too wildly in a hopeless effort to catch up with his circumstances for him to give a damn about the old man's pride.

He looked again at Molly. Trudie sat on the edge of the cot, pulling up the blanket and stroking the girl's hair as she lay on her pillow. Molly had stopped crying, but her face was still red and swollen from her ordeal. She had heard Jacob. She caught Book's eye in that moment, and he knew she felt safer with him there.

He spoke quietly to the grey man at the open door, "My knee hurts. I think I'll stay here for a little while."

Molly lay back and turned her eyes to the ceiling.

Trudie continued to lightly stroke the auburn hair just above her temples, not too differently from the way Molly's own mother would. She had also seen the exchange between the girl and Book, and she leaned in close to whisper. "You are safe here, Molly. He came back for you, dear. He will not leave you."

Molly looked again at the haggard and exhausted man in the corner. As with so much that had occurred to her since her dreams began, she did not understand from where her certainty came, but she knew that Trudie was right. She watched Book masking some secret pain in his leg, unaware that she watched him, and she wondered. Why, when she had come seeking an old man, had it been his son she found waiting in his place? She wondered who he could be or what she could be to him that he would remain at her side despite all the trouble she had brought down on his head. For the first time in many days, she thought of someone else's pain above her own. Even as the days of sleeplessness again began to overtake her under Trudie's comforting presence, she wished she had known enough to stay away from his apartment. She wished she had understood that he would stand beside her like her own personal soldier in her own private war. She wished she had known enough to spare him from all this, and what was still to come.

Book stared at the ceiling from the floor beside Molly's cot as she slept. Trudie had retrieved his blanket and pillow for him, making him as comfortable as he was going to get anyway. The old couple left them alone, keeping the light on just in case Molly woke up again.

Many things kept Book awake. There was the pain of his knee, the cold of the ice pack Trudie had wrapped it in, the myriad questions spinning in his mind about the old man with a gun, his wife who had drugged his water glass, and the murderous drifter, John. But most disconcerting and threatening of all was their sleeping prisoner. Molly.

Working Vice in Hollywood, Book had seen hundreds of runaway girls with plenty of problems. But he'd never seen problems like these. The unresolved, nagging fear that seemed to get to him the most was his understanding that Molly was not a drug addict, and she was not crazy. She was a good kid, and she was scared to death. He thought again of the invisible strings he had felt, first from the girl at the Wilcox station, then again and so much stronger from the man Jacob had called a *Shepherd*.

His head was spinning again, lost somewhere between anxiety and exhaustion. Jacob had revealed many things that added up to little more than nothing, a mixture of ridiculous speculation and facts that he could not, or should not, know. The mysteries of this troubled girl, this odd place with its very dangerous inhabitants, the fact of the Shepherd and the horrible things Book had seen him do, all combined to leave him with an over-stimulated mind and no avenue of thought that might soothe or comfort. He closed his eyes to the light of the room.

In the swirl of images that followed in his imagination, another silence began to form in him. This time, it was not the manic glare of his father, but rather something he had not seen, had not allowed himself to see for quite some time. Waiting for him in the quiet emptiness beneath his thoughts was the soft blue of his mother's eyes as she had been at the end, a frame of shallow lines around them, etched into her skin by a lifetime of smiling and laughing when she could always have found reason not to. The image warmed him for a moment, before the urgent and competing voices in his head - Molly, Jacob, and the paper-faced drifter, John, encroached again. *To make amends.*

Inevitably and at last he came to Sara. *They want me,* Molly had said. *And now they'll come after you, and anyone close to you.*

Molly slept.   The store slept.   Book pulled himself quietly and painfully to his feet. He moved as carefully as he could across the creaking floor to the door, down the groaning staircase, to the rear exit on the first floor, and outside to the alley behind the shop. It was true, what the old man had said. He was free to leave any time he wanted. But just as true, it seemed, he had nowhere to go.

From the alley he rounded the corner toward Santa Monica Boulevard, eerily quiet in the last hours before dawn.   He spotted a telephone booth, weakly lit by a flickering street light. He moved toward the only other person he could think of who needed to be warned, the only person he knew that they might still come after to get to him. At the same time, he moved toward help, friendship, wisdom and the perspective to sort out this waking nightmare.

***

Frank Harker waited. The dream had returned. The same dream that had come to him from time to time in the past, that had come more and more frequently in the last year. It was the old dream. It came with a new urgency this night.   It came with force, mysterious, compelling, and bewildering.   The old dream left him awake in a familiar room.   He recognized his surroundings only dimly. Next to him a woman slept. Her name was Marie. He knew that Marie was his wife. He knew she had slept beneath that loose pile of blankets every night for the past eleven years. Yet, he did not understand why he needed to fight so hard to recall such things. He was a police officer in Los Angeles. A detective in the Vice Division. Hollywood. But he was more than that. As he stared up at the ceiling of his bedroom, it was hard to think of the things he had always thought of before. It was hard to remember.

Though it was 3:28 in the morning, the ringing telephone did not surprise. As the woman beside him stirred fitfully beneath her blankets at the shrill bell, he rolled his heavy body toward the nightstand.

"Hello?"

"Frank, I need you to listen to me." It was the call he was told to wait for. It was Book.

***

Molly awoke with a quick inhale to find herself back in the bookstore again. As had happened with the first dream over time, it was getting easier to find her bearings. It only took a few hard breaths to calm her as she sat up in the cot, allowing the details of her dream to crystallize in her waking mind. Something she had said to her mother the day before she left was becoming clearer to her now. Her dreams were not so much like dreams at all. Molly was *remembering*.

Book heard the springs of the cot squeak above him when she moved. His eyes flashed open. After returning from his secret excursion to the street corner, his leg had stiffened until it was like having a heavy board attached below his hip. He managed to move, first to his elbows and finally to a sitting position where he could see her. She sat centered on the cot, her legs crossed, leaning against the wall. Her thoughts were far away. He wasn't certain she noticed him. "Kid?" he said softly. He put a light hand on her arm and spoke her name, "Molly."

"It's okay." She said.

Her still furrowed brow held a very serious expression that suddenly belied the look of a sixteen-year-old. She drew in a ragged breath. "I remember," she said at last as another tear escaped her eye. It was not a frantic or frightened tear, but more one of recognition, resolve, and great sorrow. Without thinking, Book reached up and delicately dried it from her cheek, leaving in its place a soft streak of dirt from his thumb. She nearly smiled then, and lifted her hand to his, grateful for the warmth of his touch and the kindness of the gesture, but knowing there was work to be done. "Her name was Rachel. They killed her."

"It's okay, kid," Book said instinctively, not really knowing what either of them was talking about. "Who killed her?"

"No," Molly insisted, calm but fishing for words with a resolve brought about by a newfound understanding. "It was me. My name was Rachel." Tears flowed more freely now but she did not sob or cry out. "They killed us all."

Chapter Thirty-Three

Shahin and the two Templars gulped water from the well as Khali filled the leather sacks. The white men blended into the village more easily and were better suited for a desert crossing in the robes Nadeem had provided. The fisherman gave final instructions to Hamal and two of his young friends, each mounted and pulling a short train of camels, as he rushed them on their way. "Ride to nightfall before you return."

Khali watched De Buci and St. Ives prepare for a desert journey with a military precision that almost made one seem the reflection of the other. Finally, each called for their camels to kneel before them. She caught the eye of St. Ives as he climbed onto the animal's shoulders. She did not like looking this young man in the eye. St. Ives possessed all of the horrible potential she had witnessed in Broussard during their flight from Ardenti's home, but none of the gentleness she had seen, or at least believed might be somewhere within him. There was always anger with St. Ives, burning just below his surface. She did not believe, if she looked hard and long enough, that she would find compassion within him. The attention he gave his weapon, the scraping caresses of his whetstone, was unnerving and seemed unnatural to her. Knowing that to St. Ives her presence was just as unnatural, Khali took an involuntary step to the side as his camel raised groaning above her. She was glad to see Broussard, returning at the run to them.

"We must ride, now," Broussard announced in alarm. Khali was further unsettled by his demeanor. He almost seemed frightened.

"What have you seen?" De Buci demanded.

"When there is time."

Broussard moved with an economy of purpose as he took the sacks of water from Khali and hastily slung them over her kneeling camel's shoulder. He turned to Nadeem, who seemed to dislike the agitation in Broussard more than any of them.

"Where are all the camels I saw?" As he spoke, Broussard eyed the two young Arabian horses that remained tied near the well.

"They are all gone from the village." Nadeem answered uneasily. "Horses are a luxury in a place like this, and these two have not been properly watered yet. But don't worry, you..."

Nadeem's words stopped in mid-breath as Broussard's sword flashed to his hand. He crossed the distance to the well in three quick strides. Before Nadeem could form a protest, before the beasts could even sense an intention, the horses were dead. In two quick, precise, and utterly thorough strokes, the blade had passed in wide arcs through their gracefully tapered necks where they were most thin, near the base of the skull. Separated from their heads, the lifeless hulks of their bodies collapsed into the dust behind him, where Broussard left them as suddenly as he had come.

Khali's eyes remained wide with shock as Broussard's powerful hands situated and balanced her in the saddle. She held on tight as her camel lurched to its feet. She saw the look of rage and horror on Nadeem's face, something akin to regret in the eyes of Shahin, and no emotion whatsoever from the Templars. Broussard struck his camel with the riding stick, causing the beast to rise awkwardly with its burden. All five animals started southward from the village at the run.

***

The Shepherd stepped out of the line of palms at the edge of the rise that overlooked the small fishing village and the sea of red sand. A Bedouin caravan moved west to east near the horizon. From the village below, four dust clouds emanated from four separate camel trains, each moving in a different direction.

***

Nadeem could listen to the shouting men and screaming women no longer. He shoved his clutching wife back into their home as he crossed the threshold into the light of the high sun.

He had seen men like this one in the many travels of his younger days, but never standing unified with Christians. Nor had he ever seen Crusaders standing with Saracens. Yet to either side of a golden-skinned Mongol in the center of the village stood two dozen fighting men, crusaders clad in the white and black of infamous orders, mixed evenly among armored warriors of Islam. All of these men seemed to look out at his village with the lifeless eyes of sharks, showing no thought as they awaited the command of the Mongol. It was an ill wind indeed his old friend had brought to his new home.

The Mongol himself was dressed in European fashion. At his right arm stood a Nordic giant, towering in the black and gold robes of the Order of St. John. The giant held a heavy sword, point down, so that it left a trace of blood where he let it gently swirl in the sand like the tail of a hungry cat. At his feet, four men, elders of the village, lay separated from their heads. All around were the helpless, who did not understand what these men wanted, or what they could do to appease them. Women wailed their torment or stayed silent with shock. It made no difference. Powerless men averted their eyes or bluffed and postured that they might attack. It made no difference.

Nadeem strode forward. "What do you want here?" he demanded of the golden man.

The Shepherd saw that he had found a leader, at last, and turned his full attention to Nadeem. "Where are the Templars going?" he asked with a quiet menace. The entire time he had waited at the urging of Fadia, Nadeem had debated in his mind whether he owed continued silence to Shahin, or if his obligation had been more than met. Upon seeing the bodies of the slain, and grasping the extent of the horror his former comrade had brought to his peaceful home, Nadeem quickly determined to tell what he could and cursed himself for not being the first to meet these men. Yet, none of his pain, rage, or reasoned decisions made the slightest difference now as Nadeem felt pulled, by the very sound of his words, toward the sinister stranger.

The words flowed from him like water from a jar this golden man had simply nudged over with his heavy foot. "They cross the Sinai to the sea, to Qulzum." Stranger still to Nadeem, a veteran of so many battles, a survivor of so many life or death struggles, he never even lifted a hand to the scabbard of his saber as, after a dismissive wave of the Mongol's hand, the Nordic giant's massive straight blade flashed down upon his neck.

"I have said, Ye are gods; and all of you are children of the most High."

-Psalm 82: 6

Chapter Thirty-Four

His heels echoed like the clicking of a heavy clock as Mathias Holt stepped from the elevator onto the wide Italian marble floors in front of his secretary's desk. Elizabeth was still very beautiful, and she still smiled a knowing, intimate smile at her lover whenever he approached. But the years she had spent waiting for Mathias to propose had begun to show in thin lines of worry, most visible around her eyes an hour or so before sunset, when the west facing windows watched the sun falling toward the ocean.

Elizabeth had been his first order of business in America, his first hire after realizing that Los Angeles was to be his home some sixteen years ago. Together they selected the location that would serve as his residence and headquarter the endeavor that was to become Pacific Enterprises.

She loved him for many reasons. Mathias had a secretive way about him that intrigued and tantalized. He also had a way of making the most mundane activities seem filled with wonder and importance. He was handsome, wiser in words than any grandfather, though still vital and powerful in body, and uniquely unencumbered by the fears that slow accomplishment and deaden life for most men. Through all these qualities, and many more subtle ones only Elizabeth could see, he not only had amassed a fortune so great even she could only guess at it, but he seemed able to create or achieve anything he might wish for, no matter how grand, no matter how bold.

But it was the secret attentions Mathias offered only to her that she loved most. When he was away or merely distant within his thoughts, Elizabeth still carried parts of him with her. She carried the sorrowful touch of his hand, so lonely in the isolation of his great mind, the private glances she alone understood, and the warmth of the wonderful stories she could sometimes coax from him as they lay in the morning sun within the womb of his bed.

Since she'd first met him, Mathias had harbored an obsession for the sea. Sometimes, when Elizabeth pressed him about his curious fascination, he would tell a very old story she loved to hear as if it were recalled for her alone. It was a Persian fairy tale told each time with the same boyish gleam behind his eyes that never seemed to fade for her, though the face around them may have aged and his black hair silvered. The deep capacity for romance in his heart brought the tale to her as if carried on spiced Arabian winds as Mathias recounted the legend of how Ashmedai, the great demon king, having once obtained the mighty and magical signet ring of Solomon, broke the object's spell over his demon-kind by hurling it hundreds of miles into the ocean. Once free of the ring's power, he then assumed Solomon's form, as only a demon could do, and sat upon the throne of Israel.

Once in the ocean, however, Solomon's ring sparkled and flashed until it was snatched into the mouth of a hungry fish. The fish in turn, was caught in the nets of a fisherman. And the fisherman, upon finding the ring and recognizing the seal, did return it to Solomon. In this way, the great ring made its own way home, and the demon king was undone.

From this towering office building overlooking the ocean from Santa Monica, Pacific Enterprises managed the largest open ocean fishing fleet and the greatest number of canning facilities in the Western United States. But Elizabeth knew that Mathias Holt's love and concern for the sea reached far beyond commerce.

Obsessed with the damage caused by waste and industrial pollution pouring into the sea, he maintained the most diligent conservation program in existence. At great personal expense, Mathias employed teams of scientists to keep a meticulous accounting of any and all incursions of civilization in the region. A legion of oceanographers and engineers perpetually scoured the ocean floor just beyond the Santa Monica pier. Within his penthouse office of luxurious marble, rare Persian carpets and the finest furnishings of leather and wood, Mathias poured over daily reports from biologists, staffed at each of his canneries along the Pacific coast, and tasked with cataloguing the stomach contents of every animal caught by his fleet. From tin cans, lost fishing tackle, foil wrappers, to lost jewelry, no signs of man's incursions onto the sea went unnoticed.

She knew it was his concern for the environment and hunger for knowledge that drove him, but Elizabeth liked to pretend that Mathias was really searching for King Solomon's old ring. After all, one never knew what wonders the sea might hold. It was their secret together, and it warmed her when he was away.

"Good Morning, Elizabeth." His words were always economical, but she knew the warmth behind them.

Elizabeth responded in the manner it must always be when she sat at her post. "Good Morning, Mr. Holt." She offered her secret smile, as he reached across her desk and subtly took her hand into his.

"Any messages?"

"Yes, Mr. Holt," she said, distracted by his touch. She produced a small stack of letters and notes. She drew his attention to one in particular, which she had set on top of the stack. "You've received a call from the police."

"The Los Angeles police?" he asked without concern, picking up the note and turning it to read.   His heels began to click again, clock-like against the marble floors, his dark cashmere overcoat flaring as he moved toward the tall stainless steel double-doors of his private office.

"Yes," Elizabeth answered, covering the warmth he had left with her other hand to keep it with her a little longer.   "Detective Harker in Hollywood."

Chapter Thirty-Five

Book watched the girl from the opposite side of the table, where he sat in a matching, heavy wooden chair. She hunched over her plate, greedily shoveling scrambled eggs into her mouth like she couldn't eat fast enough. Book ate enough to catch up from the day before, too, and without fear of any poisons on his plate or in his coffee. As clear as it was that the old couple could not keep him in their bookshop, it was just as clear now that he could not leave the girl behind. He was trapped by the mystery, as maybe they all were.

Molly was different. She had changed, grown, or matured very suddenly during the night. Her movements and demeanor showed the confidence of experience, of one tested in ways no sixteen-year-old likely could have been. To Book it seemed as though all, or at least many, of her doubts and fears had suddenly vanished.

Trudie hovered near Molly, projecting an oddly admiring attitude as she watched protectively over the ravenous girl.

Jacob made his way to the table from the stairs. He smiled a morning greeting, pleasantly flashing his darkened teeth, first at Book, then at Molly. Book watched as Molly looked up from her plate and held Jacob in a lingering gaze, studying his face until his stained smile dissolved into a thoughtful look. "Yes?" The old man seemed a little hopeful. "What is it?"

Jacob's eyes narrowed, as if trying to will what would come next. There was a soft edge to Molly's penetrating stare as it lingered on him for a moment longer. She extracted whatever information she sought from the grey man's tired and worn features, then she turned away, leaving his question to fade in the air. She turned toward Book.

Their eyes met in a sudden collision, and he received the same penetrating stare. "Have you ever had bad dreams?" She asked without warning.

Book's nerve scattered and he quickly looked away. Molly had a way of finding the most raw and sensitive of memories thought long dead and buried, and breathing sudden life into them. *How could she know?* She had put it to him as a question, but she already knew the answer. Of that Book was certain.

"A long time ago," he admitted, again feeling like a man on trial for a crime he could not recall, and now wondering if he could actually be guilty. "How do you know about my dreams?"

Molly seemed to search for a moment to find a good answer before she settled on another question. "Were they like mine?"

"I don't know. Maybe."

"They were scary?"

"Yeah."

Jacob avoided his chair at the table and remained standing. He took care not to intrude, but studied the unfolding moment between his guests with renewed interest in Book. Both men waited for Molly's next words, Jacob with fascination, Book with dread.

"Please, tell me about them."

In sixteen years, Book had told no one. Not even Sara. Year after year he had covered them over with an ever-growing mound of mundane experiences, the normal joys and pains of life. It had never occurred to him that a moment like this would ever come. He looked again at Jacob and

Trudie as they waited patiently for fresh pieces for their secret puzzle, then back to the girl. The pools of her eyes seemed to deepen by the moment, as if hard-earned wisdom could arise in an instant within someone so young. Book also found something else in those new depths. He saw warmth. Sympathy. These could have been the eyes of a woman who knew something of pain.

"Yeah," he relented at last, glancing away and picking up his coffee cup to steady his hand. "Okay."

He turned inward, searching old memories and old fears for a starting point. Then he spoke for what might have been several minutes about monsters under a little boy's bed, shadows lurking outside his window, and things that await children in the dark.

"What did they do to you?" Molly asked when he had finished.

"Nothing. They were just dreams," Book said, sensing the instability of his ground.

"What did they do?" Molly pressed him, knowing full well the instability of his ground.

"They asked questions."

"What questions?"

Book continued to study her as they spoke, his own deep fears of recalling the dreams fading somewhat with the light he now shed on them. They *were* just dreams. Yet, with all that he had seen in the last few days, he also knew they were something more. Something very dark and very powerful hid within them.

"They asked, *what did you see?* Over and over again, every night after my parents died. Maybe for a month. *What did you see?*"

"Only a month?" Molly asked. "That's all? Then it stopped?"

For a moment Book thought she might be trying to gauge how long she might have to endure her own nightmares, as if it were some kind of virus that might run its course. But he noticed the disappointment in her voice.

"That's right," he confirmed.

Molly drifted into her own thoughts long enough for Book to hope the interrogation had ended.

"What did you tell them?" She finally asked.

"Them?" Book asked. "You mean the monsters in my dream?"

"What did you see?" she asked with growing impatience.

The fact that she used the precise words of his dream monsters was not lost on him, but Book looked directly into her eyes, with an unflinching conviction of his own.

"I saw my father cut off his own finger and throw his wedding ring into the ocean."

Molly took the full brunt of Book's words with calm. After a moment she took in a knowing breath that seemed tinged with resolve. She sighed. And then she turned away from him as if she had suddenly lost interest.

Book realized that she intended to leave him in the dark, to leave his own questions to fade the same way she had with Jacob. He reached across the table and took her hand, urgently enough that she turned back to him.

"Why did he do that?" Book demanded. It was an absurd question, he knew, but he also knew that he might be looking at the only person in the world who could answer it.

Molly met his stare for a long time, going over many issues in her thoughts. Her mind told her to remain silent, that speaking any more of what she had learned in her sleep would do no good for any of these people, and had the potential to do far worse. She knew what it was that had come to him in his dreams. She knew what it was that waited for her now, somewhere in the city outside this bookshop.

Detective Book's pain and his need for understanding ran very deep. She admired the courage it took for him to ask, and she knew she could not deny him. She closed her eyes again and returned to the haze of her dreams, trying her best to clear the blurred images.

"There are a lot of things I can't remember," Molly began, sometimes talking to Book and the old couple, sometimes talking out loud to herself, "but seeing myself through her eyes, I know there were many before her as well. I was married to a man... Michael. Oh, God..." her voice filled with emotion at a sudden memory, "...we had a little girl."

Book squinted at her from across the table, again unable to follow her through the gaps she seemed to leap across. But his sense of dread, vague and unfocused, increased with hers as powerful emotions welled within her and Molly seemed to become lost in her fantasy. Or her memory, he could not be sure which any longer, but he could see how hard she worked to connect the threads, to fill the gaps.

"I could have escaped," she continued, holding tighter to Book's hand on the table between them. "I *tried* to escape, but we became separated. I went back for her... I went back... and...." Molly reflexively pulled her extended hands back to her chest, above her heart, almost defensively, and her eyes snapped open and back into focus with a sharp inhale. She had suddenly seen too much.

Rachel had entered the apartment and witnessed the aftermath. Her child was dead. Her husband was dead, still holding their daughter in his arms where he had fallen. Rachel had tried to warn him years before that this day might come, but he had loved her. He was a brave man. A good man. He understood her sacrifice, and he had died for it. As much as she loathed it, as much as its relentless weight threatened to crush her as it eventually did all whom she loved, Rachel still had the ring. Michael had seen to that.

When she had seen enough of Rachel's memories in her mind's eye, a lifetime of pain and regret battered Molly all at once. She looked again to the old couple, at the restrained longing in their eyes, at the unhealed scars of loss. Molly turned quickly away from them, assaulted by what she knew. She bit her lip, unaware as it began to bleed. The God damned ring.

Book watched the trickle of blood escape the wound she had just opened on her lip. He rose from his chair, leaning in close to her. His strong hand gingerly reached out and loosened the tension in her jaw with a touch.

"He was there too" she announced quietly. "Sixteen years younger, but he was there. The Shepherd." Molly looked at Book with the sorrow of the guilty. "I am sorry. I should never have come to you, Book. I didn't understand."

"Didn't understand what?" Book held her eyes in his, perhaps the only thing keeping her in the room with him instead of in whatever place she had been visiting. Molly brought her hand to his again, and he let it slip from her face so she could hold it.

Book waited for her to speak, while something more was communicated between them, locked as they were in the moment.

"The Shepherd," he asked, returning to her words, "was *where*?"

"Poland," Jacob broke the hanging silence between the detective and the girl.

Molly glanced at the old man. Her attention lingered on him as if he had just confirmed something for her.

"What the hell are you talking about?" Book demanded of Jacob.

"I have brought something horrible down on your head," Molly said to Book, speaking as a loved one might when breaking the news that you are terminally ill. "I had no right."

Book struggled with the impulses of fear and anger. His mind screamed at him that this was all an illusion, that Jacob had filled the girl's mind with enough nonsense to make her believe. Yet, instinct told him to take the girl by the hand and run to a place where these dangers could not find her.

"Molly," he asked at last, "why did you choose me?"

She thought about this for a moment, the much older anxiety poisoning her newfound confidence. Her eyes darted without focus, as though she were searching her own thoughts and still coming up blank on many things.

"There was a train," Molly offered, still searching. "They were pushing us all together. Karl Buchner was there on the platform." Book's brow tightened. "Your father."

Molly waited for him to process what she had just said.

"My father died the year you were born."

"Yes," Jacob interjected with an odd confidence. "But Karl Buchner was just leaving the city of Warsaw the day Rachel died."

Book was glad it was Jacob speaking so he could more easily indulge his anger. But he did not fail to notice what Jacob had said. *Rachel.* She had not spoken that name to anyone but him. How could Jacob know what she had dreamed? Question upon question formed in his mind, but he was beginning to fear the answers too much to ask them.

The story of his father's secret past had come to light only days before his mother had been killed. He had not believed what anybody had said, not the papers speaking of the "monster in our midst," and not the kids at school. Carl Book had been a volunteer in the war effort. He worked in a factory that turned scrap metal into American artillery shells. He looked to his parents for the strength to stand up to the lies, but his mother could only cry, and his father was just so afraid of the old demons now resurfacing in his new home that he couldn't face his dreams anymore. The truth had come to light in the Santa Monica Journal. That was when the old man stopped sleeping altogether.

Book was ten at the time. He barely knew what a Nazi was, other than the black clad villains he and his friends used to kill when they played war. But the truth emerged at last, and the past Karl Buchner had tried to bury in American soil was resurrected for all to see. Rather than risk sleep and the demons returning, Carl Book had simply gone out to the garage and put a bullet into his own head. That was the day when Book learned what selfishness was, how weak it could make a man, and how to fear and despise weakness in all its forms. That fear and hatred threatened to reach the surface now. Molly saw it rising within him.

"The Shepherd had found me again," she continued. "My child was dead. My husband was dead. He killed them. When the Nazis finally picked me up to put me on that train, it was almost merciful." She recalled her dream and Rachel's last breaths among the cooling bodies of the dead. She shivered in the chill of the bookstore. "Almost. It was an escape."

Molly turned at the sound of Trudie's muffled sob. The girl and the woman became locked in an oddly intense stare for a moment. Trudie held

a terrible sadness barely in check.   Molly turned away first, suddenly
shamed by the sight of the old woman's pain.

"Through it all, there remained the problem of the Shepherd," she
said, turning back to Book. "I found your father on the loading platform.
I'm sorry. It was chance. I needed someone who could freely move about
the city, someone who was not bound with me to take that train. I needed a
German soldier, and your father was simply there." Her words sounded to
Book like a criminal's confession.

"Karl Buchner was a Sergeant in the SS. For three weeks in December
of 1942, he worked at a train yard in occupied Warsaw. It was a processing
station where refugees, gypsies, political undesirables, and Jews were
loaded onto trains bound for Treblinka. A death camp."

Book sat silent.   Even as the lasting anger he felt for his father
blended with the potent concoction of fear and sympathy he felt for the girl,
he also knew that she was giving him something in this moment his father
had given him a lifetime without. Somehow, impossible as it seemed, Molly
was telling him the truth.

"He didn't know," she spoke of his father's thoughts like one who had
seen them first hand, "what would happen to those people at the other end
of the line. But he knew enough." Molly seemed to be fighting for a deeper
focus. "I can't say how it was acceptable to him. But he and his comrades
slept well enough at night, and laughed well enough over their meals, just
like the managers of any other train yard might, I suppose."

Book watched in silence as Molly went further back to that place,
seemingly deeper into the secret thoughts of a long-dead man.

"He was responsible for moving the line and sometimes he had to get
tough because they wanted to overload the cars. He knew it was hell for the

people who went in first, because it took so long. The cars were stopped on the tracks sometimes for hours and the people were packed in so tight, they couldn't even move their arms. Some of them would asphyxiate before the train even pulled out, so that the living would ride along side the dead. All of them still standing. These things he knew in the darkened corners of his mind. But you had to get tough sometimes," she repeated as if recalling a vague sense of conviction, "to get what they considered a fully loaded car."

"How?" Book's protest began with weak breath, without force. But he found his voice again, spurred by the ridiculous nature of her recounting. "How could you... or anybody know all that? What a man *thought* and *felt*?"

Molly considered her response for a long time. "Rachel was in possession of a device. It is the reason the Shepherd pursued her, the reason he pursues us today."

"What device?"

"It has a name, sort of a code word. *King's X.*"

Molly watched Book seem to freeze. He had suddenly returned to the pier, the old man, and the pooling blood.

"You said your father mentioned it to you once." She pushed him.

"Just before he threw the ring in the ocean," Book spoke the memory aloud, even as his thoughts turned to his father's final and most bizarre gift, the firing cap of 105 mm artillery shell currently resting in the pocket of his jacket upstairs. *King's X.* "He showed me the ring and said, 'this is the King's X, remember what you see here.'"

Molly paused, the end of a long course of events vaguely beginning to register. But the words were clear enough. There was no mistake. It was gone. Lost.

"But what is it?" Book demanded. *"King's X.* All this is about his *ring?"*

"It appears as a gold ring," Molly said. "But it is something else altogether. I was able to touch him within the crowd," Molly continued, unaware of the storm of memories swirling within Book, "and so reach his thoughts."

"Wait, you're saying that you... or she..." Book pulled his hand from her grip, suddenly self-conscious about the way she was touching him, "...could read people's minds?"

Another long pause ensued as Molly thought about this.

"Human beings have many untapped potentials. The opposable thumb, speech, and mastery of fire were only the first steps of a great journey." The pools of thought in her expression seemed to deepen further. "Much is yet hidden from us. The ring makes many hidden things possible. That is why they want it back so badly."

Book clung to his sense of absurdity as if it could keep him afloat. "You mean this thing is *magic?"*

"No. It comes from an age when more was known and understood. *Much* more. It is technology, held over from a time when our enemy walked in the light of day instead of hiding in shadow. They are its creators, its true owners."

"What *else* was understood?"

"Things that are coming to light again. Things they don't want you to know." She paused again, searching. "All things, from matter to thought, exist as energy in wave form. The human mind is kind of like a radio receiver that brings those waves into focus. The ring is like a powerful antenna. It brings more things into focus than you might dream are out there. But they are. I suppose that is a little like magic. But in the hands of the average man, it is more like a stick of dynamite in the hands of an ape."

Book held firm to remaining unconvinced. Her story lacked focus. Yet, he clearly recalled his first meeting with Molly and the similar pull he felt in the presence of the Shepherd. "You don't have this thing now, right? How did you get in my head like that, in the cell...?"

"There are other tools besides sticks of dynamite. There are techniques to reaching the thoughts of others. It is a skill created by practice, only slightly more complicated than learning to play a piano."

Even as the flesh on his arms rose with a chill, Book could still find his skepticism where it lingered on the edges. He turned the conversation back to something he could understand.

"Why would a man like my father just drop everything to help you... or her?"

Molly was now fully enrapt in the impossible character she had been projecting since this conversation began, carrying a weight of experience she obviously could not have.

"A weak man, fearing the face of his true nature," she began, "will cling to the veil of illusion like a child clings to a favorite blanket. Great men spend lifetimes slowly preparing to see past this veil, and some still go mad from the shock when they finally do. What Rachel did to your father that day was to rip the barrier down in an instant, exposing him to the full face of God and the true face of evil all at once."

Molly's eyes blazed in a way that further recalled images of the old man. Book felt that he stood half in the room with her and half on the Santa Monica pier, sixteen years ago.

"The lies he had clung to, the entire structure of his life up to that moment fell away without warning." The fire of her glare dimmed a little. "Try to imagine suddenly waking from a bad dream only to find yourself standing on a loading dock, wearing a Nazi uniform, and herding human beings onto a train bound for Treblinka." There was a long silence without movement or breath from anyone in the room. "Do you understand?"

Book nodded, sinking back into his chair. Stinging memories were now tantalizingly lining up with the bizarre details of her uncanny account. He tried to make his next question a demand, but it sounded more like a plea.

"What did she want him to do?"

"Once you put it on," Molly returned to the ring, "it kind of sticks to you. It becomes a part of your skin, like a metal tattoo. You cannot remove it from living flesh." Book began to see the possibility in Molly's story of something else his father never had been able to convey. Impossible as it sounded, Molly might have been offering, at last, logic within madness. Her next words came like some foul tasting medicine to his tortured mind. "You must remove the finger entirely." She watched him for a moment, mercifully allowing him to process the collision between her history and his own.

"When I encountered your father, there was very little time. In that instant, that moment between us, it was decided, a meeting place agreed upon. Some place we both had heard of but had never been. Far away from the horrors we had each lived through. Warm and bathed in sunlight." Molly nearly smiled as if at the memory of a shared moment. "He would escape with the ring in secret. To America. To California."

"So, Rachel gave it to him? The ring?" Book's face revealed little of the torment in his thoughts.

"Her husband was a doctor. She used his surgical tools to remove it."

"*Why*?"

"To keep it safe," Jacob interrupted, stirred from his own rapt attention on the girl. "To keep it hidden until she could return for it." He gazed at her with a fanatical expression. "And so she has."

Book studied the girl. She did not seem to doubt any of this. She just sat with her eyes focusing on nothing in particular.

"Molly? Kid, are you okay?" Her eyes appeared blank. "I think she's had enough of this."   Even with so many unanswered demands reverberating in his own head, Book began to rise from his chair to physically bring Molly back from wherever she was, and into the light of the room.

"A voice in my head brought me here." She said to herself. "I was afraid of it but I think I understand now." She looked back to Jacob. "It was *me* all along, wasn't it? The voice was mine."

"Child," Jacob almost begged her now. "Do you know me?"

Molly stared into the eyes of Rachel's father, many years older than last she saw them, worn down by the weight of loss and regret. She said nothing. She turned to the soft and wide face of Rachel's mother as Trudie moved close enough to touch her husband, steadying them both as they awaited the culmination of their long vigil over a lost child. Molly studied the old pair, felt the waves of love emanating toward her, and she remembered. Rachel had revealed herself to them in her most vulnerable time, when the memories first began their return. As she learned more, Rachel began to withhold the truth from them. No good can come to those she loved by learning more. Jacob and Trudie had kept what they knew of their daughter's secrets for nine years, until the Shepherd caught up to her once more.

They had not let go even after her death. With the Shepherd himself as the only trail, they followed him. Silent tears flowed from Molly's eyes, the only hint of the joy and pain she felt behind a face that remained stone cold. The old fools, not even understanding, they had believed and they had followed, for her sake.

"Do you know us?" Trudie beseeched the girl.

Molly thought of Karl Buchner. She thought of the torment that drove him to his death, the terror that caused him to dismember his own hand and hurl her ring into the ocean. At last, she began to let the full import of Detective Book's revelation wash over her. Her ring was gone. Lost. Perhaps, at last, it was over. There could be rest. There could be peace.

Molly turned from the eyes of the old woman, to the eyes of the old man. "No." She lied for their sake, for the sake of rest, for the sake of peace. "I'm sorry. I don't know you."

Chapter Thirty-Six

St. Ives watched the girl's delicate shoulders, draped in a fall of raven hair, bobbing in the slow rhythm set by the camel in front of him as they moved across the endless sands.

Pater noster, qui es in caelis, sanctificetur nomen tuum.

There was a routine to his devotions. When lodged or encamped, he might affix his eyes to the flame of a candle or the embers of a campfire as he prayed. When the armies moved, however, he would find the back of the rider ahead of him. He would watch, unwavering, until all else might fall away and leave nothing but his prayer.

Adveniat regnum tuum. Fiat voluntas tua, sicut in caelo et in terra.

Fourteen times for the hours of the day.

Panem nostrum quotidianum da nobis hodie, et dimitte nobis debita nostra sicut et nos dimittimus debitoribus nostris.

Fourteen more for the Blessed Virgin.

St. Ives' vision had long ago lost focus, bringing him only the hazed silhouette of the slender form in front of him. He was wary of her, even as he remained locked in his devotions. One hundred thirty-one times, he had repeated his cycle of twenty-eight prayers this day.   Even as the sun hammered the travelers from above, and the burning sand sent heat rising in shimmering waves to their nostrils, the words continued to slide in a flowing whisper from his lips, intelligible only to him.

Et ne nos inducas in tentationem, sed libera nos a malo. Amen. Pater noster, qui es in caelis, sanctificetur nomen tuum.

The girl did not belong here. Though small and fragile to look upon, she posed a threat. Broussard was caught in her spell and weakened by it. There is comfort that comes with taking vows. Strength and peace comes with keeping them. Broussard was no longer at peace. He was forgetting his vows.

As the flow of his sacred words continued just above silence, St. Ives' muddled thoughts drifted to the disaster in Acre. Acre had been the last Christian stronghold in the Holy Land, the final hope of the forces of Christ's army to cleanse Palestine of false prophets and gods. And it was lost. St. Ives knew that it was not God that had failed in this cause. The resolve of men was weak. Faith could be tested and vows forsaken. It was the weakness of men who could see this journey undertaken alongside heathen criminals and whores that might cause a just God to turn away. God had been with them. Now, it seemed, He was not.

With the sun less than two hours from setting, the sand began to cool somewhat under the deepening blue of the sky. As the close of their fourth day of travel in the Sinai steadily approached, St. Ives continued to watch the girl's graceful rise and fall.

Adveniat regnum tuum. Fiat voluntas tua, sicut in caelo et in terra.

It had been three nights since they left the fishing village. Three nights since Broussard had spoken to them of what he had seen on the beach. Three nights and four days of hard desert travel since any of the Templars had slept. St. Ives knew the golden man, too. He had seen him in a dream the night before the Saracens breached the wall. He had thought little of it at the time. He knew no answers to the questions this phantom had asked, and dreams had never harmed him before. Broussard's tale, however, had sent an unanticipated wave of emotion through St. Ives, creating the familiar surge of blood and prickling of flesh that always came in the final moments before a battle. Now, he learned that Broussard and De Buci had also seen the golden man that same night when they were called to Beaujeu's chamber. They all had. So too, perhaps, had every Templar in the keep. It was, as De Buci had briefly suspected but dismissed at the time, more than a dream. It was some form of witchcraft. And now, since Broussard had seen the golden man standing in the light of day, they could be certain that the witch was upon them.

They had discussed the matter little over their journey. Yet each night, the Templars remained awake. Shahin slept with the deep peace of a man who had traveled hard each minute of the day and well into the night at the demand of the Christians, who were willing to stop only for the benefit of their camels. The girl slept too, St. Ives noted, fearful of everything around her but Broussard as she pushed obscenely close against him to ward off the chill of a desert night without a fire. Broussard remained awake, watching over her, more as a man watches over a woman than as a soldier of Christ keeps vigil through the night.

What little talk there had been those nights concerned the crew of the pursuing warship, and what possible reasons could exist for Templars and Hospitallers to stand with Saracens under the command of this strange golden man. St. Ives saw no need to explore the argument beyond the obvious answer. Witchcraft.

"He was a Mongol," De Buci had offered in explanation of the gold skin and hooded eyes. "I have seen them, East of Palestine."

The idea of a warrior, even one from an exotic race they had never seen, was easier to understand for Broussard than the otherworldly creature they had thought this man to be. Yet the fact remained, as Broussard pointed out, "he comes in our sleep to learn what we know."

During the first of these sleepless nights, St. Ives, in a rare flash of insight, grew slightly more comfortable with the fact that he knew very little about where he was going or why. He began to see the logic of Beaujeu's scheme, even if he could not discern its purpose. He began to wonder, in the chill of the Sinai night and again under the constant hammer of its sun, how many visits Beaujeu had received from this Mongol witch, and how much more of his plan the golden man might know than they knew themselves.

***

As the singularity of desert sand and stone gradually gave rise to the intermittent appearances of small brown shrubs and patches of purplish leaves, Khali began to sense that there might be an end coming to the seemingly infinite expanse of nothing. Soon enough, from the horizon before them arose high cliff walls of sharp, forbidding rock on either side of their path. As the short train of camels approached the cliffs, the land around them grew more populous with smaller formations of rock that jutted through the earth's crust like craggy islands or stone ships floating on the sand. Around these islands, and increasing as they moved deeper into this new terrain, the variety of plants, red, green, and purple, growing sparsely among the rocks drew the girl's eye. Many were familiar to her from the markets of Acre.

Khali had learned many things from her mother before her death. Arming her daughter with all she knew about surviving alone, she instructed Khali at a very young age in the virtues of certain plants. She thought of Broussard as she studied the small chaotic gardens among the passing rocks. She thought of his wounds, and suddenly, faced with the possibility of helping him, she allowed her mind to linger more on the fact that they were not healing well.

"Just beyond the pass will be Qulzum." Shahin's voice drifted to St. Ives from the lead camel through the rising tendrils of desert heat. "We will reach the sea tonight."

With an effort, St. Ives unclouded his vision and pulled his eyes away from the girl's shoulders. The last he recalled, they had still been in the sea of sand. Now he found their caravan between the rocky cliffs of a mountainous pass. Through the fog of his exhaustion, he steadied his thoughts until he could achieve some level of focus. He felt a thought reverberating in his weakening mind. *King's X.*

"I was asleep!" St. Ives called out in alarm.

Broussard turned quickly in his saddle, riding along side the girl, "What did you see?"

Khali did not quite understand their conversation, but the unusual alarm in Broussard's voice made her nervous. She turned toward the agitated figure of St. Ives riding behind her, and heard the uncertainty in his voice as he spoke.

"He is near."

Shahin had stopped his camel to wait for the others to catch up. Riding along side them now he could make little sense of their words.

"What are you talking about? Who is near?"

"We must get underway," Broussard announced. "How soon can you secure a boat?"

"I don't know," Shahin protested, "I don't spend much time in Qulzum."

"We will find one, then," Broussard decided, in what Khali felt was an ominous tone that foreshadowed more bloodshed.

"They will be upon us soon." St. Ives said with some certainty.

De Buci cocked an eyebrow at the youngest Templar. "How can you be sure of that?"

"I do not know," St. Ives stammered, searching his own thoughts for comprehension and a better explanation. "He was near."

St. Ives turned in the saddle to study the expanse of red behind them. The desert was vacant but for a thickening cloud of churned sand rising from where the footprints of their own caravan disappeared beyond the horizon.

"I felt it strongly." St. Ives studied the red cloud. "He is near."

Shahin and Khali understood that all three Christians seemed to be in agreement on one thing. Despite Nadeem's trickery and the distance covered through the wastes of Sinai, their pursuer was upon them.

***

Broussard was the more nimble of the two, and he found the trail to ascend the Western rocks of the pass to Qulzum faster than De Buci. Despite the noticeable stiffening of his wounded thigh and the pain that pulsed with each heartbeat beneath the injured muscle as he climbed, Broussard quickly reached an overlook with a suitable view of the desert to the North. De Buci lagged behind, but not so far that Broussard could not hear him wheezing as his body protested the ascent.

As the sinking sun pulled a violet shroud across the dome of the sky above the red sand, Broussard watched the dust cloud following their fresh tracks. The Mongol was only a few miles behind them and heading for the pass below where St. Ives waited patiently, keeping vigil over their guide.

"They are coming!" Broussard called down to De Buci.

The older Templar seemed grateful for the opportunity to halt his climb. He paused long enough to catch his breath before shouting, "How many?" De Buci had counted only a dozen other camels in that village. He hoped that far fewer had returned from Nadeem's ruse in time for the Mongol's departure.

Broussard squinted into the distance, doubting his eyes against the fading light. One camel and one rider clad in black stood out clearly amidst the sea of red sand. The witch was coming for them, alone. Even as he mulled this in his thoughts, he watched the wind-blown dust rise behind the Mongol in a cloud that seemed unnatural.

"Come up here and tell me what *you* see." Broussard called back to him without turning away from the fast moving camel and the swirling cloud expanding behind it.

De Buci rolled his eyes at the thought of more climbing, spit once onto the rocks, and started again toward Broussard.

Broussard stepped to the side so the wheezing De Buci could put his hands on the rock and peer over.

"One rider," De Buci said as he pondered the red swirl in the rider's wake. "Sebastien," De Buci asked. "What do you know of Beaujeu's order?"

"*King's X*," Broussard musingly spoke the words. "Likely just as much as Beaujeu expects me to know. Nothing."

"Yes," De Buci said thoughtfully, as if laying out the details of a plan in his mind. "I think it's time you learned what little I know."

"What more do you know, De Buci?"

"I know the path."

Chapter Thirty-Seven

For hours after her denial, Jacob stalked Molly through the over stuffed shelves of his bookstore. She felt his presence constantly, silent, watchful, waiting for revelation to strike. Molly had claimed to remember only bits and pieces of Rachel's life. This was true, as she did not yet recall everything. But it was also true that she knew what the old couple had waited many years for. Rachel had been their daughter. They awaited her return. Molly's denial was cruel, but it was far less cruel than the realities of her life that Rachel had kept hidden from them.

Book did not trust the old man. He chaffed at the pressure put on Molly to answer bizarre questions about the impossible delusions everyone in this shop seemed to share. Molly avoided Jacob as best she could. She stayed silent and as close to Book as the young detective would allow.

"Does your knee hurt?" Molly sat on the same ottoman where Book rested his leg.

He held his eyes firmly closed, trying to sleep despite the constant, spiking throbs of pain shooting up his leg from his knee.

"No."

She regarded him for a moment, aware of his lie. She wished she could help ease his pain.

"Hey, Kid?" He opened his eyes and her gaze fell. "Can I ask you a question?"

"I told you," she warned, aware that the old man stood within earshot. "I don't remember anything else."

"Yeah. I know." He didn't want to hear any more memories.

"What question, then?"

"Don't take this the wrong way, but..." Book fished around for whatever he had been thinking about while his knee kept him awake. *The Savior of the world is about to awaken*, the crazy old man lurking just behind a bookshelf had said. "Do you think...?" With no delicate way to phrase his question, he suspected that Molly would appreciate the bluntness. "Are you crazy?"

Molly looked up at him, showing no sign of offense. "Do you think I am?"

Molly was the most obviously insane person he had seen since his father.

"No. I don't think so. I want to know if *you* think you're crazy."

"Not anymore. No."

They watched each other for several moments, trying to judge the other's true thoughts. Molly broke into a smile. It was the first time in a long while Molly had smiled at all, and the first time Book had seen it. Another level of her beauty opened to him, sudden and unexpected. He thought to look away. Instead, Book gave in to his own smile, rising as a reflex to hers. They remained locked together in this moment, sharing the odd camaraderie of this impossible circumstance, each warmed by a new face appearing on the other.

"So, you don't think you are Jesus, like the old man does?"

"No, I don't think I'm Jesus." Molly thought it over as she answered. "But there is a lot more for me to remember. I am certain of that. I have lived many times before, as have you, as have we all. The only difference between you and me is that, in time, I will remember everything."

The sound of Jacob rearranging books on the shelf, working his way closer to them, dimmed the growing intensity of their connection. Each looked away.

Molly's smile faded and Book's expression became grim once more. He was working something inscrutable through the cogs of his mind.

"That's why you seem to be so..." he fished for the smartest sounding word he could think of but only came up with, "...smart?"

"I carry the memories and wisdom of many lives within me."

"So, if you're not crazy," Book nodded thoughtfully, convinced she was at least telling him the truth as it seemed to her. "Then what's really going on?"

"A war."

"A war over what? What do they... the Enemy... What do they want?"

"They have what they want. They control the entire world and all that's in it. Except for the few people who know the first secret."

Book recalled Jacob's cryptic words about the first of *two great secrets*.

"That they exist."

"Yes. They exist. As far as I can tell, they always have, guarding their secrets jealously, watching over the rest of us, and maintaining the sad state of affairs we call humanity, by means of an illusion."

"What illusion?"

"That you were born to die and that, as they say, is that. When you're dead you're dead, you know?"

"When you're dead, you're not?"

"No. You're not. No one dies, Book. And they work very hard to keep us from knowing that. We can discuss it, create theories and religions about it, but we can't *know* for sure. That is how they keep us uncertain, afraid, and docile."

"Like sheep." Book again considered the words of Jacob. "But a *war* needs two sides. Who's on our side?"

"There are others. People like me. We are few, linked by secrets as carefully kept as the Enemy's. We are all that stands against them. A Legion of the Dead."

"Dead?"

"Anyone who has worn Rachel's ring, who has had it bond to their flesh as I described before, will return with a memory of that life time, and every life led since.

"*King's X* is the secret name chosen long ago. The King's mark. The fact of his signet ring is now known to the world even if it is only fantasy, a game known to children everywhere. On the playground it is the rule that changes all rules. And so on this battlefield, it is the weapon that burns the veil of illusion. It is proof that nothing you see is *true*."

"*All is permitted*," Book completed the verse. "My father said that was a weapon.

"Yes. It means that you are only limited by what you can be convinced to believe. And that knowledge is a very powerful weapon against the Enemy's illusions."

"The Enemy just doesn't make sense to me." Book pushed through to what he saw as the heart of his argument. "Why would anybody want to fool us all?"

"Writing a few hundred years ago, Milton put the words into the mouth of Satan. *It is better to rule in hell than to serve in heaven.*"

The words of Jacob returned to him, helpfully pushing Book closer to disbelief.

"You're saying that you've been fighting a war..." Book found all the comfort of skepticism returning with renewed strength. "...against the *devil?*"

Molly's eye caught Jacob where he stood between the shelves, moving his hand in the sign of the cross at Book's question.

"They hide in the open where no one thinks to look." The girl spoke with the unmoved tone of a master teacher, who had answered such questions a thousand times. "Their great secret is something that everybody knows, but no one knows for sure. Its meaning is something all of us have heard many times, but from voices we learn not to trust. They speak the truth through the mouths of liars until no one can tell the difference and everyone is lost. Everyone but them." She looked up at Book from her casual pose and found his distrustful eyes waiting for her. "Every prophet has known their secret. But great men can always be marginalized, burned at the stake, nailed to a cross, or shot in the head to keep you from knowing what they discovered. The devil, Iblis... all cultures speak of an enemy who is the Father of Lies." She shrugged and leaned back against the table. "Believe what you want. The enemy can always use that against you."

"And that's what *you* believe?"

"It is entirely possible that the Enemy is just like me, only far older and, therefore, far 'smarter.' But who they really are..." the girl sighed. "...just depends on your point of view."

"Okay, then. What's your point of view, Molly?"

She thought for a moment, and then she shrugged. "The wise have always used stories to convey important information, so it could be handed down from generation to generation openly, with no need to hide from the Enemy. The ancient Greeks told the story of Prometheus, who stole the secret of fire from the gods as a gift for mankind. He ran from the gods with their secret for a very long time, keeping one step ahead of the hounds."

Book listened intently to the story. Jacob shifted closer to them.

"Eventually they caught him," Molly continued, "but the secret was already out in the world, known and carefully guarded by a wise few."

Book's thoughts fixed on his father, perpetually chased by hounds only he could see, hounds which eventually caught up to him.

"What happened when they caught him?"

Her eyes strayed to a spot on the floor as she drifted through the vast landscape of her coalescing memories.

"They crucified him on the side of a mountain. There, immortal Prometheus would burn in the sun while a vulture devoured his liver every day. Every night, his wounds would heal so that the next day he would again burn in the sun while a vulture ate his liver. This went on for ten times ten thousand years." Her eyes turned once more to Book's, his brow furrowed and scrutinizing. "That's my point of view. At least, that's what it feels like sometimes."

Chapter Thirty-Eight

"We must fight," St. Ives demanded upon hearing the news when Broussard and De Buci returned from the rocks.

"We can not stop the mission," De Buci insisted, undeterred from his slow but steady plotting.

Khali had returned from a patch of flowering plants, carrying in her robe a small treasure gathered in the waning moments of sunlight - white petals, green stems and purple leaves. She watched them in silence as she approached, her anxiety growing at the tones of a heating argument.

"Broussard saw twenty fighting men on that beach. We are only three," De Buci calmly announced.

"He saw one man in the desert." St. Ives itched for the fight.

"I saw what Broussard saw." De Buci wanted to fight, too. They all did. Yet it remained his responsibility to choose the time and place, with no room for poor judgment.

Khali watched Broussard. His back was to the darkening slash of scarlet above the Western wall of the pass, his face obscured in the encroaching gloom of evening, but she knew the expression it carried. She imagined the look of the kill on him. She had seen it already many times, and it was there again somewhere within his silhouette.

Shahin stood uneasily where his camel rested in the sand. He ground his teeth absently, a reflex to distract from the knowledge that he was at the mercy of the decisions these men made. He distracted himself from the sense that their pursuer posed greater danger than even the Templars suspected, and his growing fear over the price Nadeem may have paid to ransom his ship in Cyprus. Yet he could not distract himself from the one overriding truth that had moved him steadily for a week now. If his people were to ever be safe again, these men owned him as surely as a slave, and he was subject to their will, wherever it led them. A time would come when he might change that circumstance, but for now he ground his teeth.

De Buci studied the rising bluffs on either side, which funneled the desert toward the lights of Qulzum, now burning in the distance, until his mind could gradually reach a decision. "St. Ives and I will wait for the Mongol in the desert, in the pass outside of Qulzum."

"What?" Broussard protested.

"The mission must continue, Sebastien. You are healing, but still of less use in this fight. It does no good to send the pirate and the girl on alone. I have told you the way. Now you must go. We will cover your escape, and stop the witch here in the desert."

"The camels would have returned to that village eventually," Shahin interjected, with little hope of influencing the decision. "What if there were men in the dust behind him?"

"There is always dust in the desert. And that was not enough dust for so many to hide behind. I saw one man. It is my decision. We will wait for him here. And we will kill him. If anyone else is with him, we will kill them, too." De Buci reached beneath his robes, retrieved Beaujeu's letter, and held it out to Broussard. "We will catch up to you on the path."

Khali still could not see his face, but she knew Broussard was displeased as he took the letter in silence. She knew little of their mission, but Khali still wondered which was the lesser evil, for them to stay and battle a man even these men seemed to fear, or to press on into the even greater uncertainty ahead. She found herself trusting Broussard's sword more than the road. She said nothing, and he could not read her face in the darkness when he looked toward her, but Khali was growing more afraid of the unknown and more accustomed to bloodshed. If she had been allowed a voice at this crossroads, she would have preferred to let these men do what they seemed born to do. She would have seen them stand together and fight.

***

Like smoke from a fast moving fire, the red cloud plumed behind the black figure and thickened the wind in the waning moments of light. De Buci and St. Ives stood their ground in his path, their swords driven into the sand an arms length away, rising from the earth before them like two crucifixes.

The witch slowed his camel to a walk, then stopped within twenty paces of the two Templars. As the trailing dust cloud began to swirl like a fog around him, the golden man studied them where they stood, blocking his path to Qulzum.

"Who are you?" De Buci demanded over the soft murmur of the prayer St. Ives repeated beside him. "What do you want?"

The Mongol considered the two men as the swirling red cloud enveloped them, too.

"I am a humble Shepherd on the trail of strays." He spoke in slow, methodical French, which might have seemed odd to De Buci, had he not suddenly found himself fighting the pull of an invisible thread at the sound of his voice. "Tell me..." the Shepherd continued, "where do you go now, and what is the meaning of your orders?" Then he spoke the word he had earlier seen written in the thoughts of St. Ives. *"King's X."*

De Buci stood his ground, struggling against an unnatural desire to speak. He turned for a moment to find St. Ives lost in the prayer he had begun before the witch even came into view.

St. Ives' eyes remain fixed in a narrow tunnel to the Mongol's chest, only his lips moving in silent supplication.

Et ne nos inducas in tentationem, sed libera nos a malo. Amen. Pater noster, qui es in caelis...

For De Buci, the pull of the witch was too strong. Even as he opened his mouth to speak, he saw the foresight of Beaujeu. He knew so little.

"The secrets of the Temple. What was found has been hidden away." Yet knowing so little, knowing not what was real and what was legend, he could not know what he might give away.

"What was found?" the Shepherd asked.

"Secrets," De Buci sputtered as he felt control slipping away. Yet, even as he struggled, he saw that St. Ives, still locked behind his veil of devotion and concentration, had found a defense.

"Secrets?" The voice traveled the distance over the sand like a whisper, only to reverberate like a shout in De Buci's mind.

"*Pater noster,*" the old soldier began, closing his eyes to the sight of the red sand swirling around the black form. "*Qui es in caelis, sanctificetur nomen tuum...*"

"Secrets?" The whispered word rang out like a hammer to stone.

Unable to turn his head, De Buci heard St. Ives' prayer grow louder as the storm of sand and wind enveloped them and the young knight fought to remain lost in his reverie.

For St. Ives, the familiar prickling of flesh before a fight had returned. He remained ready, his eyes locked on the heart of his enemy and not his eyes, his words directed to heaven, and his soul in the hands of his God.

De Buci abandoned his prayer against his will and continued at the Mongol's bidding,

"The Wisdom of Solomon, the eternal secrets..." As he fought for control, he tried again to interject his prayer, even as the invisible string dragged his thoughts into the open air. *"Adveniat regnum tuum."* He held onto those words in his mind with all of his fading strength, their meaning drifting vaguely to him.

Two thoughts hit him simultaneously. The first was in answer to the witch's demand, and the words continued to flow from him like water.

"The Seal of Solomon..."

"The *Seal!*" The Mongol's voice struck harder, as he had at last uncovered what he sought. "The Seal."

St. Ives paused at the mighty echo of the witch's words, but his eyes remained fixed and the power of his God flowed through him as he continued to invite it.

Adveniat regnum tuum. Fiat voluntas tua, sicut in caelo et in terra.

De Buci was powerless before this enemy. Whether he spoke of legend, truth, or secrets he did not comprehend, he knew he betrayed his Order and his Oath more with each question.

"Tell me," came the whispered thunder again. "Where is it hidden?"

"St. Ives!" De Buci called to his comrade, shouting into the gale. "The enemy is me! *Strike!*"

With the speed of reflex, a lack of hesitation that surprised even the Shepherd, St. Ives obeyed.   Before the possibility of his action even occurred to the Mongol, the young Templar snatched his weapon from the sand before him, wheeled on his heel and severed his comrade's head from his shoulders, the blade passing from the back of the neck through the front in an instant.

De Buci's body hung in the desert air for a moment before toppling like felled living wood into the sand. St. Ives stood at the ready, his sword stained at its heart by a swath of fresh crimson. He returned his stare to the center of his enemy's chest, unmoved but for the prickling flesh at the back of his neck.

Pater noster, qui es in caelis, sanctificetur nomen tuum.

The golden man remained still for a moment, sizing up the young soldier and listening to his prayer on the wind.

Adveniat regnum tuum. Fiat voluntas tua, sicut in caelo et in terra.

"Thy Kingdom Come..." The whisper returned the words to St. Ives over the warm sand. The familiar sounds of his own prayer encroached on his reverie for an instant, pulling him a little further from his God and closer to the witch. "...Thy will be done, on earth as it is in heaven."

St. Ives, in that momentary lapse, raised his eyes to the golden face, and became ensnared.

"You have no secrets to give, young soldier." The Mongol's voice rang with an odd note of compassion, and despite himself, St. Ives looked deeper into his hooded eyes.

With a wave of his hand, the red dust that had swirled around him like mist began to dissipate and part.

"Let me give you a secret, then. Let me teach you a Truth your betters have kept hidden from you all this time. Learn this well, young Templar, because even as it sets you free from your bondage, this lesson will be your last."

The Mongol remained seated. Behind him, first as moving shadows within the red cloud, then as walking men leaving behind their mounts, the impossible alliance Broussard had seen began to emerge from the depths of the swirling sand. He studied the slow approach and long stares of Durand, Leveque, Van Cuso and a host of Saracens.

St. Ives gripped his own weapon tightly, took a step forward and drew De Buci's blade from the sand where it still stood. The prickle of skin at the back of his neck turned to a stinging. A smile of anticipation came to his lips.

At last, with two dozen Assassins standing weapons in hands and within striking distance of the young man, the witch whispered his secret. "The Kingdom is here. Now. Spread upon the earth. And men do not see."

Chapter Thirty-Nine

Trudie knew that Molly slept because she had watched her, checking in from time to time in the deepest hours of the night, to see that her chest rose and fell, that her eyes darted about beneath their lids as she dreamt, that her husband was not disturbing her, and that the young policeman remained on the couch they had moved into the room so that he would not have to sleep on the floor. Trudie waited with Jacob for sleep to bring Molly to the truth they longed to hear. They waited for Rachel.

Instead, just as it had occurred so many years ago with their own daughter, the girl grew increasingly quiet as she seemed to settle steadily back into the emerging young woman she had been before the dreams started.

Sleep, in comfort and without fear, had removed some of the wild animal from Molly's face, and returned to her the look of a pretty young girl. Whatever great depths were rising to the surface within her, Molly was still herself, still a young girl, the same one she had been before the dreams began.

Once it became clear to her that the dangers which had chased her to this place and which still awaited her outside had no real strength within the sanctuary of the bookshop, Molly gradually accepted the opportunity to become clean, to wear fresh and pretty clothes, and to once again stand before a mirror with a hair brush, without concern for what may be creeping toward her from behind or lurking in shadowy blind spots. But if sleep also continued to bring with it the dreams others waited for, Molly kept quiet about them.

Instead, the girl kept a close orbit around Detective Book by day, never straying too far from where he sat with his ruined leg propped on a pillow. Trudie had seen the silent exchanges that passed between them. She had seen the young man seek to hide the pain of a terribly swollen knee, which only seemed to worsen with time. He could not seek medical care without endangering both himself and the girl. She had seen the girl awkwardly look to his comfort and delight in creating it. She had recognized the look on her face, the kind that comes from a longing in her stomach and chest, as Molly tentatively presented herself to him, as if for the first time, with those pretty clothes, clean skin, and her newly soft and shimmering auburn hair. Book, quite aware of the desire in the girl's heart, even if unaware of his own, struggled not to notice the changes Molly worked so hard to make him see.

And finally, as he studied the shock of the day's newspaper, Trudie saw the pain of his other life as it died before his eyes.

Book's progressing death in the world outside their shop had no antidote. It grew steadily worse the longer he read, until it was perfectly clear even to him, that no one outside this haven would ever welcome him again or shelter him from the righteous hunters now scouring the city for him.

Book did not seem a man accustomed to helplessness, but he did understand loss, and how to put it behind him. Trudie saw the shadow of that pain cross his face throughout the day, only to be sublimated and swallowed like so much nasty medicine. He was harsh and cold before the world, but Trudie could see that, despite his great losses, he sensed his purpose. Perhaps for the first time. Whether he could think of her as the woman she wanted him to see, or still saw her as the girl she was when she had arrived, he was here for Molly, just as Jacob had said. On some level that knowledge short-circuited the anguish he might have felt at the disintegration of his own life.

Always near him, like a bird that never strays too far from the safety of her favorite tree, Molly read in silence from Jacob's vast and dusty library or stared at nothing in particular, lost someplace far away within herself. During these times, Trudie occasionally saw her husband trying to intrude on the girl's veil of thought. Their longing, so close to resolution, was too cruel an irony. Through the tangled briars of time, she had returned to them, only to arrive as a selfish young girl with nothing in particular to say.

For two nights, Molly had slept in peace, and with sleep came many dreams. Those dreams, which had formerly left her screaming in her own bed, had slowly been replaced by new images. As it had been in her mother's house with those long-passed final moments of life, waning in the gloom of flickering firelight, her new dreams played in her thoughts more like distant memory than fantasy. Even as the others in the bookshop kept close watch over her, occasionally making her feel more like a laboratory animal in a cage than a girl trapped in this place by circumstance, Molly's growing understanding of the dream images made her less afraid. She began to see that not all of the past was made up of pain. Images flowed to her from memories so deeply tapped, they engaged all of her senses at once. For the first time in weeks, Molly saw that life could be much more than a dread of the moment of death, but rather could be filled with sensations greater in joy than even the worst instances could attain in terror.

In sleep, her mind took her through experience after experience along time's river, each moment having long ago merged with its ocean. Though much remained dark, what she could see she recalled clearly, as if she could claim past greatnesses for her own. Her unconscious mind became a playground of new but excitingly familiar thoughts. She quickly grew eager for as much sleep as she could get.

Each dream left warm impressions of one pleasantness or another. She might savor the taste of a sweet tea taken one leisurely afternoon in the shaded cool of an English wood, and find that it still warmed her even as she lay awake in her cot, or find herself waking to a sublime triumph of comprehension. She saw herself reflected in a dark shallow pool, her face looking back from beneath floating white lotus blossoms and from deeper than the lazing koi, her hair draped like black silk to frame a face of golden skin and soft, brown, hooded eyes. Above the water as her body was, and yet within it as was her reflection, she felt keenly and for the first time a part of the world. The light that created the image was the same as the power that ignited her thought, the same as the energy then trapped within the form of her body. She was. She is. She watched the reflected image silently mirror the movements of her mouth as she spoke. *Imasu.*

While Jacob waited with growing impatience for the word of God to pour forth from her each morning, Molly awakened to feelings so new and so private, she felt at times like a voyeur in her own thoughts. Michael was a kind and handsome man. Rachel had been drawn to him from the very beginning, the day she had come to him to have her broken arm set after a fall from a bicycle. She resisted him, for his sake, but he was strong and fearless. Not even the truth stopped him from wanting her and marrying her.

On the morning of her third day at the bookshop, Molly awoke flushed, feeling peaceful and content. The memory of Rachel's wedding night, and her first true embrace from Michael had come to her as a moment more tender and loving than any she had even imagined as a schoolgirl kissing boys at dances. With all the desire she had carried to be free of Rachel's body as it fell among the dead in the pit during the last moments of life, here Molly had never wanted to remain a part of something more.

She slipped back into consciousness with the lingering sensation that Michael was still with her, still at her side. Upon opening her eyes, she instead found Jacob's stern glare and brown teeth staring down at her as he leaned above the bed.

"What did you see, child?" He begged.

Molly shrunk into her pillow. "I..." she stammered, blushing at the odd sensation of having Rachel's privacy invaded combined with the feeling of getting caught at something she shouldn't be doing.

"Give her a chance to wake up first," Book warned from the couch. He sounded annoyed, either because he had just been woken up or for Molly's sake. "Why don't you just wait outside?"

Molly, greatly relieved by Book's presence, watched Jacob's head pivot between the detective and herself until she nodded to him as well. "Please?" she asked politely.

"That looked like a good one," Book smiled at her after Jacob had apologized for startling her and left the room.

Molly blushed again, wondering for a moment if he could somehow know what she had been doing. "What do you mean?" she asked, making certain her sheets covered her.

"You didn't wake up screaming for one thing. You even had a smile on your face."

"How long were you watching me?"

Now it was Book who seemed suddenly embarrassed. "I wasn't. I mean... Jacob woke me up when he came in just a minute ago. Listen, do you...?" Book stammered. "I mean, since you don't seem to need it anymore, do you want me to stop sleeping in here?"

Molly yawned lazily. She stared at Book while she contentedly stretched under the covers, letting the sound of his voice wash over her without really hearing what he said. She drifted back through Rachel's memories as if they were her own, and she felt no need at all to fight the sensation.

Book was not much like Michael. Michael was thin and angular. What she recalled most about him were his hands. They were delicate and powerful all at once, as one might expect the hands of a surgeon to be. He was gentle, while Book seemed closer to the opposite. The detective was intelligent, but not refined. Molly began to wonder what Book's hands might feel like compared with the touch of Rachel's gentle surgeon, when she caught herself slipping and grew suddenly more awake.

"What? Oh..." she saw Book's face change as he puzzled over her embarrassment and, though he couldn't possibly imagine what was in her mind, she grew even more flushed at the feeling of being caught once again. "No. Please stay."

"Okay."

He still seemed a bit embarrassed, and Molly wondered for a moment what he had been thinking. She continued to watch him until, either to ward off any further humiliation, or because he was still tired after Jacob's intrusion, he shut his eyes and quickly fell back asleep.

Molly turned her head away from his sleeping form with an effort. She slid out of bed and reached for the clean, flowery sundress Trudie had laid out for her the night before. In the mirror, the image of the sixteen-year-old girl surprised her. So real was her dream just moments ago, she might have expected to see a woman looking back at her.

Over the shoulder of the girl in the mirror, Molly saw Book again, eyes closed and struggling for comfort underneath his thin blanket. She remembered how Rachel had tried to protect Michael from the truth. Finally, she recalled the face of the Shepherd. His hair had been short and jet-black then, long bangs slicked back in the style of the day. Within the shadow of his dark cashmere coat, his gloves and shoes were of the finest leather. Curious, Rachel had thought, that he would take the time and expend the energy to dress so well. It had always seemed to her that a man of such knowledge and awareness should be beyond vanity. Despite the difference in age from the Shepherd Molly had seen only days ago, the eyes of the man Rachel had known resonated just as clearly with the same cold anger and unrelenting malice. It was the same man. He had successfully followed her trail from one lifetime to the next.

Rachel could not defeat him. Rather she had lost everything again, and had merely purchased a little more time with her own life. Even if she had somehow beaten the Shepherd in Warsaw, there would always be another such man waiting to take his place. Rachel had merely preserved the fight, again, for another day, another time. That time was coming, soon.

Molly looked into her own face and steeled herself with a steady inhale, feeling powerfully the old sense of re-birth. Butterfly from cocoon. Or, as it more darkly occurred, serpent from old skin. Yet, through the haze of her memories, one thing was certain. She was young and strong. Again.

She checked quickly to see that Book was asleep before she slipped out of the T-shirt she had worn to bed and into the dress. Even as Molly fell back into admiring herself for a moment in the mirror, part of her, perhaps the part that had been Rachel, filled her with a calming strength that left her heartbeat steady, and braced her for what lay ahead. And yet another part of her, deeper still, knew that every moment of safety stolen in this bookshop only added to the toll to be paid by her protectors, the kindly old man and his trusting wife, and the young detective who watched over her as she slept.

From that greater depth within her, Molly felt the rising of something very old, climbing into her awareness like the memory of a forgotten scent. She began to feel the familiar pull of resolve, and the calming heat of courage. Strangely familiar qualities of character, she thought, because Molly never had cause to summon them in the past. Her life had been too safe to need courage, and too easy to develop resolve.

As she looked again at her sleeping guardian, Molly knew she was sensing the death throes of fate, and the first dawning of new possibilities. The ring was lost. Her long flight had finally ended in failure. But it had ended, nonetheless. Free of her burden, she might at last be able to choose her own path.

The image of the Shepherd, of the malice burning in his eyes two days ago, twenty-four years ago, and perhaps countless other encounters still obscured in the fog of time, remained in her thoughts. Choice. Her heart quickened with desire for it. The last act of the hunted fox could be to turn on the hound and fight. Her path could be vengeance.

***

Trudie dusted the empty cash register, listening contentedly to the chorus of raindrops striking the pavement outside the store. Three sharp knocks on the wood and glass door broke her peaceful moment, sending a muffled jingle through the dusty bell and a shiver of alarm through the shopkeeper's wife. Peering at her through the glass was a middle-aged man in a wrinkled suit, fat and slightly winded from his walk down the sidewalk.

Trudie moved closer, masking her concern as best as she could.

"I'm sorry, Sir, but we're closed."

The man fished out his wallet, held it open, and pressed his policeman's badge to the glass with a definitive and intimidating tap.

Trudie's mask began to crack.

"I'll get my husband."

***

Molly stood over Book, watching his chest move with slow and silent breaths. She studied his determined face, lines of wisdom already appearing around his eyes from a short lifetime of pain and dark concerns.

Molly considered him where he lay for a moment longer, as if waiting for some event or revelation she could not foresee. When she was certain that he slept, she moved silently closer, reaching a delicate hand to touch his face. She felt the coarseness of his days-old beard and took in the scent of his hair, compelled toward him by something she could not understand or by something she could not recall.

She softly kissed his mouth, though she had not intended to. She allowed her kiss to linger on his lips, despite the danger.

A scent spiced with cedar in the air, a taste like sweet milk on his lips, Book drifted back to consciousness as if from an old memory. He found Molly sitting by his hip, on the edge of his couch, looking down at him with warm sadness.

Caught then in the unfathomable pools within her eyes, a question came to him without warning. He asked it.

"Who are you?"

She watched him, searching her own thoughts for the truth.

"I don't know. Not really." She wished she could say something that would satisfy. "Much is still secret to me."

Book saw that she would answer if she could. *Secret.* He loathed the word. He searched for a better question. "Molly," he ventured the thought cautiously, not sure what it would sound like when spoken aloud, "what happens to you when you...?" The absurdity of it made the words dry up before he could finish.

"Die?" she offered helpfully.

"Yes," he admitted.

"Our power is here, Book." Molly spoke with vague conviction. "Now and only now. What you do in your sleep means nothing. It's what you do when you are awake that counts. What happens to you after you're dead isn't the point. It's what you do after you're born that makes all the difference."

Book studied her face for a moment. "Where do you go? What's it like?"

She flashed a subtly mischievous smile before giving the only answer she could. "I don't really know." She shrugged. "Time passes. It happens in a cycle."

"A cycle? You mean it's always the same?" A new thought clicked into Book's mind. "How much time passes?"

"Twenty-four years."

The tightening of his brow threatened to reveal the puzzle as Book continued to work through it. Twenty-four years.

"So, then Rachel must have died..." Book pretended to calculate in his head, but he already knew the answer. *June 4th, 1944.* "...sometime in 1944?"

"I started to have the dreams last summer. In June."

Book's eyes were as wide as saucers and he knew it. He quickly thought of a new question. "But you're only sixteen. What about those missing years?"

"I'm telling you what I know, Book. I just don't remember anything about that."

Book dismissively sank back with his eyes closed.

Another silence hung between them. Molly watched him pretending to ignore her, and Book searched for a better question, a way to see how this girl could possibly be all of the things she seemed to be. His eyes flashed open to find hers waiting.

"What is the Second Secret?" he asked. "Jacob said that the existence of the Enemy is the first secret the Shepherds protect. But he said there was something else. A bigger secret."

Molly watched him carefully. He seemed to grow uncomfortable with their closeness. She moved her hand from where it rested on his chest to her lap. And the particular question he asked made it easy for her to remove the warmth from her voice. "That is the greatest secret I know," she quietly announced in a tone that seemed contemptuous. "But it is useless to hear the words unless you can understand them. It is useless unless you believe." She turned her focus toward a random spot on the floor, and Book grew more certain of the subtle acid in her voice. "It is useless to me, because for all I have seen and all I have known, I still don't understand. I still don't believe."

"Understand what? What is the secret?"

To Molly, his powerful body seemed to hide a child who ached to understand why a hard lesson must bring so much pain. For a moment, she thought she might be beginning to see what had eluded her for so long. But the pain of knowing what was to come brought the old anger back to her, anger that masked the terror always lurking in the silence, dread of the sheer scope of her knowledge and the weight of her burden. She could not *believe*, not then, not now, perhaps not ever. She spoke her useless secret.

"There is nothing to fear."

Book saw a shadow cross the girl's face. Was this the answer to his question? If it was, he did not understand. And he certainly did not believe.

"Why? Why the hell shouldn't we be afraid?"

Molly watched the curious child in Book recede once more before the secret fears and misplaced pride of a grown man. She wished she could offer more. She searched as deep as her obscured memories would allow. Mountains of studied and learned thought seemed to add up to no adequate response. She could find no answer but an old, vague notion that might just as easily have come from Molly's own schooling with the nuns in Virginia than from any past lifetime. "Because of God, I suppose." The words were weak and without any particular conviction.

Book's face involuntarily contorted into a derisive sneer and disdain poisoned his voice.

"What God is that?"

"I can't remember." She closed her mind to it, leaving him to the puzzle even as the sound of fast moving footsteps over creaking wood grew louder outside the door.

"Book!" Trudie called out in a hoarse whisper as she approached. Molly surged to her feet and Book was just climbing to his when the old woman rushed through the door to the room, wild-eyed and frightened. "They are here!"

"Who?" Book demanded as he reached for his boots.

"The police! Hurry! You must go. Now!"

Book led Molly by the hand across the hall to a window that overlooked the street in front of the shop.

"Jacob has turned the officer away," Trudie continued as if they hadn't understood. "But he will be back. There will be more."

From the window, Molly saw two uniformed policemen enter the grocery store across the street. She shuddered at an old memory, Rachel's memory, of a time when police walked city streets like wolves.

Book watched the street for several moments before breaking into an uncertain smile at the welcome sight of a friend. Frank Harker rounded the corner where the phone booth stood. He was leading two more uniformed officers toward the bookshop. Book's smile faded as he worked the circumstances through his mind. They were searching in a pattern that spread to every building within an expanding circle around the phone booth. Frank had traced his call.

Book puzzled over his friend, unsure if his coming was the answer to a prayer or the continuation of the nightmare. He only dimly heard Molly's words through the pounding of his own thoughts.

"Is there a way out from up here?" she asked.

"No," Trudie answered softly. "Only from downstairs."

Molly continued to watch the street below, her senses electrified like those of a hunted animal just catching the scent of her pursuers, already too close. "We've got to go." Molly insisted, quietly. "Now."

Trudie knew something of wolves at the door, as well. Even as her gentle husband arrived at her side to take her hand in his, through her rising terror at the sound of wood splintering under a policeman's boot downstairs, she managed a weak acknowledgement of defeat.

"Too late."

Chapter Forty

"That one." Shahin pointed to a masted boat only slightly smaller than the *Gull*, tied among several lesser craft along a short pier. "She's got a good sail and will give us more speed than any of the others."

Broussard rose from the shadows and strode silently toward the water. After an annoyed but barely audible grunt of alarm at the Templar's eagerness, Shahin followed, pulling Khali by the hand and swiveling about to search for anyone who might be watching as they moved under the thin light of the rising moon.

The fisherman burst awake as a powerful hand, clutching hard at his robe and a stinging handful of the black curls on his chest, jerked him from his hammock. His first thought, as he looked uncomprehendingly into the surreal tanned white skin of his attacker, was that he was dreaming. His second thought, as the wild-eyed man raised a heavy straight blade above his head, was that he was about to die.

"Wait." Khali touched his poised sword arm again.

Broussard paused. On his fourth night since the sight at the beach, his fourth night without sleep, his mind was dulled. His thoughts remained with his comrades, back at the rocky pass which funneled the desert into Qulzum. This was the second time he had been held out of a fight for the sake of the letter he now held beneath his robe. He felt so much anger inside, and so little of his wits remained with him, that he could not even be sure where to direct it. At the moment, he hated this fisherman for looking too much like the men he had dedicated his life to fighting in a losing battle, and for being in the way of his attempt to steal this boat. He hated the letter he carried even more.

De Buci's plan had been sound enough. Given time to prepare and a chance to choose the battleground, De Buci and St. Ives should be a safe bet against any foe. But Broussard had seen their pursuers. The fact that there were Templars among their number brought him no comfort. The tunics of Durand and Leveque still showed the blood of dead Saracens from the siege of Acre. Impossibly, Muslims and Christians rowed shoulder to shoulder in those long boats. Broussard had no explanation for what he had seen, but he knew that his old friends would die tonight for a cause none of them understood.

He also knew that De Buci was right. If the Mongol's forces had the power to kill two Templars, they had the power to destroy three. For now, his task was to put distance between the letter and the hunter at their heels.

Khalidah spoke only that one word, but Broussard understood her message. She did not want to see him kill this man. The power she seemed to hold over him angered him further. But his weapon remained suspended above them as long as her hand stayed on his arm.

"Is this your boat?" Shahin smiled at the quaking man now hanging in the Templar's grasp. As the pirate leaned closer to his face, the fisherman nodded. "Good. Maybe you can be of service to us then?" The fisherman nodded again.

Shahin turned his attention to the Templar. Though the pain remained mostly buried beneath the young man's practiced mask of strength, Shahin understood from his slightly unbalanced stance, and by the sheer effort he put forth to keep his weakness hidden, Broussard's injured leg was worsening.

"He can help sail her," Shahin slowly suggested. "We'll travel faster that way."

At last, whether it was Shahin's logic, the girl's touch, or pure exhaustion that moved him, the tension suddenly fell away from his body. Broussard dropped the fisherman back into his hammock, and lowered his sword until the tip rested on the wooden deck.

"By the way," Shahin continued, "where are we going?"

Broussard paused, thinking back over what De Buci had told him on the rocks.

"A village called Ajum. We must find horses there. Then, into the continent," Broussard said, wavering, the expenditure of strength now taking its toll.

Shahin turned back to the wide-eyed man. "Ajum. Do you know it?"

"Yes, I know it!" the fisherman volunteered with enthusiasm. "Three days journey!"

"Quietly, now," Shahin smiled. "Let's raise sail. You've got a big day ahead."

The fisherman watched the small girl lead the swordsman a few steps away, gently stroking his skin and whispering soft words to him until he sat on an empty wine cask. The fisherman studied the sword as the white man leaned on the hilt, the point digging into the deck of his boat. The European-fashioned straight blade, rarely seen in Qulzum, shone in the moonlight like a long silver cross. The fisherman looked again at Shahin, nodded his assent, and rushed to free the line.

Chapter Forty-One

Book hurried back to Molly's room as the footsteps of several police officers filled the downstairs of the bookshop. Molly stuck close behind him, as if waiting for him to enact some kind of plan that might rescue them. She watched him curiously as he snatched his bomber jacket off the peg and put it on.

"Book!" Frank Harker's voice boomed up the stairs. "It's Frank!" His friend's voice instilled in Book a feeling he had not felt since all this began. Hope. "Book, I know what's going on! It's okay!"

Book took Molly by the hand again, silently leading her past Jacob and Trudie into the hallway to listen.

"I know you didn't kill anybody, Book!" Harker continued from below. "We've got a suspect!"

"He's lying," Molly told him with quiet certainty.

"He's my friend," Book whispered to her. "Why would he...?"

"He's not your friend. They've been watching you for years. Don't you know what that means by now?"

"No."

"It means," Molly said patiently, "That many of the people around you, particularly anybody *assigned* to you, like a partner on the police force, are there for a reason."

"Frank Harker does not work for them." Book protested quietly. "I know..."

"*Everyone* works for them, Book," Jacob hissed as he chambered a round in his pistol. "Whether they know it or not."

Book looked at the weapon in the old man's hand and issued a stern warning.

"Jacob, they will kill you."

"They will kill us all," Jacob insisted, even as Trudie placed a worried hand on his arm.

"No," Molly said, resolved. "It's me they want. The chase is done. It ended with Karl Buchner, sixteen years ago. There is nothing of value to them but me, now."

"No, child." Jacob was urgent and determined. "We will fight them."

Molly released Book's hand and stepped up to the old couple. She put a hand on each of them, forming a ring of three.

"Everyone I love dies over me. I do not want that to happen again. Not to my family." Tears of relief welled in her eyes as she released her secret at last. "Not to my father. Not to my mother."

Tears of joy flowed freely from Jacob and Trudie as Molly revealed what they had already known. Years of fear and pain washed away in an instant as their child returned to them. Everything Rachel had told them long ago, all that was impossible, all that was so dreadful, and all that was so filled with hope, had been the truth. She had returned as she'd promised.

"You should not have come here." Molly insisted, still trying to deny feelings that could only bring more pain, regret, and complexity to the choices she would have to make.

If the reward for Jacob and Trudie's courage and faith could only come in their last moments together, then these would be moments of triumph and resolution. The circle collapsed around Molly. The love of a mother and father longing for a lost child flowed to her, unchecked. Molly closed her eyes tightly against the pleasure as it washed over her.

"Book!" Harker shouted from the base of the stairs. "I'm coming up!"

Molly turned away from the embrace and faced Book. She nodded her assent to his silent plea. She reached a steady hand back toward the old man.

"Give me the gun, Father."

Jacob looked deep into the eyes of a stranger, and found his daughter inside them, warm, sorrowful, loving, and resolved. He surrendered the gun to Molly.

Molly held the weapon. She looked again to Book as the wooden staircase creaked beneath heavy footsteps.

"He won't hurt us." Book spoke like a man clinging to the hope that everything he'd always known remained true and eternal, even as the weakening foundation collapsed before his eyes.

"Yes, he will." Molly whispered to him as she eyed the gun in her hand. "But not just yet. Wait for an opportunity. Don't miss it if it comes."

She took Book's hand in hers, stooped to the ground at his side, and gently slid the weapon along the floor. It stopped at the top of the stairs, just as Frank Harker arrived.

The fat policeman wheezed slightly as he paused to survey the four people awaiting him. He smiled in a friendly way Book had seen a thousand times as he picked up the gun, accepting it like a gift and a token of surrender.

"Damn, Book! Am I glad to see you!"

Book smiled uncertainly at his old friend.

"You said you have another suspect?"

"Yeah." Harker's enthusiasm remained. "Somebody else saw the guy you were talking about, long grey hair, well dressed, coming out of Sara Jamison's building."

All four silently watched Harker as he pulled out a rattling pair of handcuffs with an air of embarrassment.

"I'm real sorry about this, Book, but you've still got to come in, and I gotta put these on you."

Book glanced at the short chain between the bindings, then back again to Harker's warm, apologetic eyes.

"It's almost over, Book."

Chapter Forty-Two

Shahin studied the fisherman now piloting his vessel into the deeper blue waters, seeking out the southward current, and keeping the shores of Egypt at the western horizon. He monitored the water and their reluctant guide under the heat of the climbing Sun, until he was satisfied that they were indeed picking up speed.

After a thorough scan of the blue horizon to the North revealed no pursuing sail, Shahin turned his attention back to Khali, where she knelt beside Broussard. The Templar rested without sleeping, propped against the ship's single mast. Shahin approached slowly and unconcerned, allowing the Templar to see which of the two still preserved his strength, and which needed the support of a pole to sit upright. If the Templar noticed any shifting in power, he paid it no heed. Or, Shahin speculated with some disappointment, the Christian knew that one remained slave and the other master even into sleep, infirmity, or death as long as the Brotherhood of the Temple held his people in Cyprus.

"Do not let me sleep," Broussard commanded Shahin through weak breath and squinting eyes.

Khali looked to Shahin with uncertainty. Shahin knew that the nature of her whispering to Broussard had been to persuade the young man to sleep. Despite her diligence in tending his leg with a concoction of flowers and leaves chewed in her mouth, the yellowing wound appeared no better for her efforts. The Templar's diseased leg would kill him in time. He could see in her pleading eyes that Khali knew this, as well. Yet the Captain had no answer for her. If the Christian would not sleep, what could he do about it? And why should he help, if he could? Still, his indignation weakened at the thought of Cyprus, his dimming hopes, and the needful gaze of the girl.

"Sleep will restore some of your strength," Shahin suggested at last. "You will not reach much further without it."

The Templar continued to search for strength in stillness, and Shahin could not tell if he had been heard or was simply being ignored. Reining in his anger somewhat, he watched the girl roll more of her purple leaves into the white flowers until the soft petals became bruised and yellowed. He thought back to the overheard parting words between all three Christians in the pass above Qulzum, of the witch they believed followed them, and what St. Ives had said after falling asleep on his camel. Shahin looked past the Templar to the warm sea and clean horizon behind them.

"The sea is clear, Christian. There are no vessels before or after us. We are alone out here, making good speed to the south. Our guide assures me we will see Ajum tomorrow morning."

Broussard nodded even as he forced his eyes to open wider, as if taking in more sunlight might enliven them. Shahin shrugged for the girl, who had begun to chew a small portion of whatever it was she was creating. She flashed a frown of dissatisfaction at his efforts. Shahin turned on his heel to accentuate his displeasure with her, moving toward the low rail of the boat. He began to relieve himself over the side to give her time to realize he had done what he could. When he finished, he returned to her side, found her still silently displeased with him, and he began a new approach to the riddle of the mad Templar.

"What are you afraid of, Christian? What happens when you sleep?"

Khali removed the wet ball of chewed plant from her mouth. Despite suspiciously spitting the juices it had created on to the deck, she managed with further whispers to convince the Christian to eat it. Broussard looked up into Shahin's face, either dismayed at his question or repressing the urge to spit out the apparently vile tasting substance.

When he opened his mouth to reply, or to spit, the girl stopped him with a hard grip on his jaw and a scolding glare.

"Swallow it." She commanded.

The Templar obeyed. He swallowed three times to clear out the residual flavor before he finally spoke.

"The witch comes to our thoughts when we sleep."

Shahin crouched down on his haunches beside him, trying to pierce the mystery more directly.

"Who is this man?"

"I do not know."

Shahin recognized in the Templar's weakened demeanor that his answer was sincere.

"Why does he follow?"

"My brotherhood has many secrets. He seems to know more about them than I do."

"But not more than your Master. He wants to know where Beaujeu sends you?"

"He may know that already. That is why we must hurry. If De Buci and St. Ives were unsuccessful..." Broussard paused to ponder the fate of his friends.

"You don't have faith in your comrades?"

"Against any number of men, I do." Broussard met Shahin's searching eyes. "They were not fighting a man."

"What will you find where we go? Gold?"

Even as he spoke the word, Shahin knew that no secret store of gold could possibly match the wealth already held by the Templars, whose prowess in war and willingness to die for their God's cause had overflowed their coffers and won them vast boons of land equal perhaps to half of Europe. The Templars held wealth envied by kings and popes alike. The secrets of their *King's X* could not be mere gold.

"No." Broussard's strength faded further. "Not gold."

Shahin lingered for a moment before rising again to his full height above Broussard. He did not put much stock in witchcraft, but he knew very well that the Knights of the Temple did. The ignorant among his people considered the Templars sorcerers. Though he found the idea laughable, he also knew that a perfectly sound explanation for this journey, its secrecy, its foolhardiness, and its trailing enemy, could be found in the fact that the Templars might take the idea of sorcery quite seriously.

Shahin turned his back to the Christian and the girl and let his thoughts drift back to the land of his birth, when Al-andalus was yet the jewel of Islam. There existed stores of knowledge not seen since the burning of Alexandria by Caesar's armies. From his years as a student in the city of Cordova, Shahin recalled fantastic tales of King Solomon, the man whose Temple gave Broussard's Order its name and hidden purpose.

Then, as now, Shahin considered these to be tales for children or the weak minded. Yet he knew as well that the more powerful of these Templars, men like Beaujeu, held such tales to be much more. And such tales, whatever reality they may point to, were ever exactly the kinds of "secrets" that interested such men, and bade them spill what innocent blood might block them from digging unceasingly beneath the Temple

Mount. And dig, of course, they did. That much was known and certain.

"I recall tales," Shahin began as he watched the water, "carried down to my people through time, of Solomon the Great."

"There are many," Broussard offered as he shifted the position of his stiffening leg.

"Yes," said Shahin. "Some speak of his vast wealth, hidden away to this day in secret store houses."

"Yes."

"And some speak of..." The Captain paused, weighing whether or not invoking the word *sorcery* might entice Broussard to speak further, or to withhold more tightly what he knew.

"Power." Broussard finished Shahin's thought, working through the mystery in his own mind. "Such tales speak of power."

His back still turned, Shahin reflected over what manner of power it might be, that the Templars had so long sought, and perhaps found. Solomon had been a great king in the far distant reaches of his people's memory. Of this much Shahin could be certain, yet whatever truth there was to the life of Solomon was now veiled in fanciful tales. It was Solomon who was said to converse with lowly animals beneath and great spirits above as easily as he might talk with a man. It was Solomon who yoked the Jinn to his will and commanded the elements through the mark of God emblazoned on his signet ring. Shahin considered these fanciful notions with a growing apprehension, sifting through what he knew of the Hebrew King, searching his thoughts for what might bind them together.

"What *power*?" he asked at last. Turning slowly on his heel, he found the Christian unconscious, a trickle of discolored spittle at the corner of his open mouth.

"The flowers have done their work," Khali offered as she struggled to move Broussard's massive frame away from the mast and lower his head to the deck. "He will sleep."

"Ah." Shahin spit as the many questions he had prepared suddenly sputtered in his head. "Perfect. Well done."

Chapter Forty-Three

Book recognized the young uniformed police officer watching him and the girl from the opposite bench in the back of the police van. He didn't know him well, but he knew him by name. Benji. He was even younger than Book, married and expecting a child in the spring. Book regarded Benji as the chains of their handcuffs rattled against the anchoring pipe with each bump in the uneven pavement. He looked over the crisp uniform that declared the young man's allegiance and servitude to a power greater than himself, in this case the city of Los Angeles. For the first time in his life, Book wondered what else that declaration might mean, and how far beyond the city it might stretch.

Benji held a short-handled 12-gauge shotgun across his lap. The young policeman looked very much like he was watching over dangerous fugitives, and not presiding over the homecoming of a redeemed colleague.

Book turned to Molly where she sat in silence beside him. She watched their guard intently, searching for weakness.

Absurd questions formed and fell apart in Book's thoughts one after another until he finally spoke, not knowing what he would say.

"Kid...?"

She turned toward him. Suddenly he was moved to confess an action he still could not see as a wrong, but nonetheless now sensed had been a terrible error.

"This is my fault. I called Frank, and he traced the line."

Molly measured him for a moment.

"It doesn't make any difference now." Her thoughts turned inward and she studied the metal floor. "It's over." She seemed exhausted. "Your father has freed me, Book. And he has saved you from a fate far worse than his own."

"What fate?"

"Mine."

"I don't believe in fate."

Molly turned back to him once more. A sudden doubt. She heard the faint trace of something important concealed in his voice. Book was hiding something from her.

Chained as she was, she could not touch him. She thought to put the question to him directly, just as she had once tried to get him to open the door to her jail cell. It might have been fear of his anger, of the horrible way he had looked at her through those cell bars, but as the moment passed she realized that it was fear that she might find out the truth. If Book had hidden information about the King's X, her learning about it now would be disastrous. She could not escape the Shepherd, and he would soon know all she knew. Maybe Book was beginning to believe after all. Maybe he was beginning to understand what was at stake.

Of course, another part of her, the part that had just proclaimed her freedom, simply did not want to know. She would die at the Shepherd's hand once again, but then the long chase would be over.

From vast depths she watched the man seated next to her on the rattling bench, until a third possibility came to her. Her heart cracked a little more at the suffering she brought to those who loved her. Book was a fool. He might only be trying to protect her.

"Listen to me," she said, urgency becoming a wall against all of her competing fears. "Whatever else that thing is, Book, it is the enemy of Mercy. If you should ever see it again, throw it deeper into the ocean."

Book could feel that her words came from compassion and long restrained pain. These were the most honest words she had spoken to him since their first meeting.

"Do not be tempted," she continued, "not for me, not for the world, not for anything. Do you understand? To wear this thing even once is to bond with it, to welcome curses beyond comprehension, to end all hope."

Book realized that she suspected his secret.

"Do you understand?" she pleaded.

He watched her fear growing. He would not tell her what he knew, and she apparently knew better than to ask.

"Yeah, sure. I understand."

Both knew that they had said what they must say. There was only to let it play out.

Somewhere within the wisdom he had seen arise in her, the young girl lingered, and she was terrified. Book wished he could reach out for her again. The chains that prevented him from touching her only clarified his failure. His strength had been useless against her enemies.

Book knew that Frank Harker could still prove himself an ally, prove that he had been right to rely on a partner and a friend, to trust in the real world. He shoved aside his failure, and thought to give Molly what he had to give, whatever strength he had.

"It's going to be alright." Book heard the patronizing hollowness of his words before he finished speaking them.

Molly smiled, grateful for the gesture, but she took no comfort in another lie. Her smile dulled into the expression of a weary teacher.

"No, Detective Book. I will be given into the hands of my enemy. Once he confirms that the ring is lost, he will learn all he can from me about my allies hidden around the world. He will learn who they are and where to find them. I will not be able to prevent it."

Book spoke again without knowing what he might say, driven by a resolve that emanated from some unknown and untouched level within him.

"That won't happen, Molly. And if it does..." He paused, amazed by the depth of his conviction. "If it does I will find you."

Molly had the life memories of many people distilling within her, moving backward through time to an uncertain beginning at some yet cloaked time and place. She could recall no emotion that compared with the frightening bond that had drawn her to him, and which seemed to keep him at her side.

"Don't." She commanded in the tone of one accustomed to being obeyed without question.

Book's thoughts came sharply back to the present as the van slowed into a right turn. Molly felt the change, too. The sound of heavy raindrops breaking on the roof grew louder. The engine quieted to an idle as they drifted and slowed.

The terror of the hunted surged within her and Molly ached to weep before him again, to show him her weakness so that he might hold her up with his strength. But she was certain of the end. She remained steady.

"Look for the opportunity I spoke of. If it comes, take it. *Run.* Hide from them and don't look back. Ever." Her eyes implored him. "Promise me."

Book returned her stare, overwhelmed with fear, failure, and a new determination born out of the sudden, mysterious sensation that this had all happened before and he could not let it happen again.

"No." He spoke the truth this time. "I won't let them hurt you..." The nonsensical word *again* faded before he could speak it.

She could find no words to plead. Only his name came to her. She spoke it softly.

"*Book.*"

"Why are we stopping?" Book demanded of the young policeman.

"Quiet," Benji said almost politely as the grind of slowing tires on concrete finally came to a stop. "We'll have you out of those cuffs soon enough."

Book noted their guard's kindness, as if it added weight to his belief that Frank was here to help. *If you don't know about them, you work for them,* Jacob had said. Book took no comfort from the young man's words.

A key clanked open the lock and the steel double doors swung open at the back of the van. Frank Harker stood outside in the steady rain along with the driver, another cop in uniform. Looking beyond them, Book saw that the police van was parked halfway down an empty alley between two office buildings. "Okay, Benji," Frank commanded, "unhook the girl."

"What do you want with her?" Book had intended to sound indifferent, but his words came out closer to panic. "Frank?"

"Right now, Benji," Frank ordered again, ignoring his old friend.

As Benji unhooked Molly she looked one more time into Book's eyes. He studied her face. She was still the young girl, looking for protection from a man she still hoped could give it. Or she was someone else altogether unknowable, offering *her* strength to him at the moment of his greatest failure. Book yanked at his cuffs, as if he might suddenly be strong enough to break the chain. He was not.

"*Frank!*" Book shouted. Harker ignored him as Book edged closer to real panic. He watched his partner take hold of the chain between Molly's wrists and lead her down the metal steps to the street, where the cold and steady rain began to mat her hair to her head.

When Frank's massive frame moved out of the doorway, Book realized that they were not alone. Fear, deep and primal, washed over him like a wave, sweeping away what strength he had left to pull at his chains. A few yards down the alley, a slender sports coupe, a Jaguar, black with blackened windows, slowed to a stop with a low growl from its downshifting engine. Book had seen this car before in front of his apartment. And as he watched Frank Harker lead Molly toward it by her chain, he knew who waited at the wheel.

"*Frank!* Don't do this!" Book looked all about him for a weapon or a means of escape. His attention fell on Benji, still sitting on the bench across from him. The young officer watched Frank escort the girl towards the black car with a look of genuine confusion. "What's he doing, Benji?" Book demanded. "Something's wrong, and you know it!"

"Shut up!" Benji retorted, not knowing how else to respond.

"Do something about it!"

"About what?" Benji asked. "Shut up, I said."

Book could see the Shepherd's eyes beneath the brim of his hat as he stepped from the car into the rain. Molly was helpless before him, waiting for an opportunity that was not coming. She did not struggle as the Shepherd led her around to the other side of the car and put her in the passenger seat. Book watched him issue some brief instruction to Harker, before disappearing once more behind the black glass of the windshield.

The black car drifted back out of the alley with Molly inside. It was gone by the time Frank returned.

Frank stood at the open door, regarding Book with a vacant gaze.

"Frank?" Book begged him. "Why are you doing this?"

Book studied his partner's face and could see that there was no conscience behind it.

"Lieutenant?" Benji asked Harker, his confusion getting the better of him. "What's happening here?"

"Book tries to escape." Harker drew his service revolver and fired a bullet through Benji's head. Before the driver behind him could even reach the safety strap on his holster, Harker turned and fired two more shots directly into his heart. He returned his vacant stare to Book before the second officer's body hit the pavement.

Though it was happening just as they said it would, though the words of Molly and Jacob echoed clearly in this moment, Book could not understand what he had just witnessed. He choked out his horror.

"Jesus Christ... no."

Harker raised his service revolver again and clicked the hammer back. With the gun pointed directly at his forehead from the doorway of the van, Book looked above the barrel and into his partner's eyes. His hand did not waver, the gun remained steady, his aim perfect, but Frank's voice trembled as if pained by an old memory. "I'm sorry."

The two-by-four inch board, swung like a baseball bat, flashed from behind the open door at the side of the van. The sensation of the bullet blasting through his forehead that Book was expecting did not come. Instead, he heard the hollow sound of Frank's skull giving way to wood just as the gun in his hand flashed and thundered. Book saw his old friend and partner die in an instant even as the bullet meant for his own brain ripped instead through muscle and bone just below his left shoulder.

As Frank's body fell away, John took his place in the open doorway, clutching his board and breathing hard from his efforts to follow the police van on foot for several city blocks.

"You're shot." He announced.

Pain suddenly registered and Book saw his fresh blood covering the torn shoulder of his jacket. He froze, caught between confusion, despair, and rage. He turned his stare to Benji's lifeless body, then to the thick splash of his partner's blood clinging to the board in John's hand. The blow and the simultaneous gunshot still reverberated in his head, melding in a disorienting cacophony of memory with the murderous shot from his own gun in Sara's apartment. Within the swirling images and sounds, Book found Molly, led by a chain between her wrists to the Shepherd. Holding tight to this picture, he delayed despair a little longer, and turned his attention entirely to rage.

John moved with urgency and purpose. He fished a set of keys from Benji's pocket and moved to release Book.

"You're bleeding bad." John informed him.

Free of his chains, Book ignored his wound and his rescuer. He moved quickly, pulling Benji's body off the bench to reveal the box of his possessions removed when he had been frisked.

Book picked through the box with his right arm as his left hung uselessly at his side. He selected a small disk of brass and shoved it into the pocket of his jacket. He then took the sidearm from the young officer's holster, tucking it in the waist of his jeans. Finally, Book took the shotgun from Benji's hand. He chambered a round with the pump handle using the weight of the weapon against only a sharp flick of his good arm to see if he could do it with one hand. He could.

He turned back to the paper-faced drifter. Book found him patiently waiting, already staring him in the eye. "You know who the Shepherd is," Book insisted.

John nodded, and his paper-skin shifted into a smile at the possibility of a fulfilled wish too long in coming.

Book's rage was showing them their course.

"Give me a name."

Chapter Forty-Four

"What are we doing here?" Molly asked in an even tone. She studied the Shepherd in profile from the passenger seat as he pulled his car into the alley behind Jacob's bookshop.

"I am going to show you something."

Molly could not read the intention behind his cold expression. She turned away to look through the intermittent cascade of rain that appeared between slow sweeps of the wiper blades.

"They know nothing of me." Molly struggled to keep her voice steady, to give nothing away. The Shepherd's silence was the trap. It drew her to speak further. "I was a runaway and they took me in." Every word revealed more about what was important to her, about what she held inside.

"You and the policeman," the Shepherd corrected. He calmly turned his full attention and piercing stare to her. "He will die at the hands of the police if you don't tell me where it is."

"I don't know where it is." Molly fought to retain her mask of indifference toward Book. "That policeman will die no matter what I say. I know who you are. I know *what* you are."

The Shepherd paused to gauge his opponent. The familiar resolve, courage, and mental prowess had once again fallen into the form of an otherwise helpless child. He saw her power as well as her weakness and vulnerability.

Molly's rage was impotent and she kept it inside, until a time might come when it could be a weapon. Instead she consciously avoided looking through the windshield, looking toward the bookshop, the old couple.

The Shepherd continued to study her.

"You *are* great," he said with an air of admiration that may have been another trap, or a genuine acknowledgement of something he had suspected. "You came back for their ring, just as they told me you would."

Molly waited, listening for clues to weakness or an opportunity.

"Your greatness drew their attention, just as it happened for me."

For a moment, and for the first time, Molly saw something other than malice in this man.

"If I were to let you live," he continued, "in time perhaps you would grow even more powerful than they have made me," She heard the hint of something else in his voice. Loss? Jealousy? Hope? "We should be together, not at odds, girl. You needn't run forever, you needn't *always* fight. I could show you many things that you have never considered."

Rachel had never been this close to him. She had fought him and she had run from him, but she had never spoken with him in a moment of peace. In this calm, Molly sensed great depths within him. What sort of a man, she wondered, becomes a Shepherd?

"What do you mean," she finally asked, "*just as it happened* for you?"

"I remember another lifetime, Molly. Just like you."

Molly's eyes narrowed into a squint as she studied him. She remembered *many* times. She remembered *many* lives. If he was even telling the truth, she knew he was still incorrect in his assessment. His knowledge of her was incomplete. They were not the same. Nevertheless, this solidarity he seemed to feel, this sense of possibility, had prompted him to offer her something precious. Something secret. The Shepherd was *prideful*. Molly had sensed it before, but now she knew it. It was a weakness.

"What lifetime?" she asked.

He paused, and Molly guessed that he might be considering the helplessness of her plight and the dulled edge his own triumph would bring if she could not lead him to the ring. He spoke his secret.

"When I was sixteen years old, I had an unusual dream. Just like you."

Before she had ever heard of Rachel, Molly knew a great deal about using other people's emotions and desires to her advantage. She studied him, attentive to the subtle shifting of his facade and listening for the slightest hint of vulnerability in the otherwise smooth tones of his voice, searching deeper for the weakest spot. He seemed to sense in her something he must seldom find in his life. She was an equal, a peer, someone he could talk to who might have some chance of comprehending his own greatness.

Could it be that this man, Molly wondered, *is lonely?*

"After a few nights of dreaming the same dream," the Shepherd continued, "I understood that I was not dreaming at all."

"You were remembering." Molly interjected to show how well she understood.

As he regarded his captive and took his next breath to speak, his expression revealed a subtle acknowledgement of their connection.

"In 1912, I was a humble and rather average boy, growing up in the Austrian high country. But 600 years before that, I was a great hero. I was a soldier who had traveled the world and learned many of its secrets."

Molly inwardly sifted the new information as it came in to her. The Shepherd was providing dates and locations, any or all of which could be weapons if she could find a way.

"Though still a child like you are now," the Shepherd continued, "I recalled *everything* I had known, everything *he* had learned in an entire lifetime. His experiences, his battles, and his victories were all mine as well. I quickly came to know myself to *be* that great man, reborn in the body and mind of a youth, in another place, far into the future. An amazing thing."

The Shepherd smiled for the first time. It was a deeply self-satisfied smile, and he offered it for Molly to share. She did not return it, but continued to watch him closely.

"The world suddenly became a great wonder to me," he continued, "and I eagerly devoured knowledge of it. The history of the last 600 years and, my God, the *science*. It has been endlessly fascinating. The brilliance of who I once was and the enthusiasm of new found youth propelled me quickly through school, through University, and drew the attention of many men of power and influence. And then, *they* came to me."

"With an offer for more." Molly's acknowledgement was a subtle urging for him to continue.

"Yes. They came to me in secret with knowledge of impossible things. They knew what I had dreamt, though I had told no one. They knew *who* I had been, though I had told no one. And they reminded me of something else I had forgotten. Long ago, Broussard had also encountered them."

"Broussard?" The name brought a sudden chill to her, a sensation of familiarity. Molly searched the jumbled mass of thought and memory her own dreams had brought her. She did not know it.

"That was his name, long ago. My name. *Broussard*. He was a rare enough man to have something they wanted. So they had come to him and opened his eyes to many astonishing truths he could not have seen before. In my life now, I am Mathias Holt, but I am Broussard as well. That was their gift to him. Their gift to me."

"Not a gift," Molly corrected him without emotion. "This knowledge was the price they paid for your soul, 600 years ago."

"Perhaps it was," the Shepherd answered with a confident smile. "But I don't seem to be suffering too much for it, do I?" Then, he returned to the bargain he seemed to seek. "You have a great deal of knowledge Molly. I could force it from you. But the more you fight, the more the process becomes like opening an egg. I'm afraid you won't be easily put back together." He let the threat hang between them for a moment. "Or you could stop fighting, stop running. I could offer you much. They could offer even more."

To be a Shepherd, she thought through the next hanging silence. To run from no one, to fear no one. She had thought of this many times before in the past. There was much to envy in the life of a Shepherd. They were more powerful and more free than almost anyone on the globe. Yet, she knew, they were still slaves.

"Tell me," Molly probed, "what sort of man was Broussard?"

The Shepherd cocked an eyebrow as he considered the question.

"That depends on who you ask, I suppose. He was a Crusader in the Holy Land. A great hero to Christians, a murderous demon to Islam. Maybe he was both. Maybe neither." The Shepherd seemed unguarded as he spoke his inner thoughts for perhaps the first time. "From my current point of view, it makes no difference what sort of man I once *was*. Only what you are *now* matters. Are you asleep? Or are you awake to the world? Are you weak? Or are you *strong*?"

Molly could plainly see what he felt at the moment. It *was* pride, a
weakness.

As she studied the Shepherd beside her, a subtle orange-yellow glow
encroached into her vision from the side. She turned again toward the
bookshop, toward what he had brought her here to see. Through a small
window to the alley, she saw the soft pulse of fire spreading through ancient
wooden shelves, fueled by ancient books. A match, a lighter, or a candle
had been set within the last half-hour. He had been here already. The old
man and woman. Father. Mother. Dead already among the growing
flames.

Her tears moved like a mirror of the rainwater on glass beside her.
The Shepherd smiled at the sight of them.

"The past is just a story, Molly," he offered, satisfied and prideful.
"The future is just a dream." Then he turned her own words as a weapon
against her. "And you have no idea who or what I am now."

"All knowledge is but remembrance."

--Plato

Chapter Forty-Five

The Templar was insane. Of that, at least, Shahin was certain. Shahin had procured their two horses through stealth, sparing the inhabitants of the seaside village of Ajum from the Christian's indiscriminant sword. That had been the easy task. Since then they had ridden almost without cessation and to the point of exhaustion. For four days they travelled from the coastline of Eritrea inland through the dry savannahs, and eventually up to the undulating grass and stone highlands of Ethiopia.

Before disembarking at Ajum, over the last two days of the voyage on the Red Sea, the Templar had slept only briefly. But despite the efforts of the girl and her concoctions of white flowers and purple leaves, he had awakened feverish from the yellowing wound on his thigh. Since then, he had made the entire journey from the sea without sleep. As a result, Shahin watched him fall nearer to death and deeper into madness each day. Shahin and Khali would sleep during the hour of rest the Templar permitted each night, but the Captain knew from the growing hollowness in his expression that Broussard had remained awake, staring into the darkness behind them like a stone gargoyle.

Shahin watched from a horse length behind as the massive soldier swayed in his saddle. At best, Shahin thought, their path was an unseen road to a hidden destination known only to their Templar captor. At worst, the secret of their mission had been left behind in the desert of Sinai with his comrades, and the sole remaining Templar merely led them where his fevered mind directed.

Shahin considered his position now, re-evaluating as he had with nearly each passing moment since being roused from his bed in Acre. What had been an entire army of Templars in the falling city had been reduced to just three at sea, and now one in the wilderness. It had been two weeks since he had watched the *Leila*, flanked by Templar warships, set sail for Cyprus. His only hope of seeing her crew and his people again lay in successfully completing a mission he knew nearly nothing about. What little was known of it at all remained locked in the deteriorating mind of Broussard. As he watched the young man's head sag and loll with each of the animal's steps, his reflexes as dulled as his mind, Shahin wondered how much longer he could hold onto that hope. He wondered how long he should wait before cutting his losses and reclaiming his freedom.

He considered how simple it would be to inch his horse alongside and bury his dagger between the Templar's shoulders. Shahin indulged the impulse to live that moment over and over in his thoughts until he found himself grinding his teeth in suppression of it.

If this mission were as doomed as it seemed, then the *Leila* and the life Shahin had left behind were already lost. Yet, as helpless as he felt about the present, there was always a way to move forward. It may have been the coward's way, he thought, but that had never stopped him from taking it before. He could see a new beginning. He was far away from where anyone might know him. And there was still the girl.

He saw Khali wake from her own rest, tucked protectively before the Templar on his horse. Despite the constant uncertainty of her situation, Shahin appraised her as strong, and nearly as fearless as she was beautiful. She was younger, but far more woman than the coy and pouting Dalal. His hand still caressing the hilt of the short, arcing blade at his hip, Shahin considered what he knew about Templars, and wondered again at what this girl could be to Broussard.

Shahin knew little of Templars first hand, as he had spent the better part of his life avoiding contact with soldiers of any kind, but he certainly knew them by reputation. They were the worst kind of soldier, the kind who kill in the name of their God. It occurred to him now, as it had many times before, that Templars and other pious men would not be so wrathful and bloodthirsty if they did not despise women so. Pious men make war, and pious women stand against it. Therefore women suffer most at war's feet. Shahin had come to hold this as his highest truth: Without the influence of woman, be she mother, wife, or daughter, man's life is unbalanced. And further, the stronger the man, the greater the need for a woman's strength, or the greater the imbalance becomes. So important was this idea to Shahin that he had spent a great deal of time, energy, and resources insuring that if he were ever to err in this matter, it would be in having an overabundance of women around him at all times, rather than not enough.

Shahin let his mind wander from planting his knife in the Templar's back to the prospect of a new start in this far away land with Khali at his side.

Nadeem had done it. He seemed quite happy with Fadia, hidden away as he was in the Sinai. Shahin quickly pushed away thoughts of their last meeting, and the threat the men in the black-sailed warship posed to his old friend's new beginning. He watched Khali turn her delicate shoulders in the saddle to look up into the ragged face of Broussard.

Shahin wondered how long it might take for the girl to forgive him for taking her Templar away from her. He wondered if this child could be wise enough to one day see that Shahin and his dagger had saved her. As she watched the Templar continue to fade beside her, Shahin recognized another trait in Khali for which many women have suffered. She looked on Broussard with devotion. Inexplicable, resolute, it would see her follow him to any fate, to long life, or brief. Such a bond would prove unassailable, and would quickly turn to hatred for him and his knife.

He had seen such a look in the eyes of a woman before. There were few nights when the image of Leila did not haunt him. Her death was the end of his old life and the beginning of a new one. But that was long ago. Since then, he had lived each day as an outlaw, an agent against the civilized world of caliphates and Christendom.

He had come of age in the city of Granada in Al-andulus. He knew enough about true civilization to know that what the caliphs and cardinals offered was a lie. While the European kings, who spawned the likes of Guillaume de Beaujeu, still held sway over little more than encampments of mud, Cordova was opening its libraries, hundreds of thousands of manuscripts strong, to the Muslim, Jew, and Christian alike. Al-andulus had offered a culture based on the wisdom of the ages, a land once too sophisticated for Crusades, for Jihad, for fanaticism. All of that was gone now, for him, for her, perhaps for everyone else.

In his youth, men like Broussard had come in waves, south from the Pyrenees Mountains and into the body of his world like a fast-spreading disease. He did not blame the savages. It was foolish to expect savages to behave in any other way. He remembered the petty divisions within his own people, squabbling over scraps of land while a tidal wave loomed above them intent on sweeping them all away. He remembered fighting. He remembered the struggle to retain the last of the man he been, the last ideal, the last refuge of naiveté still held within his heart. It had been a long time, however, since he could clearly recall what that ideal had been. His effort to unify his own people in the face of another had left him bloodied, hated by both sides, and alone.

His eyes drifted once more from Broussard to the softness of the girl. He had so little rage left since that time that moments of reflection like these invariably took him to the same place, and the same great sadness. He allowed the memory of Leila to move through him like a breeze of familiar melancholy. He recalled the peace she gave as a gift to him upon his every return. The gentleness of her spirit reflected in her every aspect, hair that flowed through his fingers like warm liquid, wise expression beneath soft brows that offered him belonging without words.

Shahin knew that he was allowing himself too much of an indulgence. He turned away from Khali to focus on the uncertainty of their surroundings, and the immediacy of their plight. Before them to the West the land rose in steppes. Behind them it swept steadily downward so that he could begin to see how high they had risen from the savannah. North and South, he saw nothing but rolling hills. No sign of roads or paths, no smoke rising from a cooking fire within any horizon. They had not seen another man since they had left the coast.

Shahin did not hate men like the Templar. He had lived what he believed to be a life of sanity in the face of the rampant lunacy of hatred. Christian fighting Muslim, Muslim fighting Muslim, the Jew caught in between. Their battles raged even as the ancient libraries burned, the animals died, and the clear waters soured. He wondered now, as he had so many times in the past, who could be asking the questions that sparked such insipid and vile debate? Who was the instigator, the Prime Mover of the mad cycle? The believers, in their various forms and in their bloodlust, had claimed it was God. Shahin had always doubted them, but in truth had no way of knowing for sure.

In time, after loss of family, of home, and of love, Shahin began to see that if there was a God, there was only one, existing under many names. It seemed an invariable truth that God craved death for men, tragedy for women, and a balance of hatred between peoples. In Al-andalus, fighting for Muslim unity against the fast encroaching Christian hordes, Shahin bathed in a constant flow of martyrs' blood, martyrs of every individual creed and country, all coming together with their own particular lust in the maelstrom, until the veil had been washed away in the flood. It was Leila, who could not strike from the forests or from the sea as he could. It was Leila, who did not speak against the complacent leaders of Granada, or organize men in the marketplace as he had done. It was she who had paid the price when the veil was torn open for him. This is how he came to loathe the very idea of God.

Shahin had never again fought for any man's vision. He had no object for his love, not Leila, and not his own people, who had killed her as their only means of attacking him. With her death, love had dried up in him, along with hate. He was left with nothing to fight for but himself.

Common sense had taught him that fighting alone was foolish, so he took what he had learned when he fought for visions, and began to move among the foolish like a ghost they could not touch, like a hawk they could not reach. Common sense had made him outlaw, pariah, unfettered, free.

The Templars had caught him unprepared, and shown him his mistake. He had taken root again. Acre had become comfortable. He had been a fool to get so complacent and soft. As he studied the slumping back of Broussard, he nudged his foot into the side of his horse to bring the animals closer together. Shahin inched the curved blade of his dagger silently from its copper sheath like a snake tensing to strike, grateful to the Templar Order for the old lesson re-learned. Now, he was fully prepared to begin life again.

Khali gasped in alarm at the sensation of the Broussard's body falling away from hers in the saddle. Broussard hit the swaying bed of thick grass with a hollow thud and a rush of air escaping his lungs.

Frightened by the sudden movement and sound, the horse bolted. Shahin saw the look of terror on her face as Khali lunged to wrap her arms around the animal's neck to keep from being thrown. Ignoring his own confusion, he released the hilt of his weapon, still resting in its sheath, and kicked his horse in the side, leaving Broussard where he lay.

Shahin leaned over the beast and urged it through a long sprint across the uneven terrain until he could move alongside the girl's panicked horse. He wrapped his arm around her middle, shouting at her before she released her white-knuckled grip on the animal's neck. Light in his arm, he easily pulled her before him in his saddle as his horse drifted to a gentle stop.

Shahin felt her panic in the rapid rise and fall of her belly where he held her. He whispered soothing sounds to her, tightening his hold so that she might draw assurance and some comfort from it.

"What happened?" She demanded, less in need of comfort than Shahin had imagined.

"The Christian fell asleep."

Khali strained to see behind them until Shahin turned the horse slightly for her. Broussard appeared as a dark spot in the grass nearly a quarter-mile down the soft incline.

"Take me back." She insisted, as if she sensed that a polite request might not be enough.

Shahin paused while his horse lightly stamped the earth beneath them.

"Why?"

"I must go to him," Khali offered in a tone less confrontational, aware that moving from the side of this man back to the side of the other might not be a simple task,

"And if you go to him, where *then* will you go? Where is he taking you?"

Khali knew as much about that as did Shahin. She decided to say nothing. What she wanted, she had made clear. What was left, now, was to determine what the Captain wanted, and what could be done about it with her soldier far off and asleep in the grass.

"He does not know where he leads us, Khali."

"You do not know that," she answered calmly, without looking back at him.

"He never knew," Shahin countered with equal calm. "If any of the Christians knew our path, we left them behind long ago."

Khali remained silent.

"He is mad, girl. His mind is not working well. Can you not see that?" He waited through a long silence, hoping she would turn to see in his eyes that no harm would come to her in his hands, that he was sincere, and that, with or without her, he was leaving.

Khali knew better than to look. She had looked into the eyes of the Captain before, and found them warm and comforting. That was part of the spell she had imagined him casting over many women. Her place, she knew, was not with him.

"Come with me," Shahin said. It was an offer, not a plea. "I will protect you. I will care for you, and you will care for me. I will take you where no harm can come to you, ever again."

"As Nadeem took Fadia?" Khali immediately wished she had remained quiet. She turned now, despite her better judgment, and looked into the Captain's eyes. She saw the wound she had made, festering under a thin mask of anger.

The strong hand that had held her this whole time shifted now to her arm, and Shahin gently lowered her to the ground. She looked up at him now where he towered above her, blocking out the Sun.

"You are very beautiful, Khali. I do not understand why you would choose him over me. But I will not force you. I do not trust Templars. And I trust mad Templars even less. If I believed that there was any chance in hell or earth that this venture could succeed with him leading it, I would fight till my last breath to see us back to Cyprus. As it stands now, I must find another way to free my people." He paused again to give the girl a chance to digest his words, to weigh what Broussard truly offered her. "He will lead you to an unpleasant fate, I'm afraid. This is wilderness. He is likely injured from his fall, if not dead. I will hate to think of you dying here."

Shahin moved his horse around her so that she could see his face unobscured by the Sun. She looked up into his eyes and found them warm, compassionate, and lonely.

He offered his hand again. "Last chance."

Khali turned to look again for Broussard. No longer high on the horse's back, she could not see him. She felt tears cooling in the breeze on her cheek.

Whether for him, herself, or the Christian, Shahin took her tears as his answer. He removed the half-filled water skin from his saddle and dropped it to the ground before her feet.

"Good luck, sweet child." He kicked at the flank of his horse with a loud and sudden "hut-hah!" that sent a jolt through Khali, even as it spurred the beast northward at a gallop. Within moments, Shahin was too far away to hear her even if she called out to him. She watched until he disappeared over the crest of the next hill. At last, she stooped to recover the water skin and headed back to Broussard.

Chapter Forty-Six

Chuck Townsend wiped blackened grease from his fingers onto his overalls and glanced through the grime-encrusted window as the second wave of emergency vehicles roared and shrieked past his auto-body shop. He watched dark tendrils of smoke reaching up through the rain above the rooftops where the fire crews were headed. Something big was on fire a few blocks away.

Chuck was alone in the shop this Saturday morning and just beginning the removal of a crumpled sheet of steel that once was the fender of a Plymouth Fury. If it hadn't been for the distraction of the fire trucks, he might have noticed the two men slipping through the back door of the shop. Instead, he caught the first glimpse of them only after turning away from the window. The pale light from the uncovered bulb hanging behind the counter caught an old bum, a black man with skin dried to the sheen of paper from years of exposure, dripping with rainwater, moving within the shadows. Chuck, just registering indignation, froze at the sight of the second, much larger man, who walked with a noticeable limp and held a 12-gauge shotgun in his hand. Chuck recognized the weapon from its shortened stock as the kind the police carry in their cruisers. These men did not look like policemen to him. The big one was bleeding. A slow stream of blood from what looked like a bullet wound in his shoulder flowed along the inside of his leather jacket until it dripped from the waist. A trail of drops, each an inch wide and spaced about two feet apart, led from the back door to his feet.

"Shut up," Book warned in an even tone before Chuck could speak.

John moved to the front door of the shop, and peered briefly through the dirty glass before pulling the security cage closed over it. Chuck never took his eye off the bleeding man with the shotgun.

Book could feel the pulse of his heart as it pumped blood from the hole just below his collar bone. The pain was intense, which he took as a good sign. As long as the pain was still increasing, he knew he had time before he would slip into shock.

Once satisfied that the mechanic understood the danger he was in, Book began to study the inside of the place. They stood in a musty and dim garage with a high ceiling of corrugated metal and wooden support beams. It smelled of gasoline and rubber and was lit by a hooded desk lamp in a corner and two bare light bulbs hanging from cords in the broad open space. It housed three cars and two motorcycles in various stages of repair, some recently arrived, some awaiting the return of their owners. Book lingered for a moment on a bike that seemed road-worthy. He wondered if he could work the clutch with only one good arm.

"Your shop is going to be closed for a little while," he announced at last. Chuck Townsend nodded in agreement. "And we're going to need a blow torch."

"Okay." Chuck found his voice and swallowed without spit. "What do you need a...?"

Book pinned the shotgun under his elbow, reached into his pocket, and pulled out a small disk of brass. "Just get it."

Chapter Forty-Seven

Shahin had heard many tales of the Nile. Though he had never journeyed far into the realm of Saladin, now held by the Sultanate of Egypt, he knew enough of the White Nile and the Blue to suspect that a heading to the North and West, should, within a few days, bring him to a waterway that would eventually return him to the Mediterranean.

It had been an hour since he had left the girl behind. The highlands he now crossed featured hills rising upon hills, creating peaks and valleys almost like the still image of a rough sea made of grass and rock. The sound of nearby galloping horses came to his ears like far-off thunder. The riders were insulated within one of the many small valleys among those earthen waves so that he could not see them, and the sound seemed to come from many directions at once. He paused to listen before coaxing his tiring mount toward the western rise of grass. Upon reaching the top, thoughts of Khali and the mad Templar flooded back to him.

Three men rode away from him toward the Southwest so that they did not see him where his horse stood. Shahin's mind raced at the shock and the impossibility of what he saw. European soldiers clad in unmistakable uniforms. He paused as they moved past his position at an easy gallop, unaware of him. An image of the girl, alone on that hill, hammered at his carefully guarded resolve. Whether for good or for ill he could not be sure, but these riders were moving away from where he had left her. They would not find her.

***

The darkness gave way to a bright fog and then to the golden warmth of sunlight. Broussard focused on the dark silhouette above him until his sight returned. Khali looked nervous, but pleased to see him.

"You have been asleep for hours," she offered as she held the water sack to his lips. "You are fevered. Drink."

Broussard sat up among the highland grass, ignoring the water and the girl to listen to a growing rumble. His body was covered in the sweat of fever, his leg was lame and rigid, and all of his joints stung with each movement. He tried to focus on the sound, shutting out the pain and the attentions of the girl, hoping to determine if it were real or imagined. The rumble grew.

"I have heard that sound for a while now. Sometimes loud, sometimes far off. What is it?" She asked, trying to sound unconcerned.

"Horses," Broussard said as he pulled himself first to the knee of his good leg and then, with even more difficulty, to his feet. "Close by, and coming fast."

Broussard took a deep breath to strengthen and steady himself before slowly pulling his sword from its sheath. How he had arrived at this position was unimportant. What mattered was that his horse was gone, that there was no hiding place, and no escape. Khali rose and took her place at his side until his hand, hot and wet with the perspiration of his fever, found hers and held it in silence. He watched the rise where the riders would come, and waited. Khali saw the familiar look come to his eye as he steeled against what was coming. But his face was thin and hollow, and she knew he had little strength left.

Khali felt his grip tighten with each passing moment as the sound grew louder, until she thought he might be unaware of her. She was just about to cry out when she suddenly felt his grip loosen. She followed his eyes. A subtle sound of wordless surprise escaped her lips at the sight of Captain Shahin, cresting the hill on his horse.

Shahin reined the animal in at the edge of the hill, staring at Broussard and Khali over the distance. He raised his hand above his head and waited there for several moments, continuing to watch them without emotion while the rumble grew louder.

When the three riders reached Shahin, bursting into view over the hill behind him, Khali felt all of the strength leave Broussard's body at once. She moved quickly to prop him up but was not strong enough. He fell to his knees, quietly swearing or praising, "God's blood," before sickness, thirst, and exhaustion took whatever spark he had been holding onto. Broussard collapsed back into the grass.

Khali looked again at the riders, and saw now what he had seen. Coming toward them at a slow trot, with Captain Shahin riding among them, crimson crosses emblazoned upon tunics of white, rode three Templar knights.

Chapter Forty-Eight

The flame burned blue-orange at the end of the wand. Chuck lowered the level and waited patiently, dark goggles resting on his forehead. Book set the firing cap of a 105 millimeter artillery shell into the mechanic's hand. "Melt it," he commanded.

Chuck watched the bleeding man work his way into a seat on the hard wooden chair by the desk. Then he turned to the small, heavy object in his hand, shrugged, and placed it between the prongs of a hand-held steel clamp. He then raised the level of his flame, lowered his goggles, and set about doing as he was told.

Book had his name. Mathias Holt. John had provided him with the identity of the man responsible for everything that had happened to him, the man who had taken Molly. All that was left for Book was to decide whether he could believe a word John said. Of course, if he were to decide that John could not be trusted, then all was lost already. The bleeding in his shoulder had slowed, but not stopped. Without medical care, he would not be conscious for much longer, and he would not be alive much longer after that. Yet, however long he had left to live seemed unimportant to him now. This mad man was his only concern and his only chance.

Book rarely had call to use a gun in the line of duty. But he had put in many hours on the range learning how, should the need arise. He felt the weight of the shotgun lying across his knees. As he watched the flame of the torch wash over the King's X, he pictured the face of his tormentor framed in long silver hair beneath a brim of black felt. He longed to pull the trigger, to feel the recoil and the metal on metal slide and click of chambering the next round. He longed to hear the blast, smell the smoke. He longed to show the man in black the same mercy he had shown Sara. He longed to trust John's words.

"You killed my partner," Book calmly announced. He cocked his head to watch John's reaction.

John stood only a few feet away, watching the windows for signs that the police had found their overdue van in the alley a few blocks away, that someone had discovered the bodies. It was quiet outside the shop. "He was not your partner, Book. Not anymore."

He had known Frank Harker for one year. His wife Marie had fed him many times at their table. Frank was fat because he ate too much of the worst foods while at work, and Marie loved to cook. Frank was kind and generous to his friends, but had little time for the problems and concerns of the drug addicts and prostitutes they worked with everyday. He was thick headed and thin skinned. He was not smart, but he was wise in the ways a cop needed to be wise, and Book had learned to rely on him for that. Frank Harker had been Book's partner, mentor, and his friend. A dozen questions, filled with anger, grief, and shame over what had happened in that alley swirled in Book's head. But the image of the Shepherd, and thoughts of Molly in his control, brought him back to the task at hand.

"Who was he, then?"

John finally turned to look Book in the eye. There was no sense of mania or even urgency in his voice. He was delivering old news.

"He was one of many, Book. Just like me."

Book recalled Jacob's words in the bookshop, of how John had worked to make amends. *Make amends for what?* Of course, Book knew the answer to that now as well as he'd known it then. He stared hard into John's eyes, clutching the lowered weapon in his hand until his fingers whitened. He aimed his next question straight into his own fear.

"Who are you?"

John regarded Book for a moment before turning to study the orange-blue flame of the torch, either gathering his thoughts, or drifting away from them.

"I have only a few memories of the beginning," He said. "As a child I walked in dark sand by the sea, throwing stones at the waves and learning to fish." John watched the flame without emotion. "I was taken away from my mother, taken in the night by men I could not see, taken to a mountaintop. I never saw my mother again. I awoke in paradise. And there I stayed for a very long time."

As the flesh chilled along his arms, Book knew the meaning of the story. It didn't matter if he believed it or not. It didn't matter if John was the disciple of the crazy old man in the bookstore or his teacher. It didn't matter if the history he recounted now was true. What mattered was what John knew about the Shepherd. The police would start their dragnet upon finding the overdue van. Young men would soon be putting their lives on the line to take him in. John was his only guide now, and the time to decide where he stood was fast approaching. With so little of his life still under his own control, Book would uncover any madness and risk opening any wound to be certain the lives he might take in the next few hours would be the right ones.

"You remember?" he asked. "Like Molly?"

"No." John turned back to scan outside the windows. "Not like her.

She is not like us. She does not belong to them."

"Belong?"

"There were dark secrets known at Alamut, Book. The Old Man of the Mountain got his power from them."

Book squinted as he tried to recall the words of Jacob from a new perspective. *They seek out the greatest among us, like Hassan ibn Sabbah, and they offer them the world.*

Shepherds. Jacob had suggested there were many. John claimed to be providing a first hand account of a Shepherd who lived 800 years ago near the Caspian Sea, as well as the name of another Shepherd now living in Los Angeles.

"The Enemy taught the Old Man the secrets of life, of death, and how to infiltrate the mind as easily as infiltrating a city. But they betrayed him. They tricked him. Those who followed him, the *Fedeyeen,* the *Faithful unto death,* became bound to their will, to the service of the Enemy along with him. And we cannot escape. We *are* faithful unto death, Book."

"But you can not die," Book repeated Jacob's claim in a non-committal tone to see if John might affirm or deny it.

"No one dies, Book. The Old Man of the Mountain is gone. But the Enemy is still here. Their Shepherds still know how to reach his army. They know how to awaken what lies hidden within. There are thousands of us around the world. And they can call on us whenever they wish. They come in our sleep and wake us to the past. We have no choice, no thought but to obey."

"No choice?"

"Your partner was just like me, Book. That's *why* he was your partner. They *assigned* one of us to you. To be always near. Harker couldn't possibly know what he was until he was called, until it was already too late."

"They were waiting," Book said quietly and mostly for his own ears, as if speaking the words would help him to believe, to see it as real. "For Molly to find me."

Book noticed John's breathing pick up and his mania begin to assert itself.

"I was married. I was happy. My name was John. But they knew where to find me. And they wanted something done. It started with dreams." He reached up to his skull as if clutching a wound. "They come in through your head." The tormenting fire of John's eyes implored Book now. "Do you *know* what I did?"

John had murdered Book's mother. Jacob had told him this, saying only as much as Book seemed willing to hear at the time. The drifter who attacked a woman on the sidewalk on her way home from the grocery store. It was a common theme he had heard many times. The drifter who fired on the president from the book depository. The drifter who murdered Martin Luther King outside a hotel in Memphis. Sirhan Bashira Sirhan. James Ford. Lone killers without motivation, spiders waiting to strike from an invisible, impossible web.

Here was the man right in front of him, trying to confess his crime to a grieving son clutching a shotgun. Book did not move, but within the stillness, within the silence he now fought to maintain, he began to see a fuller picture of his life. He began to see form where before all had been chaos. He began to see reason where there had only been madness. He began to see the men and women who had come and gone, the events that aided or conspired to keep him in Los Angeles, that had led him to the police force, that had seemingly held him in place, waiting. He saw that *everything* that had ever happened to him might merely be the smallest threads of a great tapestry. There was one great cohesive image of his life, all focused on this very moment, the moment in which he could suddenly see it. He had caught up to it. He had overtaken the weaver and caught up to the present moment. From here he could see that whatever was to come next was unwritten, unknown, undecided. His life had become, abruptly and for the first time, *his* to direct. The time for waiting was over at last and it came to him in a rush of realization. This was his time to choose.

The humble, resigned face of his mother's murderer brought him back to the auto shop. He focused on his enemies and what he could know about them. If he was to believe all he had seen in the last few days and months, then there could be an army of Assassins, maybe thousands strong, hidden so deeply within the world that they themselves remained unaware that they could be called upon, activated like machines, to kill anyone, anywhere, anytime. Book thought again of the Shepherd, his eyes, his malevolence, the overwhelming power he had felt twice before, and he knew in both his heart and mind that the Assassins, including the one standing just a few steps away, were the least of his problems.

"I know what you did," Book answered. John did not shy away, but waited with the anticipation of the guilty for whatever would come next.

The faint cry of far off sirens encroached on the sound of the torch melting the King's X.

"I'm going to get Molly away from them." Book quietly declared with the confidence of a man without options. Finally, he turned his burning eyes, windows to the rage and despair within, to John. "I will need help."

Not as policeman and mad man, but as men with a purpose, Book and

John watched each other. And John understood. Here was his chance to make amends for the unforgivable. Book waited. John nodded his assent.

"You will not find him here," John offered after a moment's thought. "If the thing that brought him so many years ago is now lost, he will take the girl as compensation. She knows a great deal about their enemies."

"No. I can't let that happen. I won't."

"She's gone already, Book." John was certain. "Your only hope of ever seeing her again is to find a way to stay alive, and to stay *free*."

The sirens grew louder. Soon they would hear the sound of men's voices, uniformed officers moving door to door along side streets and alleys within a few blocks of the deserted van, the blood of their comrades and the scene of their murders fresh in their hearts.

"Are you ready to fight these men, Book?" John asked with calm resolve.

A shadow moved just outside the grime stained window to the shop. From where he sat, some thirty feet away, Book watched the uniformed police officer stepping up to the window, shading his eyes against the reflected light as he leaned in close against the glass, drawn by the glow of the torch or shadows moving within. Book held the shotgun tightly, but did not rise or move for cover. He knew that dozens of young men like this one were within shouting distance.

"Are you ready to call them your enemy?" John pressed.

Jacob had said that everyone who does not know the first secret, that the Enemy exists, is by definition one of *them*. But Book knew these men. He knew the worries and fears that fueled their labors. He knew about their children, their aging parents, and their mortgage payments. He knew what was in their hearts and wondered if they could really be his enemies without choosing it. He felt an unexpected pang of loneliness when he saw how easily this could be so. He was no longer one of them. He had no concern at all for what was important to them, what had been just as important to him days earlier. He was an outsider now, a stranger with already dimming memories of what their lives are.

It came to Book clearly in that instant. If he even tried to explain what he knows of the truth to the men outside this building, or to the future judges that may preside over his fate should he survive his capture, his words would be insane to them. But dismissing him as insane might not be enough. No matter how unlikely it sounds, unsought truth becomes unnerving and eventually gets under the skin. The truth is easier when it remains a mystery beyond reach. Truth must be silenced, either by lock and key or by death.

A new implication for an old wives' adage drifted to his thoughts. They say you should never disturb a sleepwalker because they may awake disoriented, frightened, and even violent. Book saw his father's old torment with sudden new clarity. When everyone but you walks in his sleep, you are truly alone.

Book hoped that none of these people would get in his way.

"I can't kill them," Book answered at last.

"Then your choice is easy," John concluded. "You must run. Escape. Or you will die here."

The young officer at the window had seen enough through the shadows. Failing to turn the locked doorknob, he pounded on the wooden frame with a clenched fist. "Open up in there! Police!"

"Okay, I got it," Chuck Townsend announced, lifting his goggles to his forehead and holding up the smoldering clamp in cautious triumph to show what had lain hidden within. "It's a ring!"

Chapter Forty-Nine

The Mongol approached Broussard along the darkened beach of his dream. In either hand he held the heads of his comrades by the hair. De Buci and St. Ives, drained of life, flesh hanging grey on the skull, mouths wide and dark.

Broussard stood still, as if his feet were anchored at the edge of where the lapping waves reached. He could not move, he could not fight, and he could not understand. All he knew for certain was that he was dreaming.

"What do you want?" Broussard was almost completely without strength, even in his dream world. His voice offered more breath than words, and he asked without power, or any real hope of an answer.

"Clever thieves," the cruel voice hissed. "Wait for me. I am right behind you."

***

Broussard slid into consciousness to the somewhat familiar sight of an old, gray-bearded man in a monk's humble robes sitting near the door. Words of warning flowed from him even before he realized that he was speaking. "They are coming!"

"So you have said." The old monk seemed unmoved by Broussard's alarm. After a moment's study to gain confidence that he was fully awake, the monk responded to the puzzled look on the young man's face. "You talk in your sleep." The old monk passed through the open doorway, leaving Broussard with only the sound of his steps retreating down a long corridor of stone and no further explanation.

Broussard squinted and blinked to clear his long-unopened eyes. He was alone in an unadorned bedchamber made entirely of red stone. To the left of the bed, a goatskin water sack hung from the corner of a table. As consciousness and strength returned to him, he pulled the wool blanket from his body, lifted the linen nightshirt from his leg, and studied the wound that had been killing him.

The long thin gash created by the Saracen blade had begun to fester along their journey. It was now beginning to scar. The flesh was discolored around the wound, but far less angry, and little pain remained. He had seen such wounds on soldiers before. None had healed as this one had.

His muscles proved sore and weak from lack of use. He pulled himself to a sitting position and let his feet touch the dry, cool stone floor next to the table. Reaching for the water skin, he tried to fit the broken pieces of his memory together. He wondered if the Templars he had seen riding in the hills had been real or imagined, and, if real, how long it had been since they'd found him.

Broussard paused to gain strength at the side of the bed, but before he could even attempt to stand, a second monk entered the room, another grey-haired European, taller than the first. A small Templar cross of iron hung by a chain above his heart. Though a deep reserve of vitality still shone clearly in his eyes, all else about him spoke of great age. The length of his beard and the way his robes hung from his arms and shoulders gave him the look of an ancient willow moving in the wind. Broussard did not recognize the man, but determined him to be a brother of great importance.

"Do not stand," the eminent Templar commanded as he crossed to where Broussard sat. Broussard obeyed, exhaling the strength he had gathered. The man stooped before him to examine the greenish-blue tissue around the leg wound. "Your strength will return quickly now. But let it come as it will." Satisfied with the condition of Broussard's injuries, he turned to regard the young man. "My name is Montbard." The name drifted in the deeper eddies of Broussard's thoughts, but he still did not know him. "This wound was the source of your sickness. It was badly diseased when you arrived. It would have killed you before long."

As the closing moments of his dream blended with his first moments in this strange place, urgency began to fill his body with unexpected strength and to assail his mind with sudden, sharp fears. "Khalidah?"

The word meant nothing to Montbard.

"There was girl!" Broussard explained in a rising tone that communicated a great deal. "And a Moor."

"Yes. You have them to thank for your rescue, I suppose. Our scouting party would likely never have found you if not for them."

Broussard surged forward, more powerfully than he might have thought himself capable, and grabbed Montbard's robe by the shoulder.

"Where is she?"

The old man withered somewhat, still like a willow in a harsh wind, but he had no fear of Broussard.

"They are gone." He reached a defensive hand to clutch at Broussard's wrist. "They left together upon delivering you. I do not know where they are now, nor is it important."

The words hollowed Broussard's resolve. He did not trust Captain Shahin, and he wondered with a gnawing pang in his chest if Khali had gone with him willingly, and if she had, whether she might be better off for it. As he began to realize the intensity of his grip and the fragility of the old man, Broussard's eyes fell to a peculiar sight.

The index finger of the old willow's hand was missing. In its place was a short stub glazed over with old scar tissue. And, stranger still, on Broussard's own hand, where it grasped the old man's garment, a golden-black ring that had not been there when he fell in the field. He released the old man's robe and fixed his gaze on the shining object.

It was half an inch wide and inscribed with many symbols, some familiar, most not, that seemed to shimmer and dim, now black, now gold, as his hand moved in the light of the room. Looking closer at the edges of the ring, Broussard noticed a phenomenon even more odd than the dancing inscriptions. He could not discern where the flesh of his finger ended and the edge of the metal began.

"What is this?" he asked.

"That," the old Templar answered, "is the reason you are still alive and standing on two legs."

Broussard did not look up from the odd piece of jewelry.

"Now then," Montbard said in the stern voice of a leader of men. "We have little time. Account for yourself, boy. Report."

Broussard came fully back to the room, realizing that he was in the presence of not merely a monk, but a warrior as well. He recalled the dreams, and the danger. "I am, I fear, the last of three come from Acre. Palestine has fallen to Islam."

The old Templar accepted this news, and the ultimate failure of nearly 200 years of fighting and dying that it represented, with impatience. He pressed ahead, as if such matters as Christendom, Islam, and control of the Holy Land meant little to him.

"You came to us with orders from a man named Guillaume de Beaujeu, orders that bore the seal of the Templar Grand Master."

Broussard wondered at the tone of the question. "You do not know the Templar Master by name?"

The first monk, who had watched over Broussard while he slept, returned with a plate of warm rabbit, placed it on the small table by the door, and then left in silence as quickly as he came. When the smell reached his nostrils, Broussard suddenly realized that he was very hungry.

"This Beaujeu is new to me," the old man answered. "I left Palestine before his time." This statement also bore a cryptic tone, but Broussard was once again distracted. "Eat," the old Templar commanded.

Broussard sat on the stiff wooden chair at the small table, pulling meat from bone with his fingers. Montbard stood with his back turned and his mind on slower moving matters as Broussard ate.

"Do you understand your orders?" the old man asked after a moment.

"Only that I am to return to the Templar keep at Cyprus with what you give me."

"And you do not know what it is I am to give you?"

"I was told nothing."

The old Templar worked on the puzzle.

"Clever of this Templar Master to send the unlearned on such an errand," he said aloud as he worked to penetrate the logic. "Clever or desperate."

Broussard had stuffed nearly half the animal into his mouth. He watched and listened to his host as he swallowed.

"I have seen many omens. With nothing but these portents to guide me, I sent riders far to the east to scout the savannahs for more than a sign of a coming change. What they found was strange indeed. A wandering Moor, a girl, and a dying knight far from home who carried the mark of the

Templar Master on a most peculiar order."

Montbard turned to face Broussard.   He found the young man studying the object on his finger.

"For three days you have slept in this room.   Since yesterday at nightfall, you have issued warnings from your sleep.   *They are coming.*" The old man reached out and covered the ring with his hand, so that he might force his way into Broussard's attention. "*Who* is coming?"

Broussard looked again into the bright eyes of the ancient tree. Though he had heard every word, he was surprised to realize how far away his thoughts had been.   He was struck in this moment by the familiar and growing sense of distrust for men who kept secrets.   The greater the Templar, it seemed, the more dangerous the secrets.

If there was one thing that Broussard had learned from the wise among the brotherhood, it was the value of knowledge.

"How many are you?" he asked, testing the exchange rate of information.

Montbard paused, annoyed as he gauged the young man.

Broussard watched the old man gather thoughts from a very deep and ancient well. *The Order is a gateway,* Vincent had said, *a hidden entrance to a secret world undreamt by the vast body of humanity.*

"Come with me," Montbard said at last and moved quickly to the door.   Broussard followed, surprised further by his unexpected strength. He snatched his cleaned Arabic robe and boots from the table by the door as he passed.

Pulling his robe over his head and hopping into his boots as they walked long corridors of the same red stone that comprised the walls of his room, Broussard felt drawn to the odd mason-work of this place.   Where the floor met the wall, and again where the wall met the ceiling, he could find no trace of the builder's hand. Impossible as it seemed, this passage, as well as the room where he had slept, seemed to have been excavated rather than built. As they walked, Broussard noted hints of the extent of this construct through small portals carved into the solid walls. The place was silent and lifeless. Yet there were several buildings visible through the carved windows, all created through the same mystifying technique. As easily as a man might scoop out the innards of a gourd to create a bowl, these rooms and corridors had been hollowed out with flawless precision from the red rock of the mountains by tools and skills he could not fathom. As Montbard led him at last into a great hall, Broussard was determined to learn the secrets of as many of these mysteries as he could.

Inside the hall were six old men, including the monk who had attended him and fed him with rabbit. They took their mid-day meal together, a stew or gruel of some kind, eaten from wooden bowls at a large, plain wooden table. The six monks looked up as they entered. None seemed surprised at the sight of the young man. They studied him only long enough to gauge his recovery, before returning in silence to their meals.

"This is a monastery, not a fortress," Montbard said in answer to the question asked moments ago. "It is a secret, silent place. We are seven. We are old. We are tired."

"Seven?" Broussard studied the old men at the table in concerned disappointment as he imagined what was to come. "Seven men in this entire place?"

Montbard regarded the young warrior for a moment, finding great courage within him alongside his quarrelsome and youthful disposition.

"You are quite young, yet, Broussard."

"I have lived 23 years, and I have been in Palestine for the last four of them. I have seen much in that time."

"Much, for a man, is relative." Montbard continued to study him. "It is unseemly for a Poor Knight of the Temple to feel anger over his duty."

"I know my duty."

"You are withholding information from me."

"I sense that my value as courier will be gone once I've made my report." Broussard returned the old man's intense gaze without flinching. "However, I can tell you with certainty that seven Templars, now eight, cannot hope to hold this ground against what is coming."

"It has been a long time since we seven have raised swords in battle. A very long time. If there is fighting to be done, Broussard, you will carry the load."

Broussard studied the ancients at the table with their ragged beards and balding grey heads until yet another peculiar sight caught his eye. On a hand now lifting a bowl, he noted another missing index finger. He looked further along the table at the troop of withered monks, each one missing a finger.

Broussard's mind crowded suddenly with the hidden history mixed with legend once whispered to him during Templar initiation rituals, and which he had so long ago dismissed as pointless. He felt small, young and foolish.

"What is this place?" he finally demanded. "What are Templars doing here?"

The old men at the table watched in silence as if already resigned to the notion that Montbard's answer would signal a long awaited moment, the culmination of long years spent at this remote outpost.

After a long pause in which he seemed to rush through a complex and disturbing decision, the old willow moved to the head of the long table and sat wearily with his comrades. The other six waited, each regarding the young man standing before them. At last, Montbard began to reveal knowledge that had seldom been spoken.

"Do you know what was found when the original Nine of the Order reached the Temple Mount at the beginning?"

Whispered rhymes and foolish puzzles turned over in Broussard's mind, signs pointing everywhere and nowhere through the paths of memory and history. "No."

"Good." What appeared to be a smile of approval flashed briefly across the wrinkled face. "If you seek knowledge, Broussard, you will find over time that there is never an end to it. There is no point at which you might arrive and understand completely. Each revelation along the course of wisdom will always lead to another, deeper secret. Much was discovered at the beginning." Montbard seemed to reflect over his own long path. "Much that we expected to find, and much that we did not."

Broussard noted the way the old man seemed to place himself within stories too old for him.

"Among the unexpected were cryptic writings in Solomon's own hand."

"Solomon's own...?" Broussard had heard no whispers of this in his training. "*King* Solomon?"

"It would be a long time before such things were revealed to one so young as you." Montbard silenced him. "The king spoke of fear, and a great secret that must be hidden away, a treasure that he dared not leave for successors to his throne. But his words were short, and though we never stopped our search for more, their trail led nowhere. It was many years after this initial find, when the Brotherhood of the Temple received an unexpected visitor from the darkness of this unmapped continent, from the darkness of an unknown history. An Ethiopian Prince, exiled from his throne at the hands of a usurper, had received instruction in a dream to come to Jerusalem, the ancient home of his ancestors, for aid."

"A dream?" Broussard asked.

"The Prince Lalibela came to the brotherhood with an ancient tale from the time of Solomon. In this tale were news of a secret lineage and the missing piece to the puzzle of the writings we had found. The famous journey undertaken by the Queen of Sheba to meet the great king had produced a child. She carried the child in her womb on the journey home to Ethiopia. Here, in this land where we are right now, the Son of Solomon was born. The Prince Menelik. When the child grew to adulthood, he came in secret to Jerusalem with tidings from his mother. Solomon saw worthiness and greatness within the young man, and knew him to be his son. It was Menelik whom Solomon entrusted with his greatest secret. He returned with it to his home in Ethiopia, telling no one of his true identity, telling no one of his boon, no one of his burden. Here it has remained hidden for 2,000 years.

"Upon hearing this story, a small force of the greatest of our Order followed the young prince, Lalibela, back to his home among these highlands, and won back for him his throne. In exchange for our assistance, we were allowed to remain, to seek answers for our own mysteries."

"Answers that you..." Broussard found himself speaking as if he were hearing a personal account. "Answers that *they* found."

Montbard nodded. "Answers that, in turn, introduced only greater mysteries. Answers that brought only more terrible burdens." Montbard paused, as if further debating the plummeting value of his secrets. "You have asked what Templars are doing here. We are hiding. We have kept guard over a secret far greater than ourselves for nearly one hundred years."

Broussard worked to further align what he had been taught long ago and the new reality of what he could now see for himself. He thought more of Beaujeu's mysterious orders, the enigmatic questions of the golden Mongol, and an eerie sense of dread began to rise from deep within.

"Am I to know this secret?"

"The object you seek is the ring on your finger. It is my charge, the ancient truth I have concealed. From your orders we thought you and your quest to be very important, indeed. And from your injuries, it was clear that only the ring could save you. Therefore, save you it did."

Broussard slowly turned his hand in amazement and watched the symbols dance in the light. "This is the Seal of Solomon? Given the King by an angel?"

"It came to Solomon not from an angel but from the shadows of a time and place where the memory of man does not reach. It is the fire of the gods, stolen by the immortal Prometheus for the illumination of mankind. For this act of rebellion, he was pursued for unknown eons, caught, and crucified upon the pinnacle of Mount Caucasus, where he suffered for age upon age. It is the Apple from the Tree of Knowledge, taken and eaten by the first man and woman, an act for which their children still suffer."

Broussard looked again at the shimmering band, now dark gold, now sparkling ebony. "Why?" he asked at last.

"The ring holds the mark of the true ruler of this world. Beyond this I know little, but he is a jealous king. It is his will that Seth murder his brother Osiris forever, that Cain murder Abel again and again. It is the tireless work of his servants that mankind live in ignorance and fear, as sheep before his shepherd's staff, knowing nothing of our true nature and true inheritance. For many years, we have kept the King's mark safe, studied it, and unlocked many of its secrets. What little of its vast power I have accessed has kept our brethren alive and well here since the beginning. But now, with your presence as further harbinger, I fear the Enemy has found its lost prize once more. Time is very short." He would have Broussard's full report. "What have you seen?"

Broussard did not know how much, if any, of what the old man said was to be believed, but he could see that the time to haggle over information had ended.

"On the beach where we landed in Sinai, I saw two dozen warriors. Saracen fighters mingled in alliance with Knights of St. John and great and powerful Templars whom I could recognize, all fresh from the battle at Acre. They were led by a Mongol who comes to your thoughts while you sleep." Broussard paused before determining that what he had to say was unlikely to sound as ridiculous to these men as it did to him. "The witch cannot reach your thoughts unless he is very near." He then added with resolve and finality, "He was near when I awoke. They are coming."

After a moment of silent thought, Montbard spoke with regret and a degree of fear. "Then, Broussard, much falls to you. You will not be prepared."

"What falls to me?"

Montbard rose from his seat, pacing slowly as he plumbed his ocean of knowledge. "Our time as guardians of the Seal is at an end. There is a great struggle to come and a great burden to carry." He looked now on Broussard with pity. "You will be as a fox before hounds, boy. You will suffer terribly for coming here." Ever deeper concerns moved beneath the years of experience etched in his face. "The thoughts of Beaujeu are a mystery to me. But if, in you, he has chosen well, these things will come to pass for you. Otherwise, all is lost already, and the great struggle will end here and now." Montbard gazed upon the unlikely savior who stood before him. "I will tell you what I can of the ring in the time we have, Broussard. But you must quickly take your charge and flee. We seven will attempt to cover your escape."

Broussard could form no more questions. He stood silently as the old men slowly and gingerly rose from their table.

"You may yet learn all I know and more, if you live beyond this danger you have brought on your heels." Montbard lingered on the young man's eyes to measure his heart before reaching out to place a hand on his shoulder. "Know in this moment that you are a Templar no longer. You have joined the ranks of an even smaller brotherhood, even more secret, and far more ancient. From the men in this room, tracing backward in time to Menelik the son of Sheba, to his father Solomon the Wise, and further back into time and legend to the eternal sufferer, the Thief of Secrets."

Broussard knew the characters. He knew the tales. But he struggled to see how they could suddenly become so real as to touch him.

"To possess the King's mark is to know the true meaning of Our Saviour's death on the cross, and his resurrection. If the Enemy catches you, Broussard, you may be tempted. If you are great enough, they may allow you to serve them. To serve the Enemy willfully is to live in all the splendors the world has to offer, and to hold great power over all men. Yet it is to be a slave nonetheless. Still, the alternative is..."

"Is what?" Broussard asked, the lines between what was real and what was not seeming less important by the moment.

"If you refuse this temptation when it is offered, you will be crucified. Like Prometheus, Osirus, Mithras, Christ, and many others before and since who have known the simple truth your ring reveals, who understood and spoke that message aloud, you will suffer, Broussard, you will die, and you will rise again."

He watched Montbard with wide eyes and only vague comprehension, like a fish with the first suspicion of being caught in a net. *The eternal sufferer. Thief of Secrets.*

"It falls to you, Broussard," Montbard repeated in the grim tone of a commander assigning a man to a most dangerous task. "Your charge is the only hope of men. You must keep it safe. This is your honor. This is your doom." The old willow's eyes brightened even as the furrows of his wrinkled brow deepened. "Open your heart and mind to me now and I will tell you what I can of its many secrets, great and terrible."

Broussard turned once more from the sad sparkling gaze, to the shimmering band on his finger, flashing now black, now gold.

Chapter Fifty

Molly paced her comfortable cage like a sullen tiger. One lap around the room had shown her everything there was to see. Yet she found herself starting fresh at the beginning each time she returned to it. The window showed her that she was in a mighty building, a tower reaching some thirty stories above Santa Monica with a view to the west over the ocean. There was one set of polished steel double-doors, a formidable barrier, impenetrable to anyone without a key. Her surroundings were lavish. Green plants accented a carefully conceived decor, heavy and masculine with dark oak, smooth marble, and supple Persian carpets that felt like short grass over spongy earth beneath her feet. On the walls hung paintings and tapestries that spoke not only of their owner's knowledge of art and of history, but of his ability to procure rare and even priceless items. It also spoke of his desire to hold such precious things and call them his own. This was his home, his sanctuary, and his fortress. The Shepherd. *Broussard*.

Molly had not often considered that Shepherds might need homes, or even beds to sleep in. So often had their relentless pursuit deprived her of such things in the past. Yet, what she learned here only confirmed what she had seen in his car and what Rachel had suspected from the first time she saw him. This man was proud and he was vain. There was weakness in him.

For all of her hatred of him, seeing the way he lived elicited another unexpected flash of pity within Molly. His wealth was not only vast, but likely limitless. Yet for all that it was, it was still all he would ever have.

And that, she knew better than any man or woman walking the earth, would never be enough to soothe the ache created by that same pride, that same vanity.

Molly pushed that nearly compassionate thought away in favor of the image of his malicious stare, and for the sake of the crushing dread that came to her, the appalling realization. She had failed again. People she loved were dead because of her. Again. What inconceivable knowledge and power she might wield, once again had come to the heart, mind, and hands of a child, and that child had led the Shepherd straight to them. All that lay underneath faded into the background, leaving only the frightened girl alone with her failure.

Unable to reach the nearby couch as images of the horrors of the bookshop assailed her, Molly fell where she stood. She lay on the soft carpet, a cry choking in her throat. She remembered the cradling embrace of her mother during those last days of home in Virginia, but the image came to her faded and from far away. Her thoughts moved unexpectedly to the rush of comfort that had swept away the demons of her memories when she awoke to find Book's powerful arms holding her tightly to his heart. She thought of these things while she wept over her burden, over her failure.

That sense of failure gave way to sorrow, sorrow to rage, and rage finally to the old hatred, just as it had countless times before. The God-damned thing. It consumed like a white fire, devouring her and what love she had to give, always and every time, leaving only this hate for it within the ashes. Her ring. The King's X.

She could not fight this man, she knew. And in knowing that, Molly grew more calm, allowing a sense of purpose to slowly rise within her where she lay on the carpet with her knees tucked to her chest.

Molly closed her eyes and began to concentrate on her breath. She listened to the sound of the air entering her body through her nose and softly leaving through her lips. She felt her lungs fill and she turned her awareness to the blood coursing like countless rivers and streams through her body. She calmed. She moved away from her anger and hatred, reaching for a stronger peace. The Shepherd was nearby, somewhere within this building, likely waiting for her to lower her guard and sleep, thus inviting him into her mind. He held every advantage, including time. He could wait indefinitely while she grew weaker. But perhaps, she reasoned, and even sensed that it was so, there was a way to fight after all. There could be someone yet hidden within her dreams and memories far stronger than herself, a champion, someone possibly even stronger than the Shepherd.

Molly breathed in this way for a few minutes more, slowing her heart, dulling the edge of her emotions, and reaching once more for the embrace of sleep.

Chapter Fifty-One

Somewhere within the rolling sea of soft grass that hushed in the night breeze, Khali stood, holding the bridle of their horse to keep it silent and still. She watched the moon in the clear sky. Since the beginning of their journey, the moon had steadily waned from half to nothing at all. Now, as she waited within this unknown wilderness, even more uncertain of her place in the world than as a lost child on the streets of Acre, the moon was re-born. It grew each night, and Khali knew that the thin silver crescent would come again within a short time to the fullness of its cycle. She took comfort in this mystery, as it seemed to offer some wisdom to her in her loneliness. Just as her life with her mother had given way to her life among Ardenti's women, so now that existence had given way to something new. It came to her as steadily as the birth of the new moon.

Shahin cursed the moon as he scrambled back to where he had left the girl and horse. Thin as it was, it still shone brightly in the clear sky. There was nowhere to run from what was coming, and no cover but the grass. They were trapped in the open and the moon was no ally.

"Quickly, Khali" he commanded in a harsh whisper as he approached and snatched the bridle from her hand, "lay down flat and quiet in the grass."

Fear moved quickly through her at the urgency in his voice. Khali did as he said and watched the Captain gently and quietly pull the enormous animal down to its knees and then onto its side. The horse grunted and sputtered nervously through the process, but Shahin held its head still, stroking its coat and whispering soft words that the beast seemed to understand. "The moon is behind us," he said, loud enough now for her to hear. "We are just more stones in the grass."

It had been two days since the old men in Templar garb had taken Broussard from her. And it had been two days since Captain Shahin had taken her from Broussard. He had said before that their mission was hopeless, and that he would take her with him to a new life if she would come. But something had changed in the Captain upon finding the grey-bearded Christians riding among the hills. He had found hope for the plan of Guillaume de Beaujeu. As harsh and dangerous as this man could be, Khali had felt the hidden compassion that burned slowly within. Unable to abandon his people while hope still remained, he had won his freedom from Broussard's quest, but still chose to follow in secret.

They had followed the trail left by the Templars, hours behind and matching the slow pace of the litter that carried Broussard. For two days they had seen no sign of man other than the tracks of their quarry. The rising savannah had been silent in all that time, until the breeze at their backs had brought a sound that caused Captain Shahin to suddenly stop their slow climb up the steppes. He had paused to listen further, more intently, even reaching a hand to cover her mouth when Khali started to ask. He had pulled her from the horse and handed her the bridle, teaching her in an urgent whisper, "hold his head still and he will stay still. Quietly now." And he had moved off toward the crest just behind them.

Now, as she lay beside the horse in the grass, listening to the deep breaths filling its mighty body, she thought of the dying animal in Ardenti's courtyard. She thought of the archer on the wall, of the marauding soldiers, of the blood and death. When she began to hear the sounds that Shahin had heard, voices of men and the slow steps of horses just beyond the rise behind them, she recalled the horrible ferocity of Broussard.   She remembered the strength she had felt at his side and the fear in the eyes of their attackers at the sight of their blood staining his sword. But he was not with her now.

The riders slowly came into view, only a few paces away. As Shahin had surmised, they followed the same trail of hoof prints and grass bent beneath a litter. What light the crescent moon provided shone in their faces, picking up the glint of their weapons and armor.

Some wore uniforms she had seen before, black tunics with a gold cross at the breast. Hospitallers. White tunics with crimson. Templars. And still more incongruously riding among the Christians, she saw the pointed helmets and curved blades of Saracen soldiers.

Another man stopped his horse at the top of the hill. He wore no uniform and appeared as a shadow of deeper black framed against the starlit sky. Khali held her breath as she watched him. He seemed frozen as he watched his men move in a steady stream. Finally the shadow turned toward the moon and the warm breeze scattered the veil of hair from his face. So close she could see his hooded eyes like pools of ink, Khali looked into the golden face of Broussard's witch. He was staring right at her.

For the first time since she had found herself alone in the corridor outside Baseema's chamber, fear surged through her so overwhelmingly, she began to forget that silence and stillness were her only hope. Suddenly her lungs seemed too small for the breaths she took. She thought to run.

Shahin's hand snatched her back to the earth just as she had begun to rise. She turned sharply. He caught her eye in his and held her there in that moment. He did not dare speak, but there was force enough in his glare that Khali remembered, *stones in the grass.*

From where his horse stood at the crest of a high hill, the Mongol closed his eyes to the passing line of his Assassins and released his thoughts like a flock of birds with his breath. Broussard slept again. *Clever Thieves. Wait for me. I am right behind you.*

They traveled slowly at night, but Broussard moved slower. To the right of the line, with the moon thus behind his left shoulder, the trail of horses dragging a litter behind them was easy to follow. Opening his eyes once more, the Mongol scanned the dark savannah to the south. He remained only a moment longer, watching the stones among the waving grass.

Chapter Fifty-Two

Free now of its heavy brass casing, the *King's X* flashed black and gold in Book's hand as he turned the ring over and over between his fingers. Even as the young policeman outside continued to announce himself in rising tones and bang on the locked door with the pad of his fist, Book studied the unfamiliar, darkly dancing inscriptions.

This was no wedding ring. Even as his eyes became more deeply fixated on the shimmering metal, Book could see what his father had done. At the munitions plant, at the height of the war, Carl Book operated the press into which the molten brass alloy was poured, cooled, and then stamped into the form of a firing cap for an artillery shell. He knew long before the hunters caught up to him that he needed to hide the ring. So, when no one was watching, he simply dropped it into the molten mix and stamped it. But even though no one had seen, Book reasoned, his father still *knew* what he had done. They would still come in his sleep to see what he had seen, to know what he knew. And the old man had also known that if what Rachel had told him was true, it would be far too long before she could return.

His father had commissioned a lawyer, Grissom, to deliver a package to his son twenty-four years to the day after Rachel's death, trusting beyond faith that 1968 would be the year she would seek him out to retrieve the thing hidden inside.

And the hunters did catch up. For those nine days after they had found him, Carl Book did not sleep. While the hounds circled, he held on.

Through the exposing of his wicked past in the newspaper, the murder of his wife, and the inevitable disintegration of his mind, he held on until the last of his strength failed.   Rather than give in to sleep and open his thoughts to his enemies, he went out to the garage with a gun and put a stop to all of his thoughts at once.

"It's time, Book," John announced, cutting through Book's fixed attention. "You've got to go."

Book closed his fist around the ring so that he might finally look away from it. The policeman at the door had walked off toward his patrol car.

"I can't. Not while there's still a chance to find her."

"There is no chance of that, Book.   But there is still a chance for everything else. *Everything.*" John's stare implored him. "She fought for us all, Book.   All that she has won, over *lifetimes,* is in your hand right now."

Book could not quite discern the fine line between mania and conviction in his voice as John's personal story merged still tighter with his own.

"This is why you are here.   It's *you* Book.   You've got to take it now."

Book's head spun from blood-loss.   He stepped out of the crimson slick gathering around his left boot and retreated painfully to sit in a chair. He steadied himself, the shotgun still tucked under his good elbow, the ring clutched in his good hand.   He sought options and saw none.

"Take it where?"

"I don't know.   Away.   And fast.   You can't let them find you.   Not now."

Book heard the echo of Molly's last words to him in what John said. *Don't look back.*

John turned to watch the young officer standing by his squad car, only a few feet from the locked door. He moved closer to the dirty glass. "Book," he said without turning. "I have suffered at their hands and brought a great deal of suffering to others because of them. But I have lived long enough to know what has happened to me, and I am grateful to them for one thing." John reached for the lock on the door. "I know a secret."

Book opened his palm and returned to studying the ring.

"What secret?" he asked, his weakening voice just above a whisper.

The young policeman was speaking into the car radio, too far away to hear. John carefully slid the bolt out of its brace, unlocking the door. He turned once more toward Book and Chuck Townsend, who sat and waited. A plan had formed in John's mind, and he didn't have much time. Still, his answer sounded reasoned and calm, as if they were not the thoughts of a mad man.

"There is nothing to fear."

Book had heard those words earlier, and he was no less skeptical of them the second time.

"The Second Secret." He offered the grand title as confirmation, but the look on John's face showed that Book's response meant nothing to him. "Because of God, right?"

John paused to wonder at the sarcasm in Book's voice long enough for the distracted detective to notice the two-by-four in his hand.

"No, wait!" Book climbed painfully and too late to his feet as John swung the door open to the street.

As quickly as John stepped outside, Chuck Townsend seized on the distraction to run. Book saw the mechanic disappear around a corner toward the rear exit, but did nothing to stop him. Instead, he hobbled after

John into the alley.

The Assassin moved with such speed and violence, the officer had no time to defend himself. He dropped the radio microphone to reach for his revolver, but the thick board caught him first in the solar plexus, then came down across his back with the force of a falling tree.

The rain had stopped. The setting sun gashed the horizon beneath the grey sky to the west.

Both men heard the concerned voice of the dispatcher on the other end of the radio. "34? What happened? Unit 34, respond..."

"Don't you believe in God, Book?" John asked.

Overwhelming anger surged in Book as he saw his own fate once more being decided by the whims of mad men. The madness of convictions that drove his father, the madness of the old man in his bookshop, the madness that Molly had brought with her, the madness that fueled his mother's killer long ago, and the madness of this moment powered his words now.

"I don't believe," Book seethed, "because I'm not blind and I'm not stupid!" He paused, thinking he was finished, but a quick breath brought even more of a lifetime of rage and disappointment to the surface. "I was a *vice* cop! No God worth believing in could account for what happens here every single day. If there is a God, then I promise you he doesn't give a damn about you, and he doesn't give a damn about me, and he doesn't give a damn about that girl!"

John heard Book's voice break at the mention of the girl. The young man's fear was plain and fully exposed. People he loves die, and there is nothing he can do about it. After a long moment, the Assassin responded in an even tone.

"I think he's just waiting."

Book had heard his own voice crack, too. He turned deeper into his anger, into his own madness to quell the rising agony of loss. He glanced back at the open door to the auto shop, no longer a place to hide. He listened to the voices of the police on the radio. They were nearby and coming fast. The agony remained. Molly was gone and there was, as always before, nothing he could do about it.

An unexpected impulse overtook him in that moment. Book's anger turned to laughter. He laughed to keep the pain from taking over. He laughed at the hole in his shoulder and his own blood on the ground. He laughed at the hopelessness of his predicament. He laughed at the things Molly had said. And he laughed at God. It was the laughter of a fool. And he knew that, too.

Stung by the laughter, John's anger rose to meet Book's.

"Did you ever think that maybe you are not just a walking, talking piece of meat, pushed around by the wind?"

Book stopped laughing and stared at him, a madman, a murderer, the broken shell of a man whose name was John, who'd had a wife and family a lifetime ago.

"Did you ever stop to think that maybe God needs you as much as you need him?" The question came with quiet, tempered certainty. "Because I have. I've thought about that a lot." John's eyes drifted around the alley, as if gathering evidence for what he was about to say. "I see him sometimes walking the street, shaking his fist at the rain like a dumb animal. Impotent. Foolish."

His eyes came back to Book's once more, the same unnerving stare.

"I hear him sometimes. He talks in a voice that sounds like mothers wailing for lost children, or men crying out for justice or even a goddamned cup of coffee. Sometimes he shouts with a voice that shakes the ground, that explodes like bombs falling out of the sky. I've heard him calling out like a helpless father kneeling by the crib where his baby sleeps too deep, sick with fever and at the edge of death. *Wake up!* Like thunder. *Wake up!* Like war. *Please, child! Wake up!*" Tears streaked the dusty surface of John's paper skin as he told Book of the God he had come to know. "Understand me." It was John's plea to be heard just one time. "I have seen him crying."

Book saw madness and no madness in him now, like his father just before the end. He felt Molly's ring, the *King's X*, heavy within his clenched hand as the heat returned to the back of his neck.

"What is he waiting for?"

"He's waiting for you, fool" John snapped, like the words of an angry parent to a selfish, complaining child. "He's waiting for you."

The two men remained locked in a stare, unflinching even as the sirens sounded in the distance from every direction. Book had understood every word and none of them.

"Run, Book!" John commanded sternly as he slid behind the wheel of the police cruiser. He slammed the door and jammed the car into gear, turning once more to find Book standing frozen in the alley beside him. "You're free! *Run!*"

The tires squealed on the wet pavement and the cruiser shuddered away as the sirens came still closer. Book stood alone in the alley, the King's X in his hand, his body weakening by the moment. Without the blood that flowed from the throbbing bullet hole in his shoulder, a fog encroached on all his senses and thoughts. As John's stolen cruiser accelerated toward the far end of the alley, toward the approaching sirens, Book came all the way back to the present danger. Whatever he was going to do, he would have to do it now.

He lurched toward the open door of the auto shop.

Alone inside, he moved for the possibility he had seen before. A motorcycle, repaired, reassembled, and awaiting the return of its owner. Struggling to drag his stiff right leg in front of the other, he stumbled. His useless arm hanging, he was unable to catch himself. Book struck the concrete floor with the left side of his face and his ruined shoulder hard enough to blast away what awareness he had left. The shotgun skittered away. The golden ring escaped his clutching hand, bounced, rolled and spun like a jingling top until it came to rest a few feet away.

An electric surge of pain through his rapidly failing body brought Book a moment of consciousness. His mind was no longer capable of holding many thoughts, but there was a new sensation beginning to drift through him just below the surface. Peace. Like a gentle stream that took him suddenly out of the vast river of pain, he seemed to move with a flow of bliss, as if it aimed to take him somewhere. After a moment or two within this soft current even the notion of longing for more of the feeling it carried began to give way to having no notions at all. He sensed that he was drowning in it. He had no strength left and no wish to fight it. Wendell Book was dying.

Chapter Fifty-Three

Shahin held the girl closer, his arms and body a shield against the pre-dawn chill. He guided the horse at a quicker pace alongside the tracks of the war party. The Mongol had traveled all night on the trail of Broussard. Shahin had followed for the sake of his people and the possibility of seeing Beaujeu's mission to fruition. He thought to tell himself that Khali had followed because he carried her, because he could keep her safe in this wilderness. But he was never adept at deceiving himself over matters of the heart. He knew well enough that she came for her dying soldier.

The sky ahead of them had slowly begun to change, star-mottled blackness giving way to violet as the sun approached the horizon at their backs. Shahin stopped the horse to listen to the rapid clang of a bell far ahead, somewhere deep within the slowly dispersing darkness.

"What is it?" Khali asked, rising a little in the saddle before him to peer further ahead.

"An alarm." Shahin listened until the bell abruptly stopped only a moment later. "We have caught them," he surmised. "And they have caught up with the Templars." The first discernable clouds in the west took shape in the growing light from the east. "The Mongol attacks with the first light." Shahin dug a boot heel into the flank of the exhausted horse. They moved on toward the crest of the next hill, toward where the klaxon had sounded and been silenced, toward the battle.

***

Templars, Hospitallers and Saracens moved in a mounted phalanx past the abandoned klaxon and onto the earth and stone pathways of the keep. Durand held up a hand to stop the march at the sight of riders ahead. In the rising light, the shadows of men on horseback began to color. First, tunics of white, then crosses of crimson. Seven Templars stood in their path. Waiting.

"*Broussard*," the witch hissed at Durand. "They protect him."

"We are twenty-four," Durand coldly replied. "They are seven."

The Mongol scanned the peculiar stone buildings as the keep became more visible in deepening scarlet.

"No survivors," he commanded as he turned his horse away from the impending clash.

Durand called out to their men. They formed a line that stretched well beyond either side of the seven. Their horses, sensing the lust rising in their riders, stamped the earth and snorted in anticipation.

The old Templars had waited in silent resolve. They drew their seven swords as one, and a single rush of metal scraping against metal hit the ears of the Assassins. The twenty-four paused long enough to watch the seven raise their blades to bowed heads in preparation, in prayer.

"We are Knights of the Temple no longer." Montbard spoke for the ears of his men alone. The old men listened, bowed heads still touching the cold weapons held before them. "Though our lives are forfeit on this field, know that we are free. The Enemy has no dominion over us. Our long watch has ended. Our new task begins. Today we die, tomorrow we fight anew, a legion of the dead."

The seven opened their eyes together. Montbard looked upon his brothers with pride as he steeled himself for the battle. "Godspeed, my brothers. We will meet again at the appointed place."

Durand let the great sword held over his head fall toward the enemy. Twenty-four horses screamed to a fast gallop and thundered toward the waiting old men.

***

Broussard moved west down a treacherous slope of mud and rocks hidden in the half-light. At Montbard's orders, he carried Beaujeu's prize on his finger, away from the Templar keep, and once again, away from battle. He paused in the short valley where the downward slope began to rise again. He listened to the sound of fighting coming from the sanctuary. The old willow and his six monks were dying at the hands of his enemies, purchasing time for his escape.

Looking back, Broussard saw movement at the top of the rise behind him. His eyes widened as another horse crested the hill and paused at the top. Black cloak and black hair whipped about him in the rising dawn wind as the witch looked down upon his quarry. Broussard drew a quick breath as he jerked the animal's head around again and spurred him on toward the next rise.

***

Shahin and Khali watched from the safety of a hilltop outside the keep, listening as the sounds of clashing swords and shouting warriors died gradually down to nothing. Hidden among the peculiar red stone structures beneath them, a battle was ending.

"We must go down there," Khali announced.

Shahin had been silently calculating their escape.

"You don't want to go down there, Khali."

"Broussard is there," she insisted.

"Broussard was near death when they took him, girl. For his sake, you should pray that his God took him before his enemies caught up to him."

Khali considered his words as she considered the silence that had fallen over the stone buildings below. If what Shahin said was true, she reasoned, tears of grief would come to her. They had not. A new sound flowed to them on the wind. It was the sound of a war horn, less than a league away to the west. Beneath them, they heard the sound of many horses moving across stone at a gallop. In another moment the Mongol's riders burst from the far edge of the mysterious compound like wolves in a pack, urging their mounts to the westward steppes, toward the sound of the horn.

"He is alive," she said with certainty.

Shahin did not reply. He watched the stream of soldiers racing away from them. Their number was still twenty-four. He cocked his head toward the quiet below, and frowned. He nudged the horse's flank once more, convincing it to make its way down the incline toward the red stone buildings.

It was an inconspicuous place, with no towers to draw attention to it from a distance, and no walls to protect it. Had they not been following a trail, Shahin speculated, they might have passed within shouting distance and not known of its existence. They moved slowly through the red stone pathways, their horse's hooves sounding in a calm rhythm among a small complex of empty buildings that seemed carved from the stone around them. Two riderless horses stood among the bodies of the dead, watching them with twitching ears. The white tunics of a handful of aged Templars shone red with stains of still pooling blood. More grey beards and wrinkled skin, and the men Shahin had first encountered days earlier lay among the dead. All the Templars of Ethiopia, it seemed, were too old and too frail to stand against Broussard's witch.

"He is not here." Khali announced again.

Eyeing the carnage, Shahin remained unmoved by her determination. "We must look to ourselves now, girl. There is nothing left here."

"No. He is alive. We must follow."

Shahin leaned around her in the saddle for a better view of her face, to see if she could somehow be privy to some secret information he could not recognize. If she was, he decided after a moment of study, he still could not see it.

***

Broussard's horse stumbled repeatedly across hidden and loose stones in the mud. The animal limped to the top of the next rise. He paused there to look back, only to find that the Mongol's war horn had been answered. Twenty-four riders rushed down the slope across the small valley, fast on his trail. Ahead of him, another treacherous descent opened eventually into a far more expansive plain. His best chance was to outrun them. Leaning over the animal's shoulder, he could see how he favored his right leg. The horse was hobbled and would certainly be overtaken in the plain below. His best chance gone, Broussard was left with one other option. He cursed under his breath and spat, the look of the kill returning to his eyes. The time to fight had come at last.

His feet hit the earth heavily as he dropped down from the saddle. The old monks had provided him with armor, and impossible as it still seemed to him, they had provided him with health. Beneath the leather gauntlet on the hand that drew his sword in anticipation of the onrushing riders, Broussard felt the weight of the darkly golden ring still on his finger. He would make his stand on the high ground.

***

Shahin had followed the trail of the Mongol for as long as he dared before leaving the path for the cover of a field of stones on a high bluff. Round and jagged, large and small, they had long ago emerged from the earth like a patch of enormous wildflowers to the north of the clashing swords and shrieking horses. There, in the safety of the rocks, Khali saw Broussard again. Though Shahin and all reason had warned of his death, he was just as she imagined he would be. Broussard stood upon a rise, fierce and indomitable, wielding his horrible weapon.

The attackers had scattered from their charge uphill at the ferocity of Broussard's stand. Five riderless horses wandered near the motionless bodies of five men. She had seen it in her mind. Broussard lived and continued to fight.

"We must help him," she demanded quietly.

Shahin squinted at the impossible scene across the valley with disbelief. The Templar was strong enough to stand, to ride, and to fight. Shahin determined to watch it play out a little longer.

He saw that Broussard had wisely chosen the location for the battle. The crest of the rise was too thin for many horses at once. Therefore, though fighting two-dozen armored cavalry, he was able to face them no more than two at once. Shahin felt Khali's body tense and her breath shorten as Broussard crossed the path of a charging horse. The Templar adroitly moved away from the Saracen rider's sword hand as he drove his own blade up through his target. The rider was unhorsed and killed by the blow, but the strength of the animal's charge had driven Broussard's sword all the way through to the hilt. Broussard lost his weapon as the horse passed and the Saracen fell away. He turned then, unarmed, into the path and the leveled pike of the next rider, a black and gold clad Hospitaller. The iron tip passed completely through Broussard's chest below the left shoulder, and the force of the charge drove him backward until the spear pierced the earth as well. Khali cried out in horror and Shahin quickly clasped his hand over her mouth. Broussard's body hung on the wooden shaft in recline, impaled and pinned to the top of the hill.

***

In the short hours they had before the arrival of the enemy, Montbard had explained what he could of the Seal. "In time we learned," the old willow recounted, "that with no knowledge at all, Solomon's Seal might keep the wearer alive through disease, age, and even grievous injury."

"What is the cost?" Broussard had pressed, with dark curiosity.

"That is simple," came the reply. "For the wearer of the ring *uninitiated* into its secrets, the cost is great pain."

Pain surged from the hole in his chest through his entire body where he hung from the pike now lodged in the ground behind him. The tip had passed through the light metal chest plate just above his lung. He struggled for breath, struggled to remain conscious, and as he watched the next rider raise his sword and start his charge, Broussard struggled to free himself from this gruesome snag.

Again, he found himself alive when all reason would demand his death. Yet Montbard had stressed to him, though his body might outlive more horrors inflicted upon it than it once would, he surely could die the same as anyone else from wounds numerous or grievous enough.

Broussard took what breath he could into his lungs, throwing all of his strength and weight into a sudden, powerful twist to the left. Using the metal of the chest plate where the pike emerged at his back as a fulcrum of sorts, Broussard snapped the wooden shaft in two just behind the metal tip still buried in the earth. He rolled to his knees, still holding the same breath, caught a grip with two hands on the pole protruding from his chest, and pulled it free.

As too much blood spilled suddenly from an open wound that surely should have been mortal, Broussard felt a level of pain no man was intended to feel. It was the pain of a killing blow that had somehow failed to kill.

With no time to react to his agony, Broussard sucked in a new breath like a drowning man just breaking the surface for the last time. He drove the dull end of the broken pike into the ground, anchoring it there even as he leveled the jagged break at the chest of the charging horse. The animal struck the point at a gallop and the earth held fast to the anchor. The horse screamed in panic as it drove itself onto the pike and came to an unnaturally abrupt halt. The rider was thrown and hit the ground heavily.

Broussard crawled to the fallen knight, another Templar. A man who had once been a comrade and a friend looked back at him with dulled eyes where he lay on his back. Broussard caught the man's sword hand by the wrist as he raised it. With only little breath to power his body, Broussard leaned on his new enemy until the long blade of his own sword pressed against his neck. With no time and no strength to question what he was about to do, he dragged the length of blade across the man's throat.

Broussard staggered in agony back to his feet, new sword in hand, and awaited the next attack.

***

Durand, Leveque and Van Cuso sat on their mounts next to the Mongol as he studied the battle, puzzling only briefly over the single Templar, still standing among the bodies of a dozen fallen Assassins.

"He has the Seal," the Mongol decided. "Dismount and attack as one. He *will* fall."

***

"Captain, please!" Khalidah turned in the saddle to face him.

Shahin watched the Templar in the distance continue to stand, continue to fight. A rush of the twelve remaining attackers turned to eight in an instant as Broussard began again his impossible slaughter. He and the girl were safe here, their presence undetected. He looked down into her imploring eyes in disbelief, both at what was occurring and at what he knew he was about to do.

"This cannot be."

***

With each passing moment, the flow of blood from the hole in his chest lessened. The *ring*. As Montbard had promised, time would be his ally. And, as Montbard had warned, "there could be no peace, no respite. Because whatever else it may be, this ring is the enemy of Mercy."

Hanging at the edges of the fight, disengaged while his men fell one by one, the Mongol waited for the Templar to die. He watched as Broussard rose again to one knee, pulled himself to standing with the support of his sword, and then finally dragged the weapon from the heart of his twenty-first kill.

The strongest of the Europeans were his last three Assassins. The lightning quick Durand, the brutal and merciless Leveque, and the giant Van Cuso stepped over the bodies to form a circle around Broussard. From three sides, they struck at Broussard in concert, like the sudden closing of a three-pronged trap.

Van Cuso saw his thrust parried, but his attack served its purpose. The second sword, a vicious hacking blow from Leveque, sliced into the Templar's leg where the chain mail did not reach. And the third found its mark. Coming unseen from behind, as straight and true as a striking cobra, Durand's blade pierced his armor and penetrated deep.

Van Cuso listened to the cry of pain. He then watched once more in bewildered astonishment as Broussard did not fall, did not die, but rather parried Leveque's sword into the ground and delivered a swift upward arcing strike that passed several inches deep through his torso, disemboweling the man within his armor. Durand, his own weapon still caught in Broussard's back, paused in dumb amazement as the Templar turned on him at close range, and struck him down.

Broussard fell to his knees among twenty-three dead enemies. He reached back awkwardly to catch Durand's protruding sword, and pulled it free of his body. Life poured from him in the form of blood, but life poured into him as well. He felt the heat entering though the top of his head, as if the ebbing force of life could be recaptured even as it fled from the torment of the fight, and hauled back to him as with a fisherman's heavy net.

Van Cuso stood only a few feet from where Broussard knelt. He watched the young man where he wheezed through punctured lungs, and shuddered through the unimaginable torment of clear consciousness before open flesh, sundered muscle, and broken bone.

"Broussard." The giant said aloud. "This cannot be."

Broussard looked up at his old rival from his knees. He thought to agree with him, but knew he might only have the strength to stand once more if he did not speak. Slowly, horrifically, he stood.

Van Cuso had fought in dozens of battles across the Holy Land. He had killed more men than he could count. He had stood side by side with death in battle, and he had stood against it. As he studied Broussard, covered from head to boot in gore as if he had bathed in it, he knew he had never seen anything like this. He also knew that he was looking into the eyes of a man who, only weeks before he had called rival, but also an ally. He tried to remember why things were different now, but no satisfactory answer came to him. Nothing else need be said between them.

Van Cuso raised his mighty sword above his head and attacked. Broussard lurched to his left on wounded legs, and found the strength to dodge and parry Van Cuso's bullish charge one final time. He deflected the massive sword away. Momentum carried the blade into the ground, and the giant off balance. Broussard spun quickly on his heel, bringing his own sword around in a full, high-arcing circle with what strength remained in his ruined body. Van Cuso had just lifted his head in time to see the blade pass through his neck. The head fell first, then the body. Broussard stumbled a few steps in the direction his sword carried him, before he toppled into the reddened mud.

The sound of approaching footsteps kept him conscious. He tried, but Broussard could not stand again. From where his head rested in the sodden earth, Broussard saw the Mongol's black boots come to a stop a single pace away.

"What have you found, Templar?" The witch seemed to take some pleasure in the question this time. "Clever, clever thieves."

Seeing that what had kept Broussard alive and fighting was now spent, the Mongol removed the gauntlet from the Templar's right hand. On his finger, the thing he had been sent for flashed darkly, now black, now gold. He studied the prize for a long moment, before reaching to his hip for a short, curved blade.

As the Shepherd set his hand to the earth and held the knife to his finger, Broussard heard through the mud where he lay, an urgent, rhythmic pulse, growing louder.

The Mongol also heard the sound, emanating from behind him. It was a horse, fast approaching and climbing the rise just out of sight. He dropped his knife and reached instead for his sword. He turned and rose to his feet just as Captain Shahin burst over the crest at a gallop. Shahin's curved Moorish blade hammered into the Mongol's parry with all the power and weight of his charging horse behind it. The force of the blow knocked the sword from the witch's hand and sent him stumbling backward over Broussard's unmoving body, and into the mud. The Mongol retrieved his weapon on his hands and knees as Shahin pulled his protesting horse around to charge again.

With the weapon of surprise now spent, Shahin sensed that he would not have many more opportunities. He sought to take the enemy quickly with a sudden and overwhelming onslaught. The witch had regained his feet as the snorting beast bore down on him. Shahin lifted his sword in a wide arc to strike, but the Mongol was prepared this time. He darted like the shadow of a fast flying bird across Shahin's path, a low sweep of his sword slashing deep into bone on the horse's foreleg. The animal screamed in pain and terror. Shahin went hard over his head as they fell together in the mud.

Stunned by the out-rush of air pounded from his lungs upon impact with the ground, Shahin fought to remain conscious. At last he filled his lungs again through a gaping mouth. He located his weapon first, only a few feet away in the mud, and his enemy second. The Mongol stalked slowly toward him, his sword held low at his side.

"This is not your fight, Moor."

"I choose what is my fight." Shahin reached his feet, wavering more than his shaken body demanded, letting the Mongol see weakness when there was yet some strength.

"You have chosen poorly." The Mongol struck.

Shahin's defense came faster and surer than expected. The Captain turned the first blow away and struck with the back of the balled fist of his off hand.

"It would not be the first time."

The Mongol turned from the stinging blow across his face and lashed out again, the hilt of his sword crossing Shahin's cheek and knocking him again into the mud.

The Mongol stepped toward him once more, smiling at the Captain's guile and still wary of further deception. He waited until Shahin raised his weapon from where he lay as a token defense. But this time the witch knocked the curved blade aside, leaving the Captain's heart open to a quick attack. Shahin rolled away as quickly as he could, but the thrust only slightly missed its mark. Shahin found himself watching in amazement as the blade passed through his chest, a hand's width to the right of his heart, and into the earth below him. The pain was astonishing, but not yet unbearable. The greater pain would come if he were to live for a few minutes longer. It was with equal amazement that the Captain found himself able to face his own impending death while simultaneously reaching to the short curved blade on his hip.

The Mongol looked into the eyes of the dying man at his feet, and saw that there was yet life in them. His strike had missed the heart. The wound would kill, but not quickly.

As the Mongol's hand turned round the hilt of the protruding sword, Shahin knew he would have only an instant. Lacking the strength to rise and strike, he reached his gloved hand to the blade in his chest. When the Mongol tried to pull it free, Shahin held tight. The blade came up, lifting him a foot off the ground, close enough to strike. The short curved blade in his left hand struck deep into the unprotected belly and penetrated far into his enemy's chest from beneath. A grunt escaped the witch's lips. Shahin watched his eyes register what he took to be surprise, before life fled from them, and the golden man fell back into the mud.

Chapter Fifty-Four

John reached the mouth of the alley an instant before two converging cruisers. His car burst through the opening, sliding between them in a tire-smoking fishtail as he angled for the open space of Santa Monica Boulevard.

The cruisers joined in pursuit. A radio message was sent. *Suspect headed west on Santa Monica.* The picture was painted. Fears were confirmed. The madman was behind the wheel of a stolen police car.

To the citizens of Santa Monica, blissfully unaware of the significance of John's flight, it was as if a great jungle cat had escaped from the zoo. The terrifying roar of a black and white police car suddenly bounding onto the sidewalk shattered the peace. Adrenaline surged through their bodies in a thrilling rush as the people fled for the safety of doorways or crouched behind the protection of massive palm trees.

It took several minutes and numerous detours for John to travel the quarter-mile from the auto shop to the ocean. By the time he reached Broadway, a block short of Ocean Avenue and within sight of the long pier beyond, his cruiser had become a battered hulk. Steam flowed from underneath the hood, accompanied by the stinging scent of coolant pouring over a hot engine. The car had little life left in it, but it had taken him where he needed to be. This was the place where he had once made his escape after a horrible crime. And this would be the place where he would make amends for it.

***

From where he lay with the side of his face pressed against the cold concrete, the floor of the auto shop appeared to Book like a grim landscape. Across what seemed from his perspective as a great distance, his shotgun rested behind the wheel of the partially disassembled Plymouth. And beyond that, waiting out in the open, the ring flashed darkly.

His father's ring. Molly's ring. *King's X.* Whatever the hell it was. Even as he stared at it, he longed for the deeper waters of the quiet stream of bliss that continued to carry him further from the pain.

But something else held his eyes open at this moment. Something more powerful than the gentle stream, more important than the flashing ring, compelled him. Molly moved through his thoughts, just as she had from the first moment he saw her.

With the girl came more thoughts to threaten the peace that pulled at him. The image of Sara collided sharply with the softness that carried him, but he continued to drift. As the current worked to sweep him away, the fog encroached more heavily on the black and grey scene of the concrete floor. All he needed to do to escape the pain was to fall asleep, simply let go and let the gentle water take him under.

The image of Molly entering the black car stung at him through the fog. He knew the man who held her now. He had stood face to face with him, and he had seen what he could do. Book struggled to hold onto that thought, until yet another came to him. He was not finished. He could not leave her. Not now.

He pulled a shallow, determined breath in through his nose. He would fight against the flow of bliss with the only tool he had left. Pain.

Book willed his eyes to open wider, to take in more light from the room. With light came awareness. And with awareness came more pain.

He reached for it. The pain of the bullet wound, the old pain of his leg, the sharp sting of open flesh against concrete as he lifted his face from the cold floor.

In the dim light of his weakened mind he watched the Shepherd, and he let anger flow into the stream of peace. He began to remember many things she had said. She had warned of the dangers and hardship it had brought her and all she had loved. He recalled the promise she had demanded of him to throw it deeper into the ocean, and the promise he had offered instead. He had promised to keep her safe. He had promised to find a way.

He recalled the unlikely stories she told of its power. Whatever else it might be, Book knew it was real now. It existed. And he knew it was a weapon.

Book began to crawl, right hand clawing at the floor, left leg pushing from behind. Pain surged through him, the only thing he could hold onto, the only thing keeping him here - awake, alive, and moving inch by inch toward the darkly shining ring.

***

John watched the black and white cruisers gather like pursuing hounds in his rear view mirror. Two more rushed to a stop on the road before him, blocking his path to the last intersection between his car and his escape. He stomped on the gas pedal. The dying engine groaned at the demand, but obeyed.

His cruiser slammed into the front fender of the right-hand car and sent it spinning violently out of the way. The flow of steam became a geyser as he pushed the car on like a faltering horse. He was on the pier now, and still picking up speed.

He looked to the sky above the fast approaching horizon, where the rain clouds had given way to glorious streaks of red and violet as day turned to night. The water would be dark and deep. The search might take days.

The hounds followed onto the pier. The sirens continued to scream. Men and women snatched up their children and shrank back as the chase passed them by. But John did not see them anymore.

Even as his howling cruiser blasted through the steel rail at the far western end of the pier, even as the cold grey water rushed toward him, John smiled, triumphant, free, seeing nothing but the colors of the sky.

Chapter Fifty-Five

Khali reached the crest of the hill, breathing hard after a long sprint and climb without the benefit of a horse. What she found there chased her breath away altogether. The mud gathered in red pools around the bodies of the dead, as if from a hard rain of blood.

Despite the horror of the scene, her thoughts returned quickly to the two men who had led her to this moment. She found them near each other, bathed in still more blood, unmoving, and with the body of the golden skinned man in between.

She rushed to Broussard first, dropping to her knees beside him, his body a gruesome heap of wounds and dark mud. He did not move.

"He is surely dead." It was the voice of Captain Shahin, weak and strained, coming from behind her.

Khali turned to see that his shallowing eyes watched her from where he remained impaled and thus propped into a half-seated position, where the Mongol's curved sword passed through his chest into the ground.

"And I will join him soon enough." He looked on her fondly, a smile passing his lips. "I fear what will become of you alone out here. But you will probably do better without us."

Even as he lay dying, Khali sensed that he was trying to ease her fear. She looked again at the still body of Broussard, before moving to Shahin. He reached out his hand and she took it, kneeling beside him. She fought to keep a serene expression as she studied the wound where the blade entered his body.

"I must remove the sword to attend the wound." She said.

Shahin felt the warmth of her hand in his and allowed the peculiar gift all women bring to wash over him, letting her touch deaden the pain like a sweet wine or some fragrant opiate.

"No." He fought for each breath with great calm, his right lung long ago filled with blood. "I am dead already, girl. The blade only plugs the wound. Remove it and I will only leave you faster."

Khali looked deeply into the Captain's peaceful eyes, marveling with gratitude over the cruel ironies of his life. Here was a man who projected many of the worst qualities of men; criminal, cutthroat, and thief. Yet, these evils were a mask. She used to wonder if he hid the truth from others as a trick, to show strength where there was weakness and weakness where there was strength. But now she could see more clearly as she held his hand. His best qualities were simply beyond his control. They had led him to this action, to this place, and to this moment.

"Stay with me a while please, Captain. Stay and keep me company."

Khali and Shahin remained for a long time like that without words passing between them. While nearby, the shock of consciousness flowed slowly into a ruined body, pulled back from the peace it had longed for by the strange power of the object still clinging to its finger, half-buried in battlefield mud, still darkly shining, now black, now gold.

Chapter Fifty-Six

The clicking of a man's heels across marble floors outside the door encroached on the silence. Sleep scattered, and Molly again found herself lying on the opulent carpet in the Shepherd's keep, listening to the cold scraping of key in lock.

Mathias Holt entered his office, closed and re-locked the heavy steel doors behind him. He turned to face the girl, who stood in the center of the room. She saw the astonishment on his face. He had seen into her thoughts as she slept. He knew what she knew.

In her desire for what strength and power she might uncover within, Molly had slept, she had dreamed, she had gone all the way back to the beginning. And in his greed for the secrets she possessed, the Shepherd had followed her. There, at the bottom of a deep well, two great enemies met once more and found the truth together.

The needling sharpness of anger suddenly weakened and obscured within her, shoved aside by something altogether unexpected and far worse. Molly held the determined mask of hatred in place to hide what she now felt in his presence, the shattering grief of betrayal, the unfathomable pain of love. She knew this man now as she had known him then. *Broussard.*

Shock and the unfamiliar touch of humility quieted the Shepherd's voice, and he spoke like a man standing on loose earth ripe for an avalanche.

"I would have killed you," he confessed in muted amazement, seeing the girl as if for the first time.

"You did kill me." Molly spoke evenly and from experience. "And you will kill me again."

Chapter Fifty-Seven

Avignon, 1307

The most sage among men have always known that power comes and goes like the tides. With the fall of Acre, the last Christian-held city in the Holy Land, the power of the great military orders quickly ebbed. Only sixteen years had passed, but the time of the Templars was coming to its end with the suddenness and finality of a flood. No longer needed by Kings or Popes to fight their wars, the Order's strength had become more feared within Christendom than without. Their wealth, their secrets, and their fearlessness before both state and church had sown the seeds of a great storm. Phillip of France had joined with Clement of Rome to stand against the might of the Order. The wisest among the Templars saw disaster's approach, and made preparations to ride the rising sea. Hundreds of miles from Avignon, a fleet prepared in secret to sail from La Rochelle at a moment's notice.

In Avignon, the land of his birth, Broussard dreamed. The pain wracking his body, now lashed to the machine of the Inquisitor, faded in the bliss of memory as his thoughts journeyed through the past. He came upon Khali, their children, and their happiness in the home of his father. Warm reminiscences flowed to him from sixteen years of a secret life, a secret love with the woman whose unintended spell over him remained forever unbreakable. Sixteen years of happiness and contentment that made the mystery and pain of his earlier life diminish with each moment.

Broussard was not alone in his dreaming. He could feel the presence of a witch, new and different, but still much like the one he had known years before, watching his thoughts from somewhere in the shadows. This presence followed as his journey took him back to the highlands of Ethiopia. The witch's need for answers guided Broussard back and back until, in his memory, he awoke on a hilltop running red with blood, and to pain unimaginable.

***

A rush of air into his lungs returned him to that ruined body. From the mud where he lay, he saw Khali sitting with Shahin. The Captain lay dying, a Mongol blade anchoring his body to the earth. In the mud between them, frozen hands still clutching a Moorish dagger beneath his chest, eyes open and covered with a yellowing film, the tormenting witch lay dead.

On his finger, Broussard watched the ring flash in the mud, now dark, now gold. It was the burden he had undertaken, the cause of all of this. Montbard had warned him that to join this more ancient brotherhood was to invite more struggles like this one in the future. And as Broussard looked about him at the bodies of the dead, former enemies and allies alike in a war of beliefs, he began to understand the Enemy Montbard described.

In Acre, the Enemy had picked up a trail that had gone cold in the time of Solomon. This dead Mongol in the mud beside him represented only the first of many hounds. He understood clearly in that moment, there could be no safety for the fox in Avignon. He could not bring the ring to Cyprus. He could not return it to the Templars.

He looked again at the suffering Captain, and he wondered at the nobility of soul hidden within. Here was a rogue criminal who had given everything for his people now held in Cyprus. Here was a Moor who had given his life for the life of a Crusader, perhaps still in the hope of saving his people, or perhaps, and just as curious, at the request of the girl now holding his hand.

As strength flowed slowly back into his limbs, he began an unsteady climb to his knees. Khali turned at the sound and beheld him. The horror of the sight was overpowered by her joy that he lived. She rushed to his side, lending all the strength of her slender body to help him stand. Too many emotions at once flooded her thoughts.

"How can this be?" She wept as they moved together. "I thought you were dead."

The hillside around them was dotted with warhorses, armored, saddled, wandering riderless. Broussard caught sight of Shahin's eyes, dimly watching them. He wondered if this pirate might make yet one more bargain for the lives of his people.

"Khali," Broussard breathed the words heavily, "bring a horse for the Captain." He watched the ring flicker as he lifted his hand, recalling what he had learned of its mysteries from Montbard. "No one else is going to die today."

***

Broussard surged into consciousness once more to find his body still in the dark chamber, stretched upon the grotesque engine of the Inquisitor. Every muscle was cramped tight or torn loose all at once. He could not move even to draw a decent breath, and what breath he could brought the unmistakable odor of aged masculine sweat, which blended with the stench of rot and excrement. He perceived men standing all around him, vague shapes cloaked in shadow, barely touched by weak and shifting firelight.

Broussard let his eyes move from figure to figure in the flickering gloom, searching for his enemy. Somewhere hidden among them was one like the golden man he had encountered many years ago. One man, among this gaggle of pious witch hunters, was indeed a witch. Contact had been broken with his returning consciousness, but this new witch was near.

"Where are you?" Broussard wheezed. "Show yourself."

A pale face that seemed to float above a scarlet cassock moved into the light above him. The thin, angular skull of the Inquisitor was further elongated by a sharply jutting beard, and framed by a weak flow of blond hair that spilled like rain from a leaking roof beneath his wide-brimmed scarlet hat.

"He is near death." the pale man pronounced.

This man was no witch.

"I would know my enemy," Broussard groaned.

After a moment or two of interminable silence, wherein Broussard hovered between life and death, another man moved among the shadows. From the darkness the figure moved closer until his face took shape among the pulsing torchlight as if emerging from a billow of harsh smoke.

Pain upon pain now assaulted Sebastien Broussard at the sight of him. He pulled at the ropes that bit into his flesh, further contorting his tearing muscles, but the old torment faded in the face of one new and still darker. Weak breath turned into a bellow no animal could muster, because no animal could know betrayal as a man undone by one beloved, as student by teacher, as brother by brother. A new Shepherd stood above him in the dim light. Vincent.

Broussard could not recapture the breath he had just raged away. His eyes flickered and threatened to go out altogether. Still, he could see sorrow beneath the steely purpose in his brother's expression.

"I am sorry, Sebastien." Vincent leaned closer to his brother. "But there is so much in this world you do not understand."

The pain in his heart caused the worst the Inquisitor could offer to drift into the background. He watched his brother above him. It was Vincent who had entered his dream moments ago. Of course, he thought. It would be Vincent, whose love of secrets and power had always been greater than his love for the Order or his respect for its laws. Vincent, who had always tried to teach his younger brother that the world was forever ruled by the learned at the expense of the ignorant. It was Vincent to whom the hounds came when the trail of their prize ran cold. It was Vincent to whom they offered all the power in the world. And it was Vincent who could not resist. It was Vincent who would fall. And it was Vincent who betrayed him.

Sebastien's glazing eyes looked on his brother with sorrow and pity.

Vincent leaned still closer, and his voice carried with it the beginning of an eerie pull. "Now, Sebastien, before it is too late. What happened to the ring?"

The pale man had donned his mask once more, a hood of black velvet to declare his work impersonal, the necessary work of his God, before returning to operate his vicious machine.

"Speak your secret!" the Inquisitor demanded from hiding as he turned the wheel a notch tighter. Aware that the pious monster knew nothing of the secret Vincent sought, knew nothing of that Ethiopian hilltop where he had last seen the ring, Sebastien would have laughed if not for the pain overwhelming his body. Instead, he let his eyes fall once more to his brother.

"Kill me." Sebastien whispered for mercy.

Vincent furrowed his brow in frustration and what appeared to be true grief.

"I am sorry, my brother. I cannot do that. I require an answer. Until you give it, I'm afraid things will only get worse for you."

Vincent somberly raised his hand, causing more movement among the shadows behind him. Sebastien watched as they led her toward him. All thoughts of what had been, what was to be, suddenly melded into a singularity of passing sorrow and infinite joy. Her presence here brought no pain for him, despite their black intent. Now drifting between their ugly world and whatever the next world would bring, he saw what they could not. He saw how truly powerless they were. A light burned within this woman even as she was made to walk among dark stone and grim torchlight. He had sensed something of this light when he'd first seen her, long ago on the parapets of a doomed city. But now, among this sadder darkness, a veil seemed to fall from her. He saw her now as he had always imagined her. Lit from within. They could not see what he saw. They could not touch it. They could not harm her.

When at last she was made to stand before his battered and faltering body, lashed to the obscene and blasphemous machine of the Inquisitor, Khali did not weep or cry out. She could offer him little aid, but what she could give, as always before, she would.

When the Inquisitor snarled a pale hand within her beloved's hair and lifted his head, Khali steeled herself as his eyes beheld her. She slowed her heartbeat for his sake. She offered all she had, the only thing they could not take. She offered him her strength through the warmth of her eyes.

"Speak your secret." The Inquisitor made his demand again.

Broussard pondered the glaze of scar tissue where his finger, lost these many years, once had been. He thought to speak of the ring, to tantalize and torture his own tormentors with a taste of it in words. But through his ebbing strength he could only offer in weak defiance, "Lost."

As the Inquisitor signaled the man pressing the blade to her throat, and even as she felt the slow sting of the edge, her beloved reached to embrace her once more with his failing gaze. Each drew strength from the other, as always before and for the last time. Through battered lips and bruised flesh, his face contorted into what she understood to be a smile, he breathed her name and spoke again.

"Do not be afraid." Unable to turn from her eyes while there was still life in them, he held her still as he offered his own last words. Strange, gentle, a tender command or a reassuring plea, Khali felt within them the unfathomable possibility of a story much larger than this moment could reveal. "Wait for me."

Chapter Fifty-Eight

Mathias Holt stood in his Santa Monica office, staring in shock at the sixteen-year-old girl before him. At the same moment, Vincent Broussard looked into the eyes of a man he had known 600 years in the past. He looked into the living eyes of the price of his bargain, the man he had dutifully killed for their sake, the man he had betrayed in exchange for power unimaginable. He looked into the eyes of his brother. For the first time in either of the two lifetimes he recalled as clearly as one, the Shepherd stood humbled and awestruck. "Sebastien..." the name passed his lips in a shamed whisper.

The shock and pain of revelation were so near that Molly quivered from the effort to stifle a lunge for his throat. The Shepherd was still bigger, still stronger, and still schooled in the dark arts of the Enemy. But Molly had found a weapon. She stood quietly and glared into his eyes until truth caused him to look away.

"I..." the Shepherd began, uncertain of his words. "Vincent never wanted to harm his brother. He always wanted him to understand." Mathias Holt offered up words that sounded true in his head, but seemed to weaken and turn false the moment they hit the open air. "This is the path of the strong."

Molly's courage began to grow in the face of the Shepherd's uncertainty. She reached again for her new weapon.

"No, Vincent. It is the way of the weak. It is the way of the fearful. They select men like you the way jackals pick out the weakest of the herd. It is the way of the sucker at the hands of the magician, the con, the liar."

The Shepherd seemed to ignore her as he moved to the other side of his desk and began to work the combination lock to his wall safe.

Molly pressed her advantage. "You still don't understand what's happened to you, do you, brother?"

"What has happened?" He asked, feigning disinterest in her answer as he dialed in the numbers.

"You believe you have lived twice, and that is their gift to you." She saw him pause at the lock. He listened and she continued. "Because of the ring you seek for them, I have the memories of a *dozen* lifetimes lived since that day in Avignon. *Think*, Vincent."

The Shepherd resumed working the lock on the safe with his back turned.

"Where have *you* been all that time?" She asked.

The Shepherd paused again, perhaps losing the combination, perhaps hearing her.

"I'll tell you." Molly pushed harder, her voice rising. "You have been their slave. You have died in their service many times. And they come to you again and again, just like they came to Mathias Holt. They offer the same promise, the world and all that's in it. *Every time,* Vincent. And every time, you fall for it. You do their bidding like a blunt instrument in their hands. You kill for them. And for what? Look at all you have, brother. Is it grand? Is it great? Or is it cheap and debased?" Her words were daggers. She drove them in as deeply as she could, the bitter memories of Avignon fueling her attack. "What is this bargain you agree to over and over again like a pig who agrees to fatten himself for slaughter for the privilege of covering himself in shit? *What have they given you?*"

The Shepherd closed his eyes as he waited for the answer, as the thing he had secretly feared since the beginning leaped out like an unseen serpent in the weeds.

Molly delivered the blow without mercy. "Thirty pieces of silver, brother. Nothing more."

The fear within turned quickly to rage. The Shepherd crossed the distance between them in one stride. A back handed slap sent a shocking jolt through the girl, knocking her to the floor. The room blurred and her ears buzzed.

The Shepherd's attack steeled him. He looked down at the girl as if she had forgotten the gravity of her situation.

"I am sorry for Avignon, my brother. But surely you can see now, in the wake of all you have seen since, that it was a smaller matter than it seemed at the time."

Molly saw her advantage wane in the face of his conviction. Like most men, it was simply too important for him to have been right all along, to fully face the truth. Once it had begun, he would need to complete any mission just to prove it was worthwhile from the beginning.

"You will kill me again," she stated flatly, without emotion.

"I will do what I must." His words were forced, intended to convince himself of their power.

"So must we all." Molly turned once more to her weapon. "You know by now that there are others who have waited for my return. Others who know how to follow the trail of a Shepherd, and who know how to wait." Molly watched a new emotion cross in shadow over his face. For only the briefest moment, there was fear. She laughed at him now with no need to contain her delight at the sight. "There are tigers in these woods, Templar.

I am not the only one of the old brethren to have worn Solomon's Ring. I am not the only one who remembers. The Legion of the Dead has been watching you for as long as you have waited for me. They have the trail by now."

Mathias Holt turned quickly back to his wall safe. Molly watched him complete the combination and open it. From within, he removed an envelope, bulging with papers. He left the safe open like a man in a great hurry, like a man who wasn't coming back to it, and he moved to his heavy oak desk. He set the envelope down in the center, where it would appear conspicuous to the next person to enter this room.

Molly looked closer. The envelope was addressed with a single name, written in large, somewhat affectionate cursive. *Elizabeth.*

Having placed his letter, the Shepherd grabbed Molly by the hand, yanked her roughly to her feet, and pulled her toward yet another locked door. Since the construction of this concrete and steel citadel, this door had remained hidden, unopened, and locked until the first and only time to use it should come. That time was now.

***

For many years they had studied the tower on Ocean Avenue in Santa Monica, knowing that it was his tower, his home, and his keep.

They were seven in all, gathered in secret from around the globe by ties that transcend time and distance. The Legion of the Dead. As the rain cleared and the light of day began to fade, they executed a plan formed long ago, that had lain dormant until the time was right, a time when they could know Broussard had arrived at last, and that the Shepherd had found him first.

Two entered the lobby. Making no sign of their intentions and taking no chances, they used pistols equipped with silencers to end the lives of two security guards near the elevators. The first were then followed into the lobby by four more. They sealed and secured the double glass doors behind them.

Two now stood guard over the gateway to the tower. The other four entered the twin elevators. And finally, the seventh stood alone and ready in the basement, where a generator supplied the building with power. He waited as the seconds passed through his wristwatch.

***

Elizabeth looked up from her work at the sound of both elevators arriving at once. She watched the doors open from across the wide marble floors. Both cars were empty.

Just as the facts of the moment began to dawn on her, and a peculiar foreboding caused the flesh to rise along her arms and thighs, the entire building suddenly plunged into darkness.

With no time to process the event, Elizabeth nevertheless knew what had happened. There was no why or how for her, but she instinctively knew that the power had been intentionally cut. Her prescience was born out in the next instant, as the sharp beams of four tightly focused flashlights swung from the open doors of the elevators. There were men in the room with her.

Elizabeth had just risen to her feet when she was caught in the beam. She froze like prey.

"Where is Mathias Holt?" a man calmly demanded from behind the light.

"Who are you?" she returned the demand, less confident than she tried to convey.

"We are the ones he fears."

The voice played on her unsteadiness. Elizabeth's skin blanched as her fear drove the blood from her face.

The voice continued from behind the light. "Where is he?"

She had often suspected that the mysterious ways of Mathias Holt might lead to unusual dealings, but she had never expected a visitation so bizarre by men so deeply frightening. She thought to lie, to protect her lover, but there was an eerie pull to the voice. She felt herself compelled as if by an unseen thread. "He is here." She listened to the words, shocked as she spoke them. "In his office."

Two of the flashlights followed as she pointed to the steel double doors of Mathias Holt's inner sanctum. She watched the shadowy figures attach something to the hinges and then calmly move back. There was a quietly hissing burst of light at the corners of the doors that seemed to burn hot enough to melt steel.

In short moments, the doors were loose. The first two shadows kicked them into his office. The second two followed quickly, leaving Elizabeth alone in the darkness to wait.

Within the sanctum, a focused beam fell on an envelope left in the center of a heavy oak desk. Addressed in graceful cursive, the name read *Elizabeth*, but the four transgressors knew it was also meant for them.

The Shepherd also had a plan formed long ago, a plan that had lain dormant until needed, a plan should he find Broussard first. They were too late by minutes. Long ago they had lain as hidden and still as prey before the hunters. Now, it was they who moved likely hungry wolves with the scent of blood on the wind.

Elizabeth still stood at her desk when the four lights returned. An envelope fell from the dark onto her desk. "He left this for you," said the voice as the four shadows returned to the elevator.

After what seemed only a brief moment or two, the lights suddenly came back on. The elevator doors were closed. The steel doors to Mathias' office lay strewn on his Persian carpet, but all else remained untouched.

She looked at the envelope, her name written in her lover's hand. The intruders had opened it already, and the contents had spilled partially on the desk where they dropped it. There were many documents of an official nature within. In time, she would find that wealth beyond her imagination, all that Mathias Holt had built since coming to America sixteen years ago, was now hers to do with as she pleased. But in this moment, her eyes fell upon a handwritten letter that rested on top. In this letter she would eventually find all of what he had never said, all of the things she had longed to hear, but they would all come too late, and bring only sorrow, longing, and regret.

From where she remained standing in stunned silence, Elizabeth could see the beginning of his letter. The first words to come after her name caused a short painful inhale, and it would be a long while before she saw any more of them. The words were direct and honest, as her lover had always been.

You will not see me again.

Chapter Fifty-Nine

Since the death of his mother, since the disintegration of his father, since the coming and going of the dreams the old man had foretold, Book had waited. He waited for something important that would change everything and lift him from his small purposes to large. His own life stalled and stagnated beneath the guidance of some strange hand that held him in place, that now seemed to have been preparing him for what was coming.

Now, that thing had come and gone. It came in the most unexpected form of a runaway girl. Book had been slow to understand, and he'd lost her. A lifetime of waiting undone by a moment of doubt.

Book approached the imaginary border between Los Angeles and Ventura County behind the wavering beam of the single headlamp of a stolen motorcycle. Only hours earlier, his right knee had been swollen and straight, rigid as old wood. His left arm had hung useless on the far side of a shoulder full of torn muscle and splintered bone, wrecked by a bullet fired from close range. Now his leg tapered along the body of the bike with its proper bend so his foot could change the gears. His left hand worked the clutch with ease. Book could feel a strange warmth in his chest and shoulder, where muscle and bone rapidly and impossibly continued to knit. In his leg he felt something other than pain for the first time since the injury. And at the top of his head, he continued to feel the bizarre heat that had come to him at the edge of death on the cold floor of the garage. It was the heat of life, of whatever it was that had almost fled his body entirely. It was still returning to him, pulled back to him against its will like a fish on the end of a line.

His mind swirled through the past and raced ahead to a future of suddenly endless possibilities.

Twenty minutes earlier, Book had stood with his back to the ocean, straddling the idling motorcycle and looking up at the heights of Mathias Holt's tower while the cherry lights of police cars covering the Santa Monica Pier flashed importantly a half-mile down the beach. Book had no plan but to attack. His thoughts had no room for any recourse but to kill for her, and most likely die for her, until something unexpected offered a new opportunity. In that moment, the mighty tower across the street suddenly went dark. All at once the lights from top to bottom fell black. The power had been cut.

He did not know how, or who could be responsible, but Book realized in that instant that the Shepherd was under attack. He lingered in the shadows across the street, hidden among the palms trees of the long, thin park that separated the city from the beach. Only a few seconds after the lights went out, the opportunity he waited for, came. The dark silhouette of a familiar Jaguar coupe emerged from the shadow of the tower, headlamps off as it drifted toward the street. Once it reached the relative freedom of Ocean Avenue, the yellow eyes of its lamps ignited, the engine growled to life and the car fled to the north.

In the open air, speeding through the dark night on the Pacific Coast Highway, Book hid many sins from the eyes of the new world in which he now moved. His torn and bloodied bomber jacket held a service revolver in one pocket to replace the one he had lost, and its broad back covered a police issue, short-handled shotgun that ran the length of his spine. On the index finger of his right hand Book bore something else. Whatever the hell else it might be, Book wore on his hand a difference maker. The rule that rendered all rules null and void. *King's X.*

The sting of failure began to fade as the rolling blacktop pulled him forward. The pain of loss became refocused through grim thoughts of vengeance and retribution. Book heard the words of his father once more, still reaching for the surface though buried beneath a lifetime of experiences that now added up to nothing. Even now, Book knew the story of the lost tiger by heart.

What do you see when the water is still?

Book watched the girl in his thoughts. Small, delicate, incomprehensible, and powerful. He saw the blank stare of his partner just above the dark barrel of a gun. He heard the sound of a single shot in Sara's apartment, witnessed the aftermath, and felt once more the searing heat of the barrel of his own gun held briefly to his temple. He studied the Shepherd.

Who told you that you were a sheep?

No one told me. It's just all I can remember. All I have ever known.

Book was unaware of the event when, for the first time in his life, he crossed the imaginary line that marked the boundary of Los Angeles County. He would keep going long into the night and eventually leave his home far behind. He focused instead on the road ahead, where a hundred yards beyond the reach of the motorcycle's beam, but just close enough that he could track the red glowing tail lights darting through the twists and turns of the canyons and cliff-sides, a black jaguar coupe made its way north.

He had found a way. He would wait no more.

Chapter Sixty

Death must come with every life. Still, Molly hated it. Only in life is there possibility. Only in life is there a chance to fight and win. What happens when you are asleep is unimportant. What you do when you are awake is everything. Yet, only in death were her secrets safe. Before very much longer, either for her or for this Shepherd, it would be death.

She studied him as he pressed the Jaguar faster than prudence would allow along the snaking black highway. There was no echo of Vincent in the lines of his face. Yet there was something familiar in his unwavering concentration on the dull swath of light cast by the headlamps.

To the right of them, the soaring stone walls of ancient mountains dropped straight down from the night sky to the edge of the pavement. To their left and hundreds of feet below, the gaping maw of the Pacific Ocean, more implied than visible in the spent light of the sun already fallen below the horizon.

The Shepherd glanced away from the shifting road ahead to his mirrors, where a lone headlamp winked at the edges of the turns behind them, matching his speed. The break in his focus was nearly imperceptible. But Molly saw it.

They were being followed. The Legionnaires. Molly had been right and the Shepherd knew it. They had watched him since Rachel's death. Longer even than the Shepherd had watched Book. All waiting for her return. And now, as the memories came faster and faster, Rachel's memories, Broussard's memories, the Legion of the Dead had stepped from the shadows. As she hoped. As she feared.

They want it too. Her ring. King's X.

Molly's thoughts turned to the familiar trail of horror and sorrow the King's X must always leave in its wake. Trudie and Jacob. Mother and father. Murdered.

And her policeman. Her guardian from the moment he pulled her from that cell at the Wilcox station. Confused, angry, yet gentle and always standing by her. The more helpless she was, the stronger he became. She had kissed him once, as Molly had never kissed a boy. Something so strange, so subtle in his manner, his voice, his scent – whatever it had been, it drew her almost as powerfully as the lure of her ring. Wendell Book. Murdered.

The King's X was gone. Lost. Karl Buchner had thrown it into the ocean and left his small son behind as a witness. All who would follow – the Shepherd Mathias Holt, Molly, the Legion – would know and understand. The chase is over. The Seal of Solomon was once more buried at sea. May it lie at the darkest levels of abyss to the end of time.

Molly also knew there would be few moments of opportunity like this one. Her mind was filled with lifetimes of knowledge the Shepherd planned to seize. The names of people, places, events, and many more secrets dangerous to the Enemy. And she would lose them all eventually in his hands. Her helplessness would prove a devastating blow to the cause.

Behind her now, the follower. If it was indeed a Legionaire, it meant a possible return to them. To the fight. To the life she hated. But the ring was gone. Her mission had failed. With failure also came an end to her burden. She could stop running. She could stop fighting and dying for hopeless causes. She could disappear and never be found again.

The dark highway coiled sharply to the left and the Jaguar's tires moaned to hold on. Molly moved too quickly for the Shepherd to stop her. She grabbed the hand break between their seats and pulled back as hard as she could.

***

Book watched the beams from the car's headlamps swing sharply to slice the black beyond the precipice. Then the car rolled. He heard the screech of steel impacting the guardrail and saw the rooster tail of sparks exploding from the darkness as it tumbled, slid, and finally fell out of sight.

The car lay on its roof against the jagged stone of the cliff wall, held suspended and insecure above the drop, its thin chrome bumper tangled with a torn ribbon of guardrail still anchored by the roadside above. The nose of the inverted Jaguar pointed straight down. One working lamp shone like a searchlight into the mist rising from the dark ocean hundreds of feet below. Somewhere beneath the reach of the light, heavy Pacific swells foamed white among black rocks.

Book dropped the bike beside the torn guardrail and rushed to edge of the abyss. Several yards beyond the edge and down among the harsh angles of jutting rock, the black coupe hung by its creaking tether. It spewed steam and leaked hot liquids into the yellow shaft of light below. A single spoked wheel slowed to a stop, like a dying animal pawing the air. Book climbed down along jagged stone, slick with the dew of a rising fog.

The wall grew steeper above the drop as he moved closer. He did not trust the car against his weight, but saw no other option but to lean against it to reach the blown out window on the passenger side. Molly.

Her body lay like a discarded doll across the roof of the upside down car. He could see that her left leg was broken above the ankle. Her face was badly bruised and thin rivulets of blood fell from many tiny shards of broken glass in her flesh. From where he stood, one hand on the door frame and both feet crowded together on a thin edge of stone, Book reached inside and touched her shoulder.

"Molly."

Her eyes opened, dim but recognizing.

"You."

"I'm going to get you out."

"No."

Her voice was weak. She lingered on him for a moment, the faintest rise of surprise and joy in her face.

"I have the ring." Book held his hand where she could see the King's X, flashing darkly in the dim light. "It can help you."

"No." She said again.

He stole furtive glances at her broken leg. The pain had not come to her yet, but it would soon. He was afraid to move her, afraid to bring her any closer to fully awake, and afraid that she would slip away if he didn't.

"I'll carry you. Try to put your arms around my neck."

"Who are you?" Her eyes penetrated him. He was caught and held in her gaze. But this was no invasion, no invisible thread controlling him. Behind Molly's eyes he saw a peculiar hope. She had no intention of leaving this wrecked car and he knew it. Her hope was directed solely at him. He was a mystery to her, one that left her warmed and comforted. She reached out a hand with almost no strength left in it. "Show me." She said.

"Show you what?" Book took her hand in his, uncomprehending.

She held his hand, at once touching him and the ring on his finger. Book felt something pass between them like a low electrical current. Molly felt much more.

He watched her expression shift from nearly blank to a sublime, sorrowful joy as something seemed to flow to her in the current.

Her voice trembled. "My beloved."

"I'm going to get you out." He repeated, but she showed no concern or even awareness of the danger. He continued to hold her, to keep her with him, even as he tried to dig the edge of his boot deeper into the thin, slick foothold that held him.

Her face contorted into what he knew to be a smile, and tears of unmistakable joy mingled with the blood on her cheeks.

"I am so happy."

Book blinked at the unfamiliar sensation of his own welling tears.

"I don't understand." He shook his head slowly.

"You will. Someday you will remember everything. As will we all." She reached her other hand to his face. She held him, and her joy turned once more grave and her tone urgent. "You must run far away and stay silent. Tell no one of me. Tell no one of your ring."

He pinned her hand tightly to his cheek.

"Molly, don't leave me here. I don't want you to die."

"No one dies, my love." The smile returned to her, and he smiled back through his fear, though he did not understand why. "You waited for me. And at last I found you again. I have touched you again. My sweet beauty. My beloved. My Khalidah."

The word meant nothing to him, but Book wept as her warm gaze slipped again, closer toward an unseeing stare. "Molly, please..."

"Wait no more, Khali." She said, fading. "You must run."

Not a word. A name. Book searched his thoughts but there was nothing familiar in it. But her warning brought a moment of realization. Where was the driver? Where was the Shepherd?

As quickly as the possibility had occurred, like a striking snake the black gloved hand surged from the dark. From only inches behind Molly where he had remained unseen, just as he had in Sara's apartment before her murder, just as he had in Book's apartment before slaying the unsuspecting policemen, the Shepherd arrived too suddenly and from too close. His powerful grip caught Book by the wrist, yanking his hand away from Molly's touch.

"Don't move." The Shepherd hissed. Within the wild tangle of silver hair flecked with blood, Book could see the hint of his eyes in what little light reflected from the head lamp on the mist. Book knew what was happening, and he tried to fight the invisible thread that compelled him.

Still, he could only watch, his body quaking with the unanswered desire to move, as the Shepherd's other hand brought forward a silver .45 caliber handgun from within his black coat. He touched the end of the barrel to Book's finger, just below the ring. The King's X flashed in the darkness, now black, now gold.

"Clever thieves," said the Shepherd. "What was stolen is returned."

At the click of the hammer being thumbed into place, a surge of adrenalin allowed Molly to lift her head to the arm just above her. She sunk her teeth into Mathias Holt's flesh at the wrist and bit down hard.

The gunshot was deafening inside the car. The spray of flaming powder stung Book's face as it flashed, but the bullet passed harmlessly into the steel door with a loud clang. Book's ears rang from the point-blank thunderclap, his eyes shut tight against the burning, and he fell from the sliver of rock.

One thought went through his head in that instant. Molly. She was alive, injured and in the hands of the Shepherd. If he lost her now, it would be forever.

Book caught the arm that had held his wrist and clamped down hard. The Shepherd tried to release him, to let him fall, but it was too late. Book's grip was iron, his 200 pound body was plummeting dead-weight, and the Shepherd was halfway out of the car before he managed to grab onto something.

The shock of pain flooded her with merciless consciousness as the Shepherd caught hold of Molly's leg just above the break. She screamed in agony as she braced her arms against the frame of the car and her slide stopped with a jolt.

Looking down, she could see Book swaying above the drop into darkness, clinging to the Shepherd who had become an unlikely link between them. She closed her eyes tight against the pain and held on.

"Book," the Shepherd shouted, attempting to command. "Let go!"

"No!" Molly shouted through clenched teeth. "Hang on!"

Despite the ringing in his ears, Book could hear the courage in Molly's voice. He could hear the fear in Shepherd's. There were no threads on him now. He held on.

It is said that at the moment of death, many things may come clear. At this moment, hanging suspended hundreds of feet above jagged rock and violent water, Book saw many things with great clarity. He saw that Molly would sacrifice herself for him, now, then, and perhaps someday again. He understood something more of what she had told him, of what John had told him moments before his sacrifice. *There is nothing to fear.* He heard the voice of his father from 16 years ago, and the words he said could be used as a weapon to fight the Enemy. *Nothing is real. All is permitted.*

The Shepherd sought a weapon. His thoughts settled with sinister understanding on what he heard Molly say moments before. The name she had called him. *Khalidah.* Both Broussards had known that name. The beautiful girl. One brother had used her life as a weapon against the other who had loved her. The girl's death had been brave. A sacrifice.

"Book!" He called out again. "If you care for this girl, if you love her you will let her live. Let go or she dies!"

"Everybody dies, Shepherd." Book spoke softly as he reached with his left hand beneath the collar of his bomber jacket between his shoulders.

The Shepherd glanced down as Book pulled the police issue short-handled shot gun from along his spine. He watched with growing helplessness as Book skillfully prepped the weapon with one hand. He released his grip to catch it again around the pump. A flick of his wrist chambered a shell. He then caught the gun again by the handle, wrapped his finger around the trigger, and looked the Shepherd in the eye.

The Shepherd tried to shake free of Book's iron hold on his wrist, but could not.

"I didn't wait in Los Angeles all this time to keep Molly from dying." Book smiled at his enemy. "I waited so I could be here, right now, to protect her from you."

Hearing his words, Molly opened her eyes, straining to hold the weight. He swayed above the blackness, just a few feet below her.

"Book! Please, don't leave me!"

Book turned to hold her eyes with his for a last moment. He gave her the last of his strength, once more. Fearless and calm, his words not a plea, but a promise.

"Wait for me."

Book pulled the trigger, the shotgun spit fire and lead, and the arm of the Shepherd that clung to the girl's leg was severed at the elbow.

Mathias Holt cried out in fear as he and Wendell Book dropped together into the mist.

Epilogue

Indian Ocean, 2 Days East of Madagascar

Shahin swung his legs over the side of the long boat into the low surf and walked onto the brown sand and black rock beach for the first time. He studied the trees, the stones, and the sand for signs of tide levels or the passage of men. This place would suit his needs.

"Return for me in one hour," he commanded. Confused, but growing more accustomed to the enigmatic ways of their leader, his crew pried the long boat from the thin beach and headed back to the *Immortal*, now anchored in the deeper waters beyond this lagoon.

Shahin began at the most permanent structure he could find, a natural obelisk of volcanic rock that stood slightly higher than a man at the edge of the tree line. He moved off the beach, counting his steps. At thirty-three paces he found the next permanent marker, a fatter and even heavier stone. A right-angled turn, another thirty-three paces, and Shahin stopped once more. He looked around beneath the canopy of trees. He was nowhere, watched by no one.

From the sack on his hip Shahin produced a small, hinged box made of thick cedar. Looking around him once more to see that no one had followed, he knelt with his box among ferns growing from dry, sandy soil. With his hands he began to dig a shallow well, deep and wide enough to swallow this box when the time came. He worked for several minutes, looking about him every so often to see that he remained alone.

When the hole was deep enough, Shahin sighed loudly. This moment had been a long time coming, the culmination of an unusual bargain made long ago with an even more unusual man. In exchange for what he now did, Shahin had received a chance to start anew. A new life, in a new world, where none knew him, except perchance by the infamous reputation of The Hawk. For what he now did, Shahin also received a promise, freedom and a chance at new lives for all those he had been forced to leave in the hands of the Templar Order at the fall of Acre. Shahin never saw Cyprus, or his people again. But word had returned to him from his own agents abroad that the *Leila* had been freed, that Broussard had kept his word upon returning. And so, Shahin would keep his word as the bargain dictated.

From the curved sheath on his hip, the Captain drew the blade he had been sharpening every day since setting sail from Madagascar in search of an island such as this one. The journey to this uninhabited shore was carefully mapped on board the *Immortal*, the landing spot scouted from among all sides of the island, and the place where he now knelt was known to him alone. Everything was as Broussard had instructed. All debts between them had been fulfilled, but one.

Shahin spread his hand in the sandy earth before him. He studied the peculiar ring he had worn on his finger since that day, now many years past, in the highlands of Ethiopia. It shone in the sunlight streaming between leaves above in its familiar, peculiar manner, now black, now gold. There were a great many odd and wonderful qualities to this particular prize among Shahin's collection. He was loath to surrender it here and now for more reasons than one. But Broussard had been true to his word, and Shahin, having learned something of a notion called *karma* during his new life on the eastern seas, was not about to let the Christian get the better of him in any way.

The Captain breathed deep through his nose and placed the tip of the blade against his finger just behind the darkly shining ring.   He took another breath. He took a third. He closed one eye, then both together. He took a fourth breath, held it, opened both eyes wide once more, and quickly forced the blade through.

All that we are, all that we have ever been, the King's X will reveal...

KING'S X will continue with new adventures and new lifetimes.

For more on King's X, visit www.kingsxbooks.com

A NOVEL ENDEAVOR BOOK

Made in the USA
Lexington, KY
13 April 2012